BODIES POLITIC

BODIES POLITIC

A novel

Michiel Heyns

JONATHAN BALL PUBLISHERS
Johannesburg & Cape Town

Published in 2008 in trade paperback by
JONATHAN BALL PUBLISHERS (PTY) LTD
P O Box 33977
Jeppestown
2043

ISBN 978 1 86842 298 2

Design and reproduction of text by
Etienne van Duyker, Cape Town
Cover design by Flame Design, Cape Town
Printed and bound by Paarl Print, Paarl, Cape Town

Author's note

*T*his is a novel, not a piece of historical research, and most of the encounters described are imaginary. However, all characters and events are based on actual historical instances, and the time scheme is generally accurate, as far as I could ascertain it. I have availed myself of the research of others, but I have frequently appropriated their findings to my purpose. Distortions and inaccuracies are therefore to be reckoned to my account.

My main debt is to Martin Pugh's *The Pankhursts*, whose traces can be found everywhere in this book. Nevertheless, he should not be held responsible for the considerable liberties I have taken with his material in fictionalising it.

The other indispensable source has been Sylvia Pankhurst's *The Suffragette Movement*. Opinionated as it is, and resentful as Sylvia is of both Emmeline and Christabel, it is nevertheless an invaluable and astonishingly vivid record of a family and an era. Here, too, I have borrowed freely, and adapted at will.

I have also drawn on, and once again adapted to my purpose, *Freedom's Cause: Lives of the Suffragettes* by Fran Abrams, *Sylvia Pankhurst: Artist and Crusader* by Richard Pankhurst, *Queen Christabel* by David Mitchell, *The Hard Way Up* by Hannah Mitchell and *The Women's Suffrage Movement: A Reference Guide 1866 -1928* by Elizabeth Crawford.

Experts on the era will note that I have often omitted figures other than the Pankhursts and their immediate circle from events that they were involved in, and even suppressed incidents from the lives of those characters I do depict. This was to prevent cluttering my narrative with characters and incidents not germane to my purpose. I apologise for the distortion attendant upon this.

List of main characters

BILLINGTON-GREIG, TERESA, born Billington (1877–1964). Early member of the Women's Social and Political Union (WSPU). Objecting to Emmeline and Christabel's dictatorial style, she left the organisation in 1907 with Charlotte Despard, and started the Women's Freedom League. Married Louis Greig in 1907.

CORIO, SILVIO (1875–1954). Italian journalist, anarchist, and anti-Fascist refugee; lover of Sylvia Pankhurst, father of her son Richard Keir Pethick Pankhurst.

CRAGGS, HELEN (1888–1969), later Mrs McCombie, then Lady Pethick Lawrence. Daughter of Sir John Craggs, educated at Roedean, and returned there as a teacher, but left her post in 1910 to become a full-time organiser for the Women's Social and Political Union (WSPU). She was imprisoned in 1912 for her part in the WSPU window-smashing campaign, and again in the same year for attempting to burn down Lewis Harcourt's country house. Married Alexander McCombie, a medical doctor, in 1914, and qualified as a pharmacist to help her husband. Married Frederick Pethick Lawrence in 1957.

HARDIE, KEIR (1856–1915). Former coal miner, who taught himself to read and write, and became a journalist. Founded the Independent Labour Party in 1888; was elected as first socialist MP in 1892. A supporter of women's suffrage groups, and an opponent of the First World War. Close friend and probably lover of Sylvia Pankhurst.

7

KENNEY, ANNIE (1879–1953). The fifth child in a family of eleven, daughter of textile workers, Annie worked in a cotton factory from age ten until she became a full-time worker for the Women's Social and Political Union (WSPU). When Christabel Pankhurst fled to Paris in 1912, Annie was put in charge of the WSPU in London. During the War she helped organise an anti-strike campaign. After the War she retired from politics and immersed herself in Theosophy.

PANKHURST, ADELA (1885–1961). Youngest daughter of Richard and Emmeline Pankhurst; fellow founder of the Women's Social and Political Union (WSPU), but banished to Australia by her mother in 1914. Married Tom Walsh, active as a Socialist in Australia, but conceived a policy of 'class co-operation' in the twenties, and moved ever further to the right thereafter; was interned in Australia during the Second World War as an active Fascist sympathiser.

PANKHURST, CHRISTABEL (1880–1958). Eldest daughter of Richard and Emmeline Pankhurst. With her mother, she was co-founder and also principal strategist of the Women's Social and Political Union (WSPU). Largely responsible for the adoption of militant tactics in 1905, but fled to France in 1912, from where she organised the militant activities of the members in England. In 1921 she went to live in the USA and became a prominent member of the Second Adventist movement. She returned to Britain in the 1930s, but left for the USA on the outbreak of the Second World War. She died in the USA.

PANKHURST, EMMELINE, born Goulden (1855–1928). Married Richard Pankhurst in 1879; member, with him, of the Independent Labour Party (ILP). Founded the Women's Social and Political Union (WSPU), and remained its leader to its demise; together with her daughter Christabel, adopted a policy of militancy. On the outbreak of the First World War, renounced militant activities and became an active supporter of conscription. After the War spent some years in the USA and Canada lecturing on the prevention of venereal diseases; returned to Britain in 1925 and joined the Conservative Party. Stood as candidate in the Whitechapel constituency.

PANKHURST, HENRY FRANCIS (Frank) (1884–1888). Son of Richard and Emmeline Pankhurst; died of diphtheria.

PANKHURST, HENRY FRANCIS (Harry) (1889–1910). Son of Richard and Emmeline Pankhurst; died of poliomyelitis.

PANKHURST, RICHARD (1834–1898). Graduated in 1858 and qualified as barrister. Married Emmeline Goulden in 1879. Tireless campaigner for social justice. Joined the Liberal party, but resigned in 1883; stood as independent candidate in Manchester. Was later a member of the Independent Labour Party (ILP).

PANKHURST, RICHARD KEIR PETHICK (1928–). Son of Sylvia Pankhurst and Silvio Corio. Expert on Ethiopia, attached to the University of Addis Ababa.

PANKHURST, SYLVIA (1882–1960). Socialist feminist, particularly active in the East End of London, where she founded the East London Federation of Suffragettes. She always had much stronger working-class sympathies than her mother Emmeline and sister Christabel. She was expelled from the Women's Social and Political Union (WSPU) in 1914. She was vehemently opposed to the War, and, unlike her mother and sister, continued the battle for the vote after its outbreak. Had a son by the Italian anarchist Silvio Corio in 1928. In her later years worked for the restoration of

Ethiopian independence, first against the Italian invaders and then against the British government. She moved to that country in 1956 and died there in 1960.

PETHICK LAWRENCE, FREDERICK, born Lawrence (1871–1961). Married Emmeline Pethick in 1901. Well-to-do lawyer and owner of *The Echo*, a left-wing newspaper. Was not allowed as member of the Women's Social and Political Union (WSPU), but was an active collaborator, and was repeatedly imprisoned and forcibly fed. Expelled from the WSPU in 1912 by Emmeline and Christabel Pankhurst. Opposed to Britain's involvement in the First World War. Later became a Labour MP, and appointed as Secretary of State for India. After the death of Emmeline Pethick Lawrence (1954), he married Helen Craggs.

PETHICK LAWRENCE, EMMELINE, born Pethick (1867–1954). Was converted to socialism at an early age; married Fred Lawrence in 1901; joined the Women's Social and Political Union (WSPU) and became its treasurer. Was expelled in 1912 for objecting to Christabel's proposed arson campaign. Started a journal *Votes for Women*. During the War, a prominent member of the Women's International League for Peace. Remained active in politics till 1950, when she was left paralysed in a serious accident. She died of a heart attack in 1954.

SMYTH, DAME ETHEL (1858-1944). Composer who, under the influence of Emmeline Pankhurst, interrupted her musical career to devote her time to the cause of votes for women. Wrote 'The March of the Women' in 1911, which became the battle cry of the suffrage movement.

Book 1

Emmeline

She threw scruple, affection, honour, loyalty and her own principles to the winds. The movement developed her powers – all her powers for good and for evil … She was capable of beautiful tenderness and [a] magnificent sense of justice and self-sacrifice. These things in the course of the struggle became damaged. We all sacrificed many things – she sacrificed her very soul.

Emmeline Pethick Lawrence to Sylvia Pankhurst on
Emmeline Pankhurst, quoted by Martin Pugh.

I

Sunday 8 April 1928

Christabel says Wapping is no place for a Pankhurst. I reply that the Pankhursts have always identified with the poor and the downtrodden. She says identifying is one thing, living in the slums another.

'Leave that to Sylvia,' she says. 'She likes dinginess and squalor. You've always wanted beautiful things around you.' She looks critically at the wallpaper, which is indeed of an ugliness to distress the soul, a floral pattern wanly aspiring to cheerfulness and arriving only at vulgarity.

'I did change the carpet,' I venture. 'I thought it might discourage the wallpaper.'

'I'm not sure that a grey carpet is an improvement, Mother. What looks elegantly understated in Belgravia merely looks gloomy in Wapping.' She puts down the little dog she has been nursing on her lap. 'I hope little Flora will cheer things up for you.'

'I am sure she will,' I say, though in truth I think the little creature is itself too despondent to inspire cheer in others. 'It is very thoughtful of you. I only hope I shall be able to give her the attention she requires.'

'Oh, she doesn't require attention, Mother. Just being around you is all she asks.'

I want to say that being around me hardly seems to exhilarate Flora. But Christabel is not really thinking about the dog: she is inspecting the room as if she suspected it of harbouring rats. 'It's not as if you *have* to live here, you know,' she says over her shoulder, too loudly; I would not want Mrs Chipperfield to hear. 'Any number of people would be only too honoured to have you.'

Any number of people – among whom Christabel is not to be numbered. 'I know, darling, but I am tired of living in other people's houses.'

'You know you hate small rooms.'

'Yes, I do, but at least I am paying for it and it is mine. As long as I have my own desk where I can work, I feel comfortable. And Nellie Hall has been an admirable secretary.'

'Nellie Hall can be an admirable secretary quite as much in Kensington as in Wapping.'

She walks to the little window, parts the flimsy curtains, and peers into the street. Her vivid colouring and beautifully cut frock make the threadbare room seem even drearier, the attempts at decoration more tawdry. She turns again, runs her finger along the mantelpiece and inspects it. There is an ornament of sorts, a shepherdess or some such bucolic fancy, on the mantelpiece. Christabel chucks it under the chin and it falls over. She leaves the figurine sprawling inelegantly, and opens the door leading into the adjoining bedroom, then quickly closes it, as if to prevent some noisome smell from escaping. 'It's hideous,' she says, with a shudder. 'You could get something nice in Kensington or even near me in Hampstead for not much more, you know, if you asked the right people.'

'But I do not want to ask people, Christabel. It is too demeaning. And Mrs Chipperfield is very attentive, when her other duties allow.'

'I'm sure she is, Mother, but with all due respect, Emmeline Pankhurst deserves better than to live on the Ratcliffe Highway and be tended by a butcher's wife during intervals between disembowelling pigs.'

'Mr Chipperfield is a barber, dear, not a butcher. And I do not see how I can aspire to represent a working-class district in Parliament when I shy away from living in one.'

'Aspire?' Christabel snorts sarcastically. 'Mrs Pankhurst

14

aspire to represent the slums of Whitechapel? In any case, Mother, how many MPs live in their constituencies? How often do you think Mr Asquith visited East Fife?'

'I trust I shall not start taking my cue from Mr Asquith at this stage of my career, Christabel.'

She returns to her chair. 'No, you never did take your cue from anybody. I don't know if that was your strength or your weakness.' There is something restless about Christabel today: normally so at ease, she seems unsettled.

'What do you have on your mind, Christabel? It cannot be only the wallpaper that is agitating you.'

She grimaces. 'Never underestimate wallpaper.' She takes a deep breath, exaggerating it to lighten the tone. 'But you're right, I do have something on my mind. I've been debating with myself whether or not to tell you now, while you're recovering from your illness.'

'It was not an illness,' I protest. 'It was just an indisposition.'

Christabel's most eloquent gesture on the platform was always a little wave of the hand, dismissing an interjection from a heckler as too trivial to merit a rejoinder. She now bestows this wave upon my feeble protestation. 'Recovering from your *indisposition*, then.'

'I shall not recover the sooner for being kept in suspense, Christabel.'

She looks at me as if calculating my chances of recovery, then nods. 'Well, on balance I do think it better that you should hear it from me rather than from some other source.'

I laugh, but even to my ears my laugh sounds nervous. 'Heavens, Christabel, what horrors have you brought me to sup upon?'

She takes up her bag from the little table next to me. 'I don't know if it's a horror, Mother, but it's ugly enough in all conscience.' She rummages in the bag, then brings out a copy of a newspaper and unfolds it. 'It would seem the *News of the World* thought its readers might want their Easter Sunday enlivened with an uplifting story of true love.' She turns the front page to me. A banner headline announces: '*Eugenic Baby Sensation. Sylvia's Amazing Confessions. Soul Mate of 53.*'

A career of public speaking has trained me never to appear at a loss in the face of the unexpected; but here, in my own rented space, with only my daughter for an audience, I feel incapable of even the feeblest rejoinder. I sit staring stupidly at the Pomeranian, who is tearing up a ball of paper. All I can think is that I envy the little creature her ignorance.

Christabel makes a gesture of rising from her chair. 'Mother, you're very pale. Are you all right?'

'Yes,' I manage to say, and wave her back to her place. 'Yes, I am quite all right, thank you. Only a little shaken, I think.'

She settles back in her chair. 'Do you want to hear your daughter's amazing confessions?'

'I do not think I *want* to hear anything about Sylvia ever again. But read me the worst bits, to confirm me in my resolve.'

She turns the front page towards herself with an exaggerated frown. 'I'm not sure that anything is worse than anything else, given the fundamental vulgarity of talking to the press in the first place – though *the press* is a very dignified term for this … *publication.*' She shakes the paper to smooth it. 'You can get an intimation of the flavour of the whole thing from the opening: "From the obscurity in which she has lived since the memorable days of the militant suffragettes, Miss Sylvia Pankhurst springs a new sensation upon the world today."' She lowers the paper. 'Thus our years of sacrifice are turned into just another *sensation* preceding this latest coup by Sylvia. The struggle for the vote for women is equated with having a child out of wedlock by an Italian anarchist. The Pankhursts have found a new mission, catering to the prurient tastes of the semi-educated.'

I interrupt Christabel, knowing that she is capable of sustaining the diatribe indefinitely. 'Do they mention the Italian anarchist?'

She scans the page. 'Not by name or nationality, for which

16

small mercy we should be thankful, I suppose. Sylvia says only, in her infinite good taste, that he is, and I quote "an old and dear friend whom I have loved for years, but who is not in a position to contribute substantially to the baby's support." In effect, she's saying she's had a bastard by a pauper.' She folds the paper angrily and puts it down on the table.

I force myself to reply calmly. 'It does rather leave the field open for speculation of the most lurid kind.' I try to sound controlled, ironic; but the thought of the masses gloating vulgarly over the details of my daughter's private life fills me with disgust. 'I do not see how I am to appear on a platform after this,' I say. 'How am I to go into the streets of the East End knowing that the world is thinking of this?' I point at the newspaper. 'I have been imprisoned and been proud of it. I have had ordure flung at me and felt ennobled by it. But *this*! Sylvia has achieved what the whole British legal system never could. For the first time in my life I shall be ashamed to be seen in public.'

Christabel shrugs impatiently. 'Now, Mother,' she reprimands me, 'however provoking the offence, don't exaggerate the effects. It's vile enough as it is, but it does not reflect on you. Everybody knows that you disowned Sylvia years ago.'

I try, but fail to find comfort in this consideration. 'In the vulgar mind all the Pankhursts are lumped together. And my whole campaign is based on the need for higher standards of sexual morality. Can you imagine what the hecklers will make of this?'

'Come, Mother, you're not going to be intimidated by hecklers at this stage of your career? You, who quelled politicians and magistrates and policemen and prison warders, and faced hostile crowds in the streets of this city and almost every other city in England and Scotland?'

No doubt Christabel is right: when the time comes I will find the resolve to face whatever slings and arrows the rabble can bring against me. But for the moment I feel exposed and weak. I get to my feet.

'Where are you going, Mother? You know you shouldn't get up.'

'I don't know. I'm feeling faint. I think I need some air.' I sound fretful even to myself.

'Sit down, Mother. I'll open the window ...' – she gets up, pushes up the sash window, sniffs critically, '... though *air* is a hopeful term for the atmosphere out there.' She rubs the tips of her fingers fastidiously, as if to get rid of the dust from the window frame. 'And the noise ...'

I sit down again; there is in any case nowhere to go. I must look like Whistler's Mother, planted on my chair in submissive neutrality: Arrangement in Grey and Black, except for the wallpaper. 'Thank you, dear. That is much better. I think it was just the unexpectedness of it. What made Sylvia do it?'

Christabel shrugs. She has remained standing, and the gesture eloquently involves her whole body. For a moment I recall my old dream of her becoming a ballerina. 'What makes Sylvia ever do anything? Somebody who lives on Egyptian lentils will do anything, even have a child out of wedlock, to relieve the tedium of existence.'

'I wish I could blame it on the lentils. But I cannot help thinking this is all a deliberate attempt to undermine my campaign.'

Christabel raises a quizzical eyebrow, another one of her rhetorical devices. 'That would be an unusually subversive kind of pregnancy, wouldn't it, even for Sylvia?'

'Oh, for Sylvia the unusual is the norm. She let me know that she regarded my *embracing* of the Conservative Party as a betrayal of the principles of her father – her father! As if he weren't also my husband! I think at bottom *that* is what she cannot forgive me – that I was married to her beloved father.'

But Christabel has lost interest in pursuing Sylvia's motives. 'You mustn't brood too much on this, Mother, it's no good breaking your head over it. You and I saw years ago that Sylvia's behaviour was beyond the pale, and we told her so.

Now she's having her revenge, or trying to. We mustn't play into her hands by seeming to take her actions to heart.'

I wonder whether Christabel has declined into cliché with age, or whether it's just *my condition* that so fails to engage her imagination. 'I'm sure you're right, Christabel,' I nevertheless say. 'I mustn't brood. I think I'll try to get some sleep.'

'Shall I stay with you, Mother?' she offers dutifully. 'Or ask the Marshalls to fetch you again? You'd be so much better off with them at Chipping Ongar.'

'No, Christabel, you have your life to attend to. I know the Adventist meetings are taking up much of your time. And the Marshalls have been more than kind, but my duty now is here.'

'I don't see why you have to live in squalor in order to qualify for a seat in Parliament. Surely you can work for a cause without sacrificing yourself body and soul to it?'

'I'm not sure that I understand your distinction, Christabel.'

'That's exactly my point, Mother' – she stabs an index finger in my direction – 'you don't understand the distinction between working for a cause and sacrificing yourself to it. I worked for women's suffrage, as hard as anybody else, and harder than most, but I never *sacrificed* myself to it. The cause needed me to be alive and strong and free; there were plenty of others who could go to prison and go on hunger strike.'

Like you, she means. 'I am quite alive and strong and free enough, Christabel. This is nothing compared with prison and hunger strike. Nellie Hall usually comes by in the evenings, and Dr Williams will be in in the morning, I should think.'

'If you truly would rather entrust your welfare to Nellie Hall and May Williams than to your first-born daughter, I shall not insist,' she says, her light tone smoothing over the implications, and making a protest seem like a lack of humour. But the unfairness of her charge takes my breath, and for a moment I am at a loss for words.

'Nellie Hall and May Williams are paid to see to my welfare, dear,' I retort with a mildness that I hope is not weakness. She says nothing, merely raises a sceptical eyebrow, which commits her to nothing.

I have something to tell her. This is not a good moment for it, but I sense that she will leave soon, and this moment will have to do. So I announce, conscious of a certain abruptness, 'I have had a note from Ethel Smyth asking if she can call tomorrow.'

I glance at Christabel. She raises both eyebrows – she has taken to pencilling them, a trifle over-emphatically, I think – and makes a little *moue*. 'Ah, Dame Ethel … a *revenante*! I thought we had done with her for good.'

I am being let off lightly. 'She has written to me from time to time, and of course in mere civility I had to reply.'

She searches for her gloves and finds them on the mantelpiece. She looks at them critically, as if they represented Dame Ethel Smyth. 'I don't see the obligation,' she says matter-of-factly. 'Some people find encouragement even in mere civility. However,' she says, with a smile as tight as it is bright, as she draws on her gloves decisively, 'since she is determined to call, I don't suppose anybody can stop her.'

Christabel is displeased after all. I could have kept the news of Ethel's visit from her, but I did not want to seem, even to myself, to be arranging a clandestine meeting. I seek refuge in a questionable universal: 'When a friendship has run its course, it is simpler just to avoid confrontations, don't you think?'

'I should have thought the simplest way of doing that would be not to see her at all.' She smiles, an ambiguous grimace halfway between forgiveness and disapproval. 'Still, you know best how to run your life. And Ethel should feel absolutely at home here, in her tweeds and pork-pie hat. She always did look more like a dog breeder than a composer.'

I am provoked to feeble protest. 'You are unkind. She was very good to me once, and she was invaluable to the cause.'

'Ah yes, the March of the Women.' She hums a few bars with exaggerated emphasis. 'Stirring, I grant you, though I always thought it would have been more appropriate as occasional music for *Coriolanus*. It's all march and no woman.'

I smile at this. 'Ethel was always more march than woman.'

Christabel leans over and kisses me. I have been forgiven. 'Get some rest before she comes; you'll need all your energy to ward her off.'

'Oh, I shouldn't think I would have to do that,' I reply as lightly as possible, though I am in fact apprehensive about Ethel's visit. 'And perhaps you could ask Mrs Chipperfield to look in later, if she is free. I trust the Chipperfields do not take the *News of the World*.'

Christabel kisses my forehead again. 'Come, that's better. You won't allow Sylvia's malice to upset you.'

I take her hand in mine and kiss it. 'Not as long as I have you, dear. You have always been a source of strength to me.'

She smoothes my hair. 'And I have found enough strength for both of us in my faith.'

'You have always been strong. And you know that I can't share your hope for the Advent. I lost all belief in an afterlife when I met that imbecile Madame Blavatsky, and I am not prepared to have my unbelief challenged after so many years.'

'You will see the light yet.' She hands me the little dog. 'And in the meantime, pending your illumination, you have little Flora.'

'Of course I do.' I feel awkward, not being used to having dogs in my lap. 'Has there been news of Adela in Australia?'

'Not that I've seen. We must assume that she's peddling her Socialist agenda as relentlessly as ever.' She takes up the newspaper. 'Shall I take this wretched rag away? It can only further poison the atmosphere.'

'No, leave it, dear. I think I can face up to its horrors now.'

In truth I want her to go. I have a sudden urge to cry, and I do not want to cry in front of Christabel. Christabel has no use for tears.

21

After she has gone, I do not in fact cry. I put the dog on the floor and take up the newspaper again. The parts Christabel read out to me are bad enough, but the rest is worse. Not content with letting the Pankhurst name speak for itself, Sylvia made a point of stressing the family connection in an unseemly frenzy of self-revelation, exceeding even the prurient appetite of the gutter press. Without being asked what the child would be called, she volunteered: *'His name is Richard Keir Pethick, after my father and two dear friends. And he will keep the Pankhurst name; his father is only too proud for his son to carry on the family tradition and the family name.'*

There is more such sanctimonious blether about *'my son, who I trust will make his mark as a reformer, or at least as a fighter for social justice like his father and mine'*; and then, to make sure that the world knows every sordid detail of her private life, a profession of hurt: *'I confess myself surprised and wounded at the failure of the members of my immediate family to respond to my attempts to involve them in my joy. My mother in particular has chosen to ignore the letter I sent her on the subject. I'm afraid advancing age has deprived her of the principles of tolerance and compassion inculcated in us by my late father.'*

I fold the paper neatly: tearing it up or crumpling it would accord it an importance I do not attach to it. *The principles of tolerance and compassion* – yes, those are what Sylvia has fashioned as her weapons of war, having first claimed them as her legacy from her beloved father. *Tolerance and compassion* – in Sylvia's hands they have assumed a power denied to mere militancy.

II

If Sylvia's sentimentality had manifested the feebleness normally associated with such a temperament, one could at least have managed if not respected it; but it was reinforced by a righteousness that gave it all the unyielding determination of abstract principle. Sylvia, in a word, was obstinate. She was too obstinate even to confess to pain. One evening, when Sylvia was about seven years old, Susannah came to me where I was sitting in my husband's study. We would have been discussing the Women's Franchise League, which we had just had a large part in forming.

'I beg your pardon, Mrs Pankhurst, but I think there's something you should see.'

'What is it, Susannah?' I did not as a rule suffer my few enough moments with Richard to be interrupted by domestic affairs.

'It's Miss Sylvia, ma'am. I think she's gone and hurt herself.'

'You *think* so Susannah? Is the matter not capable of verification?'

Susannah looked at me blankly – she was never a very intelligent woman – and Richard intervened.

'What is the matter with Sylvia, Susannah?'

'I noticed when I was bathing her, sir, that she had this big lump on her hip, just here, really swollen and all red and blue. And I asked her about it, and she said she got it running in the hallway and bumping her hip against the staircase.'

'Is it not something you can attend to, Susannah?' I asked.

'I wouldn't know what to do, ma'am. It really looks like quite a bad bump.'

23

I could see that Susannah was determined that I should witness the injury myself, so I followed her up to the bathroom, where Sylvia was wrapped in a towel, looking rather pale, but not otherwise discomposed by her injury. I was inclined to believe that Susannah had exaggerated the nature of the hurt, but when the towel was removed, it did seem that the injury could be severe: the hipbone was standing at an odd angle, as if broken, and it was badly bruised.

I was shocked and angry. 'Sylvia how on earth did you do that?'

'I was running, Mother, and bumped against the staircase.'

'But when?'

'This morning.'

'This morning? And you did not think to tell anybody about it?'

She just shook her head; her silences could at times be as provoking as the most overt challenge. And Sylvia knew, better than most children, that an injury disarms the parent and empowers the child.

'But why not?' I nevertheless insisted.

'Because you told us not to make a fuss when we hurt ourselves,' she replied. For a moment I wanted to slap her for this subtle transference of responsibility, but I thought better of it in the presence of Susannah. Besides, the injury really seemed to be of a nature requiring attention, so I suppressed my irritation and told Susannah to fetch Dr Stevenson, who fortunately lived nearby.

Dr Stevenson, like most medical men, was maddeningly circumspect, as if committing himself to any but the most general diagnosis might jeopardise the life of the patient or even his own career. Though unwilling to speculate as to the cause of the injury, he did, upon my expressing my doubt that such a severe injury could have been caused by a bump, venture to disagree with me.

'No,' he said, 'no. We must not underestimate the effect of a hard object like a banister upon the relatively unformed bones of a young person. Besides,' he added, stroking Sylvia's head, 'there would surely be no reason to doubt the word of the young person involved.'

I could hardly cast aspersions on the truthfulness of my own child, and had no choice but to accept his diagnosis, such as it was. He ministered to the bruise as best he could, but Sylvia retained a slight limp ever after, which could probably have been prevented had she not insisted on concealing her injury.

Clearly, there was always something akin to defiance in Sylvia's stoicism. When, as a small child, she was beaten for some offence, like refusing to eat her porridge because it was 'lumpy', she resolutely refused to show any emotion, other than a kind of satisfaction in her own impenitence. After a while I gave up beating her altogether, as I saw that it had no effect on her, indeed seemed only to confirm her in a self-righteous sense of her own undervalued merit. Once she refused so obstinately to take her cod liver oil that I was forced to instruct the servants to tie her to her bed until she obeyed; but she remained obdurate, and at bedtime was still tied to her bed.

What I have called her defiant stoicism later stood her in good stead in braving the rigours of hunger striking and forcible feeding, but it also did her much harm in depriving her of that openness and candour that made Christabel so much more amenable a daughter. Even in her appearance, Sylvia mutely asserted defiance of my preferences and principles. I have always believed that a woman should enhance her natural beauty, or at any rate ameliorate her appearance, by dressing as well as she can afford. A frumpish suffragette, I believed, succeeds only in confirming the prejudice of the ignorant, who choose to believe that only those women take to politics who fail to make themselves felt in their more traditional sphere. I never made a secret of the fact that whenever I

25

could I bought my clothes in Paris. The Parisian seamstress is still vastly superior to anything our own country can produce. I could not see then, and still can not see, that my appreciation of well-cut clothes and good fabric is inconsistent with my concern for social justice, as Sylvia's demeanour and apparel seemed calculated to suggest. She was in this respect, too, an unrewarding child, offering little of that refreshment to the spirit that we look to young people to provide in the midst of the all-encroaching dinginess of modern life, the sheer ugliness of the conditions of so many people, the extreme plainness of so many fighters for social justice. I detest lumpy jerseys and shapeless skirts; it was one of Sylvia's perversities to insist on wearing both, even as a child and of course much more chronically once she was free to choose her own clothes. Indeed, her clothes now are of a cut and colour that one could not imagine being *chosen*: they seem to have been inflicted upon her by a malign providence or a German godmother.

Lacking Christabel's power to charm, Sylvia strove to make herself felt by cultivating and exhibiting an overpowering compassion with all living creatures, the more helpless the better. Her younger sister, Adela, was at first the object of her charity: a strange, sickly little thing, suffering from bronchitis and from weak legs, which necessitated iron splints for the first six years of her life. Sylvia made a show of helping Adela to get about, moving objects out of her way with unnecessary ostentation, closing windows wherever Adela went. Adela, however, was an intelligent and self-sufficient child, and did not take readily to being mothered; she declined Sylvia's help with a firmness remarkable in one so young.

The next object, not to say victim, of Syvia's compassion was her little brother Frank, but he was far too cheerful a child to respond to her lugubrious ministrations. Besides, he received all the attention from the whole family that any child could have desired. As the long-awaited son after three daughters, he was the joy of my and Richard's lives, and his three sisters, small as they were, delighted in him. For them, he was a novelty, a superior kind of plaything; for us, Richard and me, he represented the future, bright with promise. He would live, we believed, to accomplish ideals that seemed impossible of fulfilment in our lifetime. He did much to lighten up the difficult years of our life in Russell Square.

We had moved south from Manchester some years before because London was so much the centre of things, but the bulk of Richard's legal practice was still in the North, and he frequently had to travel there, leaving me to care for a large house and a young family. Richard did not desire that I should turn myself into a household machine; and having made sure that my children were well looked after by competent servants, often helped by my sister Mary who was living with us at the time, I felt at liberty to resume my rightful place by my husband's side in the political struggles that were occupying more and more of his time. I thus looked after these affairs in his absence, and indeed at times accompanied him to Manchester.

The four little children had the whole large house to play in, and also the garden of Russell Square. There they devised their games and played out their fantasies happily enough, giving me no reason to doubt their contentment. Sylvia, to be sure, was always the solitary one, spending much of her time making drawings of fantastic subjects, drawings that she would hide under furniture, there to be discovered many weeks later. I thought little of this at the time; only now, thinking back, do I see the figure at the margin, the silent child in the back garden, and I wonder if thus were sown the seeds of the resentment that have now born such poisonous fruit.

One evening, returning from one of my occasional visits to Manchester with Richard, I was met at the door by a hysterical Sylvia, screaming 'Where were you! Where were you!'

Richard, who was always better at calming Sylvia than I, picked her up, while I sought a rational explanation of her extreme agitation. I found the other two girls hardly less worked up, however, and even my sister Mary in tears. All she could say was 'It's Frank, it's Frank.'

'Yes, Mary, but what about Frank?' I demanded, the truth to tell somewhat irritated by her incoherent babbling. She, however, could only point upstairs mutely, and, fearing the worst, I made my way to Frank's room. I say I feared the worst, but in fact I was not prepared for what I found: Frank was dead in his little bed.

It took Richard and me a while to establish what exactly had happened. It transpired that in our absence little Frank had fallen ill. Doctor Stevenson, for once producing a firm opinion, had diagnosed croup and treated him accordingly, but the good doctor's confidence had proved misplaced: Frank's condition had worsened rapidly, and by the time it had been established that he was suffering from diphtheria, he was dead.

Frank's death was as devastating as it was sudden. It was my first experience of death at such close quarters, and I mourned his passing deeply – perhaps too deeply, in that my grief led me to neglect tasks I had undertaken in connection with Richard's increasingly strenuous political activities. I tried to forget Frank by hiding all the portraits of him that I could find, but my surviving children reminded me of him, if not by their innocently tactless questions, then simply by confronting me daily with their presence. I found these demands on my attention painful at times, though of course I hid this from them. Frank had had beautiful eyes, and in facing the imploring countenances of his sisters, it was difficult not to compare their comparatively insipid stares with his dark, lustrous glances.

I was shaken from the inertia of grief by the discovery, very shortly after Frank's death, that I was expecting another child. I took to referring to the expected child as 'Frank coming again', in spite of Richard's cautioning me: 'It is quite as likely to be a little girl as a little boy, and it would not do to set your heart so entirely on a boy.' I feigned agreement, but remained secretly convinced that it would be a boy, and to our joy I was proved right. In gratitude we named him after his departed brother, Henry Francis, but called him Harry. He was, at birth, the most beautiful of my children, and Richard and I delighted in him – a delight that his sisters wholeheartedly shared, although as usual it was Sylvia who was most demonstrative in her affection.

My time being just then much taken up with the newly formed Women's Franchise League, Harry was left to the care of a nurse, one Mrs Watson. Though sturdy at birth, he was not a healthy child: his bottle did not agree with him, and he demanded constant attention. Mrs Watson was competent – having had several children of her own – but strict, in the fashion of the time, not believing in heeding the boy's every cry. 'He'll cry himself out of it,' was her considered opinion, and indeed, of course, he usually did. But this method distressed Sylvia, who was only seven at the time, and rather an emotional child for her age. When she failed in her attempts to involve her sister Christabel in her alarm – Christabel sensibly maintaining that Harry's care was in capable adult hands – she made a nuisance of herself with Mrs Watson. She got short shrift from her, but Susannah and my sister Mary were more tender-hearted, and inclined to intercede with Mrs Watson to allow Sylvia to pick Harry up. Their indulgence upset Mrs Watson and encouraged Sylvia in a morbid fixation on her brother, which unfortunately we did not recognise for what it was at the time. This was to lead to much graver confrontations between Sylvia and me later in life.

In the short term, her coddling encouraged a regrettable lack of independence in Harry. He grew into a timid boy, who shrank before a reprimand as if he had been whipped. When scolded for some misdemeanour, he would grow deathly pale and stare at his chastiser as if in mortal fear. As the only son, he should have basked in the favour of the whole family, but his very vulnerability made one reluctant to come too close to him:

29

his nature was like an open wound, requiring attention and yet tender to the touch and repulsive to the eye. I speak figuratively, of course, of the spiritual eye; he was in fact an almost eerily beautiful boy, with very light colouring and bright blue eyes. He was, as I have intimated, difficult; not from any innate rebelliousness – he was only too eager to please – but from a fragility that inhibited one's relations with him. He was the exact converse of Christabel, with her high colouring, her cheerful, confident manner, and her robust constitution. She at all times gave the impression of being sufficient unto herself; he seemed somehow incomplete, needing others to affirm his existence.

It follows from the relative feebleness of Harry's constitution that he became a favourite with Sylvia. Indeed, he seemed so preternaturally prone to misfortune as to tax even her powers of compassionate ministration. Before he was eight he had had both the chicken-pox and the measles, and broken his teeth in falling from a tree into which he had attempted to follow Christabel. One could not, of course, hold him responsible for these misfortunes, but it was difficult at times to suppress a sigh of exasperation as yet another mishap was announced, invariably by Sylvia.

When Harry was eight, Sylvia claimed Harry had poor eyesight and needed glasses.

'What on earth makes you think that, Sylvia?' I asked. 'Who has ever heard of a child of eight needing glasses?'

'Harry does,' she maintained stubbornly. 'He gets headaches when he reads.'

I declined to take seriously what seemed to me a whimsical and wholly uninformed diagnosis. Richard was just at this time much away from home, and I did not want to vex him with a contrived difficulty and an unnecessary expense. Sylvia managed, however, to bring the matter to his attention in a manner most gratifying to herself and embarrassing to me.

One evening after dinner Richard asked Harry to read to the

family, as all the children were expected to do from time to time, and as Harry had done well enough, if rather haltingly, several times before. On this occasion, however, Sylvia announced abruptly and dramatically, 'Harry can't read. It gives him the headache.'

'Why is that?' asked Richard, who always took whatever the children said seriously, almost gravely.

Sylvia looked at Harry, but it was clear that he was not going to answer on his own account. 'Because his eyes are bad,' she said. 'He can't read small print.'

'Is that true, Harry?' Richard asked.

Harry nodded, but still did not say anything.

Richard held out the book he wanted Harry to read from, and asked, 'Can you make out the letters?'

Harry took the book. 'Yes,' he said.

We all looked at him expectantly, but he did not volunteer any further information.

'Then why does Sylvia say you cannot read?'

Harry looked at Sylvia imploringly, and she said, 'He can read, don't you understand, but if he reads for a long time he gets the headache.'

'And what makes you think it's his eyes?' Richard asked.

'I know,' she said, with that air of total certainty that sorted so oddly with her social diffidence. Then she added, 'I know, because his eyes are like mine, and I get the same headaches.'

Richard turned to me. 'Did you know about this, Em?' he asked. His tone was not at all accusatory, yet I could not but read into it an implication of neglect, as I am sure Sylvia had intended to communicate to her father.

'Sylvia has mentioned something of the kind,' I was forced to admit, 'but not as something requiring immediate attention.'

'I would not want my children to be deprived of the means to read,' was all he said. 'Perhaps we can get Susannah to have them seen to by somebody.'

This, I think, was the first open challenge to my authority

mounted by Sylvia. It served her purpose admirably, because it grouped her with her father against me, and it established her as the protectrix of Harry. In the event, of course, it transpired that Harry did not need glasses at all.

I could not hide from myself, though I concealed it from my children and even from my husband, that Harry was not the substitute for little Frank that I had dreamed of: he was himself too dependent and diffident to inspire any hope that he might live to lead others. Apart from being physically weak, he seemed starved for attention, in spite of all the affection he received at home. Missing him from the nursery one morning, Susannah found him in a nearby park, talking to one of the gardeners. When she asked him why, he said, 'The man spoke nicely to me.' As if he weren't spoken to nicely at home!

I was indeed being brought to realise that, in looking to my boys for large ambitions and great deeds, I had been guilty of the same kind of conventional thinking that I deplored in others. A little incident brought this sharply to my mind. One evening, as was often the case, the children were sitting with Richard and me after supper. He liked to have his family with him, reading and discussing matters that came to mind. Christabel was ten at the time and Sylvia eight. Sylvia had been reading Stead's *Review of Reviews*, and suddenly exclaimed, in the over-emotional tones that she was prone to, 'Oh, but how dreadful!'

'What is it, Sylvia?' asked Richard, who believed in encouraging his children's interests and sharing their concerns.

'It says here,' Sylvia reported, as if bringing news of a new Deluge, 'that at ten the brain is fully developed and can form no more new cells.'

'I see no cause for ultimate despair in that,' said Richard, in the humorous tone he often adopted with his children.

'But that means that in two years' time I shall stop learning, and I know so little.'

While Richard was trying to explain to Sylvia the error in

her thinking, Christabel said, 'For my part, I am only too pleased that I am ten and that my brain is fully formed. I have as much sense as anybody else, and will not be treated as a child any longer.'

I was struck, though I did not say this, by this difference between my two daughters. I believe it was from that date that I mentally elected Christabel as my acolyte, or, more properly, my ally. There was in her the spirit that I would want to see in the woman of the future – self-assured, confident, positive.

The transference, as it were, of my hopes from Harry to Christabel was unmarked by any change in my behaviour, but Sylvia, with the preternatural perceptions of a resentful child, always found subtle ways of reminding me of what she regarded as my maternal duty. 'Mother, do you think Harry will be quite warm enough in that jumper?' would be a typical question.

'Sylvia, if he is not, he can say so. It is not necessary for you to mediate my treatment of Harry.'

This would elicit from her the air of a martyr, a silent setting of the mouth in lines of noble endurance, an all-but-visible casting of the eyes heavenward as if to appeal to a higher justice. I refused, naturally, to be cast in the role that she had precociously created for me, and made this clear to her; but it is to be feared that she never really reconsidered her childish interpretation of my attitude to Harry.

Richard died on the 5th of July 1898, two days before Harry's ninth birthday. Deeply as I felt his death, I realised that my remaining children needed my strength to sustain them in their own grief, and I did my best to introduce, as soon as I could summon up the emotional resources, a more hopeful note into the household. It was, then, particularly trying, in the midst of my efforts to overcome my own sorrow for the sake of my children, to have Sylvia's tearful face attending upon me as if reproaching me for not being properly grief-stricken. When not actually crying or sniffling, she exuded an aura of dampness and misery, her eyes red with the weeping that – the implication was – had kept her from sleep all night.

One day, about a month after Richard's death, Christabel and I were laughing over something, a harmless enough trifle; but Sylvia's coldly disapproving glance and tight-lipped silence seemed to suggest that we had committed an atrocity. Provoked beyond my normal policy of ignoring such demonstrations, I said to her, 'Sylvia, it would help me very much if you would contrive to be more cheerful, instead of reminding me constantly of our loss.'

She sighed deeply and said, 'I would be cheerful if I could to please you, Mother.'

I would have let this pass, only Christabel flared up and said, 'For heaven's sake, Sylvia, one would think that you were the only person who felt anything for Father's death.'

Even at this early age – she was sixteen at the time – Sylvia had mastered the art of eloquent stoicism: she simply sighed again, but very gently, as if to herself, suggesting that her feelings were too deep to be shared with the likes of us. Thus she embarked on that life-long habit of criticising me for not living up to my husband's ideals that was to issue in this latest and most public accusation.

The truth was that Sylvia could never forgive me for being married to the man she idolised. That was the most fundamental cause of our division: even after his death, she competed with me in what she termed fidelity to the memory of her father. She persuaded herself at an early age that she alone was truly in sympathy with her father's principles: the rest of us were mere interlopers with no true understanding.

But more pernicious than her jealousy was her resentment of my treatment of Harry. Battling me for the keeping of her father's memory, she was in the weaker position and knew it; but as self-appointed guardian of her brother she assumed a position of equality and even superiority. She showed, in her protectiveness of him, that she thought I neglected my duties

34

as a mother: a silent accusation that was all the more difficult to counter for being unexpressed.

Sylvia's campaign derived a spurious air of moral legitimacy from Harry's helplessness, which made it all too easy to cast him as a victim. He was in fact a difficult and unrewarding child. In addition to being physically weak, he was mentally slow. At times even my maternal tenderness failed to vanquish altogether the suspicion that he was something of a fool. Although he liked reading and studying, and indeed was all too inclined to seek refuge in some book or periodical, he lacked the power to articulate his impressions; privately, I even doubted whether he possessed to any useful degree the power to form such impressions. Ours was always a highly articulate family; in our midst Harry seemed like a donkey amongst race-horses.

Not that he was unwilling: there was nothing donkey-like in his eagerness to be of use in the causes that were more and more coming to occupy me and my daughters as they grew into adulthood, and as I became more active in the political life of Manchester, whither we had moved not long after Harry's birth. He even absorbed some of the political principles forever being debated at home, and when he was only eleven was given a beating by his classmates at school for coming out against the Boer War, to which I was much opposed at the time. He tried to hide his bruises from me, but Sylvia, of course, brought them to my notice.

I endeavoured to impress upon Sylvia that her exaggerated care of Harry was preventing him from developing his own powers, but she was never an easy person to persuade of anything contrary to her own bent, and implied, without quite stating, that she saw my concern as a form of callousness. When I sent him away to school in Hampstead she made much play of feeling sorry for the poor lad so far from home; when I could no longer afford the fees in Hampstead and brought him back to Manchester, she affected to pity him for suffering an 'interrupted education'.

In 1907, when Harry was eighteen years old, it came to be time for him to go out to work – as much to strengthen his body and improve his health as to contribute to the family income. Apart from these considerations, I had also decided to give up my home in Manchester, since I was for much of the time travelling to speak at public meetings. Thus, had Harry not gone out to work, lodgings would have had to be found for him.

Fortunately I found a small builder on Clydeside who was willing to have him as apprentice for a very modest fee. This particular builder, a member of the Independent Labour Party, devoted his energies to the worthy cause of erecting barrack dwellings for the working class. I had always admired builders, and envied them their capacity to create great structures out of shapeless bricks and mortar. In them the power of the male seemed most constructively manifested, and I thought that in apprenticing Harry to this trade I was enabling him to enter a life of usefulness to others and satisfaction to himself.

Unfortunately Harry was slow to appreciate the advantages of this position. He was ever the most obedient of children, and would not have complained, but I sensed some reluctance and reserve in his manner, and encouraged him to speak his mind, as I always did with all my children. 'You must tell me, Harry,' I said, 'if my arrangement does not suit you, or if you have something else in mind that you would rather do.'

He shook his head. 'No, Mother,' he said, 'I don't have anything else in mind.' He made this seem like a confession of hopelessness rather than an acceptance of my arrangement.

'But you do understand, don't you,' I asked, trying to hide my exasperation at his lack of cooperation, 'that you have to go out to work at some point?'

He nodded his head dumbly, leaving me to carry on. 'And you do understand that an apprenticeship is a form of education that will equip you to make a living for yourself and your family later, don't you?'

He nodded again, mutely. I was grateful that the builder had accepted him as apprentice without meeting him. He could not have shown up well in an interview.

I was by and large content, though, that Harry had accepted my reasoning with little more than his normal dullness of spirit, and there things would have ended, had Sylvia not intervened.

'Mother, do you not think it might be possible to find Harry a more intellectual kind of occupation?'

This put me in an extremely awkward position, as Sylvia could not but have known. Harry's intellect had never been strong, but how was I to say so in front of the boy? So I simply replied, 'What intellectual kind of occupation did you have in mind, Sylvia?'

'Oh, there must be plenty of opportunities for a hard-working young man like Harry – perhaps a lawyer's clerk, so that eventually he can qualify as a lawyer like father.'

This was characteristic of Sylvia's sentimentality. Richard had been a brilliant man; Harry was a boy of below average intellect. He would have been hopelessly out of his depth in a lawyer's office; but again, out of compassion for the boy, I could not say so to his face.

'I have made the arrangements for Harry to go to Mr Duns-combe, Sylvia,' I said. 'If you can contrive to find an alternative career that is as good, you may proceed to do so; but in the meantime I shall assume that Harry will report to Glasgow on Monday as arranged.'

'If you give me a week I'm sure I shall be able to find Harry something more suitable.'

'I'm not sure what you mean by *more suitable*, Sylvia. I am surprised at your disdain for manual labour, given your sympathy with the working classes.'

'It is not disdain, Mother. I have only too much respect for the hardships the working classes have to endure; but Harry has not been brought up to that kind of physical deprivation.'

'You always want to make people seem weaker than they are, Sylvia, so that you can lavish pity on them. You *want* them to be victims.'

Sylvia's eyes filled with tears. 'If that were true, I would presumably be happy for Harry to go off to be a builder.'

'Is it your implication, Sylvia, that Harry is a victim to my machinations?'

She faced me, glaring through her tears; and for the first time I realised that my daughter hated me. 'Not to your machinations, no, Mother. To your good intentions.'

As far as I could tell from his infrequent and inarticulate communications, Harry was happy enough in Glasgow. As fate would have it, however, Mr Dunscombe went bankrupt early in the New Year of 1908, and Harry rejoined the family. Unfortunately, since there was no home for him to go to, he had to join Sylvia in her lodgings in London, a proximity which was later to prove unfortunate in the extreme. For the time being, however, I was pleased to note that he seemed more robust, and I felt vindicated in having proposed a life of physical labour for him. He was less communicative even than before, but now displayed a strong interest in helping me and his sisters in working for the vote for women. I had doubts about the efficacy of men in our struggle in general, and Harry in particular struck me as an unlikely sort of champion, but since Sylvia was encouraging him quite immoderately, I held my peace, not wanting to be accused of interfering.

For the time being, however, I was still facing the practical problem of Harry's future. Christabel, in one of her rare misjudgements, suggested that he should train as a secretary. I would have opposed this course more vigorously, but Harry himself grasped at it so eagerly that, perhaps unwisely, I did not have the heart to deny him what I judged to be a wholly inappropriate career. He was accordingly enrolled for typing and shorthand at the Polytechnic, and I found him lodgings in London at a pound a week.

I did not think this sedentary life agreed with Harry. His eyesight deteriorated so rapidly at this time that it was necessary to buy him glasses for reading, which did little to improve his appearance. The glasses gave him an entirely misleading intellectual air, which would count against him in more active walks of life, and little benefit him in a sphere where the appearance could not long conceal the reality. Sylvia, however, maintained that 'for the first time in his life' Harry could now read easily.

Fortunately, at this time, Harry vindicated my ambitions of a more active life for him by evincing a hitherto unsuspected interest in the back-to-the-land movement. He gave a quite creditable address on the subject to a meeting of the Independent Labour Party, his evident sincerity making up for his lack of oratorical skill. Though at this time I had resigned from the ILP, I attended the event at Harry's request, and I happened to be sitting next to a well-to-do supporter of the Women's Political and Social Union, one Mr Joseph Fels.

Mr Fels was favourably impressed with Harry's performance. 'A serious lad,' he said, while we were having tea after the address, 'and well informed.'

'Yes,' I said, 'I have been encouraging him to take an interest in outdoor activities because his health as a child was not good, and I believe a more active existence would benefit him greatly.'

He took a pensive sip of his tea, which was, as always at ILP gatherings, execrable. 'Is he at present at all practically involved in agriculture?'

I shrugged. 'Alas, no. He has somehow conceived the idea of becoming a secretary and is taking classes in shorthand at the Polytechnic.' I did not think it necessary to tell Mr Fels that Harry had been urged to this course by his sisters rather than by his own inclination.

Mr Fels smiled and shook his head. 'Shorthand? A pity. I could use a lively lad on my smallholdings in Essex.'

This opening was too fortuitous to ignore – I have often found providence to be surprisingly beneficent in moments of real need – and on further enquiry Mr Fels disclosed that he had several smallholdings in Mayland in Essex, which he was farming on a cooperative basis, allowing the tenants a share of the profits. He would be more than willing to place Harry on one of these smallholdings, where he could be lodged with a tenant family. 'It would be simple accommodation, of course, but clean and salubrious.' He pronounced it *saloobruss*.

I was grateful to Mr Fels. I had not originally been very favourably impressed with him: he was a soap manufacturer, one of that class of floridly red-faced males whose motives for belonging to any progressive association always seem open to conjecture. I did not, however, want my prejudice against Mr Fels's physiognomy to interfere with this opportunity for Harry. I told him that I was fairly confident I could persuade my son of the advantages of his offer, and that I would be able to give him a definite undertaking soon.

I lost no time in informing Harry of this stroke of fortune. To my disappointment, he again failed to show any enthusiasm. Indeed, he evinced hardly any interest in the opportunity: instead of enquiring into the details, he merely said, 'I've been enjoying my shorthand and typing classes. And I have a reader's ticket at the British Museum.'

'Now, Harry,' I said, 'you know that the enjoyment derived from an activity bears no necessary relation to its usefulness.'

'Shorthand and typing are useful, are they not?' he asked, to my surprise and displeasure. He was not usually an obstinate boy.

'They are useful for commercially inclined people,' I explained, 'but have little of that higher usefulness your father used to commend to you, the usefulness that contributes to the greater happiness of others rather than yourself.'

'I don't see why others should be happy and not I,' he said sullenly.

As a first sign of rebellion this was alarming. I ascribed it to the regular contact he was having with Sylvia in London: yet another reason for his removal to Essex. I could, in any case, ill afford the pound a week for his lodgings.

'Harry,' I accordingly said, 'You know your father used to say "If you do not work for other people, you will not have been worth the upbringing." That is the principle on which you were brought up, along with your sisters, and which you see them putting into practice every day. It would be a sad day indeed if I were to feel that my only son had not been worth the upbringing.'

After this, he readily enough saw reason, as any appeal to the memory of his father could always be counted on to effect. Sylvia, of course, objected strenuously on the score of her brother's health. She refused to see that in order for Harry's health to improve, he would have to spend time in healthy outdoor activities rather than stooped over a typewriter.

'Mother, they say you cannot make a silk purse out of a sow's ear,' she said. 'Well, you cannot make a sow's ear out of a silk purse either. Harry's constitution is too delicate for agricultural labour.'

'His constitution always will remain delicate if left to you, Sylvia,' I replied. 'I think we have seen what nineteen years of your solicitude have done for Harry. Now it is time to try my system, which has the merit of having served generations of young Englishmen.'

Sylvia snorted rudely. 'Mother, perhaps you should confine yourself to the welfare of the women of England and not presume to legislate for young Englishmen.'

I ignored this gratuitous and pointless comment, and informed Mr Fels that Harry would be pleased to assume his duties as soon as practicable.

I have no reason to believe that Harry's sojourn in Sussex was unpleasant. He was uncommunicative, but then, he had never been a forthcoming child. I was myself very much involved with our campaign, which was entering its militant stage, and I seldom had an opportunity to see my son or speak to him. My daughters I of course saw more often, as we were all involved in the campaign together. Indeed, Christabel had assumed charge of coordinating the militancy campaign, and she, I, and Fred and Emmeline Pethick Lawrence met daily to discuss strategy.

The brilliance of the principle of militancy lay in the simple enough fact that, as Christabel said, 'Most people will give you what you want if you make enough of a nuisance of yourself.' Militancy was all about making a nuisance of ourselves: this was why we were so much disliked by male politicians, who had hitherto regarded the female sex as created by God to smooth the way of the male. Mr Lloyd George implied as much by saying to me in exasperation one day, 'Mrs Pankhurst, do you realise how *difficult* you are making things for me?' I replied, 'Yes, sir, I do. That is the sole aim of my campaign.'

Since resistance to female suffrage on the part of male parliamentarians was based largely on their terror that, once enfranchised, women would make a nuisance of themselves in the House, it was our duty to persuade them that we would make an ever greater nuisance of ourselves outside the House. This was why we targeted traditional male preserves, places like golf courses and clubs, where men had hitherto gone in order to get away from women.

But, of course, it takes trouble to create trouble, and we were kept very busy. Even as apparently simple a thing as stone-throwing, I discovered, does not come naturally to the untrained body, and Ethel Smyth, to whom it apparently did come naturally, had to give me several lessons on the golf course in front of her house – to the peril and dismay, she claimed, of her large wolfhound, which was, however, standing behind me and thus not within my line of fire. Ethel was somewhat childishly amused when in the effort of hurling my missile I overbalanced and sat down quite hard on the grassy surface. Other more technologically advanced tactics such as pouring acid on golf courses, setting fire to post boxes: all these took time to plan and execute, quite apart from the larger and more constructive effort of planning major demonstrations.

This was an exciting and strenuous time. Christabel and I, together with Emmeline and Fred Pethick Lawrence, had found it necessary to suspend the constitution of the WSPU in order to streamline the running of the Union by concentrating it in fewer and more competent hands. There were of course those who objected to this procedure on the grounds of its being 'undemocratic', as if any war had ever been won by democratic means – and it was by this time ever clearer to us that we were involved in a war requiring military discipline and military tactics. Teresa Billington-Greig, in particular, complained that our actions were 'a poor advertisement for what women will do with power once they have it'; but Christabel rejoined, 'Those who cannot follow the general must drop out of the ranks.'

With the running of the WSPU thus simplified, Christabel and I could take decisions and execute them with much more dispatch than under the cumbersome constitution. Thus we decided in October that we should try to get a deputation into the House of Commons by sheer physical weight of numbers, and immediately printed and distributed handbills which read 'Help the Suffragettes to Rush the House of Commons'. This produced a police summons on the grounds of a likely breach of the peace, 'the peace' being what the watchdogs and their masters termed their own undisturbed comfort. We were duly arrested and tried, which occasion Christabel turned into a triumph by conducting our defence in a manner to cause most embarrassment to the government, especially those cabinet ministers whom she had summoned as witnesses. The value of her performance, apart from the publicity it accorded the cause, lay in demonstrating that the instruments of oppression could be used against themselves by a sufficiently skilful manipulator.

Of course, the law always has at its disposal the means of physical oppression, and Christabel and I were duly locked up for three months in Holloway Prison. To deprive a person of sovereignty over her own body is something only criminals, diseases and governments dare do, and I resolved that I would jealously guard such sovereignty as remained possible within the limits of incarceration.

Imprisonment was, of course, not pleasant, but we saw it as an extension of our campaign, in that it gave us an opportunity to make a nuisance of ourselves more conspicuously. With my experience as a public speaker, I found that I was particularly good at simply making so much noise that the wardresses found it intolerable. 'I've seen prostitutes and I've seen murderesses,' said one of them, not unadmiringly, 'but I've never seen one as could make a racket like a lady born.'

'My good woman,' I replied, 'I am used to making a racket in the Albert Hall. Holloway Prison is no challenge for me.' She seemed impressed with this, though I do not think she had ever seen the inside of the Albert Hall.

By dint of consistently making as much of a racket as my means and circumstances allowed, I won several concessions; indeed, I believe if the politicians and magistrates who decreed that we be locked up had had personally to supervise our incarceration they would have granted us our demands much earlier. Be that as it may, though much of my time in prison was taken up in making my time there as unpleasant for my jailers as for myself, my main concern was for the fate of the WSPU in our absence. There was at this point some dissension amongst the ranks, largely fomented by the ambitious Teresa Billington-Greig, who felt excluded from the body of women who were now congregating in the Pethick Lawrences' chambers in Clement's Inn. Teresa adduced our 'take-over' of the Union as the reason for her insubordination, but she was in fact motivated by resentment of the measures necessitated by her own conduct. In the Hexham by-election of 1907 she had appropriated the occasion by such flamboyant behaviour on the platform that it quite distracted the rest of us, especially Christabel, whose style of performance was always pitched at a lower key. As Christabel commented, 'We are waging a war, not mounting a circus.' There was something vulgar about such a vying for attention and applause, and it had been necessary to bar Teresa from further appearances. Being a resentful person by nature, she might well now make use of our absence by bending the WSPU to her own purposes.

I knew we could rely on the Pethick Lawrences to keep to the policy formulated by myself and Christabel in conjunction with them, but I had been alarmed by a communication from Emmeline Pethick Lawrence to the effect that she had deputised Sylvia to stand in for Christabel, a piece of folly I had not imagined Emmeline to be capable of. It should have been clear to anybody, let alone somebody as close to the workings of the WSPU as Emmeline, that Sylvia had quite other priorities, and wanted to hitch the Union to her own socialist agenda.

'What on earth is Emmie thinking?' I asked Christabel in one of the conversation opportunities I had managed to establish as one of our prison rights. 'She must know that Sylvia's interest is entirely bound up with her East End women. She will turn the WSPU into a home for abused working-class women.'

'She will turn it into a platform for Sylvia Pankhurst, whatever else she does,' said Christabel, 'and I'm not entirely sure that Emmie would oppose her very vigorously.'

'Why not? Emmeline is hardly a working-class woman and most definitely not abused. Fred is only too ready to jump to her every whim.'

45

'I would not be surprised if Emmie had her own ambitions, and she might very well think Sylvia a more amenable ally than either of us.'

I snorted, 'Sylvia amenable? She's about as amenable as Coriolanus on a punitive expedition.'

'Emmie may not know that. Or she may count on Sylvia's being won over by the Pethick Lawrence riches.'

'Whatever it is,' I said, 'it bodes ill for the WSPU.'

'I don't think so,' said Christabel with a kind of grim enjoyment. 'I think it bodes ill for whoever interferes with the WSPU. We are not going to be in prison for ever.'

We were in fact released from Holloway three days earlier than we had expected, on the 19th of December. This was probably calculated by the authorities to forestall public demonstrations on our release, and it did in fact face us with the practical problem of accommodation, with everybody out of town for Christmas. Fortunately Christabel and I were able to take a train to The Mascot, the Pethick Lawrences' 'cottage' – in truth a sizeable house – in Holmwood, near Dorking, where we had gone before to recuperate after a spell in prison. Christabel, though in general so strong, suffered more than the rest of us from incarceration: it seemed to sap not so much her body as her spirit. By the same token, however, she recovered her strength more quickly than the rest of us, and by the second day she was fit enough to go for a long walk on the Common with Emmeline Pethick Lawrence, and with Annie Kenney, who had come to Holmwood to be with us.

I still felt too weak for a walk in the cold weather, and stayed at home happily enough by the fireside in the beautiful morning room. It was with mixed feelings, then, that I received the news from Fred Pethick Lawrence that Sylvia had arrived, uninvited and unannounced, from Penshurst, where she had been resting. Of course, it was only natural that she should want to see her mother and sister after such a long spell of imprisonment, but Sylvia's nature had always something over-intense about it that made her arrival anywhere less a matter of pleasure than of apprehension. At the best of times, with her haunted eyes and hollow cheeks, she could drain an occasion of joy; and on emerging from prison, one might be forgiven for preferring a more sprightly reception. Still, there she was, and I could not very well decline to see her.

Sylvia's entrance lacked grace. She had evidently walked from Holmwood station, and her face was flushed with exercise. Her hair, heavily framing her face, added to an impression of brooding gloom that cast a pall over the cheerful room and bright fire. Although her appearance was less aggressively plain than usual, the Arts and Crafts Movement frock she had chosen was not a happy idea, tending as it did towards the earnest in its conception of the decorative.

Sylvia looked at me as if inspecting me for damage. 'Was it very bad?' she asked.

I shrugged. 'Not worse than usual. They tried, of course, to make me abide by their degrading regulations and wear their disgusting prison clothes, but I refused. I demanded to be treated as a political prisoner rather than a common criminal, and I informed them that I would speak to my fellow inmates at every opportunity.'

Sylvia sat down by the fire and took my hand. Hers was unpleasantly cold from the walk in the cold air. 'And did they grant you your point?'

'Not just at first. They are not, as you know, in the habit of granting anything unless they are forced to. But I made so much noise in the exercise yard that they relented and allowed me to spend an hour a day with Christabel.'

She smiled at this, though a trifle wanly. She seemed, indeed, more than usually preoccupied, and I guessed that she had something on her mind. I was afraid this might be about the WSPU, her stewardship of which still filled me with some apprehension.

'There is something I must discuss with you,' she said, with that combination of resolve and diffidence that could make her such a strenuous presence.

'Is it about the WSPU?' I asked, trying to hide my anxiety.

She smiled faintly. 'No, Mother, you need have no fears on that score. It's only about Harry.'

I ignored the implied reflection on my priorities, and merely said, 'What is it now, Sylvia? He was quite happily settled at Mayfield ten weeks ago.'

'He has left Mayfield. He could no longer bear it.'

I removed my hand from her grasp. 'Left Mayfield? And with whose permission, pray?'

'Harry is twenty years old, Mother. He does not need permission to dispose of his own body.'

'In common decency he could have consulted me. What am I to say to Mr Fels? And what is Harry doing with himself?'

'He is doing French gardening at a sanatorium in Suffolk. He seems to be happy.'

'French gardening?' I exclaimed. 'I have the greatest admiration for the French, but I fail to see how their style of gardening is preferable to the English.'

Sylvia had got up from her chair and was looking out of the large window at the winter landscape outside. 'Mother, do you have any idea what conditions are like at Mayfield?' she asked.

'I understand them to be simple but salubrious. Harry must not expect the same standard of comfort on a farm as in London or Manchester.'

'I don't think he's insisting on Liberty furnishings, Mother,' she said in her driest manner, gesturing at the luxuriously appointed morning room. I refrained from replying – I never deign to respond to sarcasm – and she continued. 'Comfort has nothing to do with it. He was lodged with people who show no pity for man or beast. The husband beat his wife and they all maltreated the animals in their care. Harry was more distressed by this than on his own account, though he was him-

48

self living in the most appalling circumstances. He did not complain – as you know, Harry never complains – but he could simply not carry on any longer.'

She was now pacing the floor and wiping at her eyes. It was one of the more trying aspects of a conversation with Sylvia that she was perpetually on the verge of tears – like a house, Christabel once said in exasperation, with a basement prone to flooding: you never knew when you were going to end up with damp feet.

'I would not subject my son to worse conditions than I myself endure, Sylvia,' I said. 'I have just spent ten weeks in a prison cell totally destitute of any comforts, with unspeakable food and almost no opportunity for contact with a sympathetic human being. Can you be surprised if I say I do not see *French gardening* as a priority in our struggle?'

She stopped by my chair and glared at me, her eyes now full of tears. 'Mother, for pity's sake, the priority is not French gardening. The priority is Harry's health. I really don't think an agricultural career is what he was cut out for.'

'You talk like a dowager duchess discussing the youngest scion of the family. We cannot think of what people are cut out for, Sylvia; we must think where he will be most useful.'

'To whom will Harry be useful, digging turnips on a smallholding in Essex?'

'To himself. To others. To his country.'

'And perhaps to you.'

'I don't know what you are implying, Sylvia. I fail to see how Harry's agricultural career, as you call it, can be of use to me.'

She came even closer to me, as if arraigning me in a court of law. 'Useful to your vision of things. Your vision of your son as a strapping lad, your vision of men as manual labourers who are not to be involved in the cause. Perhaps even your vision of sacrificing to the cause.'

'I do not shrink from stating that I would sacrifice my own life to the cause.'

She seemed on the point of an angry reply, then visibly controlled herself, and said, in her most pedantic manner, 'We are all free to sacrifice our own lives, Mother, but sacrificing the lives of others is somewhat presumptuous.'

I, too, suppressed the anger I naturally felt. 'You talk as if I were planning to send Harry into battle, Sylvia,' I said. 'All I have in mind for him is healthy outdoor labour.'

'What is healthy for some constitutions can be fatal to others,' she informed me. 'The doctor in charge of the sanatorium says Harry's health is precarious. She is even prepared to treat him for a pound a week if he works in the garden.'

'I fail to follow the logic of her position: on the one hand she declares Harry's health to be precarious, on the other she is quite prepared to have him work in her garden and pay her a pound a week for the privilege. It strikes me as naked exploitation. As for his health, it has always been precarious, as you call it. The answer is not to be coddled in a sanatorium, but to remain active and happy.'

She drew a breath and assumed the expression of impassive submission that I knew so well as her attitude of capitulation-under-duress. 'I assume, then, Mother, that you will command Harry to be happy. I cannot imagine any other way of achieving that end.'

'I have given you every advantage in life; I cannot give you an imagination. I believe that Harry will be happy as soon as you let him be an independent creature and stop moulding him into an object of your pity.'

She had walked to the door. Then she looked back and said, 'I sometimes wonder at what point the means defeat the end. If we forfeit mercy, pity and charity in our struggle, we have become no better than the men who we claim oppress us.'

'Thank you, Sylvia,' I replied. 'You can keep your sermonising for your followers in the East End. They may be more receptive to it than I.'

'They certainly have more humanity than you, Mother.'

'I have dedicated my life to the service of humanity,' I said. 'And I shall not be lectured by you on its nature. I shall tell Harry that he is to return to Mayfield, and I shall write to Mr Fels to apologise for his apparent ingratitude. I need hardly remind you, I hope, that the time spent in this manner could have been expended more productively on matters of public import.'

'Yes, Mother, I don't need reminding. Public import has always taken precedence with you over the private welfare of your family.'

She turned to leave. 'Oh, Sylvia,' I said, and she paused, looking at me expectantly.

'Yes, Mother?'

'I really do think that frock is an unfortunate choice. It makes you look like the youngest daughter of an Austrian pastry cook.'

'Thank you, Mother,' she said. 'I can imagine an Austrian pastry cook making an admirable parent.'

She left. I remained in the morning room, reflecting on the curious fact that people who display their emotions publicly on every occasion assume that those who show more self-control have no feelings.

Christabel came in from her walk, her cheeks glowing, her eyes bright. It was difficult not to compare her appearance with that of the just-departed Sylvia. One would have said that Sylvia, with her drawn face and red eyes, had just emerged from Holloway prison, and that Christabel had just spent several weeks resting in the countryside.

I told her about my interview with Sylvia. Christabel was in general so intolerant of weakness, and so little inclined to sentimentality, that I assumed she would share my view; indeed, my own response had been premised partly on my sense of her probable attitude to the business. But to my considerable surprise, she seemed inclined to side with her sister.

'You must not expect more from Harry than he is capable of, Mother,' she said.

'I imagined that you would see the matter as I do,' I said, 'as a matter of practical priorities, as against Sylvia's over-protective treatment of Harry.'

'You know that in general I do think Sylvia absurdly over-emotional. But Harry is not strong.'

'My plan is exactly to make him strong.'

'I know, Mother, but is there not the danger that like the farmer who tried to teach his horse to do without grain you may fail just before making your point?'

'You are a trifle dry, Christabel,' I said. 'Is anything the matter?'

She smiled at me, not the warm, confiding smile of our closest communication, but the patronising smile she used when dealing with politically awkward people. 'Why, Mother, because I don't agree with you about Harry?'

Christabel asked this almost negligently, as if not really interested in the answer. It was clear that she was not attending very closely to the discussion. She was standing, like Sylvia, at the large window, apparently watching the waning of the short December day. 'Emmie seems very fond of Annie, doesn't she?' she asked abruptly.

I got up from the fire and joined Christabel at the window. Emmeline Pethick Lawrence and Annie were ascending the large stone staircase from the garden to the front door, hand in hand, talking animatedly. Annie was laughing at something Emmeline had said. 'Yes,' I said, 'but that's not unusual. Everybody loves Annie.'

Annie saw us at the lighted window and waved gaily; Emmeline followed suit, though less exuberantly. I waved back, but Christabel, without returning their greeting, came over to the fire and took a chair, holding up her hands to warm them. 'I would have thought, though,' she said, 'under the circumstances, with my having just spent ten weeks in Holloway, they would have the tact not to recall the *jolly times* they had while I was in prison. Annie told me with great glee of the picnic they had in November, and the bonfire.'

I joined her at the fireplace, sitting down at the other end. 'Annie takes an almost childish delight in picnics or any such outing. The poor thing could not have had many treats, growing up with ten brothers and sisters.'

'I don't begrudge her the pleasure she takes in such things; she's as ready to go to prison as on a picnic. But I think there is something unhealthy in the way Emmie Pethick Lawrence encourages Annie to hero-worship her.'

'Annie was born to hero-worship. She hero-worships us all – you most of all.'

'She has made herself very useful to me, but I don't encourage hero-worship. I can't stand that kind of exclusiveness, can you? I think Emmie would like to have her to herself.'

I was surprised and somewhat dismayed at Christabel's passion, but dared not say so. 'That would surely be out of the question,' I said with such self-command as I could muster. 'The members of the Union are not recruited as servants to one another.'

'So one would have thought. But Emmie thinks her money entitles her to special privileges.'

'The Union is a democratic body,' I pointed out. 'Nobody can buy influence.'

'Yes, Mother, in theory,' she said, impatient with my pedantry, 'but how do you tell a child not to be influenced by a new doll? Annie cannot but be impressed by the kind of luxury Emmie can offer. Emmie buys her new dresses and takes her on foreign holidays.'

She said this with such emphasis that it sounded like an accusation. 'The truth,' I said, in an attempt to lower the temperature of the discussion, 'is that poor Annie is all too apt to be impressed by almost anything, having grown up with almost nothing.'

Christabel got up out of her chair and went to the window again. 'That is all the more reason that she should not be exposed to the blandishments of spoilt rich people exercising

53

the power of their money. Now Emmie has involved Annie in the planning of this public breakfast they're organising for us, to celebrate our release from prison, and she told me to leave them alone, because they're planning all sorts of delicious surprises for us. They're like two little girls conspiring over a secret birthday party. I couldn't help gathering that I'm to be garlanded with some ostentatiously inscribed ornament in mauve, green and white, as if I were a monument on the Embankment.'

I was taken aback at the vehemence of Christabel's emotions. 'Why does it agitate you so?' I asked. 'What is it to you if Emmie and Annie take pleasure in planning a surprise for you?'

She did not turn to face me as she replied, now quite without her former heat. 'You know I never get agitated Mother, except for effect. But it's a bit provoking to be excluded from their confabulations, after ten weeks of being shut up with my own company.'

'And mine,' I permitted myself to comment.

From the window she cast me a glance, interrogative rather than conciliatory. 'In my turn I could ask you what it is to you, Mother, if I object to Annie and Emmie's conversation excluding me?'

I got up from my place by the fire. I had for one day been sufficiently addressed from a height by my daughters. 'What it is to me, Christabel,' I said, 'is a matter of no personal consequence, but of some import to the Union. As you must be aware, now more than ever, with Teresa Billington determined to seize control of the Union, we need the Pethick Lawrences.'

'Mother,' Christabel interrupted me, 'may I remind you that you are in the habit of referring to Fred Pethick Lawrence, not particularly respectfully, as the Godfather?'

'I have certainly at times found him inclined to over-estimate the power of his money, but whatever their personal peculiarities, they are unswervingly loyal to you and to me. I have not been blind to Emmeline's tendency to appropriate young women.' I paused. 'Indeed, how could I be, with you yourself as good as living with the Pethick Lawrences at Clement's Inn, while I was staying at the Inns of Court Hotel?'

Christabel had remained gazing out of the window even after Annie and Emmeline had disappeared from view. But at this she turned to me. 'Is that what you mean by *of no personal consequence*, Mother? Your resentment of the time I spend with the Pethick Lawrences?'

'It is exactly my point that I do *not* resent it, because I recognise that their hospitality is useful to you and advantageous to the Union. It is, furthermore, my point that, given Emmeline's importance to the Union, you could exercise a like forbearance in the face of her absorption of Annie. As for Annie, she is a sweet, utterly devoted follower, who would quite literally sit at the feet of anybody she admired. She is far too useful a worker to sacrifice to an unnecessary and unseemly tug of war. You know that Sylvia and her recruits are sneering that the Union has become an upper and middle-class movement, so we need Annie to give the lie to that charge.' I came closer to her, extending my hands in appeal. 'So whatever we may on our personal accounts feel for or about Emmie and Annie is irrelevant in the face of the larger struggle that unites us all. What is it all but further proof of the need to sacrifice narrow personal concerns to the demands of the battle? Should we not be thinking of the cause that unites us rather than the petty differences that divide us?'

Christabel had been looking at me in inscrutable impassivity. But as I advanced towards her, she met me and took my hands. 'Dear Mother,' she said, 'when you speak to thousands, your special gift is to make it seem as if you're addressing each listener personally. And when you speak to one person your special gift is to make it seem as if you're addressing thousands. You make me feel as if I were an audience in the Albert Hall.'

Before I could reply to this ambiguous tribute, the door opened, and Emmeline and Annie appeared. Seeing us, they paused at the door.

'Ah,' exclaimed Emmeline, 'what a pleasure to see mother and daughter so close!'

Annie gave her girlish laugh, genuinely delighted.

Harry returned to Mayfield, and if he was unhappy did not say so. I knew that if anything were really amiss he, or most certainly Sylvia, would let me know, and in the absence of any such notice assumed that he had settled down at last. There was in any case so much else to attend to that Harry's problems of adjustment seemed relatively trivial. Apart from the huge and very successful Women's Exhibition which we'd organised in May, that year – 1909 – marked the start of the policy of hunger striking, prompting in turn the adoption on the part of the authorities of the barbaric practice of forcible feeding. Christabel and I were kept fully occupied negotiating with politicians and police, contesting the legality of forcible feeding, and making sure that its inhumanity was publicised to a complacent public for the most part unaware of the extremely painful and invasive nature of the process.

It was thus at a peculiarly bad moment, in October that same year, that Sylvia came to me in the Union office at Clement's Inn, her face as usual a harbinger of gloom.

'I thought you were in Kent,' I said. She had gone to Penshurst to recuperate and to paint and write after her unremitting labour to decorate the hall for the Women's Exhibition.

'Mother,' she said, taking no account of the fact that I was involved in a discussion with Annie Kenney, 'it's Harry. He's very ill.'

'What is the matter with him now, Sylvia?' I asked, knowing that Sylvia tended to overstress Harry's ailments.

'I'm not quite sure what it is, Mother, but the people he has been staying with told Mabel McLachlan, who lives nearby, knowing that she's a member of the Union. They said Harry was dying.'

Annie gasped. I, too, caught my breath. 'Dying? Sylvia, surely you are exaggerating?'

'No, Mother, I'm saying what they said. Mabel telegraphed me in Kent. I asked her to bring Harry to London in her car, which she very kindly did.'

'But *is* he …?'

'I don't know, Mother. He is in great pain and his lower limbs are paralysed.'

'Paralysed? But where is he?'

'He has been taken to Nurse Pine in Pembridge Gardens.'

'Nurse Pine has her hands full with nursing women who have been on hunger strike and who have been force-fed. Could he not have been taken to a country doctor?'

Sylvia placed her large bag on my desk with such force that my inkstand fell to the floor. 'No, Mother,' she said, 'he could *not* be taken to a country doctor. In the first place there *is* no country doctor within twenty miles of the farm, and in the second place the Burleys are as incapable as they are unwilling to look after a sick person. In the third place, Harry is in extreme pain and may want to be close to his family.' At this point Sylvia started crying, as I had anticipated. 'Mother, Harry is *terrified* of being sent back to that place.'

Her crying was attracting attention in the office, and Annie, always inclined to be sentimental, seemed on the verge of tears herself, so I reasoned that the best course was to placate Sylvia. 'I don't know what his terror has to do with the matter,' I said. 'All I meant was that he should be seen by a doctor.'

'He has been seen by Dr Mills, Mother, but I think he would also like to be seen by his mother.'

'And what does Dr Mills say?' I asked, ignoring her aspersion.

'He says he cannot tell with certainty what is wrong, but he wants to see him every day to observe the progress of the disease.'

'Then surely he cannot be *dying*, if Dr Mills talks of observing the progress of the disease?'

'I don't know, Mother. I don't know what to think. But I do know that Harry is in great pain and is paralysed. That's enough for me.'

I went to see Harry at the nursing home in Pembridge Gardens as soon as I could get away from my commitments at the office. It was getting dark, and there was no light in his room. He was very pale and thin, as he had always been, though his eyes now seemed darker and larger than usual, an effect no doubt of the darkened room. He was very glad to see me, though to some extent embarrassed, I thought, by the inconvenience he was causing.

'Are you in great pain, Harry?' I asked. He seemed discomfited by this simple enough question, and I had to repeat it before he replied.

'Yes, Mother,' he said, 'though it's not quite unbearable.'

'Is it so bad that you could not stay on the farm?' I asked, careful to couch my question as gently as possible, lest he read a reproach into it.

He nodded mutely, and a slight shiver or shudder, I could not tell which, rippled over his slight frame. I could see he was reluctant to answer, and did not press the point. There was in any case nothing to be gained by questioning Harry. He had never been a forthcoming boy, and it was clear enough that, for whatever reason, he was extremely reluctant to go back to Mayfield.

I stayed for a while longer, but he was disinclined to talk, though he held my hand and seemed to want my presence. His hand was very hot, probably feverish, and though it was a cold night there was sweat on his forehead. It was now quite dark, and a nurse switched on a light by his bedside. She made me a sign over Harry's head that seemed to suggest that I should be leaving, so I kissed him good night, which brought tears to his eyes.

I resolved to have a private word with Nurse Pine. Though a highly compassionate woman, she had, in the course of nursing suffragettes back to health, seen enough of suffering not to be misled by considerations of sentiment. I did not, of course, think that Harry was feigning illness, but there was much talk just then of hysterical conditions, and I knew that illness and even paralysis could be induced by an extreme state of mind. I thought it at least possible that Harry's dislike of the farming environment had translated itself into a somatic condition.

'I don't know, Mrs Pankhurst,' said Nurse Pine. 'That is to say, I don't know what's ailing him. But I do know he is suffering something cruel. The pain makes him fair shrivel up at times.'

'He told me it was not unbearable,' I said.

She nodded. 'That's Harry, you won't catch him complaining. But I've seen pain in my day, and I reckon it's as close to unbearable as it can get. The doctor gives him somewhat for the pain, but there's only that much as drugs can do.'

I will not deny that I found Harry's suffering distressing. Though he had in many ways been a disappointment, he was nevertheless my son, and in his pallor and frailty he acquired an uncanny and unnerving resemblance to his little brother. His eyes, in particular, recalled Frank's glance, which had haunted me so after his death. To face now, again, those eyes, this time with full knowledge of their dark import, was more, I thought, than fate could ask of me. I did not lack courage to confront anything that I believed I could change; but I turned away from what I knew I could not.

I continued, of course, to visit Harry as often as my schedule allowed, painful as it was to see him in his wasted state. To facilitate such movement as he was capable of, it was judged proper for him to lie naked under the bedclothes, which made him seem almost ethereally vulnerable. When he was asleep, which the exhaustion of pain at times brought about, it was not difficult to imagine him dead; and even when awake, the strange immobility of his lower limbs seemed death-like. It was an atmosphere I found near-intolerable: the smell of medicine, the hushed voices, the evident agony that Harry often suffered. The beauty of his slender frame and delicate face made the suffering seem crueller, as if inflicted on a child.

At this taxing time an offer was made to me to lecture in the United States. My instinct was to remain by the bedside of my son. Reason persuaded me, however, that such a lecture tour would not only be invaluable to the cause by bringing to the attention of the larger world the plight of the hunger strikers, but also, by virtue of the large fees paid by the Americans, enable me to afford the best possible medical attention for Harry. It would also consolidate the position of the WSPU, which was, as always, under siege from Teresa Billington-Greig's Women's Freedom League. Indeed, there was some likelihood that if I did not accept the invitation Teresa would be invited in my stead, which would be catastrophic for the Union and thus for the cause.

Christabel supported me in my decision, arguing that she and Sylvia between them would give Harry constant care and companionship. Sylvia, however, made no secret of her disapproval.

'I do think that your only son should take precedence over the call to action,' she said one evening after we had both been to see Harry in Pembridge Gardens. 'The cause can do without you for a while, and will still be there for you when …' she hesitated, '…when Harry's disease reaches its natural termination. But Harry you may not have with you for very much longer.'

'Sylvia, can you not try to take a more cheerful view of poor Harry's prospects?' I asked. 'Your gloomy prognostications cannot be doing him any good. I am sure they convey themselves to him through your manner and tone.'

'Mother, I have had more experience than you, I think, of cheering Harry up. I know how to spare him the possible implications of his condition. I do not see why I should spare you.'

'That is quite clear. And assuming I do cancel the American tour, how do you propose that we pay for Harry's medical expenses?'

'Mother, he is being looked after by Nurse Pine, who loves Harry, and who would do anything for you. There is little enough to be done for him; it hardly requires the riches of America to pay for him. In case of absolute need, Fred Pethick Lawrence has assured me of his willingness to help us.'

I did not relish being beholden to the Pethick Lawrences, but that was not a topic I wanted to broach with Sylvia. 'By that argument,' I pointed out, 'he has the less need of me.'

We were standing on the pavement outside the nursing home, and I was trying to forestall one of Sylvia's emotional outbreaks. In this, however, I was defeated by her taste for melodrama. 'If you are satisfied,' she declared portentously, 'that your role as a mother can be filled as well by an efficient nurse, then indeed you are expendable.'

'You know that I must weigh up what you call my role as a mother against my public function. I cannot simply ignore the fact that my duty is now in America.'

'Yes, Mother,' she said. 'As it was in Manchester when little Frank died.'

I slapped her then, hard, as I had not slapped her since she was a child.

III

Wednesday 11 April 1928

A rainy day in Wapping. A gastric complaint, a memento no doubt of the hunger strikes of old, has kept me in bed. I demurred at first, since this is the day fixed for Ethel Smyth's visit, but Mrs Chipperfield was adamant. 'I don't care if the King himself comes to call, you don't want to be sitting bolt upright on such a day as it is today. This Mrs Smyth can come and see you in the bedroom and no harm done.'

'Dame Ethel.'

'What's that, then?'

'She is called Dame Ethel. Not Mrs Smyth.'

'I beg her pardon, I'm sure, but dame or no dame, you're not getting out of bed for her.'

I submit to Mrs Chipperfield's ruling. Having spent much of my life defying authority, I have earned the right to obey. I amuse myself by imagining a confrontation between the immovable Mrs Chipperfield and the irresistible Ethel Smyth. Mrs Chipperfield has left my door ajar, and Flora trots in and jumps onto my bed. I want to chase her off, but she settles down by my feet and goes to sleep, and I let her be.

There is a light tapping at my windowpane. I assume at first that it must be the rain, but the sound is harder and sharper than rain. I raise my head and see a pigeon on the sill pecking at its own reflection. There is something awkward about the way it is perching on the sill. I get out of bed, hoping Mrs Chipperfield won't come in and discover me. The pigeon has only one leg. It balances quite well, but lists slightly to the right. It seems rather dishevelled; I suppose one-legged pigeons are low down in the pecking order. Dear Lord, even the birds in Wapping are ugly. As I come closer, it flies away. I close the curtains and go back to bed.

I doze lightly, the sound of the Ratcliffe Highway, muffled by the thick curtains brought by Nellie Hall, for once almost soothing. Brutish human endeavour carrying on ceaselessly, regardlessly – how much difference can one really make to it? I did my best, heaven knows, and if the world is not a better place for my having lived in it these seventy years, it is not for want of my trying. I am told almost daily, by friends who mean to cheer me up, how much I have achieved. They tell me a tribute is being planned for my seventieth birthday in July, but I have let it be known that I desire no such extravagance. I have never been given to empty display, and do not intend to start now. In any case, I think it vulgar to have one's age referred to in public. Women who have achieved nothing in life except turning seventy may choose to celebrate that event as if it were some prodigious feat, sweetly dotty old ladies surrounded by hordes of children and grandchildren, relishing over tea and cakes the proof of their fecundity and longevity. Those of us who have dedicated our lives to causes outside of and greater than ourselves take little pleasure in such futile pieties. And then, too, what a mockery, if I should consent to such a 'celebration'! One daughter a ranting socialist in Australia, another denouncing me in the gutter press, who would no doubt attend from sheer perversity, to flaunt her little bastard. As for Christabel …

I must have dozed off. I am awoken by a light tap at my door: Mrs Chipperfield's deferential announcement of her presence. 'Mrs Pankhurst? Dame Ethel is here to see you.' She has clearly been awed by Ethel's grand manner, before which I have seen the most resolutely egalitarian of souls wilt. 'Will you see her?' she asks, as if I had the will to refuse Ethel Smyth.

'Of course. But warn her that I am weak and dreary.'

'Oh you're never dreary, Mrs Pankhurst,' she says; she does

not deny that I am weak. She places the single upright chair next to my bed, checks on the fire in the grate, and leaves, closing the door behind her.

Ethel's tread on the narrow staircase sounds too loud and purposeful for the little house, like an army invading a chicken coop. She opens the door without knocking, and pauses in the doorway; Ethel has always had about her an air as of inspecting the troops. While she is inspecting me, I inspect her. She is indeed wearing her tweed suit and porkpie hat, with a collar and tie. I smile, thinking of Christabel's dog breeder. Ethel does not return the smile. She comes to my bed. I lie helpless. My hands are folded on the counterpane. Flora has woken up and barks tentatively.

Ethel glances at the little dog, and seems on the point of commenting, but then ignores her. 'Emmeline Pankhurst,' she says sternly, 'what are you doing to yourself?'

'I don't know that I'm *doing* anything unusual to myself, Ethel.'

'Quite,' she says, 'you're doing what you've been doing all your life, which is to sacrifice your health and your comfort and your well-being and your very soul to a cause. You've never set any value on your life.'

'Then why should I start now, when it is all but over?'

I hoped that Ethel would retreat before this invocation of the Ultimate, but I should have known that even this would not intimidate her. 'Exactly because it is all but over,' she replies, 'and will be over all the sooner if somebody doesn't rescue you from your own perversity.' She turns to the dim mirror above the mantelpiece and takes off the hat; it is, seen in profile, more of a collapsed soufflé than a porkpie. 'It's Stygian in here. May I open the curtains?'

'Please do.'

She does so, and peers critically through the small panes. 'Not a very cheerful prospect,' she says. I do not reply. I am weary of having the prospect criticised: this is not Versailles, and I am not Louis XIV with the power to legislate myself a prospect.

Ethel comes to my bedside, leans over and kisses me peremptorily, then sits down on the chair next to my bed. Her long, untidy hair, swept back in a loose bun, is her sole concession to femininity. Her ears, I note for the first time, are extraordinarily large. They may have grown larger with age; apparently ears do, or is it the nose? 'Are you very ill?' she demands.

'Nothing out of the ordinary,' I say. 'A gastric complaint.'

'Should you have dogs on your bed?'

'There is only one dog, Ethel. And I don't think I incurred my complaint from Flora.'

She nods sceptically. 'You know I always disapproved of Christabel's dog making itself at home on the furniture.'

I do not say that was because she always disapproved of everything that was Christabel's. I say instead, 'You know I always said it was because you were an inveterate old maid.'

She pretends not to hear me, and takes my hand. 'Your hand is cold. Are you being well looked after?'

I do not resist her hand, but nor do I return its pressure. 'Very well indeed. You have met Mrs Chipperfield.'

'I have, if that's the name of the rather red-faced woman who let me in. She asked me if I was *the dame*.'

'She has been very kind and attentive.'

She removes her hand. 'That is as it may be. The point is, however, that you should not be dependent on the kindness of Mrs Chipperfield.'

'My friends have also been very kind. I am here because I want to be here.'

'And may one ask why you should want to be here?'

'You may ask, Ethel, but you should not have to. You must know that I have been nominated as Conservative candidate for Whitechapel.'

She sighs impatiently, as if dealing with a recalcitrant child. 'Indeed I know. What I do not know or understand is why the

Conservative Party should have given you, and why you should have accepted, a candidacy so utterly without any prospect of success. The Ratcliffe Highway, if memory serves, is celebrated mainly for the number of prostitutes and murderers frequenting it. Is this not the place where a whole family was most dreadfully disembowelled quite recently?'

'That was more than a hundred years ago, Ethel. And the prostitutes have also gone.'

She snorts, sounding like one of her horses. 'Still, a Conservative is as likely to be elected in Whitechapel as a Bolshevik in Mayfair.'

'When have I ever been deterred by what seemed unlikely? Did it seem likely that women would ever be granted the suffrage when we – you and I and countless others – subjected ourselves to harassment and imprisonment for its sake?'

She adopts a gentler tone, one I have heard her employ to her dog. 'I've never doubted your readiness to take on a battle against the odds, Em. But there comes a time when one has to set off the cost of the casualties against the fruits of victory. Even assuming that you can achieve the impossible and convert the labouring classes to the Conservative Party, is it worth ruining your health for the sake of another Conservative seat in Parliament?'

I am conscious of being harangued, with whatever semblance of rational persuasion; I am at a disadvantage, debating with Ethel Smyth while lying flat on my back. 'My health has never been my prime concern,' I say.

'That was because your health was excellent, in spite of your demands upon it. But you're no longer a young woman.'

'You know that I do not encourage references to my age.'

She snorts again. 'I happen to know that you're the same age as I, Em, so I'm hardly referring to your age in a spirit of youthful derision. But regardless, then, of your age, you're ill, and this dank little box is no place for an ill woman, and campaigning for election to Parliament is no activity for an ill woman.'

'What is it you would have me do, Ethel? Turn my face to the wall and die?'

'No, Em; turn your face to the beauty of the world beyond Wapping and *live*.' Her tone has been brisk, as if proposing a business deal; now, suddenly, she becomes urgent, even passionate. 'It's time to be kind to your spirit and to your poor over-taxed body. Come live with me, Em, and listen to Schubert and Beethoven and even to my own compositions as you did in the days of our struggle.'

I resist the tide of her emotion. 'Oh, *then* I could listen to Schubert and Beethoven – and even to your own compositions – exactly because they gave me strength for the struggle. Now you want me to give up the struggle and decline into my dotage listening to pretty tunes. There is a difference between great music as an inspiration and as a soporific.'

She takes her cue from me, returns to the dry irritability of her former manner. 'Great music can never be a soporific. That's what makes it great. Beauty generates energy. But don't you think you've struggled about as much as any human being can be expected to? And don't you think you've achieved more than almost any human being before you?'

'There is always more.'

'Of course there is always more,' she says, almost angrily, 'and more and more, and one can never do it all, which is why there comes a time when one has to say I've now done *my* all and I've done it well and I'm passing on the standard to the next generation.'

'I would rather die on the platform than wait out my life knitting socks.' I pause, wondering how much I can confide in this hard, peremptory woman. As if guessing my thought, and sensing that I have something more on my mind, she presses my hand, more gently than her manner has led me to expect, and I continue. 'Besides, I can't quit now. Not after that abomination.' I point at the *News of the World*, which is lying on the table next to my bed.

67

She glances at it and nods grimly. 'I have seen it. It's a calculated act of evil. Why would Sylvia do that to you?'

I am not interested in once again discussing Sylvia's reasons. 'I don't know,' I nevertheless say. 'I think she hates me because I was married to her father.'

Ethel nods, as if this were the most natural thing in the world. 'I said to my niece Jane,' she continues, 'when she showed me that … that *atrocity*, This will kill Em, I said, and that was when I wrote my letter demanding to see you.'

'To witness the killing?'

She does not acknowledge my irony. 'No, to save you from killing yourself. I'm here to offer you a chance at last to live, Em.'

'What have I been doing all these years, Ethel?'

'Your life has been all for others. It's been heroic and magnificent on a scale altogether unparalleled by anyone except perhaps Joan of Arc; but it's now enough, and I'm offering you life for yourself, a life of ease and plenty and warmth and music and beauty and love, all those things you've denied yourself and are still denying yourself.'

'Self? Why always the self? One lives for others, Ethel.'

Ethel pulls at her tweed skirt impatiently. 'How is the cause of others served by your climbing onto a platform to be humiliated by impertinent people on account of the antics of your own daughter? And even climbing onto a platform is dependent on your preserving that part of your *self* called the body from ruination. Come with me and forget the *News of the World*, and if need be your daughter Sylvia too.'

She looks about the room critically, her manner not unlike that of Christabel yesterday. I smile to think how little either of them would relish the comparison. Ethel sees the smile and misinterprets it. 'I daresay I amuse you, Em, with my schemes. But what do you have to show for a lifetime of denial?'

'The enfranchisement of my sex.'

'Yes, you have enfranchised your sex and impoverished yourself.'

68

'I have never wanted for food and lodging.'

She looks about her again, her pointed silence a sufficiently eloquent comment on my lodgings. 'I'm speaking of spiritual impoverishment. You have denied yourself love for such a long time that you've forgotten to love or how to be loved.'

She is speaking more gently now. The unaccustomed irresolution in Ethel's manner, the slight tremor of her unclasping her bag, her leaning back in the uncomfortable chair, all tell me that she recognises that between us we have once again arrived at a critical juncture. Then she snaps shut her bag: she has made up her mind. 'Before I met you, I thought the agitation for women's suffrage was an unseemly commotion in the hen-house. It was meeting you that recruited me to the cause – I wish I could say because I was persuaded by the force of your arguments, but in fact because I fell in love with you as soon as I saw you. If you'd been advocating a return to slavery, I would have followed you; if you'd agitated for the abolition of the crown, I would have stormed Buckingham Palace; in short, I was following *you*, not the standard you were bearing. Still, one could not be with you for any length of time without being invigorated for battle. The cause and you became as one; but it was you I loved, and my love for you was the inspiration of my most active years and has been the sustenance of my declining years. Now let it be the sustenance of yours too.'

I lie still. Experience has trained me to deal with almost any challenge that human ingenuity can conceive, but it has not taught me to deal with a declaration of love. I am used to delivering impassioned appeals, not to receiving them. Ethel has never made a secret of her affection, but nor has she ever presented it like this, as a fact and a proposition demanding attention, wanting to be dealt with, opposed to the claims to which I have devoted my life. Of all the thousands of women who have admired and even adored me, and would have laid down their lives for me without hesitation, this is the one who demands that I share her life. And for a moment it seems blissfully simple, just obeying, and consenting to the love and care of this dry, angular, strong woman.

But only for a moment. Because while I lie there considering this offer – either the respite from battle surely every soldier deserves, or else desertion in the face of the enemy – Ethel continues, now firmer of tone, more sure of herself. 'Em,' she says, adjusting her expressive voice to the gentlest tone at her command, 'as you know, I've never been a tactful person – tact, to my mind, is just timidity trying to pass itself off as a virtue – and I've in the past made it clear to you that I felt that your eminence, nay your *heroism*, was compromised by your unquestioning allegiance to Christabel. You were mortally offended because I told you the simple truth, which was that the attempts of your friends to provide for you by public subscription were hampered by the perception that quite enough of the Union's funds had gone towards keeping Christabel in a style to which she had come to regard herself as entitled. When I wrote that to you six years ago you returned my letter and advised me to tear it up, and that was effectively the end of our friendship, though neither of us acknowledged it in so many words.'

Ethel pauses. I sense she is waiting for a response from me. 'And you have come here today to remedy that omission?' I ask.

If she is offended by my sarcasm, she does not show it. 'No, Em, I'm here to attempt to breach that gap. But in order to breach it we must face it and call it by its name.' She takes a deep breath. 'I shall not pretend to love Christabel as you love her, but I will love you and endeavour to respect your love for her, and cherish you as you have never been cherished. Christabel may well be the most dutiful of daughters, but she has other interests – I'm told she has been preaching the Second Coming quite as passionately as she ever advocated Votes for Women – and she cannot give you the care and attention I'm at liberty to lavish upon you.'

70

'You think, then, that I am so feeble as to need care and attention to be lavished upon me, like some senile monarch?'

'You will never be feeble. But the world has seen only your strength; I've seen your vulnerability and loved you the more for it. I said to you once that it was the crowning achievement of my life to have made you love me, and that remains true, whatever you now choose to make of it.'

She leans forward, carried away with her own appeal. She looms over me, too close. She takes my hand in hers. But she has said too much, and the moment has passed. I do not want to be cherished, and I do not want to be loved for my vulnerability. I am not an emotional invalid and I am not to be nursed into submission to Ethel's will. I am no longer weak in the face of her appeal. I know how to repel her. I reply as factually as I can. 'I don't know much about love, Ethel,' I say. 'I have loved my husband and my children, and I have nothing to show for it today other than Christabel's devotion.'

She lets go of my hand, and takes a deep breath. I can see that she has recognised my rebuff for what it is, and for a moment I think she will challenge me, and test her determination against mine. But when she talks again, her tone is calm, almost pensive. 'I've often reflected,' she says, 'on the fact that you and I were never as close to each other as when we were in Holloway Prison together. Perhaps you felt then that you could allow yourself an intimacy sanctioned by the cause in whose name it came about.' She looks at me as if she expects me to respond to her proposition.

'I don't know, Ethel,' I say. 'I cannot take responsibility for your speculations.'

'But don't you feel that we were closer to each other there than ever before or after?'

I am irritated by her insistence. 'No doubt the sense of a common plight is a uniting factor. Men become very close in wartime, they say.'

She laughs suddenly, startlingly.

'Have I said something amusing, Ethel?' I ask.

She looks at me. 'Yes, dear. I am amused. I'm amused at your blitheness. "The sense of a common plight!" When I held you in my arms to warm you in that pestiferous little cell, when I pressed you to me, and you returned the pressure, when I kissed you and you returned the kiss, was that the sense of a common plight? When I told you I loved you and you returned my love, was that the closeness of men in war-time?'

I remain silent. 'Don't you have an answer for me, Em?' she asks.

'Your questions are clearly rhetorical, Ethel, and as such do not require an answer.'

'Which is as much as to say you don't want to answer them. But let that be; I have no desire to force memories upon you that you're determined not to have.'

I do not reply to this, and for a long moment there is a silence broken only by the sound of traffic outside, and the knocking of Mrs Chipperfield's broom on the stairs. Ethel seems to be lost in thought. 'Do you remember,' she suddenly asks me, musingly, as if recalling a summer picnic long ago, 'when we first met, that I quoted you Kent's words to Lear?'

I am suspicious of arguments that take refuge in Shake-speare. 'I remember something like that, yes,' I say, 'but I forget the words.'

'Kent says to Lear, on their first meeting, *You have that in your countenance which I would fain call master*. When Lear asks him what that is, Kent replies, *Authority*.'

Ethel looks at me as if she has now provided me with a key to her meaning, but I am merely bewildered. 'Why are you reminding me of that now? To impress upon me the failure of my powers?'

'On the contrary. To recall you to a sense of your own strength, which you have too easily signed over to others.'

'Like King Lear?'

'Like King Lear. Except ...' she hesitates, 'except that he at least had one daughter he could rely on.'

I marvel at the perversity or perhaps desperation that makes her play that card now. 'I, too, have one daughter I can rely on.'

At this, Ethel laughs, a dry, mirthless laugh. It makes her seem quite coarse, like, yes, a dog breeder at a county fair. 'Do you really?' she asks. 'Would you call Christabel a Cordelia?'

Her tone is lightly interrogative, as if she really were interested in my answer. But I know her well enough to feel the edge of her irony. Suddenly, for the first time, I am angry. 'You go too far, Ethel. I have thus far, in the interest of our long history, ignored your petulant allusions to Christabel, but I do believe that it's your intention to force the issue. I'm not sure what your motive for this is, but I do know that I shall not have you sit here in my own room, rented and shabby though it be, and malign my daughter to my face.'

She persists in her lightly insouciant manner. 'I'm not maligning Christabel. I'm merely pointing out that she is no Cordelia.'

'Ethel,' I say, as neutrally as I can, 'you seem to have conceived a notion that I am in some way like King Lear. I recollect Lear as an unreasonable, self-pitying old man who thought he could get rid of the responsibilities of power without sacrificing any of the benefits. Now please enlighten me as to the respects in which I resemble this man.'

'You ...' she starts, then checks herself and continues more calmly. 'Lear was a born king. You, too, were born to command.'

'Then why are you trying to intimidate me? Do you think that because I'm sick I'm feeble? Do you think I can't see that you are trying to estrange me from Christabel so that you can have me completely in your power? Do you think that I'll commit myself to the domestic equivalent of Holloway Prison, drooling obediently by the fireside while you play me Chopin?'

She is silent, and I can see that my blows have struck home. After a moment of silence she says, 'If that's what you think of me, so be it. My only crime is that I love you and want you to be comfortable and happy.'

'Your crime is that you are jealous of a mother's love for her daughter, and always have been. I remember what you said to me in Paris, that Christabel was playing God, except that she was going God one better, in that God had only sacrificed his son, whereas she was sacrificing her mother. I said then that I would never forgive you, and I have kept my word.'

'Even you should be able to see that I was speaking not from hatred of Christabel but from love and concern for you.'

'If you are concerned about my comfort and happiness, you can make me as comfortable and happy as I am at present capable of being by taking your leave of me.'

She gets to her feet. There is a little red spot on each cheek, and she is trembling slightly. 'I told you once that you had the kind of vision that embraces only the mass, and is blind to personal relations. I thought then that I was the glorious exception, but I was wrong; you will sacrifice your very soul to those who would trample it underfoot, and with it those who love you. Your natural element is combat: that's why you were such a formidable suffragette and such a poor mother and lover.'

She snatches her hat from the mantelpiece and forces it down on her head, more as an expression of exasperation than with a view to her appearance. The hat perches on her head at an odd angle: it looks like a small dead animal. This detracts from the dignity of her exit. Unaware of this, she addresses me from the door. 'It was a mistake to come here. When a profound relation comes to an unnatural end, it can attain a quite surprising degree of deadness. I should have known better than to try to revive it. What I am now most reminded of is

74

Lear's question: *Is there any cause in nature that makes these hard hearts?'*

On this, she leaves at last. My first impulse is to laugh; but strangely, I begin to cry, and the little dog, puzzled, starts whimpering. I take it in my arms and press it to my face. It smells of coal dust.

IV

Holloway Prison: Ethel's visit has revived old memories, as no doubt she intended it to. But she was confusing the closeness of comrades in arms with whatever it was she wanted from our friendship. There was, indeed, a kind of exhilaration in feeling that we were all united in resistance to a tyrannical authority, and extreme hunger does of course tend to make one light-headed. But Ethel has in her own mind magnified the significance of an intimacy that was almost entirely a function of our situation. I suppose she must be thinking of the evening when we succeeded in cowing the wardresses into allowing us to discard the disgusting prison garb and put on our own clothes.

As I remember it, I had conceived the plan of protesting against the foul clothes we were compelled to wear by the simple expedient of taking them off. Word was passed round during exercise time that at bedtime we would all strip down completely and refuse to put on our prison clothes again. As this was in January, and the prison blankets were thin, we were exposing ourselves to physical hardship and worse: weak and emaciated with hunger-striking, we had few physical resources, and there was a real danger that some of the women might succumb. This, of course, the authorities knew as well as we did; besides, with the puritanism of all repressive regimes, they would be scandalised by the thought – or, worse, sight – of our naked bodies. They could violate our bodies by forcing tubes down our throats, but they felt threatened by those bodies in their natural state.

I cannot remember how Ethel came to be lodged with me on

this night, as in general we were kept strictly apart. It is possible that she had contrived it with the cooperation of a wardress, one Mrs Smollett, with whom she had struck up an odd kind of friendship, based, I suspected, on certain traits they had in common.

Be that as it may, Ethel was lodged with me, and when the time came for us to lay off the vile prison garments, she asked to be permitted to help me.

'It's only appropriate that you should have a servant to help you disrobe,' she said.

'Disrobe?' I asked. 'Heavens, Ethel, such rags as these!'

'Whatever a queen puts on, becomes by that token a robe,' she intoned. Ethel had always been inclined to a certain grandiosity of effect, in her vocabulary as in her music, and I did not take issue with this extravagant claim.

'Arise,' she said, in the same high-flown tones.

Bemused, I obeyed. The cell was so small that on getting to my feet I was standing not two feet from her, but her eyes were fixed on some distant spot, as if I were approaching her down a long chamber. At length, having as it were given me time to arrive, she extended her arms and lifted the ugly prison cap from my head. She was much taller than I, and towered over me, making me feel less like a queen than a child being undressed by her nanny.

She placed the cap on the bed. In solemn silence she took me by the shoulders and turned me so that I stood with my back to her. My hair had been loosely gathered under the cap, for they'd taken away our hairpins; she released the hair, spreading it out over my shoulders. I in all truth felt somewhat ridiculous, as if I were being ritually prepared for some ceremony, but there was something imperious to Ethel's ministrations, as if I were both an object of reverence and a sacrificial victim. I have never been subservient by nature, but for once Ethel assumed command and I obeyed.

She kept my back turned to her and did not speak, directing

the movements of my limbs by her hands alone, each touch a caress as well as a command. First she made me sit down on the wooden stool and kneeled before me and removed the unmatched boots, the short thick stockings, as delicately as if they were glass slippers. Then, directing me to stand up again, in silence, she removed the coarse prison garments, the dirty blue check apron, the drab jacket with its black arrows, the too-wide skirt gathered in lumps at the waist, the flannel singlet, the dreadful calico chemise. After weeks and months of resistance and defiance, there was relief in simple submission of my body to the will and ministrations of someone else, to be purely passive in her strong and purposeful pianist's hands.

When at last I stood naked, she draped the rough prison blanket over me and directed me to lie down on the prison cot with its straw mattress. There was by now a gathering noise in the prison, as the warders became aware of the defiant nakedness of their charges and tried to coerce them into getting dressed again. We, however, were left undisturbed, whether by the offices of Mrs Smollett I still do not know.

Ethel's silent resolve was still exerting its strange spell over me; there was something luxurious in acquiescing so completely to her will. She undressed herself rapidly, flinging the filthy prison clothes onto the floor with a kind of disdain, and lay down next to me on the hard narrow cot.

I was not of a generation that countenanced nakedness, even between man and wife, and this was the closest I had ever been to another human being. Our smell was rank with lack of washing and with the body's breaking-down of its own tissues, but there was something comforting in the warmth of another body, in the total acceptance by another of one's own body, atrophied as it was by the vilenesses of prison.

I lay quite still, content to let Ethel explore my body with her subtle fingers and searching mouth, in truth not quite sure what at any given moment she was doing. The sensation was not unpleasant, like being nuzzled by a large over-affectionate dog, an impression reinforced by the inarticulate snuffling noises Ethel was making. If at any point she had given an indication that my own active participation was required, I would have been at a loss, but she seemed as content to retain the initiative as I was to submit to it. She kissed me, and I may have returned her kisses; but my will and consciousness remained separate from my body, attending to the noises of the prison, the dank smell of the cell and our bodies, the rough texture of the blanket.

Thus we lay, I do not know for how long. I think I must have drifted into sleep under the soothing spell of her caresses. I know that at one point I woke up, and Ethel was standing over me, quite naked. She reached for my hand and pressed it to her breast. 'Now we are sisters in arms,' she said.

'Yes,' I said, since I couldn't think of anything else to say, and went back to sleep.

I woke up to find Ethel fully dressed, with the news that our demands had been met and that thenceforth we would be allowed to wear our own clothes in Holloway.

'You see,' she said, 'what you and I can achieve together.'

V

12 April 1928

Thin sunshine today, and I am feeling strong enough get out of bed, though Mrs Chipperfield insists that I am still too weak to go out, and has made a fire in the sitting room. Christabel has sent a note saying she will visit today, and I do not want to be in bed when she calls. Flora seems rather lack-lustre this morning. It is a useful distraction from my own physical dereliction, I suppose, having a dog to look after, but it is also an anxiety I could well do without.

I take care over my toilette, as I always have done. The right to sovereignty over my own body is one I have fought for in conditions worse than these. I know, too, that it would pain Christabel to see me at anything other than the best I am yet capable of. The exertion of dressing and grooming myself is strangely exhilarating: the sense of having the power, at least, to present oneself pleasingly revives for a moment the energy of battle. The face I show myself in the dim mirror is a pale shadow of its former self, but it has kept something of its integrity in the set of the chin and the clarity of the eyes.

There is a tapping at the window. It is the one-legged pigeon. It imagines, I suppose, that it has found a mate in its own reflection – or is it an adversary? It is difficult to enter into the emotional life of pigeons.

Christabel looks brilliant, as always, in the mauve and green that in our suffragette days was part of our uniform, but that she now favours for its pleasing effect. She looks at me critically.

'You're looking well, Mother,' she says. 'I hope you've shaken off the effects of Sylvia's little demonstration.'

'Oh yes. I think I can see it in a more accurate perspective now. Should I ask Mrs Chipperfield to bring us some tea?'

She gives a mock shudder. 'No, thank you. I can imagine the over-boiled brew that's likely to issue from downstairs.' She sits down by the little fire. 'Why is Flora so undemonstrative today?' she asks; indeed, the dog has hardly acknowledged her arrival.

'I don't know,' I reply. 'Perhaps she needs exercise. I will take her out when I am stronger.'

She does not reply; I am afraid she is displeased.

'Oh, incidentally,' she says, 'there was a note from Fred Pethick Lawrence yesterday.'

'For me?'

'No, addressed to me, but asking me to ask you if he can visit you.'

'Why should he want to do that?'

'I don't know, Mother. Perhaps he's heard that you've been ill.'

'I have been ill before. Perhaps he thinks I am dying.'

'I don't see why he should think that.'

'I don't know either. But I do know that I don't have the energy to speculate about Fred Pethick Lawrence's motives. He was always just the slightest bit tedious, didn't you find?'

'Yes,' she says dryly, 'though uncommonly useful at times.'

'Is that a reproach?'

'No, Mother. I'm saying he was useful, which he was. And he was willing to be made use of, so we made use of him.'

I hoped I had done with the Pethick Lawrences. 'Please, let's not disagree about Fred Pethick Lawrence. I don't want to see him, and there's an end of it.'

She nods non-committally. 'I'll inform him accordingly,' she says. She seems bored with the subject.

'Was Ethel Smyth here?' she asks abruptly.

81

'Yes, she was.'

'Did she come bearing an olive branch?'

An instinct to please Christabel makes me want to devalue Ethel's offer. 'She came with a proposal that I should spend the rest of my days in her cottage listening to her play her own compositions.'

'That sounds like a premature exposure to the torments of hell. What did you say?'

I sit down next to her. 'I declined with good grace. Actually, I declined with bad grace. I got the impression that she had come not so much in a spirit of conciliation as to assert her own power, now that I have been publicly humiliated by my own daughter.'

'There's always an element of domination in the subservience of the disciple,' Christabel declares with her usual confidence in her own universals. 'The stronger becomes addicted to the subservience of the weaker, and the weaker knows it. The hyenas survive to feed on the flesh of the lion.'

'I would not have thought of Ethel as a hyena,' I object mildly. 'And I don't think I am addicted to her subservience.'

'Oh, it happens without one's noticing,' she says dryly. 'I think I was addicted to Annie Kenney's subservience.'

I am taken aback by her frankness. 'Well, Annie was besotted with you. It would have required an effort not to be adored by her.'

'I suppose so,' she says musingly. Then, suddenly, 'Still, it may have been a bit drastic to get rid of the Pethick Lawrences just to have Annie to myself.' She laughs, as if at the memory of a girlish foible.

I look at her, trying to gauge her intention; why the Pethick Lawrences again? 'That is hardly why we *got rid* of the Pethick Lawrences. We expelled them from the Union because they refused to adhere to the official policy.'

She laughs again, now genuinely amused. 'Yes, so we said at the time, even to ourselves. But we can be honest now, can't we? I was jealous of Emmie's influence over Annie. She could offer so much more than I could. And I had really got quite fond of little Annie when I was living in Paris and she came over weekends with dispatches from London.'

'I remember,' I say, trying to match her dryness of tone. 'She used to be referred to as Christabel's Blotting-paper.'

But my little arrow is deflected by her incomparable sang froid. 'Oh yes,' she says, sounding quite pleased, 'What a faithful little scribe she was. We had lovely times, Annie and I, in Paris.'

'That would have been when I was on hunger strike in prison,' I cannot refrain from commenting.

'Yes, about that time,' she says blandly. 'But then, it was your idea that I should go to Paris, wasn't it?'

'You know it was. The Union needed the continuity of an organiser who was not subject to arrest at any time.'

'And you needed me at a safe distance from Emmie Pethick Lawrence's influence.'

She says this matter-of-factly, blithely. I try to seem equally insouciant. 'I thought it was your point that *you* wanted to be rid of the Pethick Lawrences.'

'Yes, I did, but so did you. You resented Emmie quite as much as I did, but for the hold you thought – quite wrongly, by the way – she had over me. That was why you and I agreed so readily on their expulsion: I was sacrificing Emmie for the sake of Annie; you were giving me Annie in exchange for Emmie.'

I look at her aghast. 'You talk as if we were slave traders disposing of our latest purchases.'

She smiles, with one eyebrow raised, as if she is sceptically but amiably considering a logical proposition. 'Yes,' she then says, 'but with this difference that we didn't purchase them. We bound them to us in the name of women's freedom.'

I try to read her expression, but it has only the blithe brightness that she always affected when devastating an adversary. 'Why are you saying these things to me today?' I ask her, helpless. 'Now, when Sylvia has chosen to shame me to the world?'

'I'm saying these things because we need no longer hide them from each other, you and I. When Christ returns to earth, as He will soon do, to make his reckoning, I do not want to stand before Him ashamed.'

So I am to be sacrificed to the Second Advent. 'And do you believe He wants you to betray your own mother?'

'He will not see it as a betrayal, bringing you to the truth.'

This, for the moment, brings the discussion to a close. I cannot take issue with Christabel's religious notions: they offer me no purchase or even access. But she has opened a vein that has not run dry. I get up from my chair, walk to the window, then turn and address her. 'Then had you not better also inform Him of your treatment of Adela?' I ask her.

If she is surprised by my seizing the initiative, she does not show it. She says, calmly, 'I did not *treat* Adela. Adela was an adult woman capable of making her own decisions.'

'She was an adult woman, but she was not capable of making her own decisions. Since we are calling things by their name, we can agree, in the interests of truth, that you suggested to me, though not quite in those words, that I banish her to Australia.'

'Why would I do that, Mother? Are you not attributing your own distrust of Adela to me?'

'I am not talking of distrust, I am talking of your jealousy of Adela.'

She laughs, lightly, without conviction. '*I* jealous of Adela, poor frumpish, awkward Adela?'

'Frumpish and awkward she may have been, but she was always more popular with audiences than you. Your grand style was impressive, but Adela had more of the common touch.'

She sniffs. '*That* she certainly had. It's no wonder she's been so successful in Australia.' Her tone becomes ruminative,

84

conversational. I have seen this tactic, too, in her public appearances. All that is new is that she is using it on me. 'To be sure, she seems to have become a raving socialist, but she can do very little harm down there, I should think. I'm told that Australia is in essence a working-class country, which would suit Adela very well; indeed, I believe she's made a working-class marriage. That is at least preferable to Sylvia's inspiration to have a child out of wedlock by an Italian anarchist.'

I decline to follow the diversion she has created. 'That is as it may be,' I say. 'I am merely in all consistency reminding you that the Pethick Lawrences were not the only expulsions that you and I effected.'

'I still fail to see what Adela's going to Australia had to do with me.'

'You fail to see …? Have you forgotten how you railed at her public appearances, where, you said, she stole the audience from you with cheap jokes and common antics? And how furious you were when in Milan she was hailed as *Miss Pankhurst* and she didn't have the wit to realise that she was being mistaken for the *real* Miss Pankhurst? How you said to me *I can put up with a hundred Sylvias but one Adela is too many for me*?'

'And given your total recall, do you remember my ever saying to you Mother, please tell Adela to go to Australia?'

'It was not necessary. You knew that your wishes were paramount with me. If by your contention an agreement could pass between us on the Pethick Lawrences without a word being spoken, then so could it on the subject of Adela. It was for you that I persuaded her to go to Australia.'

She remains silent for a moment, not at a loss, merely considering her options. Then she asks me, as if enquiring after my health, 'Do you expect me to thank you, Mother?'

'No. But I do not expect to be treated as if I were some kind of reprobate who had to be brought to justice.' I pause, then add, in a more conciliatory tone, 'And I do expect, perhaps, some affection in return for my dedication.'

She is not so easily to be conciliated. 'You know that you have my affection, Mother,' she says, as a mere matter of record, without any warmth. 'Do I not demonstrate it every day?'

'You are, as far as it goes, meticulous in your observance of what you regard as your duty. But affection, real warm affection ... what the world calls *love*, that you never give me.'

'I'm sorry if you feel I'm emotionally deficient, Mother. I show affection as you have taught me to. I cannot give you what you never gave me.'

'Did I never give you love? Was my whole career not dedicated to you? Did I not say countless times that you were the best thing I ever did? You, my dauntless, brave, beautiful daughter, body of my body, the only one of my children that I nursed myself? Who could face any challenge and laugh it to scorn? Who proved by her own example that women were the equals of men and more, that a woman could suffice to herself and be strong? Did I not, only yesterday, turn down an offer of a life of ease and plenty for your sake? Have I not loved you above everything in my life?'

She remains quiet for while. When she speaks, it is calmly, without passion. 'Mother, I'm immensely touched that you should attach such importance to my place in your life, and I'm of course infinitely grateful for all you have done for me. I, too, have heard the world talk of *love* as if it were the supreme thing on earth; but when you ask for it from me as something distinct from my gratitude and devotion, I do not know what you mean, unless it be the kind of emotional outpouring that Sylvia is so good at.'

'If you do not know what I mean, there is no point in my explaining it to you.'

'Come, Mother, let us not quarrel. This is a difficult time for you. You're not well and you are, quite naturally, upset about Sylvia and about Ethel Smyth.'

She gets up from her chair, takes my hand and smiles at me.

I have to accept her condescension in the place of the love she cannot give me.

'Incidentally,' she says – and I know she is about to broach a subject by no means incidental – 'incidentally, I saw Sylvia yesterday.'

I wonder if I am supposed to show a polite interest in Sylvia's welfare. I opt instead to say what I feel. 'You know I have refused to see Sylvia, even when she came knocking at my door, and you go of your own free will and seek her out? Why? To congratulate her on the birth of her child? To offer to be its godmother?'

'Mother, please don't react so violently. I went to see Sylvia to ask her not to give her child the Pankhurst name.'

'And Sylvia, being Sylvia, immediately saw the justice of your request and acceded to it.'

She smiles wryly. 'No. But I did think it was at least worth trying.'

'I cannot imagine why you thought that. You simply gave her the satisfaction of refusing you, and through you, me.'

She remains provokingly calm. Christabel never loses her temper, unless for a calculated effect. 'Well, it's difficult to tell. Sylvia's satisfaction has never been of a very demonstrative nature. But she does dwell on the joys of motherhood to a rather irritating extent.'

'That, too, you could have foreseen. Did she not offer an explanation of her extraordinary conduct?'

'You mean having a child?'

'No, I mean leaping onto the front pages of the gutter press with it.'

'I don't think Sylvia feels she owes us an explanation.' She pauses. 'She had many other things to say, though.'

'Are you going to tell me what they were?'

'Are you interested?'

'*Interested*, no. But if they relate to me I suppose I should know what they are.'

'Oddly, they did not really relate to you. They related mainly to me.'

'I would have thought that we were, in Sylvia's mind at least, to some large extent fused with each other.'

'No, she discriminates quite finely in her resentments and reproaches.'

'What is it she reproaches you with?'

She lets go of my hand, walks about rather aimlessly. 'Oh, as you can imagine, a quite exhaustive list. Everything and nothing … I don't know, Mother,' she says; she is for some reason evading my question. 'Mere human truth is so fickle, and attaches herself so lightly to every passing human motive. That is why I've placed my faith in the eternal truths.'

Christabel knows she has placed herself beyond the reach of reason. 'I won't take issue with you on that,' I say. 'We would seem to have enough to disagree about without bringing religion into the question.'

'We have always had enough to agree about, Mother.'

'Yes, I used to think so. But today you have made me feel that we never agreed. Our different purposes just happened to coincide.'

'What united us was that we are both militants,' Christabel informs me. 'When we had a common enemy, we united against it. Now that we no longer have that enemy, we must guard against turning against each other.'

'*You* are warning *me*? You who have as good as destroyed our common past today?'

'Our common past cannot be destroyed,' she says serenely. 'It is what it is, and what it achieved is there for all to see.'

I am conscious of appearing fretful in the face of her unshakeable aplomb. 'I don't know. I don't know what we have achieved, if at the end of it we sit here in this little … *cell* exchanging accusations.'

'We have won the vote for millions of women. And we have won the admiration and support of thousands.'

'We have lost each other. You have lost your mother and I have lost my last child.'

She laughs, trying to make light of my despair. 'Come, Mother, it's not like you to be so gloomy. It's this wretched room that's dejecting you. Will you come for a walk? Little Flora would enjoy that, wouldn't she?' She claps her hands and the little dog runs up to her, pleased at the attention, but with drooping tail. I think she is ill.

I try to smile. 'I hardly think Mrs Chipperfield will allow me out. She is very fierce with me.'

'You've never taken meekly to imprisonment, Mother. Come, you need the fresh air, and for once there is some sunshine out there. There must be a little patch of park somewhere, even in Wapping. Put on your hat and come with me.'

I obey. I am weary to death, but perhaps Christabel is right; perhaps I need the fresh air. Christabel chatters to Flora, trying to cheer her up. I have failed even the dog.

'Incidentally,' Christabel says again, as I am putting on my hat, 'incidentally, while I was visiting Sylvia, who do you think came around?'

I don't know and I think I don't want to know. 'Teresa Billington-Greig?' I nevertheless suggest, as the worst horror I can think of.

She laughs. 'No, thank heaven. Helen Craggs.'

I put out my hand to the mantelpiece to steady myself. Helen Craggs.

'I am ready for my walk,' I say.

VI

Helen Craggs was just such a young woman – hardly more than a girl – as I would have expected Harry to become infatuated with. She was attractive enough in that rather wispy way beloved of the painters of my youth: she was intended by nature, perhaps, for sentimental pursuits like gathering rosebuds or feeding small birds, and by birth for genteel pastimes like pouring tea and visiting the poor. Now Fate, in the person of my daughter Sylvia, had plucked her out of her proper station and placed her by the bedside of a dying boy. Only Sylvia could have imagined that Miss Craggs would be capable of offering Harry any comfort or support. Only Sylvia, for that matter, could have taken Harry at his word – if indeed he had really expressed this bizarre wish to have a strange woman by his bedside. Sylvia was quite capable of half-imagining it, or somehow imparting the notion to Harry, susceptible as he always was to her influence.

I was, in fact, never apprised of the full story. What I knew was what I was told by Christabel and what I could piece together from Sylvia's effusions and poor Harry's inarticulate statements, and of course what the girl herself told me. It is not my fault if these do not add up to a coherent whole.

Upon my returning from America in early December, my first thought was naturally of Harry. Christabel had promised that she would telegraph me if there was a serious change in his condition, and in the absence of any such message I knew at least that he was no worse than when I left. My instinct was to go immediately to Pembridge Gardens, where Harry still was, but I was interminably delayed by reception committees who wanted to make the most of the occasion to publicise the immense success of my American tour. Since part of the purpose of the tour had been to demonstrate at home the support we enjoyed in the greater world, I felt I could not default at this point, and I submitted with such good grace as I could muster to the interviews, the photographs, and the congratulations of hundreds of well-wishers. It was, in one sense, a triumph; but uppermost in my mind was the thought of my son lying in a clinic a few miles away. Christabel assured me that he was 'comfortable' and 'no worse', but these phrases did not convey the reassurance they were intended to. Conspicuous by her absence was Sylvia, who could have been counted on to give me the unadorned truth in its least palatable form.

Eventually, late in the evening, Christabel undertook to give some last interviews on my behalf, and I took a cab to the clinic. It was almost eleven o'clock of a violent winter's night when I at last reached Pembridge Gardens. The place seemed in darkness, but my knocking brought out a rather sleepy night nurse. Nurse Pine had gone to bed, but the night nurse directed me to Harry's room, a new one to which he had been moved in my absence. She did not offer to relieve me of my wet coat, and I left it on a chair in the entrance parlour, a kind of makeshift waiting-room.

'If he's asleep, please not to wake him, Mrs Pankhurst,' the nurse said. 'It's all we can do to get him to sleep.'

'Of course,' I said. 'I do have some experience of sick-beds.'

The nurse mumbled something under her breath that did not sound like an apology, but I let it pass, anxious to see Harry at last.

There was a faint light burning by his bedside. He seemed to be asleep, but sitting next to his bed, reading by the dim light, was a young woman I had never seen before. I assumed at first that this was another night nurse, but as she looked up from her book and got to her feet, I noticed that she was not wearing a uniform. Her general demeanour, too, was not that of a functionary; there was something diffident about her, and yet she was also socially assured. She extended her hand.

'Mrs Pankhurst?' she said, almost whispering. 'You may not remember me. I am Helen Craggs.'

This told me nothing, and as she volunteered no further information, I resorted to whispering at her, 'How is my son?'

She looked at the slight form on the bed – his head was turned away from the light, so I could not see his face, but the pulley above the bed and the other sick-room apparatus told their own tale. 'He suffers much,' she said, 'but he is very cheerful and hopeful.'

'Hopeful – of recovery?'

'Yes,' she said, and her eyes filled with tears.

I found it intolerable, having a whispered consultation with a strange woman whose business next to my son's bed had not been explained to me. I gestured her to accompany me to the waiting-room by the front door. She came readily, though with a last glance at Harry that suggested she would have preferred to stay. I was, however, in no mood to consult her preferences.

'I must confess myself puzzled, Miss Cragg,' I said when we were alone and had occupied the sole two chairs in the chilly parlour, 'as to your function and identity.' We still had to keep our voices low, since the parlour abutted the room where the night nurse, of whom I had formed no favourable opinion, was sitting.

'I can understand that,' she said. 'I'm almost equally surprised to find myself in this situation.' She was softly spoken, but with the clear tones of a good upbringing.

'Perhaps you will enlighten me, then,' I encouraged her.

For the first time she seemed at a loss for words. 'It's a long and strange story, and I'm not sure that I'm the best person to tell it,' she said.

'You are the only person available to tell it,' I pointed out, 'so I will thank you to do so.'

'I'll tell you my side,' she offered, 'and perhaps you can have the rest from Sylvia.'

'Sylvia?' I asked, trying to hide my displeasure. 'What does she have to do with it?'

'Well ...,' she began rather hesitatingly, 'let me tell my story, and let Sylvia's part in it emerge.'

I nodded, not trusting myself to say anything. Sylvia's part in it was not likely to be soothing to my agitated senses.

'You must know,' the young woman said, 'that Harry came to Manchester to help in the by-election two years ago.'

I nodded. 'Indeed I do.'

'And that he drove the suffragettes' four-in-hand.'

'I was not informed of the exact nature of his duties.'

'Well, that was what he did, and I was appointed to go with him on his rounds. I had gone to Manchester from Brighton to help, you see. I felt that ...'

'So that was where you met my son,' I said, to forestall unnecessary detail. I was not interested in this young woman's motives; I had seen enough girls from privileged homes find their 'vocation' in the women's movement.

'Yes, that was where I met your son,' she repeated with what I thought a slightly ironical mimicking of my phrase. She was clearly accustomed to taking the lead in conversation. I guessed that she was a schoolteacher. 'And that would have been all, for my part ...'

'He made no impression on you?'

'He impressed me as a lonely and sweet young man,' she replied, 'with a lively sense of humour and a quick wit. We had great fun and became good friends. But I would not have thought of it in any other light than that, and I'm afraid that, returning to the school where I taught, I had so many things on my mind that I would not have given Harry much thought.'

Unexpectedly, I felt slighted on Harry's behalf at the blandness with which this young woman was prepared to put him out of her mind. 'And what brought him to your ... over-charged mind again?' I asked.

She hesitated. 'Well, I was summoned – that is, I was called to Harry's bedside by Sylvia.'

'All the way from Brighton?' I guessed that she had been teaching at Roedean.

'No, I was in Manchester by then, working as an organiser for the WSPU. I don't know how Sylvia knew I was there, but she sent Annie Kenney, whom no doubt you know ...'

'Of course. Though I did not know that Sylvia had taken to using her services.'

'I naturally knew nothing about that. I was asked, as a great favour, to come to London to see Sylvia about an urgent matter. Coming here, I was informed by Sylvia that apparently Harry had, in the course of our acquaintance ... Harry had fallen in love with me, and that his dearest wish was to see me again.'

'And it was Sylvia's idea to indulge this whim?'

'Yes. I believe she did not see it as a whim as much as ... well, as in the nature of a dying wish.'

I got to my feet. 'Dying wish?' I exclaimed. 'But this is beyond all comprehension. On whose authority did Sylvia declare her brother to be dying?'

The young woman looked rather afraid. 'I don't know, Mrs Pankhurst,' she said. 'I naturally did not question her as to that, but I must assume that she was acting on medical opinion.'

'You *naturally* ...? I would have thought that the *natural* thing would have been to ascertain the true state of affairs before committing oneself to such ... such an ill-considered notion. However, be that as it may, please just tell me without equivocation: *is* he dying?'

She looked at me with what seemed – somewhat unpleasantly – to be curiosity. 'Don't you know?' she asked.

'Of course I don't know, young woman, otherwise I would not be asking you. I have this day returned from America, and it would seem that I have not been kept informed by my daughters of the condition of my own son.'

A quick flush coloured her cheeks; it appeared that Miss Cragg had a temper. I was about to point out to her that a temper needed firmer ground to stand on than she commanded, when there was the rattle of a key in the front door. It opened to a gust of rain, and with a damp flurry of mackintosh and umbrella Sylvia appeared. The night nurse rushed to meet her and take her coat and umbrella.

'I am sorry I'm so late,' said Sylvia, 'I was addressing a meeting in the East End and there were so many questions ...' Then she saw me, standing in the doorway of the waiting-room. 'Mother!' she said and came to me. We stood awkwardly facing each other for a moment, then she stepped forward and embraced me, wet as she was; her umbrella seemed to have been singularly ineffectual. 'I'm so glad you are back,' she said. I could see that she was on the point of tears. Fortunately, at this point she noticed the strange young woman.

'Ah, Helen, you are still here. How good of you to stay. I would have come earlier but ...' she shrugged, and water dripped from her wet hair. She could not possibly have walked from the East End, and yet she looked as if she had. It was a strange thing about Sylvia, that she always looked as if she had *walked* from wherever she had been to where she was.

The young woman came forward and kissed Sylvia on the cheek. 'It was no hardship. It's much colder out there than in here.'

Sylvia shivered. 'It is indeed. How is he?'

'Quiet. Sleeping well.'

'And how has he been tonight?'

She grimaced slightly. 'Cheerful.'

I felt disregarded in this discussion: they had appropriated my son's illness. Sensing this, Sylvia turned to me. 'Was he awake when you ...?'

'No,' I said. 'No, I was also detained till quite recently.'

'It is a pity. He was looking forward so much to your return.'

'Yes, Sylvia,' I said. 'I came as early as was humanly possible.'

'Of course, Mother, I wasn't implying …' She broke off. It was clear that her mind was elsewhere. 'And did he eat?' she asked Helen Cragg.

'The usual.'

'Pain?'

'No more than usual.'

Sylvia had evidently appointed herself commander-in-chief at my son's bedside, and was now receiving her deputy's report.

'Miss Cragg tells me …' I tried to interject.

'Craggs,' Sylvia corrected me. 'Helen Craggs.'

'I beg Miss Craggs's pardon. Miss Craggs tells me that you are not hopeful of Harry's recovery.'

She looked at me and, inevitably, her eyes filled with tears. 'Oh, Mother, there has never been much hope. It was always clear that Harry would never be able to walk again; the poliomyelitis had advanced too far. But in the last three weeks the bladder complaint has returned, and the doctor does not think he can live long.'

I stared at her pale, tearful face. It seemed to me then that Sylvia had been put on earth for no reason other than to be the bearer of bad tidings. 'I find it unaccountable,' I said, 'that I should have been kept in ignorance.'

'Mother, you knew how ill Harry was when you left.'

'I did not know about the bladder complaint.'

'No, that has returned of late.'

'And we thought he might walk again.'

'We hoped he might walk again.'

'If you will excuse me,' said Helen Craggs, 'I'll return to Harry's bed. He may have woken up.'

She left us. I was aware of the night nurse in her little office, no doubt eavesdropping on our conversation, but anger drove me to indiscretion. 'And may I ask why you chose to install a strange woman at my son's bed?'

She flushed, and for a moment she seemed about to offer some justification for her behaviour. But then she visibly checked herself, and set her features in the obstinate defiance I knew so well. 'No, Mother,' she said. 'No, you may not ask. You have forfeited your right to ask questions or to issue directives as to the proper conduct of Harry's bedside. If there is somebody other than you by Harry's bed, that is by your choice. While you were being applauded in New York and Boston, while you were addressing tumultuous crowds on the sufferings of women in your home country, Helen has been watching by the bed of your dying son, and she has given him more joy and more life in three weeks than you gave him in a lifetime. She has given him a will to live which, if he had been inspired to earlier, might have changed the course of his disease.'

Her accusation hung between us; I waited for her to reconsider and retract, but she simply stared back at me, her face rigid and intransigent. 'And it is your implication,' I at last said – it was not a question – 'that *I* might have given him this will to live.'

'Yes, Mother, I think you might have.'

I took a deep breath to calm myself. 'Why, pray, should I have this power of bestowing or withholding life?'

Sylvia had her answers ready. 'Harry has always wanted above all to please you. I think he would have lived if he had thought you were interested.'

'So I stand accused of causing the death of my own son through a lack of interest.'

'Not of causing it. Of doing nothing to prevent it. I do believe that all this talk about the Cause as if it were some religious crusade has affected your thinking: you are playing at being God, sacrificing your only son.'

I ignored the sheer malice of this charge. 'And it is to punish me for this that you have placed that woman by his bedside in my place?'

This, at last, seemed to sting Sylvia into angry refutation. 'Mother, I'm not the vindictive harpy you seem to think me. I have *placed* Helen at Harry's bedside, as you put it, because Harry asked for her. If he is not dead yet, that is because he has been fighting so hard to remain alive for her.'

'Am I supposed to thank Miss Craggs for keeping my son alive against my return?'

'No, Mother. I don't think your return was uppermost in Helen's mind. What she did, she did for Harry's sake.'

'And yet you keep reproaching me, directly and indirectly, for not staying here by Harry's bedside instead of going to America. Do you know what I have achieved for the cause by going to America? Do you know how many thousands came to listen to me and pledged their support?'

'I have read the newspapers, Mother, and I know that your tour was a triumph. Harry also knows it and rejoices in it. I am not denying that you have achieved something immense for the cause. You will be celebrated in years to come as a heroine of feminism. I hope it will sustain you in the weeks to come. Now I must go and relieve Helen. Are you coming to see Harry?'

'I have seen him. I will see him again tomorrow, when he is awake. I have kept my cab waiting outside.'

'Ah yes, you must not keep your cab waiting.' Her voice was carefully neutral.

'And you?'

'I?'

'How will you get home?'

'I sleep here. They have made a bed for me in one of the storerooms.'

I hesitated. 'Do you think it is right that Harry should have to lie in such an … unclothed state in the presence of a strange woman?' I asked. 'It is not healthy.'

'Not healthy?' she asked, and to my dismay she started laughing, quite vulgarly, as if I had said something uproariously funny. Sylvia laughed so seldom that when she did, it seemed quite grotesque, but this was worse: it was a mirthless kind of laughter, obviously sarcastic in intent. I had been laughed at in this way by working men in the East End. After a while, when even she could see that I was displeased, she calmed down, wiped her eyes, and said, 'I'm sorry Mother, for my hilarity. But Harry is *dying* and you think Helen's presence is not *healthy*?'

I was unpleasantly conscious of the presence of the night nurse very much within earshot, and said nothing further, but resolved to speak to Nurse Pine on the subject.

I left for the Inns of Court Hotel, where I was staying. The cab driver, sulky on account of having been kept so late, perversely stopped a distance beyond the hotel, and refused to go back for me. I would normally have refused to pay him, but I was tired and dispirited. Facing down an impudent cab driver after confronting Sylvia was more than I should have to deal with in one evening.

I arrived in my room cold and wet. Christabel was waiting for me, sitting in front of the gas fire. She was staying, of course, with the Pethick Lawrences at St Clement's Inn nearby, but wanted, I suppose, to share with me her impressions of the evening. She was evidently excited: from a publicity point of view, my return had been successful beyond our most optimistic calculations, and she had made the most of it.

She came up to me and hugged me, wet as I was.

'Mother,' she said, 'that was a complete and utter triumph!'

I looked at her glowing face and tried to enter into her ebullience, but I felt only cold and empty.

'I have been to see Harry,' was all I could say.

'Yes, I know, Mother.' Her abrupt change of expression suggested that her gaiety had been partly a front for the disquiet that now surfaced. 'And how did you find him?'

'I found him dying,' I said, while taking off my wet outer clothing.

'Yes,' she said, 'yes. He is dying.'

'And I feel betrayed – betrayed and misled.'

She returned to her seat by the fire. 'Why, Mother?' she asked, without looking at me. 'Because I did not telegraph you to return to Harry's sick-bed?'

'That is what you promised – to let me know if there was a turn for the worse.'

She now at least looked at me. 'His condition has been so unstable that it wasn't always possible to say whether he was taking a turn for the worse or the better.'

'When I left, his bladder condition seemed to have cleared. You could at least have let me know that he had had a relapse.'

'Why, Mother? To cause you fruitless anxiety and distract you from your real reason for being in America?'

'To inform me, as you promised.'

'And if we had informed you, what would you have done? Cancelled your American tour halfway through?' She looked at me in a way that I recognised as her taking the initiative in an argument. 'And given that it was practically impossible for you to return, would it have been a kindness to tell you that your son was dying?'

'I could at least have been given the choice.'

Her tone became less challenging; she seemed to be informing me rather than arguing with me. 'No, Mother, that's exactly what I did not want to give you. Out of consideration for you.'

'Consideration? To leave me in ignorance?'

'Yes, Mother, consideration. I believe it was a kindness not to burden you with the moral dilemma of such a choice.'

'And I have to live with the consequences of your decision.'

'That is preferable to living with the consequences of your own decision. I have made it possible for you to say *I did not know*.'

'Thank you very much,' I said bitterly. 'And to whom shall I say it? To Harry? To Sylvia?'

'Harry understands. You need not say anything to him. Sylvia will never understand. There is no point in saying anything to her.'

'So that leaves only myself.'

She rose to her feet again and came to me, a picture of filial concern. 'Yes, Mother, and I think quite soon you will be grateful that I made it possible for you to say to yourself *I did not know.*'

I did not reply to this. Christabel, perhaps thinking she had convinced me, stretched her arms above her head. 'It's been a long day. I think you should get to bed.' She turned as if to leave, then turned back to me. 'And I'll tell you something else that may be of consolation to you. I did not want you to know about Harry because I did not *want* you to come back from America. I'm speaking not as your daughter or as Harry's sister, but – in your absence – as the leader of the Women's Social and Political Union. The Union needed you in America more than Harry needed you by his bedside.'

'And you felt empowered to take such a decision on my behalf?'

She was putting on her hat and gloves, not looking at me as she said, 'I was not taking it on your behalf, Mother. I was taking it on the Union's behalf.'

Christabel left. I had been tired, but now did not want to go to bed. In general I try not to brood on things over-much; my instinct has always been to act rather than mull things over. But here action would achieve nothing: there was nothing to do. I could not even sit by my son's bedside and hold his hand while he was dying; that role had been taken from me. I was never to know his last thoughts.

I have given suck, and know how tender 'tis to love the babe that milks me …

But Christabel was the only one of my children that I had suckled.

101

VII
Saturday 14 April 1928

A cramp convulses my stomach. I struggle out of bed. My pale face stares wide-eyed at me from the mirror, my hair hanging grey and lifeless: the indomitable Mrs Pankhurst, who refused to be subjected to forcible feeding, and, refusing, quelled the most brutal functionaries of the state! Vanquished at last, not by my enemies, but by the betrayal of my own flesh and blood and the abdication of my body. Another convulsion. I try to retch, but nothing comes. My body is as empty as my spirit.

There is a strange smell in the room, a smell as of putrefying flesh. It is in my night clothes, it clings to the furnishings of the room; but most of all, it is part of me: it comes from within me. I recognise it from the hunger strikes of old: the body, deprived of nutrition, starting to consume its own tissue. It is the smell of corruption and decay.

Harry, at the end, did not smell like this.

At the end, what did Harry think?

One of my earliest memories is of my father coming into the nursery one evening when we were all deemed to be asleep. I was awake, but for some reason feigned sleep. My father paused by my bedside, and said to my mother, 'She's the most talented of our children. What a pity she's not a boy.'

I have devoted my life to proving my father wrong. And now I wonder if he wasn't right. If I had been a man I would have been spared this.

Nought's had, all's spent, where our desire is had without content.

Christabel has decided that I must be moved to a nursing home in Wimpole Street. I shall miss Mrs Chipperfield. She has been kind to me. I do not know what is to happen to little Flora. Perhaps Christabel will take her.

The pigeon taps at the window – whether from an obscure impulse of aggression or affection, I shall never know. I open the window and it flies away; but when I crumble a morsel of toast from my uneaten breakfast, it returns and pecks at the crumbs on the window-sill, its hunger greater than its fear.

Monday 16 April 1928
I have had a curious little note from Sylvia, asking to come and see me. My impulse is to refuse: what insult can she add to the injury she has inflicted upon the Pankhurst name? What injury can she add to what Christabel has inflicted upon me?

Is there any cause in nature that makes these hard hearts?

Wednesday 18 April 1928
I have never shied away from the malignancy of Fate or her agents. I shall not do so now. Let Sylvia come.

Book 2

Sylvia

You are unreasonable, always have been and I fear always will be. I suppose you were made so!

Emmeline Pankhurst, letter to Sylvia Pankhurst,
January 1914.

I

Spring has been dawdling unconscionably this year. Today, however, compensating for its late arrival, it has erupted brilliantly, almost excessively. I went out into the garden early this morning, and found Silvio scattering crumbs on the bird table and staring at the gaudy profusion with that bemused expression that all things particularly English can still evoke in him.

'It is beautiful,' he said, 'especially for your birthday.' He reached to pick a stem of hawthorn, but I stopped him. 'Please don't,' I said, 'it looks so right there. In my study it would just get lost under piles of paper.'

He smiled and shrugged. 'Here it gets lost under …' and he gestured with extravagant helplessness at the unchecked proliferation of vegetation, 'under all that.'

'I know,' I said, 'the garden is a wilderness.'

'It reminds me of our walks in Richmond Park in spring,' he said. 'Do you remember?'

It is more than thirty years ago, but I remember. 'Yes,' I said. 'But it also reminds me of Manchester.'

He lifted an eyebrow sceptically. 'Manchester was known for its flowers?'

'No. But when we lived there, when I was, oh, about twelve years old, we had two red hawthorns in our garden, perfect cones, like this one, so beautiful that in spring I would stand and look at them for minutes on end, wondering where such beauty came from – since, of course, we didn't believe in God. But then, when I went with father on Sunday mornings into the working-class districts, places like Ancoats, Gorton and Hulme, with their row upon row of smoke-black houses, and no trees or flowers at all to relieve the ugliness, those two red may trees in our garden came to haunt me with their beauty. I used to ask myself how I could enjoy such splendour, when the poor children had hardly enough to eat. There were moments when I could have dashed my head against the grimy walls of those terrible streets.'

He said – his Italian accent lending an oddly pedantic stress to his admonition: 'You have always been too little willing to grant yourself pleasure.'

'Possibly. And yet I have had much pleasure.'

'And now?' he asked, 'Now that you own the garden and all the flowers in it?'

I shook my head. 'No,' I said, 'I no longer feel guilty about beauty. Perhaps I have dashed my head against enough walls.'

'That is good,' he said. 'We need the beauty to give us strength. Out of the strong shall come forth sweetness – but out of sweetness shall come forth strength, too.'

I laughed. 'I never thought I would hear you quote Scripture.'

Now, I am in my study, in its way as disordered as the garden. Mother used to say my untidiness was an image of my mind. That was nonsense, of course, my mind was quite tidy enough once it was made up. But it is true that it was usually made up in opposition to some self-satisfied system that imagined itself to embody order and harmony. *Miss Pankhurst believes that everything that is, is wrong, and must be changed*, one of my critics – Winston Churchill? Bernard Shaw? – said. Have I only confirmed the establishment in its belief in its own rightness? *Oh, Sylvia – the dotty one*, they say in the Foreign Office, as they file yet another of my letters in what I am told they call the Loony Bin.

Richard comes in, bearing a telegram. 'Another one,' he says, smiling, then leaves. I watch him closing the door gently behind him so as not to disturb me. I thank that God in whom I do not believe that I have brought up a gentle child. I remember his perplexity when, as a boy, he put out cheese for the mouse, crumbs for the birds and milk for the cat, and it was explained to him that all three could not dine together because the cat might prefer to eat the bird and the mouse. 'But I love them all,' he objected, as if that example should inspire them to a like universal love.

I open the telegram. It is long. On one's seventieth birthday it is something, I suppose, to receive a telegram from the Emperor Haile Selassie, Elect of God, Conquering Lion of the Tribes of Judah, King of Zion, King of Kings, Emperor of Ethiopia, Chevalier sans Peur et sans Reproche and Epitome of True Nobility. I wonder if the Emperor habitually includes all his titles on telegrams, or whether this is an extravagance in my honour. I wonder, too, if Father would have approved. He was never much impressed with kings, emperors and God, though he might have liked the *sans peur et sans reproche*. Mother? I think she would have wanted to know how much Influence the Emperor of Ethiopia had; and for her, Influence was always with Westminster. And no, the Emperor of Ethiopia has no influence with Westminster, a fact I have spent a not inconsiderable portion of my life publicly deploring.

I fold the telegram. I must keep it, I suppose, but where? File it under *Esteem, marks of*? Odd, as one gets older, how the marks of esteem start to accumulate. Is esteem what one's erstwhile enemies profess when one has lost the power to discomfit them? Who knows, somebody may yet erect a statue of me somewhere near Mother's. I hope not. The clothed human form does not lend itself to statuary grace. As for the unclothed human form, I cannot picture that in the Victoria Tower Gardens. Since the demise of Ancient Greece, a statue has become but a dead body imbued with political significance.

The phone rings, for the fifth time this morning. I sigh. Apparently alone among my contemporaries I do not rejoice in the invention of the telephone. Its undeniable usefulness seems to me severely compromised by its presumption in demanding one's attention at its convenience. Of course, the telephone is but the instrument of some human agency, but even quite like-able people tend to become demanding and ill-tempered at the other end of it, reduced to little querulous bleats. I thus try to make it clear to whoever telephones me that I am not to be assumed to be indefinitely available merely because I have been reduced to a disembodied voice.

Unfortunately, on occasions like a birthday, the telephone calls one would normally have given short shrift have to be tolerated as gestures of good will. My usual formula – *'I am a busy woman, please be brief'* – would, I suppose, be taken amiss by some well-wisher intent upon pressing birthday wishes upon me.

So now I suppress my impatience, and say merely, 'Yes?'

Instead of the more or less studied effusiveness of another birthday greeting, there is a pause at the other end, and a slightly hesitant voice asks, 'Is that Sylvia Pankhurst?'

'It is.'

'Oh.' Another pause, which I am about to terminate with my reminder that I am a busy woman, when the voice identifies itself. 'Sylvia, this is Teresa Billington-Greig – from the WSPU, you may remember.'

Teresa Billington-Greig. Bulldog Billington, as Christabel called her, though not to her face. 'Of course I remember. You and your friends left the Union to start the Women's Freedom League.'

'Yes, although that is now all behind us, is it not?'

'That depends on your view of history. Is anything ever behind us?'

There is a silence, which I take to be one of puzzlement, then a nervous laugh.

'Well yes, I daresay, we do remember,' she says at last, 'but one hopes in a spirit of conciliation rather than bitterness.'

'One hopes, indeed.' I do not think I need lessons in conciliation, nor indeed in bitterness, from Teresa Billington-Greig.

She laughs without conviction, as if I had attempted, not very successfully, a witticism. 'Now, to get to the point ...'

'Please do,' I encourage her.

'Yes. I should perhaps explain that the *Manchester Guardian*, knowing of course of our association in the past, has seen fit to – well, not too put too fine a point on it, has asked me to write your obituary.'

'I see.' Various questions suggest themselves, the most pertinent one being *Why you – of all people*? I ask instead, 'And when is it that the *Manchester Guardian* has determined that I will die?'

She laughs again in her unconvinced manner. Laughter has never been Teresa's natural mode. 'I believe,' she says, 'that it's standard practice for newspapers to prepare obituaries of prominent people well in advance of ... the actual event in case of ... well in case of the unforeseen happening.'

'The unforeseen then becoming, of course, the foreseen.'

She turns this over for a moment. 'Yes, yes,' she says nervously, as if suspecting another joke, 'I suppose you could say that.'

'And in this spirit of prudent foresight the *Manchester Guardian* has commissioned you to pronounce posthumously upon me.'

'Well yes, while appreciating, of course that this may seem to you presumptuous.' Apology comes as awkwardly to Teresa as humour.

'My dear Teresa, the one presumption we none of us can seriously object to is that of our own mortality.'

'Quite.' I can hear that Teresa is with difficulty sustaining her unaccustomed meekness of address. 'And hoping to ensure that what eventually gets published is in all ways as you would like it.'

'Would have liked it,' I say.

'Would have? Oh yes, quite, would have. Quite.' Her pause bristles with suppressed irritation. 'Hoping to ensure your satisfaction, then, I was wondering if it would be possible for me to come and see you in order to clarify some points.'

I have no desire to see or be seen by Teresa Billington, nor to clarify her points for her. I remember her as a rather obstinate young woman. She is presumably now a rather obstinate old woman. Well, so am I.

'I must tell you candidly, Teresa,' I say, 'that I remain, in spite of my advanced age, failing powers and approaching death, a very busy person, too occupied with the demands of the present to dwell much on the past, especially with a view to a future event that I shall not, in the nature of things, be in a position to appreciate.'

I can hear Teresa breathing. She is either suffering from a chest complaint or taking a deep breath in order not to lose her temper. When she speaks, the tightness of her voice supports the latter interpretation. 'I understand that, of course, Sylvia,' she says, 'but I imagine you do care, if only … proleptically … about what is written about you after … in your obituary.'

'I'm not sure that I do care,' I say, truthfully enough. 'So many lies and slanders have been printed about me in my life-time that a few more after my death can change the minds of neither my friends nor my enemies.'

Teresa tries unsuccessfully to suppress an exasperated sigh, then tries equally unsuccessfully to turn it into a light laugh. 'Honestly, Sylvia,' she says with unbecoming skittishness, 'you're incorrigible! Well, even accepting that it's a matter of indifference to you how you're represented after your death, may I not appeal to you in the name of … of our common cause to help me to write something that will do justice to your con-tribution to it?'

Our common cause? What is Teresa Billington's cause? What does she know of mine? But I am wearying of this exchange, and it is evident that Teresa will not give up until she has gained her point. Better get her to declare her intention. 'What was it that you had in mind, Teresa?'

'I was hoping that it might be possible for me to interview you, at your home or any place of your choice, and entirely at your convenience, of course.'

My convenience? My convenience is to be left alone to get on with my work. Nevertheless, I reply as graciously as I can. 'I can be found at my home in Woodford Green. West Dene, 3 Charteris Road. Perhaps you'd better come today, I have lost so much of it already. Shall we say at two o'clock this afternoon?'

She makes an inarticulate noise, signifying, I think, gratitude. I hope the *Manchester Guardian* knows what it is doing.

II

Teresa arrives in the early afternoon, looking flustered and hot. 'I'm sorry I'm late,' she says. 'I couldn't find your house. The number and name seem to have disappeared. Fortunately the gentleman in the garden, whom I take to be your gardener, assured me that this was the right house.'

'That would have been Silvio,' I say, 'whom I would certainly have dismissed if he had been my gardener.'

She laughs, again her uncomfortable acknowledgement of what she takes to be my attempt at wit. 'To be sure, the garden is quite ... abundant. But that is ...' she gives up trying to find some extenuating circumstance in the condition of my garden.

Time has not been kind to Teresa. In youth her solidity of feature lent weight and force to the vigour of her opinions, at times quite overpoweringly so. Christabel used to complain that her lips curled rather too much, which is to say that her opinions were strong but crude. Now that her features have softened, indeed melted, she seems also to have lost her firmness of opinion. There is something tentative about her, as if life has drained her of confidence. It is strange to think that this is the woman who accused Mother and Christabel of emotionalism, personal tyranny and fanaticism. She now looks as if she could not accuse a cat of neglecting its kittens.

Teresa looks about my study and then at me, and her mouth tightens. There is, after all, a spasm of disapproval left in the slackened features. For a moment I see my study and myself as she must see it and me, in our dishevelled condition. She glances at me as if expecting me to apologise for the state of the room or perhaps even for my appearance. This I shall not do.

As a young girl I was made unhappy on account of my appearance. Once I accepted that there was very little I could do about it, I stopped feeling apologetic about it. There are more important things in life than brushing one's hair.

Teresa takes the seat I indicate, an upright chair opposite my own. There are no comfortable chairs in my study, except the one occupied by Cedric, my Persian cat. I do not have time for comfort, and I do not want to encourage visitors to stay beyond the capacity of the average human body to sustain itself in an upright position.

'Well,' Teresa says briskly, as she sits down, as if to say *Let's get this over with*. But she leaves it at that, waiting for me to respond. I hope she will not expect me to conduct the interview with myself. I wait for her. She is rummaging in her handbag, and at length produces a notebook and pen. She looks at me expectantly, as if the manifestation of the notebook should inspire me to utter something worthy of its blankness, but I remain silent, and eventually Teresa capitulates: 'I realise, from what you said on the telephone, that my ... differences with your mother may seem to you an obstacle to our free communication ...'

'Not at all,' I interrupt her. 'I never made common cause with my mother's differences merely because they were hers.'

'I was not sure, from your references in your book to the split ...'

'I suppose you mean *The Suffragette Movement*. I thought I'd made it clear that I regarded my mother's actions in disregarding the constitution as – *ill-judged and undemocratic* were my words, I think.'

'Disregard?' Teresa surprises me by all but snorting. 'She simply tore it up.'

I do not want to be drawn into an alliance with this woman so many years after the battle, but nor do I want to defend Mother's behaviour. 'Mother saw the WSPU as a kind of volunteer army,' I say, 'and members were expected to give unquestioning obedience at all times to the decisions of the leaders.'

'Yes, I know that,' Teresa says. 'It was the unquestioning obedience that I ventured to question.'

'As did I,' frankness obliges me to confess. 'I never signed the pledge, you know.'

'The pledge?'

'You see, after your departure, the remaining loyalists were obliged to vow, in effect, to obey the office bearers in all things.'

She shakes her head. From the renewed tightening of her lips it is evident that, more than forty years later, Mother still has the power to enrage. 'I was hoping,' Teresa says, with a visible effort to calm herself, 'that we could consider what you regard not so much as the main *events* in your life as its main *influences*. Other than your mother, of course.'

'Why other than my mother, and why of course?' I demand.

She looks uncomfortable. What she does not want to tell me, I can see, is that she has been instructed to be uncontroversial. The obituary of Sylvia Pankhurst should not read like a posthumous attack on Emmeline Pankhurst. 'One rather thought,' she says, 'that Mrs Pankhurst was ... well, taken for granted.'

'My dear Teresa, taking Mrs Pankhurst for granted was always a mistake.'

'I do not, of course, mean to deny her immense influence over almost everybody who came to know her. It's exactly because that influence has been so well established that I was interested in perhaps less self-evident influences. But of course, if you do regard your mother as a major influence in your life ...?'

'That is not what I said.'

A slight knitting of the brows suggests that Teresa is becoming exasperated with what she must regard as my sparring. I feel little for Teresa's exasperation, but indirection can only prolong this interview. I decide to enter as fully as possible into

116

Teresa's questions, and let her reduce it to a thousand-word obituary if she can.

'I am sure that Mother influenced me a great deal, indirectly,' I say in what I take to be the tone of a cooperative interviewee. 'But I was, and indeed still am, far more conscious of my father as an example and guide. In everything I did I tried to live up to his principles and his actions.' I point at the portrait on my wall, a beautiful photographic study. 'He used to repeat to us his father's maxim, which he had adopted as his own: "If you do not work for other people, you will not have been worth the upbringing."'

She absorbs this information placidly, passively, like a large pink sponge. 'And do you feel, now, that you have been worth the upbringing?'

'Yes,' I find myself saying without hesitation. 'Yes, I think in all honesty I can say that I have worked for other people.' She makes a note in her little book: *feels she was worth the upbringing*, I suppose. 'I think I have for a few people made life a more pleasant affair than it would have been without me, and I suppose that is as much as anybody can aspire to in one lifetime.'

'You do not feel, then, that you might have achieved more?'

'Oh, one can always achieve more, and indeed, I intend to achieve more before I die, which I am afraid will inconvenience the *Manchester Guardian*.'

This time she does not acknowledge my attempt at wit, merely frowns at her notebook as she jots down a curtailed version of my reply – *wants to achieve more before she dies*. When the time comes, she will render that as *she had hoped to achieve more before her death*.

'What?' she asks suddenly, abruptly, and as I stare at her no doubt stupidly, she repeats almost impatiently, 'What exactly is it that you hope to achieve?'

What *exactly*? What kind of imagination measures off aspiration as if it were a yard of calico? A draper's imagination, no doubt, which is what Teresa has. And which Mother never had, as witness the failure of Emerson's. The repeated failure of Emerson's. Poor Christabel, how she hated Emerson's.

Teresa is looking at me quizzically and I realise I must be smiling. 'Oh,' I say, 'forgive my abstraction. I was lost in contemplating all the things I hope to achieve before my death. But for the time being I am limiting my ambitions to the unification of Ethiopia with Somalia and Eritrea.'

She looks at me as if suspecting a joke. Like most English people, she probably has only the vaguest idea of where Ethiopia and Eritrea are and why they should be unified.

'I have just completed a substantial book on the subject,' I inform her. 'It is to be called *Ethiopia and Eritrea*, and I shall let you have a copy when it is published. I think you will find it informative.'

'I'm sure I shall,' she says without conviction.

'And there were three others on the subject,' I add relentlessly. If Teresa means to write my obituary she will have to do her homework. 'They were called *The Ethiopian People*, *Ex-Italian Somaliland* and *Eritrea on the Eve*. I shall arrange for copies to be sent to you.'

'Thank you, that is most generous,' she says faintly.

'Not at all,' I say. 'I think it only proper that as, in a sense, my first biographer, you should have access to all my writings.'

'Of course,' she says, ever less enthusiastically. 'Of course, an obituary does differ from a biography in scope and ambition.'

'Indeed,' I concur. 'An obituary is a kind of distillate of the biography, I would say, would you not?'

'That is certainly one way of looking at it.' It is clearly not hers.

'And as such, must be so much more *concentrated* than a biography, not so?'

She nods feebly, but I persevere.

'And therefore does not omit information so much as compress it?'

'I do believe you're right,' she says.

'Well, then,' I say. 'What aspect of my life do you want to know about next?'

Teresa shifts on her chair. It is not, as I have said, a comfortable chair, and Teresa is a large woman. But if she was hoping for a pre-selected florilegium of Main Events in the Life of ..., ready-potted for transplantation to the columns of the *Manchester Guardian*, she is doomed to disappointment, not to mention tedium. If I am to be represented to the public after my death, I intend to be represented accurately and fully.

'What,' she asks me, 'would you consider your greatest achievement?'

'Without a doubt, my efforts on behalf of Ethiopia.' I am surprised at the readiness of my own reply; it is not a question I have ever asked myself. No doubt my promptness is a reaction to Teresa's sceptical manner. 'The struggle to bring justice to the Ethiopian people, in the face of the criminal indifference of the British government, has been by far the most worthwhile and I think successful thing in my life.'

'More worthwhile than helping women get the vote?' she asks.

'Yes,' I say. 'It was no doubt only a matter of justice that women should have the vote. But I must confess myself disappointed with the use to which they have put their hard-earned privilege.'

'You mean ...'

'I mean, amongst other follies, returning that dissolute old hypocrite Winston Churchill to power once again. But in general women seem to have succumbed to a kind of universal frivolity. In my day, women's periodicals told their readers how to force men to give them the vote. Now they tell them how to ensnare a man. I find myself wondering whether they deserve to have the vote.'

She solemnly makes a single mark on her notepad as if ticking off an item. Does she have a check list? Did the *Manchester Guardian* give her a Guide to Writing Obituaries?

119

Then she looks about her, as if searching for inspiration. I don't want to see my study through her eyes – it has served me well for years – but I do so for a moment anyway, noting the left-over furniture, the crammed bookshelves on three walls, the odour of cat and old paper. Her gaze rests on the watercolour portrait behind my desk. 'That is Keir Hardie,' she says.

Since this is a statement, I do not reply. She looks at me for confirmation, however, and I nod. In a sense, it is of course Keir Hardie.

'Who painted it?' she asks.

'I did.' *Painted.* What an inadequate term for the process by which I tried, faithfully and without the distortions of partial vision, to rescue from transience the power of the living features of the man I loved – not just his features, but his humour, his compassion, his strength. Teresa wants to ask about my relationship with Keir, but she lacks the courage, or the effrontery, of the true journalist.

'Of course,' she says. 'Forgive me; you achieved so much in other fields that one forgets you were – are – an artist.'

'And yet if you had asked me at eighteen what I most wanted to become, I would have said an artist.'

She seizes with relief on what she clearly regards as a safe topic. 'Did you think of yourself as primarily an artist or a political activist?'

'I did not think of myself as choosing between the two. My art was to me part of what you call my activism. I dreamed, perhaps rather naively, of using my one talent to bring beauty to other people, especially to those in circumstances less fortunate than mine.'

'You won a scholarship to the Royal College of Art, did you not?'

'Yes, and spent two years in South Kensington. Except for a short spell – a summer and autumn – in Venice, the practice of my art was always in conjunction with my political activities.

120

My most ambitious works, artistically speaking, were the designs I did for the ILP's Pankhurst Hall in Salford.'

'Ah yes,' she nods, and I am surprised to see her smile as if at a fond memory, 'I remember seeing them. Huge murals, weren't they? With flowers?'

'Yes, all very symbolic – roses for love, lilies for purity, that kind of thing. Since the hall was named after my father, the decorations were something of a labour of love. I found it pleasing, too, to think that I was adding some colour to the lives of the people of Salford. I was only twenty-one at the time, and very idealistic. I believe the place was recently turned into a bingo hall.'

Teresa does not know whether to deplore the bingo hall as an affront to Art or to hail it as a victory for Egalitarianism, and changes the subject. 'You say you spent some time in Venice. How did you come to be there?'

'I won a studentship from the Manchester School of Art.'

'And you were happy there?'

'It was the happiest time of my life.' Saying it, I fully realise it for the first time, or allow myself to realise it. 'I seemed to be surrounded by beauty, and it was all there for me to see and feel and hear, and in a modest way make my own through my painting. There was poverty, too, of course, in Venice, but there wasn't the grinding ugliness of England, the sense that all existence is hopeless that one so often felt in Manchester, the blight of one's helplessness in the face of so much squalor. At home I used to wonder if it was *just* that I should be permitted to devote my life to the creation of beauty while others were caught in the trammels of unrewarding labour. In Venice it was possible to believe, however ingenuously, that by creating beauty one was adding to the sum total of happiness in the world, and alleviating, however infinitesimally, the hardships of other people. When I went out painting I used to be followed around by children and even some adults, all of whom had something to say about my work. One could feel, there, that as an artist one was part of a community in which beauty had a natural place. I made a dear friend too, Madame Sophie, who had had a tragic but heroic life in the liberation struggle in Poland. In the evenings she played and I sang – arias from *La Traviata*.'

I realise that I am losing myself in retrospection. I look up. Teresa is regarding me apprehensively, as if she fears I may subject her to an aria.

'It must sound very absurd now,' I say.

'It sounds wonderful,' she says in her unadorned, factual way – what Mother used to call *blunt*. 'Why did you return?'

'I was needed in Manchester. You see, Mother had opened a shop – Emerson's – a very worthy but not very successful venture. It was her idea to make available at a reasonable price well-designed, attractive objects, to liven the homes of women who would not normally be able to afford anything beautiful.'

'Could one say that your mother's motive in opening Emerson's was not so dissimilar from yours in your painting?'

I suspect Theresa thinks she has caught me out, but I do not give her the satisfaction of disputing her comparison. 'I suppose so, yes, though at the time I must confess I took a less indulgent view of Emerson's – when Christabel wrote to me to come back and *do my bit*, as she put it.'

'Why Christabel?'

'She'd been obliged to run Emerson's in my absence, which she hated, and apparently did not do at all well. Then she decided to study law at Manchester University, and there was nobody to look after Emerson's.'

'Did you resent having to leave Venice?'

'Resent it?' I consider this. 'I don't know. Resentment was not a luxury we had been taught to indulge. I very much regretted it. Madame Sophie begged me to stay, and I felt at home in the art school in Venice. But I considered it my duty to return, and we had been taught never to carp at our duty. It is true that when I did get back to Manchester, it was only to find that, with her more active involvement in politics, Mother had lost interest in Emerson's and my presence was not really required. But I did, soon afterwards, win the scholarship to the Royal College of Art.'

'Did you never regret the sacrifice of a career in art?'

'It was never my decision to give up art. I assumed an active part in politics only because of the urgency of the moment; and I thought that when our objectives had been met, I would return to the course I had planned for myself.'

'As an artist?'

'Yes. So there was, I suppose, a sacrifice. Only, the causes presented themselves in what seemed a natural way, and there always seemed to be something more to be done.'

She is scribbling busily now. 'Would you say that causes took the place of human beings in your life?'

'I don't think I understand your question. Causes mattered to me only as they were embodiments of human needs.'

'But, say, the Women's Social and Political Union was surely a kind of abstraction, uniting people as different in outlook and temperament as … as your mother and me, for instance. Or as you and your sister Christabel.'

'In so far as it united people and effaced differences, it did so only temporarily, as witness your defection from the Union.'

She taps her pen on her book. 'I did not defect. I was given no choice.'

'Your resignation then, or even expulsion. The point is that the differences did eventually surface.'

'As they did between you and your sister?'

She is probing, now, but I shall not be coy about personal questions. 'Between me and my sister the differences were always there. Perhaps not so much in our objectives as in our vision of methods. I deplored the high-handed way in which she rejected loyal friends and supporters because of trivial differences of opinion.'

'Perhaps, to her, the cause did override the individual.'

'That is what she would have said. But the cause was to her inseparable from her own person and her own prominence. Of course, you must remember exactly how prominent she was.'

'I remember very well.' Teresa's tone is rather dry. 'Thousands of young women adored her. I myself ... admired her.'

'One could not but. Her presence on stage was electrifying. Her gestures were so beautiful, and she used her voice to such effect.'

'So in following her, were women inspired by her or by the principles she was propounding?'

'It's exactly my point that the two could not be separated. The Union was an aggregate of individuals, and had reality only as that.'

'All those cheering phalanxes?' she asks, sceptically. 'The rowdy meetings, the triumphant processions, the roaring crowds in the Albert Hall? Were they aggregates of individuals or a body politic with an identity of its own?'

I recognise this as a real question, not a mere debating point. Looking back at it all now, I want to say: I see, not the processions and the crowds; I see Mother at her desk, frowning over statistics, Christabel pacing the floor, gesticulating, Keir passionately arguing a point; I see poor worried Fred Pethick Lawrence in the charge office with his briefcase between his knees, I see his wife Emmeline clutching Annie Kenny's arm more tightly than is strictly necessary. And, ever more clearly as I get older, I see Harry on his bed, covered with a single sheet, dying. But instead, I say, slowly, 'To me the processions and the crowds had very little reality. Of course, they were there and they were effective in that they attracted public attention; but what *is* a crowd really? Once it has dispersed, it will never exist again. Whereas the individuals, of course ...'

Teresa has a way of pulling up the left corner of her mouth when she is considering a statement, that makes her seem almost insultingly sceptical. I am not sure if this is an unconscious effect or deliberate. It is at any rate not encouraging, and I pause. If she wants to pursue the topic, she can.

'The individuals, then,' she says. 'One knows, of course, about your mother and sister, and you have mentioned your father. What other individuals would you single out as particularly important in your life?'

She glances at the watercolour on the wall, confirming my suspicion that it is Keir Hardie she is pursuing. Well, best dispose of that.

'You no doubt know about my friendship with Keir Hardie,' I say in my most business-like and uninterruptible tone, 'so I shall not dwell on that topic. But not my brother Harry. You don't know about Harry. Few people do.'

'I knew him, of course, in the old days. And I've read the chapter on him in your book,' she surprises me by saying. 'Would you like to tell me about him?'

No, I would not *like* to tell you anything, Teresa, I want to say, but I say instead, 'Few people were aware of Harry, even while he was alive.' I pause. 'You yourself, I remember, amused your friends by referring to him as *the only girl in the Pankhurst family.*'

'Your memory is remarkable,' she says, her face stony.

'It's not the kind of comment one forgets,' I say, enjoying for a moment her evident embarrassment. But I do not really wish to use Harry's memory as a way of discomfiting Teresa. If she sincerely wants to hear about Harry, I'll tell her. 'I was hurt for Harry when your remark was repeated to me,' I continue, 'but then, I understood that he never made a strong impression on people used to greater forcefulness of manner. You see, because he suspected that he was a disappointment to Mother, he developed to a remarkable extent the power of shutting off his responses and adapting to what he thought were other people's expectations. He was the least *insistent* person – in a physical sense – that I ever knew. His own comfort, his own convenience, his own health even, he simply disregarded in his desire

125

not to be a nuisance. It was strange, though, that instead of admiring him for this self-abnegation, Mother, I think, took him at his own estimate. I suppose Mother did not understand self-abnegation, except as a well-publicised political act, like starving herself in public.'

'Did Harry experience this as a rejection?' Teresa has regained her composure; she is again the interviewer.

'He must have sensed at least a relative indifference.'

'How did he deal with that?'

'By trying, in everything he did, to please her. That is, I think he genuinely embraced her political principles as he understood them, and attempted in his way to advance them. The desire to please her may not have been fully articulated in his mind. He was a clever boy, but lacking confidence, slow to speak. Mother, of course, spoke without effort, not to say without thought, and she found his laboured speech a trial. She tended to interrupt him and complete his sentences for him, when quite often one could see that that was not what Harry had intended at all. This, of course, hardly added to his confidence and fluency. There were times when he could hardly bring himself to speak in front of Mother.'

Teresa has sat through this account impassively. It is possible that she is bored. This does not perturb me. 'In your book,' she says, when I pause, 'you seem quite critical of your mother's decision to send Harry to work at an early age.'

'Do I? Yes, of course I was critical, only I hadn't realised that I'd made it so evident in my book.'

'I think it's difficult to read your book without sensing a tolerably strong resentment on your part.'

'Really? Well, yes, I did feel that poor Harry was being bundled off for Mother's convenience to quite unsuitable employment.'

'How did Harry's removal minister to your mother's convenience?'

'Of course, things were difficult for Mother, and Harry was

126

a worry, but it was more than that. It was as if she thought she could make him stronger by forcing him to do manual labour. She always detested weakness of any kind, and she thought Harry was physically weak, which he wasn't really, he was simply reluctant to put himself forward, and Mother all her life admired assertive males, for all that she fought them tooth and nail in her youth. In middle age, of course, she joined them.'

Teresa makes another note and I wonder how that statement is going to sound in my obituary – *to the end of her life she resented her mother* – but I am past caring.

'It's said,' she ventures, 'that your mother admired Mussolini. Is that true?'

'As you know, at first many people did, even on the left, and by then Mother was far indeed from the left. So I do think she admired what she saw as his aim to restore Rome to something of its former glory, and, of course, that was a military glory – for, as you know, Mother had always admired the military. At heart she worshipped and coveted power.'

She smiles wryly. 'Yes, as witness her running of the WSPU.'

'Yes. And her support for conscription during the Great War.'

'I remember that Mrs Pankhurst advocated conscription more or less from the moment war broke out.'

'Yes. I pointed out to her that she'd fought like a tigress for what she called the right to sovereignty over her own body – and now she expected young boys to sacrifice their bodies to a war they didn't believe in. And she said, "I fought for a just society and I expect these young boys to be willing to do the same." Of course, as I pointed out to her, the people who'd forced tubes down our noses and throats and broke our teeth had thought they were doing so in the national interest. We were enemies of the state. They may even have persuaded themselves that they were doing it for our own good. Now she wanted to declare a young boy an enemy of the state because he refused to give his life or take the life of another young boy in a cause he did not believe in.

'Of course, we neither of us convinced the other. We never did reach any kind of accord on the subject of the War.'

Teresa has been listening attentively. 'Would you say that was the ... decisive disagreement with your mother, her ... vigorous, not to say enthusiastic support of the War, and your pacifism?'

'I don't know about decisive, there were so many disagreements. But it's true that it was perhaps the issue on which we were most diametrically opposed. We had our differences, of course, about the running of the WSPU, but there at least we were more or less agreed on the objectives. On the War we differed absolutely.'

'Was it an open disagreement?'

'Oh, very much so. One morning I happened to come across Mother in Oxford Street handing out white feathers to young men she thought should have been in uniform. She and, I think, Mabel Tuke were, with a certain amount of publicity, forcing these wretched things upon unfortunate young men who happened to be passing by. Mother had just stuck a feather into the lapel of a young man accompanied by a young woman. He blushed furiously, and she was in tears. As they walked past me, I noticed that the young man had a slight limp; looking down, I saw that that he had a built-up shoe.

'I went up to Mother and said, "Mother, have you forgotten Harry so soon?"

'She looked at me with those blue eyes of hers and replied, "I have no idea what you are talking about, Sylvia. Please remove yourself. You are creating a nuisance."

'I was, of course, not to be got rid of so easily; how was she to know whether the young man she had just humiliated might not have some medical reason for not enlisting? She dismissed this, saying, "Then he won't feel humiliated. Besides, he was perfectly fit; it was evident from the way he carried himself."

'I'm afraid I rather lost my temper then, seeing the bland confidence with which Mother pronounced her certitudes.

"Yes," I almost shouted at her, "just as it was evident to you from the way Harry carried himself that he was perfectly fit."

'I was pleased to note that for once she seemed almost cowed by my passion. "I decline to be screamed at by you in a public street," she said, but of course there wasn't very much she could do about it. By this time we had attracted quite an audience. To be honest, I did not mind denouncing Mother in public – she had, after all, repudiated me in the Press just the week before for my views on the War – but I did not like the attitude of the onlookers. They were really just hoping to see a scrap. A dog-fight would have done as well.'

'Why, do you think, did your mother change her principles so radically?'

'If you think of it as a matter of temperament rather than principle, then she did not change at all: she was always a militant first and foremost, she merely fought on different sides. Mother thrived on violence. And I think she wanted to show the men that she could be a better patriot than they were. I was horrified. Indeed I still am, forty years on.'

Teresa inclines her head as if considering this, but does not comment. Instead, she says, 'May I return to the matter of your brother?'

'Yes, indeed, though in a sense all this does pertain to him. I am saying Mother admired strong men – and she saw Harry as weak.'

'Which he was not?'

'By no means. Physically he was not robust, but no weaker than many young men in the growing stage, until, of course he got ill. And mentally he was as strong as any of us, only Mother would not believe it.'

She hesitates, glances down at her notebook, and then asks, in a studiedly neutral tone: 'Would it be true to say that you hold your mother responsible for your brother's death?'

'Is that kind of speculation not beyond the purlieu of an obituary?'

She flushes, either with embarrassment or annoyance. 'It's certainly not something that I would think of mentioning in an obituary. But it may help to give me that larger picture of which the obituary is a concentrate.'

She is quoting me against myself, though her impassive expression signals no ironic intent. I realise that I have been drawn into making very unguarded statements. This in itself would not perturb me, never having been in the habit of turning over my words before speaking, but I am unsure of Teresa's intentions. 'I think,' I therefore say, 'we should confine ourselves, in our construction of the larger picture, to matters of fact rather than speculation.'

She nods. 'Of course, if you so prefer. But you will know that in any life fact and speculation are not so cleanly separable.'

'In this instance they are. The fact is that Harry died of complications attendant upon poliomyelitis, a relatively common disease for which there is no cure. How he came to be so weakened as to be susceptible to the disease and so little resistant to its effects, is a matter of speculation.'

She nods again, not convinced, but submissive for the time being to my opinion. I do not care whether she is convinced. I am beginning to tire of this interview, which has brought me too close to much that I thought I had put behind me.

Without comment, Teresa scrawls something on her pad (perhaps *Says she does not blame mother for Harry's death*). When she looks up, her face is expressionless, but her heavy jaw is set in a way which I now recall from her suffragette days as signifying Teresa's most obstinate mode.

'Reading your book,' she now says, 'one cannot help being impressed and moved by your evident respect for Keir Hardie, from a very early age; indeed, he seems to have been a kind of father figure to you.'

I look at her, I hope, as blankly as she is looking at me. 'You are again referring, I take it, to *The Suffragette Movement*,' I say, after a pause.

'Yes, indeed, I beg your pardon,' she says, and looks at me expectantly.

'You have made a statement about your response to my book,' I point out, 'not asked a question.'

A slight frown flickers over her broad forehead, but with admirable restraint she forces a smile. 'Of course. I meant it really as an invitation to reflect on the place of Keir Hardie in your life.'

'Pardon me,' I return, 'I do not wish to be uncooperative, but as you have just intimated, I treat of the matter at some length in my book. I think I make it quite clear what an immense debt I owed to Keir Hardie in the development of my own political thinking.' Relenting slightly, I add, 'I think I would rate him second only to my father as an *influence*.'

If she is grateful for my concession to her probing, she does not show it. She nods non-committally and makes a note in her book. Then she faces me again with the Billington jaw, and asks, 'A more important influence, then, than your brother Harry?'

I stiffen in my chair. 'You are asking me to compare a political relation and a family relation,' I say.

Her smile is a thin, joyless affair. 'You of all people would surely not insist on an absolute distinction between the political and the familial. I understand, for instance, that your connection with Mr Corio is as much one of political conviction as personal affection.'

This is impertinent, and I resolve to ask Teresa Billington to leave. But I hesitate for a moment too long before making my request, and she avails herself of the pause to push her advantage. 'I mean,' she continues, 'in reference to your brother and Mr Hardie, whether you do not now feel that perhaps your closeness to your brother at the time was compromised by your friendship with Mr Hardie.'

I more than ever want to ask Teresa to leave, but to do so now would be interpreted as confirmation of her suggestion.

So I affect unconcern. 'Not at all,' I state. 'I cannot imagine that anything in my book sanctioned such an interpretation.'

'Interpretation does not necessarily require sanction,' she replies bluntly. 'It's fairly clear from your account that whereas you and Harry used to spend his Sundays together, once Mr Hardie moved to London, you took to spending them with him.'

'Yes – taking Harry along,' I point out. 'Since you have apparently studied my book with a certain minuteness, you should know that.'

'Of course. But from what one gathers about Harry's sensitivity to rejection, is it not possible that he may have felt his own presence to be redundant or even irksome?'

'Given that what you gather about Harry's sensitivity is derived entirely from my account, don't you think that I could be trusted to be sensitive to his feelings and to act accordingly?'

'One doesn't always act in accordance with one's best insights,' she says placidly and imperturbably.

'I could consent to your generalisation and yet deny its application in this instance,' I reply. 'But really, I do not think that I owe you any answer at all to what is an unwarranted intrusion upon my most cherished memories.'

She nods, as if assenting to a wholly uncontroversial proposition. 'Of course,' she says, 'I can see that it must be painful to be reminded of old conflicts of conscience.'

She frowns slightly at her pad, as if trying to make out her handwriting. I play with a pencil on my desk, look out of the window at the blue day outside; does Teresa think I have nothing better to do than sit and watch her frown at her own notebook?

'It's a curious thing,' she says at last, 'that one notices in reading your book, that all three of the men whom you cite as particularly influential in your life – your father, your brother and Keir Hardie – were in a sense, shared with your mother.' Having produced this, she looks quite pleased with herself, as if she has just shared a pleasant observation on the weather with me. I say nothing; I wonder whether she expects me to congratulate her on her discovery.

'I say *shared*,' she continues, 'but of course, what is more striking is that you were in a position of opposition to your mother in relation to all three.'

I stare at her blankly. 'The thing is,' she explains to me, 'that in all three cases there was a kind of battle for possession.'

Sitting there, peering at me pointedly, with her pen poised over her silly little book, she looks absurdly like some police investigating officer: *anything you say may be taken down and used as evidence against you.* I can see she is going to insist on an answer. Slack and shapeless as she seems to have become, she has retained something of her sharp edge, and can still draw blood if she wants to. And, not getting from me the support she was hoping for in her dislike of Mother, she has turned that edge against me.

But I force myself to remain calm, even affable. 'I am at a loss to understand your interpretation. Possession was in no way an issue in my relation with the three men you mention, and certainly not a matter of a contest with my mother.'

'Perhaps not from your point of view,' she says, 'but who knows what your mother's feelings were?'

I have at last reached the limit of my patience with Teresa's pig-headed persistence. 'Teresa,' I say, 'If you are truly seeking to write a worthwhile obituary, read my books on the Ethiopian question.' I take the telegram from my desk and hand it to her. She is reluctant to take it, but I leave her little choice. 'I have this morning received a telegram of congratulation from Emperor Haile Selassie. If I am remembered at all, I should hope it would be for the part I played there, rather than for fanciful fabrications regarding my private life.'

She takes in the contents of the telegram and returns it to my desk, unperturbed. 'Ah, but as no doubt you know, there is a theory that our so-called public actions are subconscious strategies to fulfil emotional needs or to counter private insecurities. You've yourself suggested in your book, albeit indirectly, that your mother's defiance of the establishment was but a displaced desire to claim attention from a father figure; would it not be possible to see in your championing of the Ethiopian cause a similar drive? A defiance on the one hand of the British establishment, and a desire to please the Emperor on the other?'

I get to my feet. 'No doubt anything is possibly to anybody ingenious enough and trivial enough to want to reduce the work of others to a matter of petty gossip. I repeat, if you are truly interested in my life's achievements, read my books, all my books, not only *The Suffragette Movement*, which was written thirty years ago and deals with a relatively unimportant part of my life.'

She raises a sceptical eyebrow, but remains seated. 'I was hoping to ask you some questions about your relations with your sister Christabel.'

'I am afraid I must ask you to leave,' I say. 'I had not anticipated such a minute interrogation, and I find that we have far exceeded the time I allocated to this conversation.'

She gets to her feet. 'Thank you for your time,' she says, though there is little gratitude in her tone. As she reaches the door, she turns round. 'I gather from that telegram that today is your seventieth birthday. Do allow me to wish you many happy returns.'

'Thank you,' I say. 'That is kind of you.'

When Teresa has left, I sit for a while at my desk, contemplating nothing in particular: my cat stretching his paw; a bird fussing at a flower outside my window; the sun slanting in on the watercolour of Keir Hardie. I feel … what? Not really as indignant as I made a show of being. That was really more a matter of feeling I *should* be indignant. I realise now that Mother and Christabel might have saved themselves the trouble of hounding Teresa out of the WSPU. As a public performer, she could never have posed a threat to them. They were consummate actresses, both of them, whereas she was and is – helplessly, finally – just Teresa Billington, later Teresa Billington-Greig: worthy, dedicated, inspired even, but limited to the truth of her own being. Mother could embody the suffering of thousands, give voice to their plight, make her audience see their tears. Christabel could make her audience share her vision, enter into her scorn as well as her rapture; she could make the merest movement of a finger speak. Teresa could convince her audience only of her own dedication and her own sincerity. Of course, she had her followers, those few who valued dedication and sincerity, but Mother and Christabel drew the crowds, those who relished a performance and liked to feel ennobled while they were being entertained.

I could quite easily have told Teresa about Christabel. I just did not feel she should have it for the asking. Perhaps had she shown more of a sense of the privacies she was violating, I would have been more cooperative, but she walked through my life like a large herbivore through a meadow, selecting the juicier patches at will. And I was, after all, irritated with her insistence on reducing my life to its first thirty years. I have progressed as far beyond the suffragette movement as that movement was itself an advance upon Victorian notions of women's place in society. I suppose in a different sense Christabel, too, will see herself, with her discovery of the Advent, to have progressed beyond the merely temporal and political.

But perhaps my irritation was not with her asking about Christabel. Perhaps it was with what she said about Keir Hardie. Keir Hardie and Harry.

III

I cannot remember a time when I did not know Keir Hardie. He was twenty-six years older than I, and his friendship with my parents predated my birth. I am not sure when he first noticed me as a human being distinct from the crowd of adoring children surrounding him, and whom he adored in turn, though somewhat indiscriminately, as he adored animals. His advocacy of women's rights, even, was to him a natural part of a larger humanitarian concern. And to him humanity was not an abstraction, it was embodied in every human being. Indeed, most living creatures excited his compassion: when he was working as a miner he did all in his power to minimise the suffering of the pit ponies. Faced with the weak, the helpless or the voiceless, he was the gentlest man I have ever known. Faced with complacent privilege, blind prejudice or brute cruelty, his gentleness would ignite into an anger that would stop at nothing. There was a story that he once beat up a miner who was maltreating a pit pony. The man was taken to hospital with multiple injuries, and Keir supported his wife and children while he was laid up, but he never did speak to the man again.

For somebody with such a capacity for love in general, I can now see, he was remarkably inept at love for a particular person. He loved his wife, of course, as he loved his pit pony, but of love as a passion that inflames the mind and drives the body I do not think he had much of a notion. Nor did I, of course, at first; but I at least was aware of a need that was not fulfilled through my labours on behalf of justice and equality. That was all I had to offer Keir Hardie, a need; and he first had to recognise his own need before he could recognise mine.

136

When I first came to London, he took pity on me, I think, as if I were one of the crippled pigeons he fed in the little strip of garden he cultivated on his window sill. This was while I was at the Royal College, where, after the easy camaraderie of the Manchester school, I was lonely amongst the other students, who all seemed so much more worldly-wise than I. I was also intimidated by the teachers, who looked only to criticise, never to praise. Furthermore, after the brilliance and radiance of Venice, I was oppressed by the eternal fogs and dirt of London.

Hardie's rooms in Nevill's Court off Fetter Lane were a haven of warmth, quiet and companionship. The city noises did not penetrate the solid old building, and the ox-eye daisies growing in his little garden and arrayed in jugs and measures around the room brought a hint of country wildness. The walls were hung with pictures of his heroes – Robert Owen, William Morris, Robert Burns – and a small figure of Dr Johson stood on the mantelpiece alongside busts of Emerson and Whitman. There was a Union Jack in one corner; when I commented on his patriotism, he laughed and said, 'Now, *that* I won't claim for that particular flag. I took it from some rowdies who tried to break up one of my anti-war meetings during the Boer War.'

To sit with him, even while he was reading a book, was to feel oneself part of a household, a circle of companionship and fellowship. The candlelight he always worked by made the whole room seem welcoming and warm, especially when he had a coal fire burning in the grate. He inhabited his lodgings as he inhabited his body: comfortably, unquestioningly, naturally.

I stormed in one evening, out of all patience with Augustus Spencer, the pig-headed principal of the College. Hardie was sitting, reading by candlelight, as usual.

He looked up, smiled, and said in his comfortable manner, 'Oh aye, Sylvia, you come in here for all the world like a storm off the North Sea. You want to sit by the fire and blow yourself out.'

I sat down, but could not suppress my anger. 'There's this new regulation obliging us to spend six months out of our two years doing architectural drawing! What on earth is the use of that?'

Hardie looked at me over his glasses, put down the book he had been reading, took up his pipe, lit it, and said, 'And what would you rather be doing, then?'

'Life drawing, of course!' I said. 'The human body is the basis of all pictorial art. What do we need with six months of architecture?'

He gestured around him. 'Aye, but the human body needs architecture to shelter it and give it a frame. We are all bodies in a setting.'

'Let architects provide the setting, then. I'm not in training to construct buildings.'

'But you may want to draw them, and just as you need to study anatomy in order to understand the human body, so architecture will help you understand the structures you draw.'

He got up from his chair and walked to the inglenook, where he kept his tea caddy, and where a kettle was almost always boiling on the hob. 'Will you be taking a cup of tea, then?'

'Yes, please,' I said, not yet mollified. 'The point is that I went to see Spencer about it, and instead of explaining it to me rationally, he threw me out of his office with no ceremony whatsoever. He said he had had enough of troublemakers. And now I'm told that he doesn't like women students and that women students very seldom get scholarships in the College, no matter how well they've done elsewhere.'

If I had been trying to involve Hardie in my vendetta, this was a much more promising tack. 'Do you have any figures to prove that?' he asked, scattering tea leaves on the boiling water, which was his method of making tea.

'No, because the College does not publish such figures.'

'Somebody must have them. I'll ask a question in the House about it.'

138

Hardie duly asked his question, and got his answer: College scholarships were awarded to men and women in the proportion of thirteen to one, which even in those days could not seriously be presented as proportionate to the distribution of talent. The answer, of course, did not improve the situation, but it was some comfort to have these statistics to back up our suspicions. I tell this anecdote to illustrate Hardie's ability to distinguish between futile resistance – my rebellion against the school's curriculum – and a worthy cause – the school's discrimination against women.

To this refuge I brought Harry every second Sunday, when he was allowed out of his school in Hampstead. Hardie welcomed him as he had welcomed me, without effusiveness, but with warm affection. Harry was powerfully drawn to Hardie's love of animals, and would elicit from him stories of the pit ponies he had known. The boy was fascinated by the tooth marks on Hardie's watch made by Donald, his favourite pit pony, whom he had rescued from the attentions of some other miners who were trying to get the poor beast to move by making a fire under him. 'I just touched his nose like that,' said Hardie, 'and he upped and started working and never stopped till I left for another pit. Then the poor little thing drowned itself in a pond.'

This last detail upset Harry inordinately. He had imbibed from his father a compassion for all living things, and Keir's reminiscence of the sufferings of the pit ponies aroused in him a pity akin to anger. 'Why do people do such things to animals?' he would ask. 'Especially people who know what it is to suffer hunger and cold themselves?'

'Oh aye,' said Hardie, 'it's not often our own sufferings teach us pity for other creatures.'

'But that's all wrong!' Harry said, tears of anger and frustration in his eyes.

I watched Harry with a heavy heart. I could see in him my own helpless rage at the injustices of the world, but without, I thought, my confidence to take up arms against them.

The three of us would spend the day reading and talking and eating the simple meal of bread, butter, bannocks and Scotch scones that Hardie enjoyed, along with the leeks that he grew in his little garden. He tried always to make this frugal meal as appetising as possible in its preparation.

'Food's not worth getting agitated about,' he would say, 'but we need to eat to keep our bodies going, and we might as well enjoy it.'

'I wish you would tell that to the matron at school,' said Harry. 'I think she believes that just because we have to eat anyway, it doesn't matter what it tastes like. And it's true that we eat everything that's put before us, just because we're so hungry. And because we eat it, she thinks we like it.'

'There's only one way to prove that you don't,' I teased him, 'and that's for all of you to refuse to eat.'

'Not that,' Hardie said, with unusual earnestness. 'Hunger is a terrible thing. You cannot willingly inflict it upon your body.'

'I shouldn't think the other boys would do it, even if I suggested it,' said Harry. 'Their idea is any food is better than no food.'

This was, of course, before hunger striking became part of the strategy of the Women's Movement. When it did so, Keir was never comfortable with what he regarded as a deliberate violation of the self, though he had to concede its political efficacy. 'It doesn't seem right to withhold nourishment from your own body in order to spite Asquith. You can be sure he'll not be put off his food by your fasting.'

But that was afterwards. For the moment, there, in the mellow light of Hardie's candles and in the warmth of his old-fashioned fireplace, watched over by Emerson and Whitman, food and drink seemed a natural part of an existence that embraced Keats and Byron, Ibsen and Shaw with equal amplitude.

On some evenings and on those Sundays when Harry was

not allowed out, I would visit Hardie on my own. The impersonal atmosphere of London made this possible without untoward comment from neighbours or acquaintances. Besides, Hardie was himself so impervious to petty gossip that the propriety or otherwise of my visits never arose as a topic.

It was nevertheless true that I found, with the growing intimacy between us, that the man whom I had been in the habit of regarding as a substitute father, forty-eight years old to my twenty-two, was assuming an importance and attraction that went beyond the affection of a child for a parent. He had encouraged me from the start to sit next to him, in the easy physical proximity of parent and child, but in time I found that I was more conscious of his body in itself than as merely a comforting presence. I started noticing, for instance, how strong his hands were, and yet so fine; scarred with the accidents of manual labour in a coal mine, and yet kept immaculate, the nails carefully cut with the sharp blade of his old penknife. I could take pleasure in the strength with which he picked up a bucket of coal to put on the fire, but also in the gentleness with which he unthinkingly stroked his beard. I became aware also of his mouth under the full beard, the lips curiously moist under it. He would often place a hand on my shoulder while talking to me, or lean over me while explaining something in a book I was reading. I had always been aware of the smell of his tobacco, pungent and yet sweet. I now became aware of his bodily smell underlying it, strong and yet not unpleasant.

It so happened on one rainy Sunday afternoon that I knelt next to the fire as I came in, cold and wet after having walked from Kensington in an unexpected shower of rain. He came and knelt next to me, and gave me a towel to dry my face and hair. As he did so, my hand touched his, and he held it in his, then put it to his lips and kissed it gently.

'You want to get off your wet clothes,' he said.

He said it so naturally that it did not occur to me to be outraged. Only, I was shy, and said, 'I could not undress in front of you. My body is not beautiful like Christabel's.'

He smiled, kissed my hand again, and said, 'Your body is beautiful to me, because I love the spirit that lives in it.'

I was wearing an impractical kind of frock with all its buttons behind. He started undoing these buttons, very deftly for somebody with such large hands. I submitted willingly. I had never been undressed so gently, even in childhood. When, at last, I stood naked in front of the fire, he said, 'Your body is very beautiful. You must never be ashamed of it. And you must not be ashamed of looking upon my body. It's not beautiful like yours, but it's shaped to serve you and bring tribute to your beauty.'

He took off his own clothes, then, placed them neatly next to mine on the floor, and, very gently, made me lie down on the carpet in front of the fire.

I thought of the two hawthorn trees in our garden in Manchester, and how much I had loved them, but also how ashamed I was of enjoying such beauty while the poor children had none. Now, too, lying in the warm flicker of Keir's fire, I wondered if it was right that we should have such beauty and such pleasure in our own bodies when there were others who did not have food even to feed their bodies. But when I tried to say something about this to Keir, he put his hand on my body, and leaned over, and put his mouth on mine, and that seemed to dispose of the question. As he put his whole weight on me, and entered me, I felt, in the sharp pain of his entry, the legitimating ritual sealing our allegiance – or it is possible that that is how I presented it to myself afterwards. At the time, perhaps, I felt only the pain and the pleasure.

It so happened that at this time my evenings were taken up with life classes at the College, so I could not see Hardie after hours during the week, as I had sometimes managed to do. Since on Saturdays I had to sell my designs, that left only Sundays, and Sundays were of course also Harry's day off from his school. This presented me with one of the most difficult choices I have ever had to make. Having experienced the closeness of physical love with Keir Hardie, I could think of little else – that, and the opportunity to relive the experience. But the following Sunday was Harry's day out, and of course his presence would give an entirely different cast to the day.

Harry used to wait for me at the gate to his school, and even though I always tried to be earlier than our arranged time, he was invariably waiting for me when I arrived, impatient to tell me of his week and to hear of mine before we went off to spend the day with Keir.

On this occasion, I was so divided in my own mind that I deliberately tarried, and I was about twenty minutes later than our agreed time. Perhaps I wanted to prepare him for the disappointment I was about to inflict upon him. He was standing by the stone entrance to his school, looking pale and anxious. When he saw me, his face lit up – a sight so beautiful as to be quite heartbreaking – and he came running towards me, full of joy and anticipation.

'Harry,' I said, 'Harry,' but he was so excited that I had to instruct him, 'Please, Harry, just listen to me.'

He saw then, from my face, that I had bad news, and he said, 'What is it, Sylvia? Has anything happened?'

'No,' I said. 'That is, yes. We have been given a project to complete by tomorrow, and today is the only time I have to do it.'

'Oh,' he said. 'Oh. Does that mean we can't go to Mr Hardie's?'

'I'm afraid so,' I said. 'You see, I'll have to spend the day in the studios at the College. It's not work I can do anywhere else.'

'Oh,' he said again. Then his face brightened again. 'But I could go with you if I'm very quiet and just watch, couldn't I?'

'The problem is, Harry,' I said, 'that this project involves life drawing, with models …'

He looked at me uncomprehendingly, and I had to spell out my falsehood in all the details of its mendacity. 'That means, you see, that we work with unclothed models, and of course outsiders are not welcome.'

He kicked at the stone gate post. 'But what about me?' he asked. 'What about my Sunday?'

'It is unlike you, Harry, to ask such a question,' I replied, impatient with my own inability to answer his question, and knowing his conscience could always be appealed to.

He looked shamefaced. 'Yes, I'm sorry, Sylvia,' he said, 'I know that your work is more important than my pleasure. It's just that I had been looking forward …'

'I know,' I said, and embraced him. 'I know, and I am so terribly sorry to disappoint you.' He hid his face in the collar of my coat, wanting, I think, to hide the tears in his eyes. For my part, I was close to tears. My sorrow at disappointing him was genuine enough; it was only the reason I gave him for doing so that was a lie.

My day with Hardie, won at the price of a lie to my beloved brother, could not, after this, be anything but joyless. I was distracted and fretting. I did not have the courage to tell Hardie what I had done, and told him instead that Harry had been kept in by his school.

'Harry kept in?' he asked, not in disbelief – he would never have doubted my word on anything – but in surprise. 'I can't imagine Harry guilty of any misdemeanour meriting such punishment.'

'Oh, you know what schools are like,' I muttered uncomfortably. 'Any minor transgression is pounced upon and punished as if it were a heinous crime.'

'Do you know what the minor transgression was?' Keir asked. For once, his passion for justice was irksome to me.

'No, he did not say. I think he feels sensitive about it. It may be better not to refer to it.'

I felt ashamed now, not only for having lied to Harry, but for

144

having lied to Hardie. It seemed to me that this was a sign that in committing one wrong I was led into further wrongs. Had I not entered into a physical relationship with Keir, I would not have lied to Harry and to Keir. I resolved to extricate myself from this web of lies and deceit, but I could not do so without telling Keir why, and I lacked the courage for that. So once more I yielded to his caresses, but it was tainted with my lie, and I never could recover the beauty of that first night by the fire.

IV

R ichard's light tap at my door.
'Are you tired out?' he asks.

'No,' I say. 'Should I be?'

'She was here for a long time, that last one.'

'Yes. Somebody from the old days. One of Mother's ene-mies. Or erstwhile enemies. Everyone seems intent on letting bygones be bygones now. It's rather dull, if truth be told.'

He holds up another telegram. 'And still they come.'

'Thank you, dear.'

'Do you want a cup of tea?'

'That is exactly what I do want, yes, thank you.'

He leaves. I sit and ponder the strange arithmetic of life, which has added so immeasurably to my existence by giving me Silvio, then Richard, and continued to multiply its gifts, and which never gave poor Harry anything but division and subtraction.

Richard brings my tea, finds a clear spot on my desk for the cup.

'Thank you, dear,' I say.

'Who is your telegram from?'

'Oh. I'd forgotten.'

I open it: *Many happy returns. Am in London. Hope to see you. Will let you know. Christabel.*

'It's from your Aunt Christabel.'

'In California?'

'No. It appears she is in London.'

'Does she want to see you?'

'It seems so.'

146

'When?'

'She does not say. *Will let you know*, she says.'

'Mm. Peremptory.'

'Well. Christabel.'

'How long since you last saw her?'

I calculate. 'It was at Mother's funeral. Almost twenty-five years ago. But my last real conversation with her was shortly before that, when she called to persuade me not to give you the Pankhurst name.'

Richard laughs, more amused than curious. 'Was it her idea that I would discredit the family name?'

'Oh, most definitely. Not of course through any action of yours, but because you were born out of wedlock.'

'And of course you declined.'

'Of course. As witness your surname.'

'And she left in high dudgeon.'

'Christabel's dudgeons were always higher than anybody else's.'

He looks at me quizzically. 'You know,' he says, 'I find it hard to believe that you were as indifferent to your separation as you claim.'

I try to remember. 'I was relieved, more than anything else. After all, Christabel had established herself as a kind of conscience over me, which I did not need or want. And just then, with you as a newborn baby, I felt that I had everything that I wanted, and I seemed to myself far stronger than I had ever been.'

'And now?'

'Now?'

'Do you want to see her?'

I need to think about this. 'Not particularly,' I then say. 'My life is elsewhere now. But I don't mind. She can no longer upset me.'

'Are you sure?'

'Yes, dear, I am sure. I have you and Silvio and my work in

Ethiopia. Christabel is … well, Christabel is only Christabel. She no longer has Mother and Annie Kenney and the whole of the WSPU behind her. I think I can face her with equanimity.'

'You talk as if you anticipate a battle.'

'No, I don't. I should think Christabel has also changed with the years. But if she does want to do battle, I no longer fear her.'

Christabel. As I told Richard, my last real conversation – which is to say real disagreement – with her was soon after his birth, and indeed prompted by that event.

We were staying in the Red Cottage on Woodford Green, and I was used to people dropping in from the bus terminus opposite, often on their way from outings to Epping Forest. I was not surprised, then, when there was a knock at the door one day. I *was* surprised, however, to find Christabel standing on my doorstep.

My first impulse when I opened the door was joy. I actually thought for a naive moment that Christabel had come to see the baby, to explain Mother's refusal to see me, in some way try to act as mediator between Mother and me. I suppose it is typical of new mothers to assume that the whole world is eager to share their joy.

'Christabel!' I exclaimed, 'How good to see you! Do come in.'

She did come in, but in a dignified fashion that was meant to imply, I think, that she was not committing her spirit to the whereabouts of her body, that she was only very provisionally present in my house.

'I can't really stay,' she announced, in a voice husky with unuttered reservations. 'I have come merely with a solemn request.'

Only then did I take in her appearance: she was all in black, as if for a funeral or at least an extremely grave state occasion. It occurred to me to wonder who was paying for her clothes now that the WSPU no longer existed, but it would of course not have done to raise the question.

I gestured instead at the three not-very-easy chairs that con-
stituted our drawing room, and said, 'Will you take a chair?'
She hesitated, as if uncertain whether to entrust her elegantly-
clad person to the rather shabby chairs. I asked, 'Or would you
like to see the baby first?'

That decided her. She sat down in one of the chairs, having
first examined all three, presumably to select the least rebarba-
tive.

'Thank you, Sylvia,' was all she said, still in tones presaging
matters of the gravest import.

I took a chair opposite hers and waited for her to announce
the purpose of her visit. She folded her hands on her lap,
looked, as if pensively, at a picture on the wall – it was my
watercolour of Keir Hardie – then looked down at her hands. I
recognised the gestures: this was Christabel Thinking, a
tableau that often preceded her more solemn performances. It
was calculated to impress upon an audience the extreme
seriousness of what she was about to say, and it only worked
if the audience could be relied upon not to be rowdy. I had
once seen the effect ruined by a heckler shouting 'Din't yer do
yer thinkin' afore ye came?' For a moment I was tempted to
avail myself of that line, but I suppressed the impulse, and
waited. I anticipated that her first word would be a variant on
'This is a very serious matter.'

'I come to you on an errand as urgent as it's delicate,' she
announced, and paused again. I knew that the required response was rapt attention, and I gave it to her, or assumed an
expression that I hoped would pass for it.

She took a deep breath and exhaled delicately – not quite a
sigh, but eloquent, in its exquisite control, of the depth of her
disappointment. 'Mother, and indeed I, are in almost equal
measure perplexed and outraged by your behaviour.'

The pause that succeeded this announcement was near-
audible, indeed near-tangible.

'What aspect of it perplexes and outrages you?' I obligingly asked, 'Or do different aspects perplex and outrage you and Mother respectively?'

She lifted a pained gaze at me. 'I need not rehearse to you, I take it, the bizarre sentiments which you disseminated recently through the medium of the popular press.'

'If you mean, did I read the report – yes, I did.'

'Of all the reprehensible things you chose to reveal to the world, none grieved Mother as much as your declared intention to defile the Pankhurst name by attaching it to your illegitimate son.'

'Defile? How can a newborn baby defile anything? Or do you now subscribe to the doctrine of original sin?'

'The child, I concede, is innocent. But he is tainted with the situation of his parents, and that taint will attach to the name you bestow upon him.'

I stared at her. The majestic cadences, as much as the magisterial sentiments, were a new departure for Christabel. I realised now what the black clothes and the dignified manner were meant to signify. Christabel had become Victorian.

'Christabel,' I said, 'you sound like one of those unhappy women in Dickens who blight all about them with their ferocious respectability – what is the name of the old woman in *Little Dorrit* whose house collapses on top of her?'

Unshaken by my levity, Christabel bestowed upon me another look, and continued. 'It may suit you to be frivolous about this matter because any more serious reflection would oblige you to share in the shame you're inflicting upon your family and friends. I do not in fact expect of you to view your own behaviour in the light of civilised morality. I do think, however, that we are entitled not to be implicated in that behaviour by having our name attached to the product of a union sanctioned by neither man nor God.'

'Is it the embarrassment of family and friends or the displeasure of man and God that I am most invoking in giving my child the name of Pankhurst?'

'It is both, of course, but my concern is not personal. The name of Pankhurst transcends mere embarrassment. It is a legacy which has been entrusted to us and which must be handed down intact.'

'Handed down? By whom, pray? Father had two sons, neither of whom survived. You are unlikely, I take it, to produce a son, and even if you did, he would have to take the name of the husband that you, of course, would want first to acquire. So I fail to see how the sacred name of Pankhurst is to be passed down by anybody but my son Richard.'

She waved aside my argument. 'Does your … does the father of your child not object to being disregarded in this manner?'

'Silvio does not see it as being disregarded. He is proud for his son to be named after Richard Pankhurst.'

'And after Keir Hardie, I gather.'

'Yes. And Fred and Emmeline Pethick Lawrence.'

'Does your … *Silvio* know that his son is named after a former lover of yours?'

This was the first indication Christabel had ever given that she knew of my relationship with Keir. I refrained from showing my surprise.

'I decline to discuss Keir Hardie with you.'

'That does not surprise me. It must be a part of your life that you can hardly bear to contemplate now.'

'I have said that I decline to discuss it with you.'

Christabel, however, had never needed a willing participant in order to discuss something she had put her mind to discussing. 'I suppose,' she continued unperturbed by my interruption, 'it's possible that you really were blind to your own motives, but to anybody else it was really only too clear that your relationship with Keir originated in your resentment of Mother and was intended as a blow against her.'

Christabel levelled these accusations as if she were sharing with me a humdrum but mildly amusing disclosure about some absent third party. I succeeded – with great difficulty, and by dint of pressing my nails into the palm of my hand – in matching her composure.

'Only a very disturbed mind could suspect that a relationship such as the one I shared with Keir Hardie might have concerned anybody at all other than the two of us. I cannot see by what logic that relationship can be interpreted as in any sense a *blow against* Mother.'

'As I say, it's possible that your motives were not clear to yourself. But consider the facts: Keir was a friend of Father and Mother, the same age more or less as Father, and probably Mother's closest male friend. He was in effect, to you, a substitute father. By claiming him for yourself, which after all is not very difficult for a young woman to do by appealing to the vanity of an old man, you moved into the position of wife to the substitute father figure. You were at last breaking Mother's hold on Father.'

She announced all this as if recounting an uninteresting train journey. I sat still, staring at the toe of her shoe, which was elegantly pointed in a way that just then I found difficult to countenance. Before I could say anything, though, Christabel continued, the edge of her malice now entirely apparent: 'And of course, in bringing forth a Pankhurst son, you're reminding Mother of the son she lost. The new Richard is your revenge for Harry. I'm surprised you did not include his name in the little clutch of memories you bequeathed your son.'

I was lost in admiration at the sheer nerve of Christabel's performance, but not so much so that I felt I wanted to prolong it. 'You have the strange and unenviable ability,' I said, as calmly as I could manage, 'of poisoning every human relationship simply by touching it with your ingenious but diseased mind. I need not defend my friendship with Keir against your aspersions. He is dead and gone and mercifully beyond the reach of your malice. But I shall not tolerate your attempt to contaminate by your proximity the single most

152

precious possession I have, which is my son Richard. I must ask you to leave.'

I must have talked more loudly than I realised, because Richard started crying in the next room. Christabel looked at me as if vaguely puzzled by my behaviour. 'My dear Sylvia, do calm yourself. You know you're prone to hysteria. It was always what prevented you from playing a significant part in the Women's Movement.'

I ignored, for the moment, her imputation, and went to see to Richard. He was crying, but calmed down as soon as I picked him up. I thought to take him with me, but I felt a superstitious dread of exposing him to the atmosphere of violence and recrimination around Christabel. She was capable of invoking a curse upon him. So I stayed with him till he was quite calm, and then went back to the sitting room. Christabel was standing now, examining one of my watercolours of Venice. It seemed centuries ago that I had made it. She was about to comment on it, but I interrupted her. I did not want her aspersion to pass unchallenged.

'I am surprised that you feel qualified to pronounce on my part in the Women's Movement, as if you knew anything about it,' I said in deliberately measured tones, 'and as if you didn't spend the most crucial years ensconced in a luxurious apartment on the Avenue de la Grande Armée, like a general behind enemy lines issuing orders, or really more like a dictator converting whims into duties for others. Burning down castles, slashing paintings, bombing cathedrals: all you had to do was think up some new scheme, and you knew some poor underling would imperil her own life and liberty in executing it, submitting to imprisonment and hunger strikes and forcible feeding, while you were walking in the Bois de Boulogne with your Pomeranian and your Annie Kenney.'

Christabel, as always, kept her composure. 'You know perfectly well,' she said, pretending still to be examining my watercolour, 'that the affairs of the WSPU had to be run by a competent person from a place that the British police could not reach.'

I nodded. 'Yes, that was the reason Mother advanced, and it made enough sense to pass muster, I suppose, in the cloak-and-dagger atmosphere of the time. It was a great thrill for everybody to think that we had secrets so potent that they needed the English Channel to protect them. But has it ever occurred to you that Mother wanted you in Paris for reasons of her own?'

Christabel still refused to betray any discomposure, but I could see that she was piqued from the way that she looked at me as she asked, 'What reasons of her own, apart from concern for the WSPU, could Mother possibly have had to want me in Paris?'

'Not necessarily to have you in Paris. But to have you out of London. She wanted you out of Emmie Pethick Lawrence's way.'

Christabel flushed slightly, always a sign of annoyance with her. 'That's preposterous, Sylvia. Why would she want me out of Emmie's way?'

'Because you were spending all your time with Emmie and too little with her.'

'So, by your logic, feeling that she was seeing too little of me, Mother sent me to Paris where she would never see me?'

'Not never, by any means. She was often in Paris, and she had you to herself when she was there. Besides, you know Mother: she would rather not have something herself than be forced to share it.'

'You forget that Emmie and Fred Pethick Lawrence were paying for the apartment in Paris. Why would they finance a move that was directed against Emmie?'

'One possibility is that they did not know it was directed against Emmie. Another, and one to which I incline, is that, fond as Emmie was of you, it suited her as well to have you out of the way.'

154

She gave her lightest, most dismissive laugh. 'You seem intent upon making everybody act contrary to their own interests. What on earth could Emmie gain by sending me to Paris?'

'Annie Kenney,' I said, trying to match Christabel's lightness of tone. But Christabel just looked at me interrogatively, and I continued. 'Annie was too fond of you. And Emmie, as you know, was besotted with Annie.'

'As I know? I don't in fact know anything like that, and certainly cannot imagine how you can.'

'I take it you know that I was and still am close to the Pethick Lawrences, the more so after we were all three cast out of the WSPU.'

'You always did cling together, you and poor Fred and Emmie. And Emmie has actually told you that she was besotted with Annie?'

'It was hardly necessary for her to tell me. And more from what she has *not* said than from what she has, I have gathered that she and Mother had a perfectly good understanding about your presence in Paris. After all, without Emmie's support even Mother could hardly have sustained for so long the fiction that the WSPU needed you in Paris.'

'So it's your contention that Emmie Pethick Lawrence traded me for Annie Kenney – a sweet enough girl, but when all is said and done, a factory girl?'

'Oh, any number of people were infatuated with Annie. And Emmie always was a democrat.'

'And if by your theory Emmie wanted me in Paris to separate me from Annie, how did it come about that Annie Kenny came so often to me in Paris?'

'What nobody foresaw, I think, was that Annie might have a mind of her own, and that, suddenly deprived of you in London, she might actually express the wish to go to you in Paris. And since it was, after all, necessary for contact to be kept with you, somebody had to go. Mother would have preferred to go herself, but could not quite justify her absence every week, and Emmie suggested Mabel Tuke. For the first time in her life, though, Annie put her foot down. So Emmie had to agree. She stipulated only that Annie and Mother would alternate. Since she was Treasurer of the WSPU, and thus in sole command of expenditure, she did have some power over how the Union's money was spent. It was a relatively mild adjustment of the truth, to argue that the welfare of the Union depended on not having too predictable a pattern of move-ment between London and Paris.'

It gave me some entirely ignoble pleasure to note that Chris-tabel was deflated. Her High Victorian manner had yielded to something more tentative and defensive. She attempted, how-ever, to salvage her dignity by getting to her feet and saying rather grandly, 'I repudiate your aspersions. You shall not alienate Mother and me through your vile imputations.'

I also got up from my chair. 'You are of course free to repu-diate whatever you wish, Christabel,' I said. 'But I think you will find it difficult to forget.'

'You will understand if I decline to stay for tea,' she said, drawing on her gloves.

I refrained from replying to the facile sarcasm of this and merely opened the front door, which gave direct access to the garden. We went out, and I said, 'I think we must accept that we have nothing constructive left to say to each other.'

'Yes,' she replied, 'you have admirably demonstrated that. I had hoped that you would be amenable to reason.' She paused, and I could see that she was gathering her rhetorical resources for a final, very telling riposte; but just then the gar-den gate opened noisily – we had never got around to oiling it after moving in – and a woman entered. I did not immediately recognise her. The garden path was long, and though the face seemed familiar, that was all too common from my daily con-tact with hundreds of women whose names I never learnt. She was too smartly dressed for one of my East End acquaintances. It was only when she approached that I recognised Helen

156

Craggs. I was surprised to see her – we had by common agreement ceased to see each other after Harry's death – but mainly I was relieved to be spared Christabel's parting peroration.

Christabel hesitated, and for a moment I thought she was going to deliver the peroration anyway – it was not like Christabel to be deterred by the presence of an audience – but fortunately Helen's arrival seemed to have disturbed the momentum of her eloquence. She nodded at me briskly, as if concluding a minor and slightly unsatisfactory business transaction, and left. She had, of course, to pass by Helen, and I was interested to note that she paused, as if to engage her in conversation – but I wanted to attend to Richard and did not wait to see what ensued.

After that, I saw Christabel only once, at Mother's funeral, that dismal day almost twenty-five years ago. It was her day, her opportunity to display her grief. A grief displayed is, of course, not necessarily insincere, and I do not doubt that for Christabel Mother's death was a very real loss. But not for her the drab misery of the damp nose and the hectic flush of sleepless nights: rather the proud bearing of tragedy, the black cloak, the dramatic hat that managed to be the largest object in sight. Great comedienne that she was, for that one day she did tragedy, not only the tragedy of irrevocable loss, but also the hauteur, the unuttered reproach of the consciously immaculate in the presence of sin and error. And once again, she had an audience, many of whom would have seen her in happier days and thrilled to her rhetoric and admired her spirit. They would now admire the dignity and composure of her impeccably costumed grief.

Irritated as I was with Christabel's elaborate charade, I nevertheless found to my surprise that what I most felt was simple sadness. My feelings for and about Mother had never been uncomplicated, but now, suddenly, I felt only a deep sense of loss, a loss as much of an opportunity to get close to

157

Mother as of her presence. Whatever had been lacking in my relation to her could now never be restored. Whatever had been unsaid by us could now never be said, and what had been said could never be unsaid. Mother had been the most remarkable woman I had ever known and I had failed utterly with her. I had succeeded only in alienating her.

I disgraced myself, or at any rate embarrassed Christabel, by breaking down and weeping. She said, 'Oh, do control your feelings, Sylvia,' but other than that, ignored me. It was left to my Aunt Ada to say, 'Of course, Christabel thinks you killed your mother' – to say it, too, in a tone that neither committed her to Christabel's opinion nor yet distanced her from it. The implication was clear: my grief must be insincere, given how I had treated Mother while she was alive. How little people know about grief.

I replied merely, 'If that is what Christabel thinks, no doubt she will find occasion to say so.'

In the event, she never did say so in so many words. She opted rather for the expedient of not speaking to me at all, which I suspect cost her a pang or two, Christabel never having been half as good at being silent as at speaking. A silence, after all, can only be eloquent to a quite limited degree.

And now, it would seem, the silence is about to be broken.

V

Christabel has changed, of course. I can see her taking note of the changes in me. I can even see her refraining from commenting on them. I know how I must seem to her: old, dowdy, unkempt. She is looking at me as Mother would have looked at me, except that Mother would not have refrained from comment.

But looking at her, I am grateful that I have not had as much to lose as she: youth and energy and movement have been so much part of her beauty, that with their departure very little remains of that, too. And her exquisite movements are now hampered by the voluminous clothes she wears in an attempt, perhaps, to hide how much weight she has gained, how heavy the body under the gorgeous drapes. The clothes are still superb, of course; but the effect is as of a beautifully draped object. The cloth no longer hangs and clings with the sinuous motion of old. The face, too, is old – not in wrinkles and blemishes, but in its hard impassivity, having outlived the shifting play of emotion that once animated her features. She is an old woman, but that would not have mattered. What matters is that she is an unknown old woman, one I would have passed in the street without recognising.

She looks about her. I have chosen to receive her in my study, partly because it is a more congenial room, partly because I want Christabel to realise that I am a working woman. 'I'm told you're a busy woman,' she says, as if apprehending my implication, 'so I shall not detain you long.' She takes the chair facing my desk, where Teresa has recently sat. 'I wanted to see you before I die. We have become strangers to each other.'

'We may always have been strangers to each other,' I say, sitting down at my desk.

She looks at me, and something of the old mobility of expression returns: a raised eyebrow, a slight smile, a twitch of the lip. Then she laughs. 'Strangers we may be, but I recognise some of your old obstinacy.'

I, in my turn, recognise something of the old power to charm. She has kept her beautiful flexible voice, though it is deeper and darker, with a crack in its depths. But I resist the charm. I bear Christabel no grudge, but I will not, at seventy, pretend that we can undo the history of a lifetime in order to equip and sanitise her for the Advent – for that, I am sure, is at the bottom of this visit: Christabel's uncomfortable sense that Christ returning may find her not in all respects as He might wish.

'You are looking very elegant,' I say.

'One tries to look decent,' she says, and again her eyes flick over my shapeless dress. 'Your house seems … comfortable,' she continues.

'Do you mean untidy?' I ask. 'I find that is what people usually mean.'

'If that was what I had meant that is what I would have said,' she rejoins, dryly but not sharply.

Unabashed, she continues her examination of my study, as if searching for clues. Her eyes rest for a while, as of old, on the watercolour of Keir Hardie, but she does not comment.

'How wretchedly cold England is, after California!' She exclaims. 'The sheer *discomfort* of this country must have something to do with the crabbed faces one sees on the streets. They love neither themselves nor their fellow man nor God. It's a country of misanthropists and atheists.'

She gets up and examines the low table on which the telephone perches somewhat uncertainly.

'I do believe I recognise this hideous object. It's a milking stool from Emerson's.'

'Is it? I have furniture from so many different houses and places.'

'Yes, I recognise the shade of mauve. Mother and Aunt Mary had decided that mauve would be the fashionable colour that year.' She touches the little object. 'Milking stools, *figure-toi*. In St Pancras! What did Mother imagine?'

'How you hated Emerson's!' I say.

'Indeed,' she says, with a certain reticence. I have touched the chord of reminiscence too freely. But, running her finger over the stool, she suddenly turns to me, her face distorted in a grimace half-satirical half-resentful. 'Didn't *you*? Those rolls of tasteful fabrics and piles of exquisite cushions that nobody wanted? The strange objects Mother bought because they would appeal to "the ordinary woman", when if the ordinary woman of St Pancras could afford meat and potatoes of a Friday it was as much as she could do? And when that failed, to revive the idea in Manchester!'

I am surprised at the intensity of her scorn, at this distance in time. 'I hated it too, but not as much as you, I think.'

'That may be because you were in Venice while I was minding the store.'

'Until you went to University to become a barrister.'

'That was probably as much to get out of Emerson's as to qualify myself in the finer points of English law. I think I wrote you a rather pert letter summoning you back from Venice to come and do your bit. Did you resent that?'

'Did I? I don't think so, not at the time. I remember finding a certain piquant irony in the fact that Mother's pursuit of beauty should necessitate my removal from Venice to Manchester. But I could see that it was only fair that you too should be free to pursue a career. I had been very happy in Venice, but I came to see it as a self-indulgence.'

Christabel is still standing, examining my books and my pictures. She now turns to me, and with that dismissive wave of the hand I remember so well, she says, 'Poor Sylvia! Always ready to sacrifice yourself!'

I ignore the mockery in her voice and eyes, and say merely, 'I did not see it as self-sacrifice. Father always said, you remember, "If you do not work for other people ..."'

'"You will not have been worth the upbringing",' Christabel interrupts me abruptly, almost brutally, and laughs harshly. 'How could I forget? How that blighted our childhood, the notion that we should *work for other people!*' She starts pacing, gesticulating, as if once again addressing an audience. 'Why? Do other people work for *us*? And how do we know that other people *want* us to work for them, and that what we're working for is *what* they want? Would it not be simpler if everybody just worked for himself, then we could all know what we were working for and why?'

I am surprised at Christabel's passion. 'You are still so angry, Christabel,' I say.

'Angry?' she exclaims. 'Of course I'm angry. To be pursued all one's life by the threat that one *will not have been worth the upbringing*, a waste of effort and scarce resources, like an un-profitable hen or a barren cow! As if being brought up was some kind of *reward* paid in advance which one had to keep on earning!' She stops in front of me, placing one hand on my desk. She smells quite strongly of perfume. 'And really, Sylvia, what *was* this upbringing for which we were supposed to be so indebted? Being dragged from one unsatisfactory school to another, according to father's financial status or political aspi-rations, never staying for long enough to learn anything or make any friends, having strange governesses inflicted upon us whose idea of education was taking us to museums and gal-leries?'

'Father may not have given us a conventional schooling, but he gave us something far more precious,' I say. The worst things about Christabel is that she reduces me to tendentious-ness. 'He gave us a moral education, and he gave it to us in the first place through the example he set.'

'Bah!' she exclaims, flinging both her hands up in theatrical outrage. 'He set us a fine example, indeed, in failing in almost everything he undertook, and expecting his family to fail along with him and glory in it as a proof of high principles.'

'He was the finest man I ever knew, and I shall not listen to you demeaning him. I don't know why you have now, in your old age, invented this grievance against father.'

'I have not now invented my grievance. I've only waited till now to vent it because all my life you've made me feel guilty for not loving father enough, for not mourning his death as I should have, for not remaining faithful to his principles. And what did those principles amount to? Drudge and drill, drudge and drill – do you remember how he used to harangue us as we pored over endless dull volumes? *Drudge and drill, drudge and drill,* until I thought I would go mad with it! Well, I am now, *in my old age,* as you point out, old enough to reject the moral blackmail that imprisoned me all my life.'

'It was my impression that even in your youth you arranged your life very much to suit your convenience.'

She waits for a few well-timed seconds. When she resumes, it is in the measured tones of rational discourse. 'It seems to me, Sylvia, that you're the one who has not forgiven, who has pathologically cherished every actual or imagined slight. Why not come out and declare your anger, and allow it some air? You know that you've never forgiven me and Mother for bringing you back from Venice quite pointlessly to work in a shop that was about to close down. You would be quite entitled to be angry about that – I would have been furious – but you refuse yourself the honesty of anger, and instead have your revenge in covert ways.'

'What covert ways do you have in mind?'

'Well, first there was your much-publicised child out of wedlock, and then your hardly less ill-conceived brainchild, which you had the effrontery to name *The Suffragette Movement*, as if you were authorised to speak on behalf of a movement of which you had been at best a tolerated member.'

I force myself to retain the appearance of calm. 'What is pathological is your interpretation, not my conduct. The desire to have a child – like, indeed, the desire to write a book – is surely natural enough not to need some sinister explanation.'

She shrugs impatiently. 'The test of that is the use to which the child or the book is put. You shared your child and its cosmopolitan origins with the all-too-avid readers of some penny paper – what was it? *The News of the World?* – and you used your book to discredit the Women's Social and Political Union and all its deeds, not to mention Mother and me. If it had not been so unreadable it could have done real harm.'

'You are fond of referring to "Mother and me" as if you were a kind of double act of equals. In truth, by the time you expelled me from the Union, she was acting entirely on your instructions.'

'I never issued a single instruction.'

'No, it wasn't necessary. You expressed your preference, and Mother acted in accordance with it.'

'Mother and I happened to agree on most things.'

'As on my expulsion from the Union?'

'Yes, as it happens. We were entirely agreed that you were in contravention of the rules of the WSPU, and that the East London Federation had become a rival rather than a sister organisation.'

'You were always inclined to see sisters as rivals.'

She laughs, not a sarcastic or affected laugh, but a deep laugh of genuine amusement. 'Really, Sylvia, you surprise me. I cannot remember ever, in our childhood or later, competing with you in any respect. It was always you who had to prove to yourself and others that you were my equal or my superior. You used Father as your means to prominence by trying to establish yourself as his favourite child, even competing with Mother for a place in his affections. Then, when he died, you tried to sustain the partnership by claiming that you alone were true to his ideals. I do believe you were competing with

Mother for ownership of Father's dead body. So if we are to talk of rivals …!'

She has retained her air of amused detachment. While she talks, she examines the interior of my study as if it were a mildly boring museum. Her gaze alights again on the portrait of Keir Hardie. She seems on the point of saying something, but visibly checks herself. I think I know what it is she does not say, but I do not want to hear it.

I ask instead, 'Is that what you came here today, after twenty-five years, to say?'

'No, Sylvia, I came here in an attempt to put behind us the differences that separated us, and to recover the shared vision that should have united us.'

'And in order to put behind us these differences, you have first to revive them?'

'Pardon me, I've not revived our differences, you have.' She says this factually, not argumentatively. Christabel has always been better than I at not showing her temper, just as she has been better than I at showing it, when it has suited her to do so. For the moment, it suits her to be reasonable. I am the hysterical sister, the one who has no control over her emotions.

I am not interested in this division of roles. I am as bored with her assumption of rationality as with her imputation of irrationality. That, finally, is the effect of Christabel's visit: boredom, and irritation at the waste of my time. I will not tell her so. I do not want to give her the impression that I find her presence uncomfortable.

I am ready to ask her, too, to leave. Surely a seventieth birth-day should be an occasion to welcome one's guests, not chase them away? But then again, why should one suffer fools on one's birthday any more than on any other day?

'What I came here to tell you,' she says unexpectedly, 'is the real reason for your expulsion from the WSPU.'

'You have just told me the real reason behind my expulsion

165

from the WSPU. You and Mother resented the influence of the East London Federation.'

She shakes her head slowly, a strange smile on her face. 'There was that. But the East London Federation was never a danger to the WSPU, whatever you wanted or believed. No, it was something quite different.'

I do not want to encourage her, but she carries on in any case. 'Consider Ethel Smyth,' she says abruptly.

'Ethel Smyth?' For a moment I have to search my memory, then I remember. 'Why should I consider Ethel Smyth?'

'She was your real enemy.'

I wonder if Christabel has become unhinged in America. Her theory is as far-fetched as the reports on flying saucers that have been emanating from her adoptive country. 'I had almost nothing to do with Ethel Smyth. All I know about her is that she was at one stage a close friend of Mother's and that they then drifted apart.'

'Exactly. Can you remember exactly *when* they were close friends – that is to say, at their closest?'

'No I can't.' I consider for a moment. 'But I do remember she was there when you and Mother summoned Adela and me to Paris in – when? – early 1914.'

'Exactly. And you think it was just coincidence?'

'Why do you not think so?'

'Because I was in Paris at the time, and could see Ethel making her bid to take over Mother's life. She had some strange notion that she was Kent to Mother's Lear, and you can deduce for yourself what that made the three of us.'

'Then,' I say, 'in strict consistency one of us at least gets to play Cordelia.'

'I suspect Kent did not have much use for Cordelia.'

'But why should Ethel have wanted to get rid of me? Even if she was never very fond of me, as indeed she had no reason to be, she did not seem to have any particular grudge against me.'

'Not particular, no: general. Or at any rate not unique. She had the same grudge against Adela, who was, as you have said, summoned to Paris at the same time, and as summarily dismissed.'

'But why?'

'I've told you, Ethel was at this stage making her play for complete domination over Mother, as only a truly servile person knows how. She had an irrational distrust of Mother's offspring. I remember once coming into the sitting room of my flat in Paris, to hear her say to Mother, "You don't understand what I suffer in having always to take second place to these women just because they're your daughters."'

In spite of my distrust of Christabel's rhetoric, I find her version of events strangely compelling. She always did have a way with an audience. 'Even accepting that,' I say, 'I cannot see how expelling us from the WSPU could benefit Ethel Smyth.'

'Mother's life, as she saw it, *was* the WSPU. It was the site of all her intimacies and antipathies. As long as you were in the WSPU, according to Ethel, you were sharing her life.'

'Then that included you.'

'Of course it included me. And in due course came to mean only me, after she had prevailed upon Mother to get rid of you and Adela.'

'As you know, I think *you* prevailed upon Mother to get rid of Adela.'

Christabel bestows a pitying smile upon me. 'I know you think that. But I'm telling you what really happened.'

'If, by your argument, Ethel Smyth was all-powerful, why did she not prevail upon Mother …?'

'To get rid of me? Because in fact she was not all-powerful. I think initially she was too cautious to attempt to oust me. She did not know her own strength. And by the time she did risk it, she no longer had the power, and she was banished instead. But it was a closely-fought battle. I think in all my long association with Mother, that was the only time I felt my pre-eminence challenged. You and I and Adela may hardly have presented a united front, but yes, we were all up against Ethel Smyth. She was strong because she was single-minded. She cared only for Mother, not for the Union or the Cause.'

'But what did you have to fear from her?'

Christabel favours me with a grimace, a grotesque relic of her smile of old. 'What did I have to fear? My very sanity,' she says, with an abrupt sincerity. 'Unsure as I was of my own power, I knew that Ethel was a force to be reckoned with. If Mother turned against me, I would be called back to England to face imprisonment and what went with it. And you know that I could never tolerate incarceration.'

'Unlike the rest of us, you mean, who thrived on it.'

My sarcasm makes no impression on her. 'Well, yes,' she says, then repeats with emphasis, 'Yes. I know you think you're being satirical, but in fact I do think that any number of you positively asked to be locked up, got some kind of perverse satisfaction out of the awful food, the filthy clothes, the dank cells. It was all proof to you of what you were prepared to suffer for the cause, and you sustained yourselves and one another by telling yourselves that somehow the awfulness proved the righteousness.'

I stare at Christabel as much in incredulity as outrage. I have sometimes wondered how she justified to herself her luxurious sojourn in Paris while in England the women she ordered to set fire to public buildings were being force-fed. Now I know: she cast herself as a magnificent exception.

'Whereas I ...' she continues, 'I felt only abhorrence and terror and claustrophobia and the most terrible loneliness I had ever experienced, a sense of my own body as being not only redundant but somehow impure, *abominable*, to be the seat of so much pain. And around me were all these women exhorting each other to disregard the body as a lower thing, an obstacle to the spirit, and singing songs and pretending it was all a lark, when all I could think was that I was hungry and filthy and *ugly*. Sylvia, I would have gone quite literally mad if I'd had to go to prison again.'

168

There is, suddenly, a note of anguished confession in her voice which I have never heard before, and which is, as far as it goes, sincere. For a moment, an impulse of pity makes me want to reach out, take her hand, express some understanding of a fear that makes her seem more human than her vaunted boldness and intrepidity. There has been at least this moment of truth between us. But then, her horror of confinement and fear of madness reminds me of the suffragettes who in fact did go mad, being fed with pipes forced down their nostrils, or having their teeth broken with a feeding tube. So I say only, 'That was because in prison you had no audience. Mother, of course, arranged an audience even in prison.'

Christabel has recovered from her moment of weakness. Her manner assumes its old brittle edge of irony. 'Mother could arrange an audience because she could act the part. It was the one part that was physically beyond me. I knew that I must not go to prison, as much for the sake of the Union as for my own, and that staying in Paris was my only real safeguard. How could I serve the Union with my intellect and my spirit, with my body locked up, abused, *tortured*?'

I think I could have comprehended this extreme of self-preservation as, after all, an honest statement of priorities, had there not been something complacent in Christabel's manner, an evident belief that her fastidiousness was somehow proof of a superior constitution, a finer grain of being. So I say, somewhat brutally, 'So Adela and I were sacrificed to your wish to stay in Paris?'

'My *wish* to stay in Paris? It was a necessity, a matter of life and death.' With age, Christabel's habit of elevating her own preferences to absolutes has hardened, is no longer accessible to her sense of humour. 'There were other reasons for your expulsion, of course, none the less valid for being convenient. But yes, that was mine. I had to retain my unquestioned status in the WSPU and in Mother's regard in order to stay in Paris, and siding with you and Adela would have jeopardised that.'

169

I sit back and consider; how insignificant all this now seems. 'Why are you telling me these things?' I ask her. 'Ethel has been dead these – how many? – years, and I have all but forgotten the WSPU. Like you, I have found new fields of endeavour and entered into new relations. To be honest, even Mother is no longer very real to me. Why should I now, on my seventieth birthday, care whether Ethel Smyth engineered my expulsion from the WSPU almost fifty years ago?'

She has regained her grand manner. 'Because I think I can allow you at last to rest, to stop trying to outdo me and Mother. Don't you see, all your ridiculous posturing on behalf of countries nobody has ever heard of is so *unnecessary*, once you accept that you didn't really fail at all, that had it not been for Ethel Smyth, you could have shared in the honour?'

This may be Christabel's most exasperating role yet, Lady Bountiful distributing favours from her own abundance of rewards and blessings to the morally indigent and the ideologically crippled. Christabel is mad, I am now convinced. Whether she is sincere or not hardly matters. If she is sincere, she must be taken to believe that I have dedicated myself to the unification of Ethiopia to compensate for the fact that I have not entered the feminist pantheon along with her and Mother, and if she is not sincere, she is maliciously trying to deprive me of any sense of achievement I may have by reminding me of the distinction I did not gain.

'I tell you these things,' she carries on, quite carried away with her vision of her own motives, 'because I think they may serve to console and strengthen you. They no longer matter to me. I've found meaning and purpose Elsewhere.' She points upwards, vaguely, the Bride of Christ foretelling her own apotheosis. 'But you may derive comfort from the knowledge that it was not in the first place because of any defect in yourself that you were banished from the WSPU.'

'Of course it wasn't.' I reply. 'It was in the first place because you wanted pre-eminence. All this talk about poor Ethel Smyth

170

is just your attempt to cover up your own part in my expulsion.'

She remains calm, gives me a half-smile suggesting weary tolerance. 'You must believe what gives you most comfort,' she says. 'That is all I want for you. I think you should try to confront your anger honestly and find some resolution. You can't go through the rest of your life being angry with Mother.'

'Nor can I go through the rest of my life being condescended to by you,' I say. 'I suffered enough from your condescension and domination when we were young women; I now have my own life in which you have no part to play. And as for my banishment from the WSPU, I have no regrets on that score. I believe that your and Mother's militant policies, by alienating the people of England as well as their leaders, did nothing but delay the granting of the vote to women. I am glad for you if you find fulfilment awaiting the Second Coming of Christ; I would rather concern myself with more rationally attainable ends.'

'Like the unification of Ethiopia?' she asks, the air of gracious tolerance yielding to something more acerbic, close to a sneer.

'Yes, like the unification of Ethiopia.'

She shakes her head. 'Poor Sylvia,' she says, 'still working for other people, still pursuing Father's approval all these years after his death. Can't you see, I'm trying to tell you to accept that you have achieved quite enough in one lifetime, that Father will forgive you if you say, I'm seventy years old, and I've achieved as much as can be expected of anybody in one lifetime, and I'm now tired and I'm going to sit in the sun in my garden?'

'And you?' I ask, 'What about the Second Coming? Are you going to sit in the sun in California and wait for it?'

'The Second Coming will happen with or without my participation. All I can do is tell people about it. But you seem to feel that the unification of Ethiopia is dependent upon your labours alone.'

This is a futile argument, and I decide to withdraw from it.

As I should have anticipated, though, Christabel is too taken with her own contribution to heed my withdrawal. 'That was always your tendency,' she informs me, almost conversationally, 'to want to take charge, to stage-manage, to coordinate, ultimately to preside.'

'Always?' I ask, in truth astounded by this charge.

'Well, from quite an early age, but especially after Father died, you took it upon yourself to ensure that the household was sufficiently grief-stricken. And then, of course, when Harry was dying ...'

'I don't think you should talk to me about Harry's dying,' I try to warn her, but Christabel has never deferred to anybody in her choice of topic, sublime in her conviction of the rightness of her cause and the soundness of her insight.

'The poor boy,' she continues. 'All he wanted to do was die in peace, but you organised a lugubrious Dickensian tableau around his bedside with yourself and Miss Craggs as the weeping women in attendance. Mother and I, of course, were excluded as unworthy of having roles in the tragic spectacle of your devising.'

I stare at her in horrified disbelief. Even Christabel can surely not be so deluded as really to believe in this fantastic theory of my conduct. But seeing the glint of conviction in her eye and the high colour of her cheek, I must conclude that in fact she is entirely sincere. This is how she saw, or has come to see, my part in Harry's death.

She looks at me enquiringly, as if considerately giving me an opportunity to reply to her charge, but hers is not the kind of argument that admits of rational refutation: consisting in flat constatation, it offers no purchase to criticism or analysis. All that it permits is contradiction, as puerile as itself.

So I say nothing, merely stare at her, conscious of appearing stupid. But Christabel has always thought me stupid.

'I hope you will not start weeping again,' she says. 'You always had an unfortunate propensity to tears.'

172

'No, Christabel, I will not start weeping again. I shall never again weep in your presence.'

She nods. 'There is that much gained, then,' she says. 'I really think at our age we can afford to be honest with each other, don't you?'

'Yes,' I say. I cannot think of anything else to say. If I were to allow myself, I would tear my hair and beat my breast and scream at Christabel: 'No, not if what you call being honest means visiting upon each other the distorted visions of our youth, desiccated and warped beyond even their original deformities by the habits and complacencies of old age. No, not if you think that by speaking to me what you regard as the truth, you are doing me a kindness. And above all: no, if you think that you can now, fifty years on, speak on behalf of Harry, whom you never knew and never valued. Do not insult me with your condescension that you call honesty and with your patronage that you call kindness. Do not presume to tell me how to run the rest of my life. You want me to retire from the public stage because you want at last to be the only Pankhurst in the public eye. You have taken to proclaiming the Coming of Christ, because that is the only position that could satisfy your insane craving for predominance, the Chosen Bride of Christ, his harbinger and handmaiden, except of course that you imagine something more exalted than servile. I do believe that all that will satisfy you is to be Queen of Heaven.'

Instead of which I say 'Yes' again. I shall allow her once more to condescend to me. It will be the last time.

Christabel has left. I recover my own space gradually; the pen and ink in front of me, the piles of paper, Keir's watch, his portrait. Christabel has always been able to make me doubt the validity of my own achievements and even existence. I can see now that the effect was calculated, on her part. She hated sharing with me and Adela, ultimately even with Mother, the name of Pankhurst. This was why she was so angry at my giving my son my father's name. I had created another Pankhurst for her to contend with.

But Harry? Why should she cherish such a perverted image of my efforts to make his last days more bearable? The most insidious part of Christabel's effect on me is her ability to make me suspect a bitter kernel of truth in her accusations and denigrations. Having from early childhood controlled my perception of myself, she could thereafter invoke the authority of her judgements at will. Even now, knowing what I know about Christabel's desire to have power, to manipulate others through her judgements, I nevertheless find myself cowed by the moral authority she arrogates to herself.

I look at Keir's watch, the watch he had given Harry. Is it true, in even the remotest degree, that I had organised a tableau around Harry's death-bed? It is warm in my study, but I shiver. The thought is so monstrous, so uncharitable, so vindictive. But I cannot banish Christabel's mocking face from my mind; when I try to remember Harry, all I see is that face, with its pencilled eyebrows and its hideous accusations.

Harry, Harry, I say to myself, how can anybody think *that*?

VI

In the first place, I tell myself and the absent Christabel, it was not my idea that Helen Craggs should come to Harry's bedside. I did not even know who Helen Craggs was, until Harry mentioned her one night in Pembridge Gardens. He was just then in great pain, and insofar as the pain allowed him any consciousness of anything but itself, he kept dwelling on the conditions on the smallholdings at Mayfield. He seemed in part terrified that he would have to return there and in part remorseful at having left. The more terrible the conditions, the more strongly he felt his responsibility to alleviate them.

He told me, while I sat with him, how ashamed he had been at not being able to fulfil the tasks set him, because of his physical weakness. 'I didn't mind the hard work much,' he said, 'I mean I didn't mind the hardness, if you understand what I mean. What I minded was that sometimes I really couldn't do it, just because I was too weak, and the supervisor, Mr Gasson, called me a "muff" and would tell the other workers I was "shirking". So I couldn't complain when the work was too hard for me, because that would just have confirmed his opinion. Besides, the other workers were suffering the same hardships, so there was no point in complaining, really.'

One incident in particular haunted Harry. He had been set to filling sacks with turnips, sewing them up, and carrying them some distance to where they would be collected for delivery to the train. Because of the need to catch the train, time was limited, but Harry worked quickly, and finished in what he thought was plenty of time.

'But then, you see, I realised that in my hurry, and in my

stupidity, I'd overfilled the bags, so they were now too heavy to carry to where they'd be collected.'

'But couldn't you open the bags and take out some turnips from each?'

'Yes, I could, but unpicking the stitches would have made me late for the collection.'

'And weren't there other people who could help you carry?'

'Not right where I was, and in any case, they had work of their own, and no time to help me.'

'My poor Harry! And what did you do?'

'I just dragged the bags one by one as best I could, but it was very hard. I fell down once or twice with exhaustion, and I hurt my back quite badly. When I first became ill I thought it was because of the strain of that day.'

But it was uncharacteristic of Harry to dwell on his own deprivations. What had made Mayfield particularly terrible to him, was the suffering of others. He was lodged with a poor family brutalised by poverty and hard work. The husband drank heavily, and when under the influence of liquor, would beat his wife and children.

'I tried to intervene, but that just made the man angrier, and he beat the poor woman all the harder, and she took her husband's side if I showed any pity towards her. She said to me one night, "I suppose you mean well, but you don't understand anything of what's between Bill and me. You come here from the city and think you can run our lives according to your city notions, but we have our own ways and our own notions." She seemed to be almost proud of being the man's property, and she resented my interference as somehow denying a kind of bond between them.'

Of course, with humans being subjected to such treatment, the farm animals had very little mercy shown to them. 'I woke up one bitterly cold night,' he told me, 'and I heard a strange noise outside, half bleat, half cry. I dressed myself and went outside. It was snowing heavily, and there, in the outdoor pen where the animals were kept, was a goat giving birth. She was in distress, I could see, not so much on her own account as on account of the kid that she had to expose to the elements. It was as if she wished she could keep the kid inside her to protect it, but nature had to have its way, and the little thing was entering the world, I feared, only to leave it almost immediately. So I went into the shed and made a little place in a warm corner and carried the goat and her kid in and made them comfortable. And the next day they were fine, only the supervisor said they would have survived anyway and I had made a mess inside the shed unnecessarily.'

'My poor Harry,' I said, 'it's not right that you should have suffered so.'

'The thing is,' he said, 'that those people and animals are still suffering just as much, I'm just not there to help them.'

To keep Harry from dwelling on these things, I tried to elicit happier memories from him, asking him about times that he seemed to speak of with pleasure. It was in this way that he came to tell me about Helen Craggs. Indeed, he might not have told me about her at all had I not noticed that he returned repeatedly to the Manchester by-election the previous year, where he had made himself useful by driving the suffragettes' four-in-hand. In telling me about this, he often referred, with evident pleasure, to 'we'; I asked him who had been his companion on these jaunts. He blushed – it was heartbreaking to see the colour return to his pale cheeks – and at first demurred, but in fact proved only too eager to talk about this young woman. Apparently he had met her on her first day in Manchester, and they had spent all their working hours together after that. 'But she is above and beyond me,' he said, dejected. 'I'm told her parents are very rich, and she's teaching at Roedean. She called herself Miss Millar then.'

'Did you ever see her again after the by-elections?' I asked.

He blushed again. 'I did travel to Brighton one Saturday last summer, when I was still in London. I didn't think I could just go up the school and ask to speak to her, so I waited outside, hoping she would come out. But she never did, on the Saturday, so I spent the night sleeping on the cliffs, and the next day I did catch sight of her on her way to church with a troop of girls.'

'And did she see you?'

'No, I don't think so, they were too far away. But it was something, seeing her. She is so beautiful, you cannot imagine it, Sylvia. I think if I could see her again I could bear ... everything else.' He turned to me and took my hand. 'Oh, Sylvia, I want more than anything else on earth to see her again.'

This was as close as Harry would ever come to a direct request, and it was clear to me that he hoped I could arrange for this young woman to come and see him. I thought deeply about it. Apart from the practical difficulty of finding Miss Craggs, there was a very real doubt in my mind as to how she would receive such a strange request. If she refused, Harry would surely guess it, and that would be worse than anything for him.

Then, too, I had to recognise that there was some core of selfishness in me that resisted the idea of bringing a stranger to Harry's bedside to share the last few precious weeks that I would ever have with him. In perplexity I mentioned the matter to Christabel, hoping that her incisive mind would resolve the dilemma for me.

'And what do you propose to say to this woman?' she asked me. 'That your brother is dying and would she kindly come and witness the process?'

'In effect, yes. But if she was only half as much taken with Harry as he with her, she would surely be more than willing to spend time with him now.'

'It's one thing gallivanting with a young man on a four-in-hand, and another thing altogether sitting by his death-bed. Is it fair to ask a young woman to saddle herself for life with the memory of watching a young man die a painful death?'

Harsh as this was, I could see the force of Christabel's objection. But I was suspicious of my own receptiveness to her argument: was I not conveniently grasping at it for my own selfish reasons? And could I face a future in which I would have to ask myself whether I had disregarded Harry's dying wish out of a misguided and possessive love? I must confess, too, to a certain inherent perversity that shied away from following a course of action urged by Christabel, perhaps exactly because she was characteristically so convinced of the rightness of her own opinion.

I decided to leave the matter to circumstance. I would try to get hold of Miss Craggs: if I succeeded without difficulty, that would be my sign to proceed; if not, I would let matters be. As a first step, I made enquiries from the Manchester office about the young woman who had helped there during the by-election. Harry had told me she was a teacher at Roedean, but I wanted this confirmed before approaching the no-doubt formidable institution. In the event it proved most unexpectedly easy to find out the whereabouts of Miss Millar/Craggs. The Manchester office told me that she had given up her teaching post to take up a position as WSPU organiser in Manchester.

This, by my own logic, seemed to suggest that I should proceed with the business, and I lost no time in writing Helen Craggs a letter. I did not state the nature of my business, merely asked her as a matter of urgency, and as a great favour to me, to come to me in London. *'When I explain to you,'* I wrote, *'the nature of my really quite unusual request, you will understand why I take the liberty of asking you to come to London, rather than go myself to you in Manchester.'* I asked Annie Kenney, who travelled regularly between London and Manchester, to deliver the letter to Miss Craggs personally.

Within a day, Helen Craggs was in London. She came to my lodgings, as I had asked her to do, since I did not want to discuss such a private matter in the hubbub of the WSPU offices in Clement's Inn. She was, as Harry had said, beautiful, perhaps

179

rather conventionally so to my taste, with large blue eyes and a pale complexion. Her blonde hair, though, was cut shorter than was the fashion just then. I could see how Harry might have been attracted to her, both for the extreme regularity of her features and the hint of the unconventional. She was slim, but her frame seemed strong and athletic, I was pleased to note. What I had to ask her was not something I would willingly have asked of anybody at all fragile.

In behaviour, she was such a young woman as one would have expected her to be, given her background and circumstances. She was self-assured and polite, with that slightly questioning manner that the upper classes adopt when addressing those they regard as their inferiors. I guessed that she was completely unaware of this, indeed probably regarded herself as egalitarian in the extreme. I did not apologise for taking her away from her duties; I had learnt that people of a certain class neither extend nor expect apologies.

She seemed oppressed by the smallness of my lodgings, as indeed I myself was, so I suggested a walk on the Embankment. It was a bright, cold day in November, and we walked fast, partly to get warm and partly because I, at least, felt the need for exercise.

'You will wonder, of course,' I said, 'why I have brought you here all the way from Manchester.'

She nodded. 'Yes, though naturally I assumed it had something to do with the Union.'

'Naturally. But not, as it happens, correctly.'

She said nothing, just turned her head and looked at me interrogatively. 'What I want to ask you,' I said, 'is as presumptuous as it is unusual. It is, though, a task that nobody else on earth can perform.'

She maintained her air of polite interrogation. Even curiosity seemed too vulgar a sentiment for her to betray. It was awkward, addressing her in half-profile. I stopped walking, and turned towards her.

'I believe,' I carried on, 'that you met my brother in Manchester during the by-election there.'

She frowned slightly, evidently trying to make the connection; then, unexpectedly, her face brightened. 'Oh of course – Harry! I had not recalled for the moment that he was your brother.'

I suspected that she had not for the moment recalled Harry himself, but it suited my purpose not to challenge her amiable hypocrisy.

'Yes; he remembers you with a great deal of affection.'

She nodded graciously, but gave no other acknowledgement of my information, which in truth she must have found puzzling.

'You must wonder why I am here telling you these things, Miss Craggs. Well, not to put too fine a point on it, my poor brother is very ill. Indeed, he cannot be expected to live much beyond three weeks.'

At this, she went slightly paler. 'Ah, poor Harry …!' she exclaimed, but to herself rather than as a public declaration. 'Is he in much pain?'

'Yes, he is,' I said. 'He is suffering from advanced poliomyelitis. But the doctor gives him an analgesic.'

She looked at me silently for a moment. Then she said, 'That is immensely sad. I'm afraid I don't understand diseases, but I've heard that poliomyelitis is a particularly devastating illness.'

'It is indeed. Harry is almost completely paralysed. From the waist down.'

'Aah,' she murmured, a mere whisper of dismay. I suddenly felt that I had no right to bring tragedy into this young life. But then I recalled Harry's pleading glance, and I hardened my heart.

'The really awkward thing,' I said, 'is that he has set his heart on seeing you again before he dies.'

'He has …?' I could see her retreat before this suggestion, as in all conscience was natural enough. What young person would willingly rush to a death-bed?

'I know that this is very painful to you,' I said, 'but you see, it would mean so much to him, and there is so little left that I can do for him, that I presumed to disrupt your life like this.'

She did not deny this, merely stared fixedly out across the river, as if engrossed in the activities of the Thames barges. I got the impression, surprising in somebody so young, of understated determination. Once committed to a course, she would keep to it with tenacity and courage. As an opponent, she would be formidable; as an ally, invaluable.

Then she looked up at me and asked, simply, 'What is it that you want me to do?'

'Two things,' I said. 'First, to come to his bedside and spend as much time there as you can bring yourself to do. I'm sure we can arrange with the Manchester office that you be transferred here temporarily. The second, and more taxing, task is to respond to his declaration of love, if he should make one.'

'Respond ...?'

'Yes. And by respond I mean, I suppose, that you should pretend also to love him.'

It would be too strong to say that she recoiled from my suggestion, but her reaction was in truth quite physical, a stepping back from me as if to distance herself from the extravagance of my demand. 'But ... I liked Harry very much, but there was never any question ...'

I sensed that I should now cease to be solicitous and apologetic. I should state my demands baldly and factually: she seemed robust enough to deal with that.

'I know. But the question has now arisen. And I feel I should warn you that it may arise again. Harry is, understandably, very ... emotional at the moment.'

'Has he asked you to speak to me?'

'No, and he would be mortified to know that I am doing so. So you see, if you were to refuse, he would never know. Only,

I beg of you not to refuse. Think of him as your young brother, if you cannot love him in any other capacity. Tell him you love him; he has only three weeks to live.'

For the first time she seemed uncertain. She pulled at her glove, and turned again to look over the Thames.

Then she faced me. Her face, given colour by the walk in the cold air, seemed suddenly irradiated. 'I remember Harry with great pleasure,' she said. 'He was such a bright and smiling boy.' She flushed. 'I'm sorry, but I do think of him of as a boy, though he is probably older than I am.'

'I know. He does seem very young. He has been made to suffer more than any young person should ever suffer.'

'Yes, and if you really think my presence would make more bearable his … his last days …'

'I am convinced of it.'

'… then I will undertake as best I can to help him.'

I took her gloved hand then and pressed it to my cheek.

'I think you will not regret it,' I said. I saw tears in her eyes, and realised that I was crying, too.

'Come,' I said, 'let us go and see Harry.'

If there had been any doubt remaining in Helen Craggs's mind, it must have evaporated when she saw Harry's response to her arrival. True, she had not seen him just before, so she could not, as I could, measure the transformation from his previous wan pallor to the joyous blush with which he greeted her. There was some awkwardness, of course – questions, explanations – but I tried to smooth over these by admitting to my part in recruiting Helen. She, in her turn, made it seem only natural that she should have wanted to come to him once she knew of his plight.

Helen Craggs was, as I had guessed, a determined young woman, and she took her duties very seriously indeed, becoming a kind of second nurse, especially at night when Harry was in pain and needed not so much nursing as companionship.

Quite what they said to each other when alone I did not know, and Helen did not offer to tell me. They did share with me a fantasy of going to Venice if Harry should recover – 'when Harry is better,' as we tacitly agreed to refer to that mythical time – and taking me with them, to show them my favourite places, which Harry knew from the drawings and water-colours I had made when I was there. I think it heartened him to imagine Venice with Helen and even with me, and we all three found strength in our joint deception.

A heartening and yet distressing consequence of Helen's arrival was that Harry fancied himself now capable of doing without the regular pain-killing injections Doctor Mills had prescribed for him.

'I feel so much better,' he said, 'that I do believe I can get by quite well without them.'

If I had really believed that his physical suffering was alle-viated by his evident happiness in Helen's presence, I should, of course, have felt nothing but joy. But I was haunted by a sus-picion that Harry's declaration was a kind of innocent bra-vado, stemming from a misplaced reluctance to seem weak to Helen, and a determination to suffer the terrible pain of his condition for her sake. I suspect a lifetime of being made to feel that he was not strong enough had made him determined to prove to himself and to Helen that he could endure the pain. I suggested to Nurse Pine that she might mention this to Helen, which apparently she did, but I don't know with what success. 'She's not an easy one to make a suggestion to, that one,' Nurse Pine. 'She has a mind of her own.'

'But what did she say?' I asked.

'Couldn't get a straight answer out of her. We'll have to see what her ladyship decides.'

I was perturbed by this, and found myself wishing that Helen had not come, if the result of her coming was that Harry suffered more pain than was necessary.

In spite of this distressing development, these days were as happy as Harry's state permitted. He himself was radiant in Helen's presence, and she responded, as one could not but do, to his warm spontaneity. It was clear that he adored her, and she soon entered without inhibition into his belief that her presence would make it possible for him to recover, through the sheer strength of his will to live. It was too precious a delusion to destroy; and yet I wondered if it would not make the inevitable end so much harder to bear. Still, I was happy in Harry's happiness, and grateful to Helen Craggs for making it possible. Her presence inevitably meant, of course, that I would see less of Harry – and probably never on my own again.

Of all the sacrifices I have had to make in my life, this was perhaps the hardest. It was not one that I begrudged either Harry or Helen, but what made it particularly difficult for me was the fact that I feared that I might now never have an opportunity to tell Harry about the lie I had told him that Sunday morning. The memory of this was assuming an ever more dreadful prominence in my mind, and I believed that by confessing to Harry I might find some relief for my troubled conscience.

To complicate the matter, Keir Hardie at this time found time in his busy schedule to make regular visits to Harry's bedside. It might be thought that this would make it easier for me, in enabling me to confess to both men at once, but in fact the prospect of facing them together was far worse than facing them separately. I could also tell myself that I did not want to intrude my personal anxieties upon Keir's time with Harry, which was precious for both of them. The two men had been fond of each other from the days in Nevill's Court. Harry loved Keir, I think, for his gentleness, so unlike the treatment he was used to receiving from the world, and Keir was attracted to Harry by the boy's warmth and by his own compassion for all suffering creatures.

I was present one day when Keir took out his treasured watch, the one that bore the tooth marks of his favourite pit pony. He held out the watch to Harry, and said, 'I want you to take this.'

'To take it?' asked Harry. 'But why?'

'To do with exactly what you want,' said Keir. 'Every young man needs a good watch.'

'And what about you, then?' asked Harry.

'I'm an old man now, I don't need a watch any more.'

It was all I could do not to intervene. I knew how Keir treasured his watch, and I thought his generosity had got the better of his prudence. But then I thought that it was not for me to interfere with an impulse so generous, and I said nothing. Afterwards, seeing the joy on Harry's face as he held the watch, I was pleased that I had trusted Keir. I should have known that he seldom made mistakes of the heart. Besides, the sad thought occurred to me that Harry's tenure of the watch would, in the natural course of things, not be long, after which Keir's watch could be returned to him.

All this time, Mother was absent in America, and quite unaware of these developments. I asked Christabel whether she had written anything to Mother about it, and she said, as if displeased at my question, 'Of course not. She will soon enough find out for herself.'

I'm afraid I did not look forward to Mother's return, except as it would give Harry pleasure. I do believe the poor boy was anticipating introducing Helen to Mother, proud of having won her love. I hoped that he was right, and that Mother might take pleasure in his joy, but instinct and experience alike predicted otherwise. Even so, my gloomiest previsions did not prepare me for Mother's reaction when she did return.

On the evening of her return from America, I came in late from a meeting in the East End, to find her apparently interrogating Helen Craggs. Strangely, my first impulse on walking in and finding Mother there was one of affection. Without premeditation I walked to her and embraced her. But it was like hugging a pillar of salt. She was hard and bitter, not having expected to discover Helen by Harry's bed, not, indeed, having foreseen finding Harry in such an extreme condition. She reproached me with having kept her in the dark and with having placed, as she put it, a strange woman at his bedside. I, angry in my turn at her peremptory manner, no doubt expressed myself more strongly than was tactful under the circumstances, and for several days after that she did not speak to me. She came to see Harry the morning after her return, but thereafter infrequently, it apparently being her implication that she had been rendered redundant by Helen's presence.

Only once during this time did we mention Harry again between us. Coming out of his room early one morning, I found her just arriving. She seemed to be on the point of sweeping by me with a chill greeting, as she had been doing ever since our confrontation on the evening of her return, but then she evidently bethought herself and stopped.

'Sylvia,' she said, 'I find there is something I need to discuss with you. May I walk with you?'

'Yes, Mother,' I said. 'I was just going out. Perhaps we can talk outside.'

'Yes,' she said, unsuccessfully suppressing a shudder. 'This place ...' she shook her head. 'I always feel that I have no place here, that I come here as an intruder.'

We stood outside, on the little sheltered step leading up to the front door. It was a brilliantly sunny morning, but there was a cold wind blowing, and we were both shivering slightly as we spoke.

I did not know whether Mother was once again reproaching me for Helen's presence or merely sharing with me her own sense of desolation. I decided on the latter interpretation, and in that spirit, replied: 'I think Harry is always so glad to see you. He certainly does not see you as an intruder.'

Pursuing her own train of thought, she but half attended to my words.

187

'Sylvia,' she said, and I could see it cost her much to say it, 'you are very close to Harry.'

'I think I am, Mother.'

'What I want to know, Sylvia, is: what is he thinking?'

'Thinking of what, Mother? Of his own chances of recovery, do you mean?'

'No. Of me. What is he thinking of me?'

In the bright light of morning her face looked drawn and anxious, the brilliant blue eyes dimmed with perplexity, and there was a moment when I pitied her. She had sacrificed her maternal duties and privileges to what she saw as her higher duty, but she had not succeeded in severing the bond. She had disregarded Harry's claims to her attention, and now she had become aware of him not only as a sentient being capable of suffering but as a rational being capable of judging. And she stood exposed in the light of her new knowledge, alone and vulnerable. But then, also, recalling Harry's account of Mayfield, I felt a revulsion against my own instinct of pity, curdling it into anger. I would save my pity for Harry. Who but Mother was responsible for his being there, had sent him back when he had said he could bear it no longer? So why should she now be concerned about what Harry was *thinking* of her? Had it ever occurred to her, while he was a lonely boy, to wonder what he thought of her? Did she really expect him to think of her with love and gratitude now, after what she had done to him?

So I said, 'I don't know, Mother. Perhaps you can talk to him yourself and find out.'

Her face hardened. 'Yes, Sylvia,' she said, 'I should have known that it would be futile to appeal to your humanity. You *have* no humanity, only a dry, abstract conviction of your own rectitude.'

'Mother,' I said, 'if that is what you think, I can hardly persuade you otherwise by argument. I shall have to live with your opinion of me, and you will have to live with mine.'

For the first time in my life I turned my back on her before she could turn hers on me.

The improvement in Harry's condition after Helen's arrival was marked, but the doctor warned me that it was probably more a function of his mental state than any actual physical improvement, and that in the long run the poor body could not hold out against the ravages of the disease. This proved to be sadly true. By Christmas Harry was forced to resort to the analgesics again, and it seemed doubtful if he would see in the New Year of 1910.

On Christmas day I went to his room with such gifts as I thought he could appreciate. He had very little appetite, and swallowed with difficulty, so anything good to eat would have been a trial rather than a pleasure. I took him a book of mine that I knew he loved – a beautifully illustrated edition of *Tales from Shakespeare*.

He was very pale, and though he tried to hide his pain, I could see from the sweat on his forehead that he was suffering. He took the book from me and paged through it lovingly, putting a gentle finger on a much-loved illustration, reading snatches from his favourite parts.

'Sylvia,' he said suddenly, 'Will you promise me something?'

'Of course, Harry,' I said, though in truth I was somewhat apprehensive. A promise to a dying person is so final, so inviolable and irrevocable, that it would seem rash to commit oneself in advance without knowing its terms. But I could not, of course, say so to Harry, and I professed myself, and indeed felt myself, unconditionally prepared to bind myself to any promise he might want to exact.

'It's not a big thing,' he said, 'only there may be a bother about it – afterwards – if everything isn't perfectly clear.'

'What is it, then, Harry?' I did not pretend not to know what he meant by *afterwards*, even though this was the first time he had openly acknowledged that grim anticipation.

'It's Mr Hardie's watch,' he said, taking it from the bedside table where it always lay.

'Yes, Harry. I'll see to it that it is returned to him. You need not worry your head about that.'

He shook his head, and a light blush appeared on his pale cheeks. 'Well no, you see, that's just it. Mr Hardie said it was mine to do with exactly as I wished – those were his words.'

'And what do you want to do with it, Harry?'

'I thought … I thought I'd like Helen to have it.'

'Helen?' For a minute I was so taken aback that I'm afraid I may have reacted rather sharply, for Harry looked at me in dismay.

'Why, Sylvia, do you think she would be embarrassed?'

'No, no,' I said, recovering my composure. 'Only I was wondering whether Mr Hardie could have meant that.'

'"To do with exactly as I wished" – those were his words,' Harry repeated doggedly. 'And that, really, is what I wish. You see, I've nothing else to give her, to show her how grateful I am.'

I must confess that I felt a twinge of bitterness. Keir's watch, if he was not to have it back himself, would have been infinitely precious to me, with its reminders of our days in Nevill's Court, and of Harry himself, his face lit with amusement or fired with indignation at Keir's stories of Donald and the other pit ponies. To Helen it would be just another trinket – rather battered, at that. It was impossible that she could value it as Harry had valued it, as I valued it, as Keir valued it.

But all this I could not say. What mattered now was what Harry wanted. He had spent his life trying to please other people. It was little enough to ask, that after his death somebody should please him.

'If you are sure that that is what you want, I shall see to it that she gets it,' I said. 'And I shall, of course, tell her that you particularly wanted her to have it.'

'Thank you, Sylvia,' he said. 'I knew you would agree with me.'

After this, Harry's decline was rapid. Hard as he tried to hide his pain from me and especially from Helen, it was clear that in spite of the drugs he was suffering, and we none of us could wish him to linger for long in that awful drug-induced twilight. He held my hand and Helen's, and spoke, when he could speak, only of the past. To me, he recalled outings we had had in London, the Sundays in Nevill's Court. With Helen, he reminisced about the days in Manchester, an outing to Boggart Hole Clough, the four-in-hand. He said little to his mother, and she had as little to say to him. On those occasions when she came to see him, she would sit mutely, sometimes holding his hand, sometimes wiping his forehead with a damp cloth: the only personal service I had ever seen her perform for her son.

Harry died late one night when Helen was alone with him. I had wanted to stay, but he had seemed distressed at what he called 'inconveniencing' me, and I had thought it better to leave him to sleep, if he could, with Helen watching over him. The presence of other people by his bedside evidently tired and distressed him. It cost me a pang to think that he would rather have Helen by his bedside than me, but I reminded myself that I had forfeited my right to being first in his regard by the lie I had told him. As I walked down the darkened corridor to my room, I was startled to come across Mother, standing in the entrance parlour in uncharacteristic indecision.

'How is he?' she all but whispered. She looked haggard.

I shook my head. 'He seems a bit stronger. But it can't be long now.'

'Can I go to see him?' This was the first time Mother had appealed to me for my opinion, let alone my permission.

'I don't know, Mother,' I said as gently as I could. 'He is very tired, and seems to want to be alone with Miss Craggs.'

Something of her old fire returned in a tightening of her jaw; she seemed to want to say something, then visibly restrained herself and shook her head. 'I'll ask Nurse Pine if there is somewhere I can wait,' she said. 'I suppose I can do that much.'

I went to my room and tried to sleep, but couldn't, knowing that Harry was probably at that moment dying. Even if he would prefer not to have me witness his death, it was a physical impossibility for me to remain in bed, a physical need for me to be near him. I got up. I had not undressed before lying down. After an hour, the longest hour of my life, I could no longer bear to be shut out. I went to his room.

Harry seemed to be asleep. Helen was sitting by his bed, looking strangely self-possessed. For a moment I felt a twinge of anger at this woman, for the fact that Harry had chosen her to be by his bed now.

'How is he?' I asked.

She shrugged and gestured to me to be silent, but I was not to be denied.

'How is he?' I asked again, but she ignored me, apparently absorbed in her own reflections. I could no longer allow my actions to be dictated by Helen; I took Harry's hand in my own. Helen seemed to want to prevent me from holding his hand, but I did not let go of the poor hand, feverish as it was.

Helen must have left the room, because when I looked up again she was standing above me with Nurse Pine. 'Harry,' I said, trying to ascertain whether he was conscious; it seemed possible to me that he was in a coma. One glance at Nurse Pine's face told what she was thinking: that Harry was beyond her help and our appeals.

So the three of us mounted a kind of guard at Harry's bed, waiting for death. It was not an easy death. The body's involuntary will to survive battled the disease and the drugs to the very end. I don't know quite when Mother entered; I looked up at one point and saw her standing in the doorway, her huge eyes dark caverns in her white face, her hair in disarray. She seemed unaware of everything except the narrow bed on which her son lay dying.

When at last he had gone, I stood staring at his mute face. With the departure of pain, Harry's boyish beauty returned unmarred by his suffering. He lay like some flawless monument to youth. It was difficult to believe that he was now only a body, from which all value had departed for ever. Helen was sobbing quietly. 'I didn't know it would be like this,' she kept saying.

'Like what?' I asked, though in truth I did not want to have to talk at all.

'So *difficult*,' she said.

'Did you think death was easy?' I asked.

She shook her head. 'I don't know what I thought. Perhaps I did not think at all.'

Then she got up from the chair she had sat in for so long, and left.

As if she'd been waiting for Helen to leave, Mother came to Harry's bed. She stood there, looking at him for a long time, but said nothing. She looked old, defeated, empty. I had never seen her look so completely without purpose or even volition. She sat down in Helen's chair looking at Harry's face as if she thought he might wake up. Then she got up, brushed his hair from his forehead, and said, 'I wonder what he thought.'

VII

I come to myself, forcing myself out of this mood of reminiscence. Christabel has brought back the sadness of that time, but also some of the bitterness. I do not like having to justify, even to myself, my care of Harry in his last days. It is something that I have cherished as inviolate, one relation in which I was not dictated to by either Mother or Christabel.

It is seven o'clock by the watch on my desk – Keir's watch, with Donald's tooth marks still there, later Harry's watch; how much can be contained in a material object! But no, it is not the object, it is the human content we ascribe to it.

The sun is setting, and I am still sitting idly, with my hand folded on the desk in front of me. Even Cedric seems haughtily intrigued by my unaccustomed immobility. He has jumped from the chair and is rubbing himself against my leg. It may be affection, but it is more likely that he is simply hungry. I shall go and feed him.

I leave my study, go to the kitchen and find Cedric's saucer. Silvio is slicing carrots for tonight's meal. He looks up as I enter, smiles.

'You've had a long day,' he says.

I nod, absorbed in thoughts of the day.

'Are you hungry?' he asks.

'Hungry? I suppose so. I haven't really thought about it.'

He shrugs and sighs, a humorously exaggerated sigh. 'What a fate for an Italian, to live with a woman who does not care for food! I wanted to cook you a special meal for your birthday, and then I realised you would not even notice it.'

'Poor Silvio!' I say. 'I do appreciate your meals very much.

It's just that I don't seem interested in the processes by which you arrive at them.'

He shakes his head. 'That is bad thinking for a socialist, to be interested in the product but not the process.'

'Did you see Christabel?'

He nods and shrugs. 'Yes, but she did not see me. Or she pretended not to see me. She is a very grand lady.'

'Yes,' I agree. 'She is a very grand lady. She believes that Christ is coming soon to see her personally.'

'Ah, that is truly grand.'

He continues chopping, absorbed in the task. He has something of Keir's unconscious ability to lose himself in a simple task, to become at one with the action. I give Cedric his food, watch as he fastidiously sniffs at the dish, then, satisfied, starts eating with rapid pernickety little movements of the tongue. How self-sufficient cats are, how unlike us poor humans with our needy spirits and our unreliable bodies.

'Where is Richard?' I ask.

'He was reading in the garden, but I think he has now gone for a walk.'

'I'll see if I can find him.'

'Don't be too long. Dinner will be ready in about half an hour.'

I go into the garden. It's turning chilly. Spring has not taken hold properly. Under the large elm there are a few chairs. Richard's book is lying in one of them – a proof copy of *Ethiopia and Eritrea* – but of him there is no sign. No matter: he'll come back to find his book. He has never left a book outside overnight.

I sit down in one of the chairs. I like the sounds of the garden preparing for the night, birds scuffling, chirping peevishly, gradually settling.

I am today older than Mother was when she died. There was to have been a celebration of her seventieth birthday, all the friends and enemies of old united in praise of the grand old lady of the WSPU – all except me, I imagine. How much more abhorrent to the delicate conscience is an erstwhile ally betrayed, than an enemy. They didn't even invite me to the unveiling of Mother's statue, which did not, however, prevent me from going, taking Richard along as company. There was a general scurry amongst the suffragettes of old not to have to confront the Scarlet Woman.

I rub my eyes, trying to clear my head of thoughts of Christabel. She has gone, I tell myself, and I shall in all likelihood never see her again. But there is Mother, dead these twenty-four years, and still as present to me as she ever was; perhaps even more so.

Again Christabel, I think – Christabel, who was responsible for my going to see Mother soon after she had herself been to see me that last time, to try to get me to change Richard's name.

Christabel's letter, as always, was short and to the point: like Mother, she disliked writing, possibly because it deprived her of the advantage of her beautiful voice. It was dated 12 April 1928. I still have it somewhere amongst my papers.

'*My dear Sylvia, It may be a cause of satisfaction to you to know that your act has all but destroyed Mother. It is not for me to interfere, but as you have always professed to take your duty seriously, I would say that your duty in this instance is to go to Mother and ask her forgiveness. It may be the last thing you ever ask of her. Your sister Christabel.*'

There was a P.S. with Mother's address – she was staying with people called Chipperfield somewhere on the Ratclifffe Highway, in the East End. How strange, that Mother was living in my old territory, while here I was, living in Winston Churchill's constituency.

I read Christabel's letter several times, then put it aside. I had no desire to be forgiven by Mother, and I certainly did not take my notion of duty from Christabel. But the next day, seeing the letter still there, I tried to consider it, not as an impertinent missive from Christabel, but as an impersonal piece of information: your mother is ill, and she is at this address.

Perhaps, even now, a basis might be found for a reconciliation with my mother, a basis perhaps in the love we bore each other in spite of all our differences, in our common love of my father, in the shared experience of imprisonment and of the violation of our bodies in the name of a common cause. We had been comrades in the struggle, though we had been adversaries at home. To have suffered hunger and thirst together, and the vile intimacy of squalor, was to experience a closeness more physical than civilised amenities permit or encourage. To smell the stench of another's body is to recognise in it one's own mortality; to tolerate that stench as one is in turn tolerated is an instinctive solidarity far more powerful than any so-called sworn allegiances and political pacts. All *that* had been between Mother and me: in the face of such closeness, matters of political principle seemed abstract and disembodied. And yet, political principle had intervened and nullified that closeness – unless it were more true to say that with the withdrawal of physical closeness, political principle had come to assume an absolute importance.

I wrote Mother a note proposing a visit. It was perhaps cowardly, leaving the decision to her, but I knew her well enough to recognise that she would decline to see me if I turned up without warning. Two days later, a reply arrived. It said: *Dear Sylvia, You must come if you think anything can be achieved by it.*

I took the train and the omnibus to the Ratcliffe Highway. It was an area I knew well from my work amongst the women of the East End before the War. It had then been a place of wretchedness and squalor, teeming with drunken sailors and destitute women intent upon exploiting one another with an awful single-mindedness. Since then, it had to some extent been cleaned up. Though still poor, it seemed to be no longer as popular as it had been with the sailors from the London Dock at Wapping, and thus no longer boasted as many gin shops and houses of ill repute. I found it, as I always had, strangely congenial. It reminded me of Father and the poor parts of Manchester to which he once took me, and, later, of the friendships I formed among the destitute and the desperate.

It was, nevertheless, not a setting in which I could readily picture Mother. Such shops as there were, dealt mainly in the paraphernalia, memorabilia and detritus of a thousand sea voyages, objects bought cheaply from desperate sailors, to be sold expensively to gullible sailors. Even where not positively grimy or worse, Ratcliffe Highway was dowdy, with that kind of dispirited ugliness that of all things Mother had most abhorred. Whereas I could find in the sheer shabbiness of it all a not unpleasant reminder of my days and nights of working in just such an area, I knew that to Mother it must be a mortification of the flesh to call this home. Even politically she must be ill at ease here. She had never shown any interest in my work in the East End, and had made no secret of the fact that she did not value the women of the East End as members of the WSPU. And now she was standing as Conservative candidate in the East End – I could not imagine with what hope of success. Indeed, I could not imagine why she should have chosen an area so alien to her political and aesthetic inclinations, unless she was hoping to prove to me that my old constituency, in a manner of speaking, could be won over to her way of thinking by her powers of persuasion. *Mrs Pankhurst wins Whitechapel for Conservatives*: how Mother would relish that. And how little she knew the East End.

Mother's lodgings were above a barber shop. There was no separate entrance, so I opened the door to the shop. There was a single chair, in which an elderly man was having his hair cut by an only slightly younger man. The barber looked up as I came in, clearly puzzled as to my business in this male preserve.

'I am looking for Mrs Pankhurst,' I said.

'I should have guessed,' he said in a pleasantly unsurprised way, and carefully put down his scissors and comb. 'I'll just call the wife for you, so's she can take you up.'

He walked to the back of the shop and shouted up the stairs.

I was not expecting a warm welcome from Mother's landlady. I knew from experience that there were none as ferociously high-minded as the respectable working class, and Mrs Chipperfield was likely to be influenced by her regard for Mother. It was fortunate that I had acquired over the years a healthy indifference to the disapproval of others. Mother had helped me in that: I could not have survived morally if I had remained receptive to her criticisms.

A middle-aged, red-faced woman came out of the kitchen, wiping her hands on a cloth.

'Mrs Chipperfield?' I asked.

She did not reply immediately. She was evidently examining me, comparing me with the picture she had formed of me beforehand.

'You must be Miss Pankhurst,' she said, in a tone suggesting that I had in some respect disappointed her. Perhaps I did not look sufficiently like a Scarlet Woman.

'Yes, I am here to see my mother, who is, I believe, expecting me.'

She nodded, put down the cloth and, to my surprise, extended her hand.

'I'm pleased to be making your acquaintance, I am, for all they're saying about you now. There are many around here as remember you from the old days in the Great War when they were hungrier 'n they are now, and you helped them to eat. I myself, if it hadn't been for the Cost Price Restaurant, I mightn't've been here today.'

Little weight as I had in advance given to Mrs Chipperfield's opinion of me, this was unexpectedly pleasing, or pleasing in its unexpectedness.

'Thank you,' I said. 'I remember the years in these parts with affection.'

'It's not a place as everybody wants to live in, but once you're used to it it's comfortable enough. I wouldn't change now, even if you gave me the choice.'

She led the way up a narrow staircase. On the landing she paused. 'You'll not find your mother looking well,' she said. 'It's not for me to say, but it's my opinion that she shouldn't be left on her own here. I do what I can, but she needs her friends and family around her all the time now. But it's not for me to tell her so, else she may think as I'm trying to get rid of her. But perhaps she'll listen to you, if you reason with her.'

'Perhaps,' I said. It would be the first time.

She knocked at a door, waited for a reply, which I could not hear, and opened the door gently.

'Your daughter is here to see you Mrs Pankhurst,' she said; then she stood back, held open the door for me, and gestured with her head that I should go in. She closed the door behind me.

The room into which she had shown me was evidently a sitting room, but in one corner was a desk, presumably placed there for Mother's use. Apart from that, the room was simply furnished, in a style that I knew Mother would find oppressive: 'dingy utilitarian' was how she had described it in the days when she was trying to bring beauty to 'ordinary' homes. I found the simplicity soothing, and I respected the honest refusal to attempt decoration beyond the potential of the little square box of a room, but I could imagine Mother's discomfort.

Mother was standing by the open window of the little room. She looked up as I came in.

'Oh, Sylvia,' she said. 'Perhaps you can help me close this window. It seems to be stuck.'

I walked to the window and tried it. It was indeed sticky, but after a few tries it slid down.

'Thank you,' she said, 'I've been feeding that pigeon. It comes every day, I know it by its having only one leg.'

I looked out of the window. The one-legged pigeon had flown up when I closed the window, but returned almost immediately to eating its crumbs, untroubled by the human presence behind the pane. 'You seem to have tamed it.'

'It wasn't difficult. Hungry creatures tame easily.'

We were both grateful to the pigeon for providing us with something to focus on other than the discomfort of this reunion. It had been – how many years?

'Ten years,' said Mother, as if in reply to my unspoken query, and for a moment we examined each other with the unabashed frankness not of affection but of custom. Mother appeared to have shrunk: always a small woman, she now seemed tiny. She was meticulously turned out, as always. I wondered who had helped her with her hair. She had not, over the years, mellowed into tact or merciful oblivion: she was examining me with the same mixture of dismay and perplexity as I remembered from my youth. She could never quite hide from me her own puzzlement at having produced so unprepossessing a daughter.

'You have not combed your hair,' she said to me.

'Haven't I? I thought I had. It may have got blown around on my way here.'

Her eyes strayed over the rest of me, but for once she did not comment. Perhaps even she hesitated to tell me what I knew, that childbirth had made me even heavier of body.

I knew that I had always been a trial to Mother, with my heavy features and my refusal to make the best of such advantages as I had. She herself always looked beautiful. She had a gift for creating beauty, and she suffered actively from the proximity of anything ugly. 'Just because we are dedicated to social justice,' I once heard her proclaim, 'that does not mean we have to look like Old Testament prophetesses. We do not want to give the impression that we are trying to

201

attract attention which we are too plain to attract in any other way.'

'Come,' she now said, 'come and sit down.'

There were only two chairs in the room. I took the seat nearest me, and Mother took the other. There was something painfully artificial about sitting opposite Mother on an uncomfortable chair in an unfamiliar room. There was not even a fire in the grate to help us pretend that there was a point to our sitting just there. Mother, too, was distracted. She moved about on her chair even more than its hardness merited, and she kept her handkerchief clenched in her hand. Of course, I had not seen her for ten years, and perhaps this was now her normal mode.

'What is the matter, Mother?' I nevertheless asked. 'Are you in pain?'

She shook her head, and to my surprise her eyes filled with tears. I say surprise, but it was closer to shock. I was not used to seeing Mother in tears. Indeed, she had often reproached me for my own tears, saying they were the marks of weakness. Now, in the frailty of her old age, there was something immensely touching in the sight of the indomitable Mrs Pankhurst breaking down.

'What is it, Mother?' I asked. 'Is it something you can tell me?'

She made a visible effort to draw herself together. 'I don't know, Sylvia. I don't know if you will understand.'

I was accustomed to being shut out of my mother's emotions, but this time, I thought, I would persist. 'Why don't you test me, Mother?' I asked, trying to put into my voice the tenderness I truly felt.

She sighed and dabbed at her eyes. 'I don't know if you'll understand,' she said again. 'It's Flora.'

'Flora?' I racked my brains but could not recall any such person. 'Who is Flora?'

'There,' she said, and pointed at the little dog asleep in its basket. 'That's Flora. And I think she's ill.'

202

I was too taken aback to reply immediately, and my mother, perhaps mistaking my silence for sympathy, continued. 'You see, Christabel gave her to me as a companion because she thought I might be lonely. And now I'm afraid that if she's ill she will think that I neglected the poor little thing.'

This was so unexpected and so absurd that I had to I prevent myself from laughing. 'Mother,' I said instead, 'I don't understand: is it pity for the dog or fear of Christabel that upsets you so?'

'I told you you would not understand,' she said petulantly. 'You have never really understood.'

'What is it I never understood, Mother?' I asked.

She did not look at me. 'Why I favoured Christabel over you.'

'No,' I said, 'I did understand. You favoured Christabel because she was strong and beautiful and clever. I did not mind, not really, though it sometimes made me sad. I, too, would have favoured Christabel.'

'And now you have avenged yourself on her and on me too, by having this son of yours.'

The note of reproach quelled the sympathy I felt for her. 'Mother,' I said, probably too impatiently, 'if you had known anything about sexual passion you would have realised that in succumbing to it one's mother and sister are the last thing on one's mind.'

'I shall not be lectured by you, Sylvia, on *sexual passion*' – she pronounced the phrase with a little shudder; it was not one that had ever been used between us – 'or on anything else.'

'I shall not lecture you, Mother. I doubt if you would be a receptive audience in any case.'

'Then I fail to see why you should come here today, after publicly disgracing the Pankhurst name and making it impossible for me to appear on a platform. I don't think I have ever, in all my years of exposure to humiliation, been as demoralised as I have been by this.'

I looked at Mother as if I were seeing her for the first time. She was old and she was tired, but that was not what struck me. Her strength had always been that her most uncompromising utterances were bafflingly compatible with an impression of great gentleness. Her appeal had been altogether to the better nature of her audience. But now she seemed merely hard and querulous. The mellow timbre of her voice had been stretched by time into something shrill and petulant. But she had lost more than the physical appeal of her manner: she had lost the moral basis of her power. I felt myself at last liberated from her influence.

'Mother,' I said, 'you who have lost two sons; you who sent the second off to suffer in loneliness and cold – *you* tell me that the most demoralising thing that ever happened to you was the birth of my son and the joy I have taken in him? What strange perversion of maternal feeling, what insane distortion of humanity, can turn its back on the suffering of her own son and then be shamed by the birth of her grandson? Mother, for all that you have succeeded in doing for the cause to which you devoted your life, you have failed as a mother and as a human being.'

I stopped, horrified at my own words. I had come to seek reconciliation, and instead I had allowed my old feelings of resentment to spill over. But Mother seemed unperturbed. She looked at me, quite dry-eyed now. Then she got to her feet, and I recognised, as so often before, the fighting spirit taking possession of her – unless it was merely the habit of public delivery, in which the performance was the substance and the emotion the shadow.

'Sylvia,' she said, 'I would have thought that a daughter of mine would have known me well enough to spare me the conventional sentimentalities of the age. What I suffered through the death of Frank, what I suffered through the death of Harry, you have no way of knowing, because it was not to my purpose to reveal it to you or to the rest of the world.'

My temper got the better of my remorse. 'It was not to

your purpose. Yes, Mother, that is what you taught me, that in political action sentiment is subordinate to *purpose*. I saw you pursuing your purpose, and I resolved then that my own political purpose would never disregard the lone sufferer, and that I would not forget to mourn my losses in pursuit of my victories.'

She shook her head, with the kind of sorrowful dignity she reserved for well-meaning error. 'And you assume,' she said, 'that grief can make itself known only by public lamentation; and because I did not break down, you assume that I did not mourn. Those who took the trouble to understand me, who were not animated by a petty spirit of envy and of spite, *they* knew what I suffered without my telling them. They knew, without my telling them, that by a cruel but absolute irony, in order for us to fight for the rights of women, we had to give up most of what is deemed most womanly. There were times when I literally prayed for the source of tears in me to be dried up, for the well of pity to be stopped. I could not weep, not because I would not weep, but because I dared not weep.'

The little light in the room all seemed concentrated on her pale face and in the large violet eyes. Her voice, that voice which in its prime could fill vast spaces, was now soft, but full and resonant, sustained as always by the cadences of her speech. And on her face, an expression not of entreaty or appeal, but of scorn. It was an expression I had seen there when she was berating Lloyd George or Winston Churchill. But now I was the enemy, to be denounced and to be defeated by the force of her rhetoric.

'And if you did not know that,' she continued, 'if you could not see that I had to violate what was sacred to me for the sake of a cause greater than my own sublime sensibilities, then that was a failure of imagination on your part, not a failure of humanity on mine. And if you cannot see that through your deed you have undone a life's work and sacrifice, then that is a failure both of imagination and of humanity on your part.'

She was standing as I had often seen her stand at the end of a particularly taxing appeal: immobile, her face glowing with conviction, her eyes strangely mild in the firm set of the head. And as I looked at her, I could feel her appeal work its old spell, against my better knowledge, against my every conviction and determination. Even in denouncing her very daughter, she could summon up the voice of that compassion that I was sure she had never truly felt for me. She was a consummate actress, and I knew it, but I was nonetheless moved by the performance.

'You are right, Mother' I said. 'I truly cannot see that in what you call my *deed* I have undone any of your work. If that is how you see it, I am sorry for you, and I am even sorry that I have caused you grief, but I cannot for a moment feel repentant or apologetic over this most natural embodiment of my love for Silvio and of my faith in the future.'

She seemed not to have heard me. She was caught in the wave of her own eloquence. 'Either you are morally stupid,' she said, 'or you are deliberately spiteful. I don't much care which; all I know is that you are, as you have been for most of your life, a trial and a burden to me. Now please go and leave me to my work and my thoughts. Get out of my house. Get out of my house and never return. And may a mother's curse rest on you and your son and his progeny till the end of time.'

I stared at her. I have said that her expressions were familiar to me from her stage performances, but now, in pronouncing this curse, there was an expression altogether new, a grimace of pure hatred contorting her features, seeming even to shake her very body.

I felt not so much cowed by it as repelled. I turned from her, ready to leave with her curse upon my head. 'You sound like an Old Testament prophet, Mother,' I said. 'You have been seeing too much of Christabel.'

But I, too, was borne along by the force of my own feeling. 'And as for banishing me from your house,' I continued, 'that you did years ago. Then there was space for such gestures, because in my naivety I still thought I might gain your affection and admiration. But I have a life of my own now, and I no longer need your affection and admiration. So you see, you have nowhere to banish me from.'

At that I left. But at the door I looked round once more, and saw, not the imperious Mrs Pankhurst casting out yet another apostate, but a lonely, bent old woman in a dingy room. She was clutching her stomach.

'Is anything the matter, Mother?' I asked.

The look she gave me repudiated my concern. All she said was, 'It will pass. I have these cramps.'

She clearly resented having me witness her pain. But just then she was seized by another cramp, evidently worse than the first. She doubled over and seemed unable to stand erect again. I went to her and put my hand on her shoulder.

'Is there anything I can do, Mother?'

I could feel her resistance to my touch in the stiffening of her body; or perhaps it was just another convulsion. We stood like that for a while – she bent over, me with my hand on her shoulder – until eventually she said, with a visible effort of control, 'I find I cannot walk. Will you help me to my bed, please?'

She was so small and thin that I could all but carry her to her bed. I could feel her body being racked by the cramps, and the grip of her hand on my arm tightened almost painfully. I lowered her carefully onto the bed, and she lay back, pale, her eyes closed, her face covered in perspiration from the effort and the pain. I bent over her.

'This old body,' she whispered. 'Why must the spirit drag along the wretched body?'

I stood silent before the question. There was no consolation to be offered. I could have told her that the spirit survived the body, but that would do for neither Mother nor me. That, after all, we had in common, a belief in the here and now; not some Advent or Revelation, but the tangible present, in which pleasure and pain are felt with a like immediacy, and in which we have to achieve whatever it is given to us to achieve.

Mother was very quiet. I thought for a moment she had lost consciousness, but, with her eyes still closed, she started speaking again. 'I think, nowadays,' she said, 'of Harry. Of his pain.'

I still said nothing. There was nothing to say. I took her hand in mine. There was again the instinctive tightening, the incipient withdrawal, but then the hand relaxed and remained in mine.

'I think,' she said, 'and I wonder.'

'What do you wonder, Mother?'

'I wonder: what did Harry think?'

'What did he think about what, Mother?'

'About me. Did he ever tell you? I know you will tell me, because you have never spared me the truth.'

'No, Mother,' I said. 'He never said anything.'

For the first time she looked at me. 'I believe you,' she said. 'You would not spare me if he had abused me. But I wonder if he knew … that I had meant so well.'

'I am sure he knew that, Mother.'

'I had meant so well,' she repeated, still looking into my face as if wanting to see whether I believed her, 'and yet I failed with Harry.'

'You could not help his disease, Mother. Nobody could.'

'I could have given him the unconditional love that a child is entitled to from his mother, the love that nurtures its own offspring above itself. I did not do that.'

'No, you did not, Mother,' I replied. 'That was never your kind of love.' Except towards Christabel, I wanted to say, but something prevented me. I at last felt for her what she had never allowed me to feel: pity. I did not in fact know what Harry had thought of Mother as he lay dying, but I could not see how he could have felt anything but pain at her rejection of him. This, though, I could not tell Mother.

'You ask what Harry thought, Mother,' I said at last. 'As I say, he did not tell me that. But he did tell me, when you were in America and he was so bad, that I should not let you know, because your work was more important than his sickness. He made me promise not to tell you about his condition. So you see, we must assume that he thought you would have come home if you had known.'

She lay there, considering this. Her face became calmer. I could see her accepting my lie and drawing comfort from it. Then she asked, 'And Christabel?'

'What about Christabel?'

'Did he ask her too, not to tell me?'

'Yes.'

'Then that was why she did not tell me?'

'That was why she did not tell you.'

Mother's eyes filled with tears. 'Thank you,' she said.

It came to me then that in all the long years, that was the first time that Mother had *thanked* me for anything. But if her gratitude was out of character, its occasion was not: it was still Christabel who mattered most. For a moment I wanted to break out in anger again, ask her why what Christabel thought was more important than what Harry thought. But some calmness came to me, a memory of Keir Hardie saying one day, 'People do not elect the people they love; they are elected by something outside their own control.' Mother had not chosen to love Christabel. But how much sadder for her, then, that she had placed her affections and expectations on someone as incapable as Christabel of bestowing love or even pity on anyone other than herself. And that in doing so she had disregarded the dumb appeal of one who was himself seeking her love, if not her pity.

She seemed calmer now, though exhausted. I looked at the tiny figure, neat in its black dress and pretty mauve blouse. She had demanded so much of her body in her years of struggle: incarceration, hunger strikes, sleepless nights, cold vigils, long marches, rooftop escapes in the rain, endless meetings, and her body had faithfully served her for all those years, its pain subsumed in the fierceness of her purpose. But it had been biding its time, and now when she wanted to make further calls on it, it was refusing to obey the command to action. Its organs and processes, its muscles and sinews, no longer responded to the signal from the strong mind and the unbroken spirit: they had had enough. Having shown no mercy to her body or to those of others, she was now being let down by the body that had served her for so long.

'I think you must sleep now, Mother,' I said softly, in case she was asleep. 'Shall I help you undress?'

Her eyes opened with something of their old sharpness of focus. 'No thank you, Sylvia. I will rest for a while and then go to bed.'

I sensed that she did not want the intimacy of my undressing her. I would ask Mrs Chipperfield to come and help her later. I took a blanket from the chest of drawers. 'Shall I cover you?'

'Thank you,' she said. 'And bring Flora to me. She likes to sleep on the bed.'

I pulled the blanket over her, then gathered the little dog and put it on the bed. It found a comfortable place, curled up, and went to sleep.

'There,' I said, 'you will both be comfortable now.'

VIII

It is almost dark now. Silvio will wonder where I am. Perhaps Richard has forgotten his book, and is inside the house.

But as I get to my feet and take the book, Richard appears. He has been walking; his face is flushed with exercise.

'I was thinking you must have left your book outside,' I say.

'You know you taught me never to do that.'

I give him the book. 'Children don't always learn what their parents teach them.'

'Perhaps you didn't,' he smiles. 'I always did.'

'Let me not teach you to be late for dinner, then.'

We walk towards the house. As we reach the front door, I stop.

'Richard,' I say, 'I shall go to Ethiopia.'

He looks at me quizzically, wondering whether I am serious.

'Why now?' he asks.

'Because now is all the time I have. I don't want to die sitting in the sun with Cedric on my lap.'

'And what is to happen to Cedric if he is not to sit on your lap?'

'Oh, he will come along.'

'And to me?'

'You too, I hope.'

'And Silvio?'

'He too.'

'Then that is all decided,' he says.

'Yes,' I say. 'If only so that Teresa Billington-Greig will have to revise her obituary.'

211

Book 3

Helen

I saw thee, beloved,
And having seen, shall ever see,
I as a Greek, and thou,
O Helen, within the walls of Troy.
Tell me, is there no weak spot
In this great wall by which
I could come to thee, beloved?

Harry Pankhurst to Helen Craggs, 1908.

I

London, 28 September 1960

Fred lowers his copy of the *Manchester Guardian*. 'Sylvia died yesterday.'

For just a moment I have to think: *Sylvia who?* But of course, for Fred there was only one Sylvia. 'Sylvia Pankhurst?' I nevertheless ask.

He nods reflectively, drifting off into his own memories, as he's now more and more inclined to do. 'In Ethiopia.'

'Yes, I knew she'd gone there. Was she all on her own?'

With a small start he heeds my bid for his attention. 'No, apparently her son and daughter-in-law were with her. Strange – I had not thought I would outlive her. She seemed so … immutable. Is there more barley water?'

I refill his glass. 'Oh, you'll outlive us all yet. When last did you hear from her?'

He thinks. 'It must have been after Emmie's death, in '54. I don't think she wrote when you and I got married.'

I hand him his barley water. 'I don't remember that she did. But she was probably in Ethiopia by then. How old was she?'

He looks in the paper. 'Seventy-eight, apparently. Survived by one sister, Adela, now living in Australia.'

'Yes, poor Adela,' I say, but he doesn't respond to my prompt, either because he's preoccupied or because he doesn't want to revisit poor Adela's wrongs.

'And now?' I ask, perhaps a mite sharply.

'Now?' He recalls himself to the present. 'Well, I suppose the Foreign Office will sleep more soundly for Sylvia's departure, but apart from that, her passing will hardly cause a stir.

215

Not in this country, at any rate. She's to have a state funeral in Ethiopia, apparently.'

'Will you have to do a tribute again, as you did for Christabel?' I try not to stress the last part of my question too pointedly. We've been over the tribute to Christabel before.

'Good heavens, no. Imagine the consternation if I should drop dead while delivering my tribute. And besides, if she's having a state funeral in Ethiopia ...' He shrugs as if to imply that that's all anybody could want.

'That needn't prevent,' I say. 'They could have a memorial service for her in Westminster Abbey, as they did for Christabel.' On a second time of trying, I manage neutrality more convincingly.

'St Martin in the Fields.'

'Some national shrine, at least.'

'Mmm. They could, but I doubt whether they will. Poor Sylvia was never accorded the same hullabaloo as Christabel.'

Quite inconsistently, I'm assailed by an impulse to be fair to Christabel. 'Christabel didn't have a state funeral,' I point out.

He takes a sip of barley water. 'Well, you can't have it all. Besides, a state funeral wouldn't have impressed Christabel. She imagined, I think, that Christ would descend for the occasion to escort her up to heaven. And she did have a pretty cushy time of it in California, apparently. After California a state funeral would have been an anti-climax.'

This I interpret as licence to vent my feelings, as if poor Fred hasn't had the benefit of them before. 'What with one thing and another, Christabel had a pretty cushy time of it much of the time, didn't she? Issuing orders for us to set fire to buildings while she was walking her dog in the Bois de Boulogne?'

Fred resolutely maintains the air of benign accommodation with which he has all his life confronted the irrationality of others. It's intensely irritating. 'Strictly speaking, she didn't walk the dog, she carried it.' He shakes his newspaper to open it out. 'Well, I suppose some people are born to lead and some to follow. And the leaders go to Paris, while the rest of us have pipes pushed up our nostrils.' He considers his own statement critically. 'Mind you, not that Emmeline fled to Paris.'

'Except for shopping expeditions,' I can't resist adding.

'Yes,' he concedes. 'But she was as ready as anybody to be locked up.'

Having been fair to Christabel, I don't find it necessary to be fair to Emmeline. 'Not that she ever had pipes pushed up her nostrils either,' I say.

He chuckles. 'No, she didn't, did she? Nobody dared assault those nostrils.'

I'd not intended this to turn into a tribute to Mrs Pankhurst. So I ask him, abruptly, 'Why exactly did Emmeline and Christabel expel you from the WSPU?'

He takes off his reading glasses, puts them down on the table in front of him, and rubs his eyes with both his hands, a gesture he uses to delay answering an unwelcome or difficult question. Then, to my surprise, he laughs. 'Do you really want to know, more than forty years later?'

'Yes, I do. I've wanted to know for more than forty years.'

'Do you want the official reason or the unofficial?'

'The unofficial. The official I think I know: that you and Emmie failed to adhere to Union policy as promulgated by Emmeline and Christabel.'

'Yes. Emmeline favoured ever more extreme militancy, we favoured moderation. Christabel had decreed – '

'– from her stronghold in Paris –'

'– a policy of intensified arson, which Emmie and I thought could win us no friends and alienate our supporters. So Emmeline got rid of us.'

He says it as matter-of-factly as if he were explaining the effect of the early rains on the potato crop. 'That's one way of ensuring a united front,' I say, 'getting rid of the dissenters.'

'Well, we could hardly complain,' Fred says. 'Emmie did want to take the matter to the members of the Union, but I said to Emmie, we stood by Emmeline and Christabel when they abolished the constitution and seized power; we can hardly now appeal to the other members in the sacred name of democratic process. We were the victims of an autocrat we'd helped create.'

How like Fred to assume blame even for the injustices done to him. I want to hear him voice something of the resentment he surely must feel, certainly is *entitled* to feel. 'So because you were loyal to her when she needed you,' I ask, 'she was justified in jettisoning you when she didn't? Isn't loyalty supposed to be reciprocal?'

He smiles wryly. 'I suppose it's a lesson other people have learnt more painfully than Emmie and I, in this century: that autocrats, once in power, show little gratitude to those who put them there. Perhaps it diminishes their sense of their own omnipotence, being reminded that they were once weak enough to need help.'

'Oh well, if you want to justify the methods of Emmeline Pankhurst by likening them to those of Hitler and Stalin ...'

'I'm not justifying her methods, I'm merely placing them in perspective. But perhaps it was simpler than that. Emmeline never much liked me.' Fred hesitates; I know that he is holding back some information, but I also know that, given time, he will divulge it. Fred is discreet, but not secretive. He takes a sip of barley water, wipes his mouth, and says, 'You see, Emmie was of course Treasurer of the Union, and had started to question the need for Christabel's presence in Paris. It was expensive, and it was becoming increasingly obvious that she was not *doing* very much, apart from decreeing highly dangerous duties for her myrmidons in England to perform.' He chuckles. 'Christabel even instructed Sylvia to burn down Nottingham Castle, which Sylvia had the good sense to refuse to do.'

'I know,' I say. 'She had more sense than I. I tried to burn down old Lewis Harcourt's country house.'

'At Christabel's behest?'

'Not really, though she had been saying for some time in her weekly bulletins from Paris that it was time women *struck at the heart of the establishment*, that is to say, its property. So the idea was in the air, and I seized it. I was young and eager for ideas to seize. In any case,' I say, to bring him back to our subject, 'so Emmie wanted Christabel to return from Paris.'

Fred nods, but pensively, as if unsure. But I know that his memory, as formidable in its way as the filing system for which he was famous, will turn up the item complete with all its cross-references. I stir my tea vigorously to nudge him. 'You see,' he says at last, 'originally, I suspect, Emmie had reasons of her own for wanting Christabel in Paris; but with time those reasons may have lost their force.'

'You *suspect*? You're being very cryptic, my dear Fred.'

'Am I? Well, it was never entirely clear to me even then. But not to put too fine a point on it, Emmie had seen Christabel as a rival for the ... discipleship of Annie Kenney. Oh, nothing as indelicately stated as that, of course, but you must remember, these were highly emotional times and relationships were, well, intense.'

'Ah. Emmie wanted Christabel in Paris so as to have Annie to herself?'

Fred looks mildly distressed. 'Oh dear, that does sound so avid. But yes, in effect. It suited Emmie to have Christabel in Paris. It transpired, however, that sending Christabel to Paris, instead of separating her from Annie, only increased her allure for our Annie, who took with great alacrity to the pleasures of weekend jaunts to Paris, not to mention the thrill of eluding the police and crossing the Channel in disguise. The fact that she thought she was serving the cause of the WSPU allayed any conscientious qualms she might have had about enjoying it so much.'

'So what purported to be a battle for the soul of the WSPU was in fact a squabble for the body of Annie Kenney?'

He gives my comment the consideration it doesn't deserve.

'Well,' he says at length, 'the distinction would not have been so clear at the time. Issues were … *embodied*, quite literally, to an extraordinary degree. To Emmie, the idea of suffering womanhood was embodied in Annie Kenney, the girl from a cotton mill, who had lost a finger to a whirling bobbin. Annie was guileless girlhood personified, and where Christabel saw only a devoted servant and a useful disciple, Emmie saw a noble soul.'

This sounds like an idealisation of Emmie's part in the tug-of-war, but I let it be. I do permit myself to ask, though, 'And Emmie, in vulgar parlance, was preparing to pull the plug on Christabel?'

He nods. 'Yes, though she would never have put it like that. Emmie hated vulgar parlance. Let's say then that she was preparing a report, as Treasurer of the WSPU, in which she strongly recommended, on grounds of great financial urgency, that Christabel be recalled to London.'

'And Christabel knew about this?'

'Her mother knew about it. And what Emmeline knew, Christabel knew.'

'And Christabel, I take it, did not want to return to London.'

'Christabel most certainly did not want to return to London. What was there for her here? Imprisonment, hunger strikes, forcible feeding.'

I find this line of analysis more congenial. 'Whereas there,' I pursue the line, 'she had the Bois de Boulogne, the Champs Elysées, hobnobbing with the Princesse de Polignac and her Sapphic set.'

'Yes,' he says looking amused. 'Christabel had nothing of the martyr about her; she could have delivered a moving peroration from the stake, but she would have found an understudy to be burnt in her place. So she played the loyal lieutenant, standing by the general in her purging of disloyal troops.'

His tone is far too neutral to my liking. 'And the general

who purged you,' I say, 'who connived at Christabel's subterfuges – this is the woman whose statue you unveiled?'

He holds up a protesting hand. 'Please, I unveiled nothing. I was but one of several speakers, not to mention Ethel Smyth conducting the Metropolitan Police Band. I was hardly noticed.'

'You know that's not what I mean. Your mere physical presence there was a public tribute to a woman who in private had treated you disgracefully.'

My heat expends itself upon Fred's imperturbable equanimity. 'I think great causes simplify themselves in time, don't you?' he asks.

'What do you mean?' I ask, suspicious of his generalising tendency.

'Well, posterity seldom has the time to cherish old controversies, and so it agrees on a common estimate for convenience's sake. In Emmeline Pankhurst's case the simplification started early. She was pronounced a heroine of female suffrage, and that is how she will be remembered. Perhaps that is what statues are for: to reduce complex personalities to bronze effigies. I was simply playing my small part in the process.'

'Then I think I prefer Emmeline in bronze to Emmeline in the flesh. Seen dispassionately, after all, what was Emmeline Pankhurst? A self-righteous self-promoter with a gift for public speaking.'

I want him to deny Emmeline, to repudiate her, in some way to break the hold that she had over him, still has over him after all these years. But if I'd hoped to provoke Fred, I'm disappointed. He remains imperturbable. 'Ah, but you see, we never saw Emmeline dispassionately; we saw those deep blue eyes, that earnest expression appealing to the best in us, and we heard that deep, thrilling voice that she could play as if it were a cello. The most eloquent sculpture cannot render the effect of that body, those eyes, that voice.'

I snort. 'Oh fiddlesticks. She was a humbug and you know it.'

He shakes his head. 'No, that's also a simplification, in its way as inadequate as the heroic one.'

I do not pursue the point. Fred and I will never agree on Emmeline. 'And Sylvia? How will she be simplified?'

'Oh, Sylvia is the great exception to the simplifying process. She can't be reduced or elevated to a single cause or principle. Even the obituary calls her, you see, a crusader for many causes. She was pointedly not invited to the unveiling, but she came anyway, bringing along her illegitimate son lest anybody should mistake her presence for a tribute to her departed mother.'

'And where was she while you and Emmie were being expelled?'

'She wasn't present, but she made no secret of her support for us, which may have contributed to her own expulsion a year or two later.'

I ponder this for a while, sipping my tea. 'I'm still mystified by Christabel's actions.' I say. For some reason, Sylvia's death has perversely brought back memories of Christabel. 'I accept she had her reasons for wanting to be rid of you, but I can't understand how anybody with any pretence to morality or even consistency could turn against her benefactors like that.'

He takes his time, cooling my indignation with his circumspection. 'I have,' he says at length, 'at times wondered whether in fact Christabel was a mystery or an extremely simple person.'

'I would never have thought of her as simple,' I say. 'She was too self-contradictory for that.'

'Well, one might say that her apparently unfathomable actions and disparate causes become quite explicable if we accept that everything Christabel did was single-mindedly dedicated to the advancement of Christabel's career, as she saw it.'

'And how did she see it, her career?'

He gestures with his hands, large, eloquent gestures, oddly

mimicking Christabel's own flamboyance. 'As a public persona, as having in some way to produce herself, quite literally and physically, to an admiring public. The cause was not exactly immaterial, but it was the occasion, the screen on which she projected her image.'

At last we seem to be in accord: Christabel was essentially a public entertainer. 'Speaking of screens and projections,' I say, 'I saw her occasionally in California, you know, with Mary Pickford and May Whitty. She was very much at home there.'

'Oh yes,' says Fred imperturbably, 'she was a great actress *manquée*.'

This was not what I had in mind. 'I used to think,' I say, 'that she was a great courtesan *manquée*.'

Fred ponders this only long enough to extract the sting from my comment, then shakes his head. 'No, she didn't have the warmth for that. She compelled people, she didn't attract them. She needed to possess her own body, not to have somebody else possess it. Her life was a performance; she didn't need individual admirers, she needed an audience.'

'And whether the script called for votes for women or the second coming of Christ didn't matter very much?'

Once again I'm defeated in my attempt to provoke Fred. 'Not very much, no,' he says without rancour. 'Of course, she would have preferred to await the Second Coming in Paris, but unfortunately the French cared less than the Americans for the Second Coming.'

'They were all, in their different styles, actors, weren't they, the Pankhursts?'

He ponders this; it is one of his more disconcerting traits, to treat even my most flippant comments as if worthy of serious consideration. 'Even Sylvia?' he asks.

'Oh. I wasn't thinking of her, but now that I do – yes, even Sylvia. Though she was inclined to break up her lines to weep, as the poet says.'

Fred gets up from the table. 'Sylvia never could follow a

script,' he says. He folds the paper neatly. 'Would you like the *Guardian*?'

'Thank you, yes. I'd like to see what they say about Sylvia.'

Fred closes his reading glasses and puts them in the pocket of his cardigan. He will forget where they are, but before I can point this out, he says, 'Of course, you were also quite close to her at one stage, weren't you? How one forgets. About poor Harry.'

I pour myself another cup of tea and open the paper at the obituary headlined *Crusader for Many Causes*. 'Yes. About poor Harry.'

II

I remember thinking how odd it was, that the first Pankhurst I met should be one that I'd never heard of. I'd arrived in Manchester from Roedean, where I was then, in 1908, in my final year. After the damp green Sussex spring, Manchester with its smoke, its grime, its grey skies and blighted streets, was like a city with no connection to the natural rhythms of life; one couldn't have told that it was April from anything in the place itself.

It was, though, an undeniably lively city, and bracing, compared with the genteel complacencies of Brighton. There was an air of purpose and resolve about the suffragettes gathered in Manchester to support their candidate in the by-election. Mind you, it was always more a matter of opposing than of supporting. I was surrounded by women who clearly, if they ever did have the vote, wouldn't be voting for the same party as I, who simply wanted the vote as a means of entrenching their privileges without being beholden to their husbands. But opposition is more enjoyable than support, when you're young and impatient and not overly concerned with taking responsibility for your choices. That was surely Christabel's genius, knowing how to mobilise the anarchic streak in us; she would have been far less successful if she'd tried to convert us to any sustained programme of political reform. But breaking up Winston Churchill's meetings required only a certain amount of dare-devilry and an indifference to consequences.

For whatever reason, then, I'd come to Manchester determined to do my bit, whatever my bit might turn out to be. I had a theory that my life of privilege had left me morally undernourished and underdeveloped, and that I should put myself on a course of worthy hardship. I was, I suppose, looking for a mission. To signal to myself – and to such others as could be assumed to be interested – the changed identity I was assuming, I called myself Miss Millar, which I judged sufficiently austere for my new vocation, though I told myself my motive was to spare my father the embarrassment of having it known that he had a daughter with the Panks and Peths.

As it happened, Harry was the first person I met in Manchester. I'd arrived by a late train and, having been told that the WSPU would arrange accommodation for me, I asked my cab to take me to their headquarters. The driver muttered something uncomplimentary when I gave him the address: the Union had clearly had time to make itself known in Manchester. When we drew up at the WSPU office, it seemed deserted, but I didn't want to ask my driver to wait, even if he had seemed inclined to do so – so I paid him and approached the closed front door. I pushed at it, and to my surprise it yielded to my touch. The front room was dark, but there was a light somewhere in the back. Leaving my case in the front, I went in search of the light. I had to traverse two small rooms stacked with pamphlets, banners and streamers, the appurtenances of hell-raising, as I was to discover. In the very last room there was a rustling sound; I knocked at the door and went in.

There was a young man inside, tracing letters in black enamel on squares of calico. He looked up as I entered, straining to see me, with something of the frown of the short-sighted. As I moved into his range of vision he smiled. He got to his feet and came towards me; he was tall and thin and fair, with something of the delicacy of a shy-stepping forest creature.

'Hello,' he said. 'I'm Harry.'

'I'm Helen Millar,' I said, extending my hand. 'I've come for the by-election.'

'Then you're in the right place,' he replied, shaking my

hand. His was cool and damp, his grasp surprisingly firm. 'Well,' he added, laughing, 'not right now. Everybody else is at a meeting.'

'Don't you go to meetings?'

'Oh, no.' He was suddenly very serious. 'I do the backroom and I drive the four-in-hand.' There was something touching about the solemnity with which he said this, as if anxious to establish his usefulness. 'I have to prepare these for Mr Churchill's meeting tomorrow.' He pointed at the pile of little calico squares. I saw now that they read VOTES FOR WOMEN.

'Well, I'm pleased you're here,' I said.

'Yes, Mrs Pethick Lawrence said you'd be coming and said to take you to your lodgings.'

'That's a relief. I thought I might be sleeping outside tonight.'

'Oh, no,' he said, again very seriously – his humour evidently did not extend to any aspect of the WSPU. 'The Union is very well organised, they would never let anybody down.'

'And you?' I asked.

'Me?'

'Yes. What's your function in the Union? I thought they didn't allow men as members.'

'They don't. But I'm tolerated because my mother and sisters are all so active in the Union. I drive the four-in-hand,' he repeated with shy emphasis. It was clearly a matter of some import to him to have a function and an identity.

There must have been other mothers and sisters in the Union, but the slight self-consciousness with which he referred to his suggested that he expected me to recognise the allusion. 'Your mother ... is Mrs Pankhurst?' I asked.

He nodded, blushing with pleasure. He was evidently very proud of his mother.

'I have to take you to the Waverley Hotel in Oldham Street,' he said. 'Quite a few of the women are staying there. I think you'll like it. Should I take you there now?'

227

'Yes, please, if you can interrupt your work here.'

'Oh, this can wait till later,' he said, assuming an insouciance that I suspected didn't come naturally to him.

'Thank you,' I said, 'I really am very grateful to find you here.'

He blushed again. 'I'm very glad that you found me here.'

In the days to come I was to see Harry often. He was known as 'the honorary suffragette', and was a great favourite amongst the women, who enjoyed teasing him. He accepted their banter good-humouredly, though at times he evidently felt that he wasn't being taken seriously. Not that he took himself particularly seriously, but he did see himself as working for a cause, whereas some of the women seemed to think he was indulging a whim. The fact that he so clearly enjoyed what he was doing may have contributed to this impression, in particular his taste for the more prankish aspects of our task, like chalking pavements with slogans. In speech he seemed nervous, with none of Emmeline's organ-like tones, and in manner quick and light, with nothing of Sylvia's basset-hound gloom. He had a deep and ringing laugh, bright but mellow like a soundly made bell, and the women vied with each other to elicit it. In moments of intense feeling he could seem distressed almost to the point of tears, but much of the time he had an irresistibly merry manner about him. It was impossible not to warm to his candour, though in my earnestness I thought him rather insubstantial at the time.

He loved driving the four-in-hand, and when he did so, he was transformed: his cheeks glowed and his eyes, which were a deep blue, were radiant with enjoyment. Though not solidly built, he had a sinewy strength, and his large, slender hands had a surprisingly firm hold on the reins. It soon became obvious that when we went out in the four-in-hand he would keep the box seat next to him for me. I was uncomfortable with this, as I knew that any number of the other girls would have been glad of the seat, but I could hardly turn it down. When, on occasion, I deliberately loitered, so as to give some other girl the chance, Harry would make a point of keeping the seat for me, which of course made the distinction, such as it was, even more invidious. He insisted, too, on helping me onto the box seat, which I thought quite unnecessary, but it would have been churlish to turn him down. Besides, there was always a pleasant shock in the decisiveness of his grip, so at odds with his appearance of delicacy.

One girl in particular, Clarissa Benson, had set her cap at Harry, and had, I gathered, been the box-seat favourite before my arrival. I was not to know this, and was only alerted to her ill will when I overheard her say to a crony, 'No doubt Miss Millar thinks to advance in the WSPU by the male line,' which at first puzzled and then infuriated me. It seemed to bode ill for the women's movement if we fell to vying for the only male in sight, and I suppressed my irritation, but no longer felt obliged to hang back in accepting Harry's invitations.

I think he liked the fact that I was also young, and that he could talk to me.

'You listen to me,' he once said to me.

'Don't other people listen to you?' I asked.

'They're more interested in teasing me than in talking to me,' he said, 'so they'll always try to find something amusing in whatever I say.'

'That's because they're fond of you,' I said.

'I know,' he replied. 'And I'm fond of them, but sometimes I feel as if I'm ... I don't know, their favourite pony or something, that they feed sugar lumps to.'

The thing was, that with his large blue eyes and translucent skin, he was the kind of boy that women wanted to spoil, and I think that without realising it, he'd started lending himself to the role, not exactly playing up to their blandishments, but responding – in fact like a pony being fed sugar lumps. He was evidently hungry for affection, even while striving to seem strong and independent.

229

There were times when I regretted the sexual polarisation of our campaign; I was nineteen, with the curiosity of a girl of nineteen, to whom a young man presented himself as something other than a political adversary. Most of the other women there seemed to see men as an undifferentiated mass, at best ineffectual, at worst hostile; but looking at Harry's strong hands, feeling them linger slightly longer than was necessary when helping me onto the box seat, I couldn't help thinking about the strange thing that was the male body, so different to my own. And Harry, for all his gentleness and diffidence, was very masculine, or what I thought of in my inexperience as masculine. It was a matter of his movements, which were far more peremptory than his hesitant manner made one expect, and his smell, which, from his handling of the horses, was vaguely acrid, but not unpleasant.

The one woman who seemed immune to his appeal was his mother, who treated him with a certain dry brusqueness as if to avoid too personal a note. I think this distressed him, though he seldom talked to me about her, other than to recount stories of her triumphs – in truth rather more than I wanted to hear. He did talk at length about Sylvia, and recalled with evident delight the outings they'd taken in London. He had imbibed from her, I think, his strong sense of social justice and his fierce defence of any helpless creature. He loved working with the horses, and he was visibly apprehensive when anybody else took charge of them, as if he didn't quite trust another person to handle them properly. There was about him, in short, a certain over-exposed, vulnerable quality that made one feel slightly apprehensive in his company, rather like handling a fragile vase.

Once, on one of the few lovely spring days that Manchester vouchsafed us, he took a group of us for a picnic in the Boggart Hole Clough, which, apart from its natural attractions, was celebrated as the scene of one of Mrs Pankhurst's early triumphs, in 1896, when she conspicuously lent her support to the stand of the ILP against the City Council's ban on public speaking in the Clough. Harry regaled us all with the stories, passed down in his family, of how Mrs Pankhurst had used her parasol, upended, to collect money for the socialist cause: 'It was quite a smart new parasol, too,' he said, 'not at all the big black brolly of socialism. And she had a very smart pink straw bonnet, a real bobby-dazzler, which caused a bit of a stir, you can imagine, among the Socialist sober-sides, especially since the meeting took place on a Sunday. There was some dour muttering about unseemly frivolity, but that soon enough died down when Mother began to speak. Nobody who'd listened to Mother for five minutes could ever think of her as frivolous again. There's a family story of an old chap saying, "To hear that one speak, you wouldna think she woz wearing a pink bonnet an' all."'

The rest of the company professed themselves delighted with this story, but as a somewhat reticent admirer of the Pankhurst charisma, I was aware mainly of what seemed to me Harry's exaggerated respect, bordering on awe, for his mother. It was my slightly exasperated impression that whatever he did was with an eye to pleasing her, or at any rate to not displeasing her. Even while he was evidently enjoying every minute of the outing, he was anxious that we should not prolong our picnic too much, lest he be missed at the office.

There had been some jokes about the perils of picnicking in a spot with a resident boggart, and one of the girls suggested exploring to find the Boggart Hole itself. Normally, this was just the kind of slightly far-fetched activity that would have appealed to Harry, but he said, 'Mother will be wondering where we are.'

I thought, but refrained from saying, that Mrs Pankhurst surely had more urgent matters to consider than her son's absence on a picnic. I did, however, say, 'I should think she could assume you're safe from the boggart, with six suffragettes to look after you.' He looked so hurt that I regretted my tartness immediately, but I was myself too young and awkward to make amends, and the outing ended in a rather uncomfortable silence between us. We came back earlier than we wanted, and of course without Mrs Pankhurst's even noticing; the saddest part of Harry's efforts to ingratiate himself with her was that she seemed quite indifferent to them. Whereas I was sorry for him, I was also impatient with him for not having a stronger sense of his own person. He made himself so small in her presence that it was no wonder, perhaps, that she could so easily disregard him.

But this was a minor distraction from what was, somewhat to my surprise, and even to the disappointment of my earnest wish to engage in 'something serious', a distinctly merry, not to say frivolous, time. My disappointment, such as it was, yielded soon enough to the sheer energy of the mostly young women gathered in Manchester. We were there to make life difficult for Churchill by heckling and creating disturbances, and by canvassing votes for 'anyone but Churchill'; the most constructive thing we did was to paint and unfurl banners, and write on pavements. We had a simple message: *Votes For Women*, and we repeated it endlessly. My main task was to ring the bell to summon audiences to our meetings and to sell suffragette postcards, neither of which was a particularly strenuous occupation, especially since Harry was usually in attendance to help me.

In short, I discovered that I was having fun. The WSPU had recently been purged of dissident members like Teresa Billington-Greig and Charlotte Despard, and Mrs Pankhurst and Christabel had installed themselves with the Pethick Lawrences as the leaders of what they ran as a military-style operation, demanding absolute compliance from all its members. Whereas this made for a certain grimness at meetings, it also made for much merriment after-hours, when the leaders were asleep or otherwise occupied. We tended to congregate noisily and joyfully in Lockhart's café late at night for coffee and cakes. There were, of course, never any disrespectful references to Mrs Pankhurst; but late at night there might be a tang of irony in somebody's saying 'We must to bed, I suppose, and prepare for the new day's battles' – *battles* being what Mrs Pankhurst liked to style our fracas, in the military parlance much affected by her and Christabel. And in the hilarity of our late-night sessions there was something anarchic, putting into question – in spirit if not in conscious intent – the rigid discipline of the campaign as it was being waged.

It was at these late-night gatherings that Harry most came into his own – with neither his mother nor his sisters present to overshadow him, his natural high spirits, stimulated by the women's teasing, asserted themselves: flushed with pleasure and the heat of the café, laughing his merry laugh, he seemed as free of care as any nineteen-year-old boy. I felt, then, that that was what he might have been, had he not been born to a destiny of being the only man in a militantly feminist family.

I got to know neither Mrs Pankhurst nor Sylvia during this time. I didn't expect them to notice a nineteen-year-old novice from Brighton: they were much in demand to make appearances, along with Christabel, leading groups of women heckling candidates, and generally, as Mrs Pankhurst declared, not without satisfaction, 'making a nuisance of ourselves'. I was content with my own obscurity: basking in the favour of the Pankhursts seemed altogether too strenuous a distinction, and I found my pleasure in immersing myself in the day-to-day running of the campaign. One couldn't help being impressed, hearing Mrs Pankhurst and Christabel speak: in their different styles, both were irresistibly eloquent, with an uncanny instinct for an audience. For myself, though, that was where I preferred to see them: on a platform, addressing a crowd, rather than at close quarters addressing me. I did not openly express this view, which would have been received as heresy in some quarters, it being generally assumed that proximity to Mrs Pankhurst was the closest approach to beatitude this side of heaven – an assumption she graciously permitted if not encouraged.

The by-election was a victory for the WSPU, in the negative sense in which we counted victories in those days: we contributed to Winston Churchill's defeat. There was much rejoicing, and in the hubbub of departure and leave-taking, having some last-minute chores to complete, I lost sight of Harry, who was in constant requisition to transport departing suffragettes to the station. But emerging from my hotel, thinking to take a cab if necessary, I found the four-in-hand waiting, filled with impatient suffragettes, and the box seat as always reserved for me.

'Thank you,' I said, as Harry helped me onto the seat, 'but you shouldn't have waited. Some of the women may lose their trains.'

He shook the reins with extra emphasis, 'Oh, I'll get everybody there in time,' he said, with a confidence in his own abilities that was touching; he so rarely made any claims for himself.

At the station he helped me down from the seat. I held out my hand to him and said, 'I hope we can work together again.'

I was sincere enough in this: Harry had been a pleasant if at times slightly tiring companion, and his lightness of touch had helped to dilute the sometimes over-fervent conversation of the suffragettes. I couldn't deny, either, that I'd found his warmth towards me appealing, its youthful ardour carrying with it intimations of a world of adult passions that I had yet to explore. Still, I didn't mean very much more than politeness by my commonplace, and I was thus disconcerted when he responded as if I'd made a most significant declaration. He blushed, and stammered something about my being 'most kind'. He pressed my hand in his and said, 'I would like that more than anything.'

I found his fervour difficult to deal with under the some-what sardonic gaze of six suffragettes, and I tried to make light of it in the scramble for trains and seats. My last view of him was on the platform of London Road Station, waving slowly at the departing train. He remained standing there till I lost sight of him.

Returning to Roedean, I confess that Harry rather slipped my mind. Having recently started teaching there, I was preoccu-pied with my new duties and with the multifarious demands of a group of young girls. I did fancy I saw him once, on a Sunday, when I took a group of girls to church: he was stand-ing at a distance looking as if he wanted to speak to me, but I could hardly abandon my crocodile to speak to what my charges would certainly have bruited abroad as 'a strange man'. In any case, I wasn't sure that it was Harry, and I didn't bother my head about it. Manchester was behind us, and I was at an age when every day seemed to bring new opportunities. I was just then much vexed with trying to decide whether to carry on teaching, or to join the WSPU in a permanent capacity. My parents were strongly opposed to the latter course, and I was reluctant to hurt them, but also determined to make my life as I saw it. In the turmoil of making my decision and then implementing it by joining the WSPU in Manchester, I didn't really spare Harry a thought.

So when Annie Kenney – then Union organiser in the West Country but apparently also a general messenger for the Pankhursts – searched me out in November of the following year to inform me that Sylvia wanted to see me, I was as much intimidated as intrigued. True, Sylvia was reputed to be more approachable than her mother or sister, but still, she was a Pankhurst, and I could only assume that she wanted to speak to me in some official capacity. Indeed, there was really no other capacity in which we could have anything to say to each other. Since I was in Manchester and she was working in the

East End of London, I thought she might have some question about our work amongst the factory girls.

'But why on earth?' I asked Annie. For answer she rummaged in her large and overfull handbag and brought out a letter, visibly scuffed from its journey in that reticule. Annie's bag had clearly seen more than its share of service.

'I'm sure it's all in there,' she said with the air of a messenger whose task it was not to reason why.

I opened the letter. It was headed *45 Park Walk, Chelsea, London SW*, and it was, for a Pankhurst, almost abject: *I must ask you, with sincere apologies for the imposition, to come to London as soon as you possibly can, to this address. I must also ask you to take my word for the extreme urgency of this request. When you do come, you will understand why it has not been possible for me to travel to Manchester to see you personally, and why it is necessary for you to be in London. Yours beseechingly, Sylvia Pankhurst.*

I went, of course. To be honest, in spite of my resistance to the Pankhurst charisma, there was something flattering for me, as a novice member of the WSPU, in receiving such a request from Sylvia Pankhurst; and then, it was but natural to be curious.

Having left Manchester very early in the morning, I arrived exhausted and hungry at Sylvia's lodgings in Park Walk in Chelsea. I hoped she would offer me at least a cup of tea, but she was evidently preoccupied with what she wanted to ask me; I was yet to learn that food and drink were mere incidentals to Sylvia, necessary, of course, in the long run, but very low on her list of priorities. So I stood on her doorstep cold, hungry, thirsty and nervous.

Her manner was not calculated to reassure. Indeed, I don't think her manner was calculated to achieve any effect whatsoever: it was as plain and unadorned as her person. She was not unfriendly, but she had no charm: one felt that she would have regarded charm as a form of frivolity or even dishonesty, the kind of thing 'society ladies' went in for. I appreciated this as indicative of the seriousness of her dedication, but I couldn't help feeling that a warmer manner might have helped to put me at my ease without any loss of purpose or sincerity.

It was a cold November day, and I would have welcomed an opportunity to warm my hands at her gas fire, but she seemed reluctant to receive me in her admittedly cramped lodgings – I think Annie was staying with her at the time – and suggested a walk on the Embankment. Her manner didn't invite alternative suggestions, and I agreed with such good grace as I could muster, though I was now probably even more nervous than before.

An advantage of Sylvia's abrupt manner was that I didn't have to wait long to learn the nature of her business. It came almost as a shock when she mentioned Harry: it required an effort of the imagination to connect the delicate, light-hearted boy with this heavy-featured, intense woman. And then, to be told that he was dying – it seemed inconceivable, and for a moment, standing in the thin sunshine on the Embankment, looking into Sylvia's tragic countenance, I wanted to say, 'But no, you can't be talking about the Harry I knew, there must be some mistake.'

I'd hardly had time to come to terms with the fact of Harry's illness, when she confronted me with her strange request: that I should in effect consent to watch Harry die; not only that, but I should pretend to respond to the love that he claimed to feel for me: 'Think of him as your young brother,' she pleaded, 'if you cannot love him in any other capacity. Tell him you love him; he has only three weeks to live.'

I stood gaping at Sylvia. My first impulse, surely a natural one, was to refuse point-blank, from sheer terror: how could I willingly undertake to watch a young man in mortal agony drift into death, and keep up a pretence all the while of returning a love that could be no more than a youthful fancy on his part, intensified, no doubt, by suffering?

But Sylvia was not someone to whom one could lightly

refuse anything: though visibly doing her best to leave me free to make my own decision, there was such urgency, such suppressed despair, in her manner, that it overpowered the dictates of mere common sense. Her rather dry manner – she was manifestly making an effort not to be emotional – added a poignancy to her appeal, which, for me, a more overtly sentimental approach would have forfeited.

Still, it was an immense thing to ask of anybody. I stood for a while, irresolutely watching the activity on the river. I remember seeing a bargeman feed his dog and wondering why bargemen kept dogs; in its very irrelevance the thought seemed to offer me a respite from responding to Sylvia's request. I was in fact not conscious of taking a decision; I turned my face from the little tableau on the barge to Sylvia's imploring face, and started speaking without being sure what I would end up saying. 'I remember Harry with great pleasure,' I said; this seemed a safe enough opening to whatever outcome was to follow. 'He was such a bright and smiling boy.'

Something in Sylvia's face, a small grimace, suggested that she did not like this description of her brother. 'I'm sorry,' I said, 'but I do think of him of as a boy.'

'I know,' she said feelingly; she was not, after all put out by my description. 'He does seem very young. He has been made to suffer more than any young person should ever suffer.' For the first time she got tears in her eyes, and my sympathy hardened into something more resistant. I've never responded well to other people's tears, and Sylvia was known to shed them prodigally.

And yet, how does one refuse such an appeal? Partly I was angry with Sylvia for facing me with the choice, but I suppose that somewhere, too, I was beguiled with my unexpected eminence: here was something that only I could do, that Sylvia Pankhurst had to beg me to do. I think poor Harry himself was not very present to me at that moment: I was more taken

238

with an image of myself nobly attending a death-bed, one of those angelic Dickensian presences, presiding over the death of others.

So I stood there on the Embankment, stupidly turning over this welter of considerations. In the end, I may have said yes because I found it impossible to say no. I heard myself say, 'Yes, and if you really think my presence would make more bearable his' – I hesitated, not wanting to call the ugly fact by its name – 'his last days ...'

I stopped again, and as if to encourage me she said, 'I am convinced of it.'

'Then I shall undertake as best I can to help him.'

Sylvia took my hand and pressed it to her cheek; I found myself moved by the gesture, so at odds with her brusque manner heretofore.

'I think you will not regret it,' she said. 'Come, let us go and see Harry.'

As we turned, I cast a last glance at the barge. It had hardly moved; the dog was still eating its supper.

III

*I*find I'm sitting at the breakfast table, my tea cold, the *Manchester Guardian* open before me. Watson is lingering, wanting to remove the breakfast things. I gesture to him to go ahead. Suddenly, I feel chilly, though there is a pool of sunshine on the carpet next to me. I go in search of Fred, and find him in his study, reading a book; he has not misplaced his reading glasses after all. He looks very serene, sitting there surrounded by the beautiful things he's salvaged from a life of collecting and dispersing. A lamp with an amber Murano shade casts a warm light on his book.

'There was something I wanted to ask you,' I say.

He looks up and gives me his mild smile. 'I am at your disposal.' He puts down his book, and I notice the title.

'You're reading *The Suffragette Movement.*'

'Just paging through it, refreshing my memory.'

'I remember it as very angry.'

He takes off his reading glasses. 'There is anger. But there's also love. Isn't it typical of Sylvia that she should call her book *The Suffragette Movement* and then subtitle it *An Intimate Account of Persons and Ideals?*'

'You mean the intimacy was more important than the movement?'

'Well, at least as important – and the persons as important as the ideals – a difficult balance to maintain. But what was it you wanted to ask me?' He pats the sofa and I sit down next to him.

In truth I did not really want to ask him a question; I just wanted to talk to him. So I say, 'Perhaps you've answered my question. I wanted to know what you *really* thought of Sylvia.'

Fred leans back on the sofa. For a moment I think he may drop off to sleep, as he nowadays not infrequently does. But he's thinking. Then he says, 'I don't know if anyone ever *really* knew what they thought of Sylvia, if by that you mean having a completely unambiguous opinion. Her worst enemies at times admired her, her best friends at times detested her.'

'You're evading my question. What was, then, your *dominant* feeling about Sylvia?'

'Oh. Awe. Admiration. Pity.'

'That's three. But why pity?'

'So much passion, so much dedication, so many causes, so little satisfaction.'

'I should think she died satisfied. In Ethiopia. With her son and daughter-in-law.'

'Yes, perhaps after all she was satisfied. But you asked me what I felt for Sylvia then, before Ethiopia.'

'True. And did you pity Emmeline and Christabel too?'

He glances at me; he knows that my question is not as neutral as I'm trying to make it sound. 'Heavens no, they demanded pity as little as they showed it.'

'I'm not sure I believe you. I think in your heart of hearts you found room even for pity for Emmeline and Christabel.' I take his hand in mine. 'Perhaps that was in the end what most infuriated Emmeline and Christabel – your gentleness.'

'Why should gentleness have infuriated them?'

'Consider.' I hold up my free hand, pedantically count off on my fingers: 'Pledged to militancy, intent upon provoking violence from men, their whole campaign based on the alleged crudity and belligerence of the male sex – they simply couldn't afford such an example of male forbearance at such close quarters.'

He presses my hand. 'That's too easy. They were not so crude as to see the enemy as merely belligerent. They reserved their special contempt for the men who tried to fob them off with gentle words.'

241

'Yes, quite, don't you see, it's as if they *wanted* men to be crude and violent, and were flummoxed when they were kind and gentle.' But I'm not really interested in Emmeline and Christabel; I return to what is now uppermost in my mind. 'How else explain Emmeline's treatment of Harry?'

He answers promptly, as if he, too, has been thinking about it. 'I've never been able to explain Emmeline's treatment of Harry.'

I consider this. 'The real mystery, though,' I say, 'is Harry's treatment of Emmeline.'

'He *treated* her?' he asks, not so much sceptical as puzzled.

'Yes. And Sylvia.'

'Sylvia treated …?'

'No. *Harry* treated. Sylvia. And Emmeline. Neither Emmeline nor Sylvia really *saw* Harry, if you know what I mean.'

He frowns. 'I'm not sure that I do.'

'Emmeline didn't want to see. And Sylvia saw what she wanted to see. Which was Harry as a victim of his mother's callousness. But Harry himself, as a live, essentially joyful young man, passed them by. And he knew it. And consented to it.'

He is listening gravely. 'You've never told me, really told me, the full story of that rather bizarre episode.'

'Do you really want me to?'

'Only if it won't give you pain.'

'Pain? No, not at this remove. Even at the time, it was not exactly painful. It was troubling, and sad, of course, but it was also, I don't know … dare I say *exciting*?'

'I can see how it might have been.'

'I don't know. It shouldn't have been. It should have been only painful and sad, and it was that, too, but, after all, I was only twenty-one at the time, and at that age everything comes to you as experience, something to save up for later, that will make you a more mature and worthwhile person. I know it sounds horribly calculating – yet it wasn't really in the least, at the time; but any intense experience – I suppose one cherished

242

it, even though it was painful, as evidence that one was growing up.'

He nods. 'I remember, the first time I saw a dead person – it was my grandmother, whom I had loved dearly – I remember feeling a sense of … accomplishment, almost. Does that sound ghoulish?'

'I don't think so, not at all, or not more so than what passes for perfectly normal human behaviour at most funerals. So if you ask me was it an utterly awful experience, I have to say no; in fact I have to say that, given a choice, I would not *not* have had it. But it was hard, too, in ways that I was too young to anticipate.'

'What ways?'

'Oh, so many.' I pause to think. 'But in the first place just Harry's *connectedness*. I suppose I'd imagined him as lying on his own in a darkened room waiting for me to appear. But of course he was surrounded by other people, some of whom certainly felt they had a prior claim to being there.'

'Family?'

'Yes, but not exclusively. You see, Harry was lying in Nurse Pine's nursing home – you remember Nurse Pine?'

'Of course. She nursed me back to health after my hunger strike.'

'She nursed us all. I remember thinking she looked very much like a warder.'

'I suppose their functions weren't that different – nurses and warders.'

I laugh. 'Yes, even to making one eat what one didn't want to eat.'

'And Nurse Pine?' Fred gently reminds me.

'Yes, Nurse Pine. You do know that Sylvia summoned me from Manchester to come to Harry's bedside?'

'Yes, that much I know. I knew it even at the time from discussions at Clement's Inn.'

'And having been summoned, I obeyed. Of course …'

Like many children of my class and time, I grew up having Dickens read to me. Quite what our elders hoped to achieve by subjecting their children to such a gallery of horrors, I don't know, but I remember the almost physical revulsion I felt from many of the characters my father evidently relished. Apart from the comic monsters leering forth from the interminable pages, what I remember most is the acute *embarrassment* Dickens was so good at conveying; can there be a more painful catalogue of embarrassments than *Great Expectations*? In particular, I remember the moment when poor Pip is bundled up and shaken out as Estella's new playmate, and Miss Havisham commands him: 'Play.'

Sylvia would have been mortified by the comparison, but something in the manner in which she brought me to Harry's bedside, and then stood back to observe our interaction, reminded me of Miss Havisham's 'Play.' She seemed to assume that we'd spontaneously establish some rapport, as if we were once again on the box seat of a four-in-hand rather than in a chamber of death. And I suppose that in the anxiety of persuading me, she'd not had leisure to reflect on how Harry would react to my sudden appearance at his bedside.

Harry's probable response, in fact, occurred to me as a question only when we walked into the room where he was lying. He may have been asleep; in any case, he did not hear us enter. He was lying with his eyes closed, and I was grateful to have a moment to register the change in him without his seeing me do so. He'd been such a lively boy, and now the boyish animation was quite gone from his face: there was a pale gravity about his features that suddenly made him seem like a man. The lines were more deeply drawn, the mouth more firmly set. He seemed resolute and ascetic: the effect, no doubt, of pain, or perhaps just of the unaccustomed immobility of his features. He was thinner, if possible, than he'd been, but somehow what there was of him counted for more.

Though very small, the sick-room was as cheerful as books

and flowers could make it, and it had a window facing onto a courtyard just large enough for one plane tree, now with only a few leaves in the late autumn sun. There was some contraption suspended from the ceiling – intended, I assumed, to help Harry draw himself up to a sitting position. The room was very hot. I learnt later that this was to enable Harry to do with as few bedcovers as possible, since heavy blankets caused him pain. He was not wearing a nightshirt. His bare arm, lying on top of the covers, was smooth and white; the veins showed blue under the pallor of the skin.

Sylvia went up to his bed and touched his hand gently. 'Harry,' she said, 'Helen is here.' She beckoned me closer to the bed with a small gesture of her head. He opened his eyes; I'd forgotten how deep a blue they were. He looked at me, a frown of concentration or puzzlement between his eyes, and for a moment I saw a flicker of sheer terror, even panic. He tried to raise himself on the pillow, but fell back.

'I'm … sorry,' he said, 'I can't seem to be able to get up.'

'Just lie back, Harry,' Sylvia said.

He lay back again obediently, his eyes fixed on my face, I couldn't help thinking, like a timid animal – a deer, a horse – uncertain of the intentions of an approaching human.

'Hello, Harry,' I said. 'I heard that you weren't well, and wanted to come and see you.'

A smile trembled on the pale lips. 'No, I'm not well,' he said. 'Thank you for coming.'

There was very little to be said after this. I could hardly announce that I'd come to share his last days with him, and yet I was so aware of this fact that I could think of nothing less momentous. I wished I'd brought something with me, a book or a bunch of flowers, to serve as a pretext for my presence. Sylvia for once showed some sensitivity to social awkwardness, and intimated that she wanted to go and introduce me to Nurse Pine.

'Will you come again?' Harry asked.

245

'Of course,' I said. 'I've come from Manchester on purpose to see you.'

I was then taken to meet Nurse Pine – whom I would later get to know well when she nursed me back to health after a bout of hunger-striking. But at the time, the practice had only recently been adopted and I hadn't yet been on hunger-strike myself. To me, then, she was just a rather grim-faced woman, part of this strange institution to which I'd so unexpectedly been committed for who knows how long.

When Sylvia introduced me to Nurse Pine as 'Harry's friend', she looked me up and down, visibly suppressed a sigh, and said, 'Well, I wouldn't want to stand in the way of anything Harry wanted.' She made no attempt to pretend to be pleased at my presence. She was not intent on accommodating Sylvia either, and Sylvia didn't seem to expect her to: it was altogether a transaction conducted in Harry's name.

'I don't know, miss,' she said, 'whether we can have a young lady sitting around all day.' She'd taken me to her little office, clearly with a mind to speaking frankly. 'Nursing's not something you can do with your pocket-handkerchief. There are things as need to be done that a young lady shouldn't be witness to, and as no young man would want his sweetheart to witness.'

'I am not Harry's sweetheart, and I am not a young lady,' I said, with perhaps unnecessary emphasis. 'I'm here because Harry wants me to be here, but I cannot imagine that he wants me to be a bedside ornament, too delicate to be subjected to the realities of a sick-bed.'

'I shouldn't think Harry's in a fit state to give much thought to what it means, your being here all the time,' she said. 'And I shouldn't wonder if you haven't given much thought to *the realities of a sick-bed* either.'

I found her assumption that I was a spoilt daughter of privilege rather provoking, but then reflected that from a certain perspective that was what I was. So I said merely, 'I've been present at sick-beds before. Indeed, I would have chosen nursing as a career had I not decided on teaching instead.'

But Nurse Pine was not to be mollified by such assurances. 'Eh,' she sniffed, 'I've seen many a young lady in my time taking a fancy to nursing after reading about Florence Nightingale and her lamp. They only last till they have to wipe their first bottom.'

I knew she was intent on shocking me, and I was determined not to be shocked. 'I think I can answer for my own fitness to undertake such menial tasks as will save the time of the qualified staff.'

She snorted rudely. 'We'll see about that. Easy to talk of menial tasks. It's a fancy term for shitting and pissing.' I must have registered some shock at this, for she visibly suppressed a smile of satisfaction and said, 'You'd better get used to calling a spade a shovel. Most of my nurses were in the Boer War, where they saw and heard soldiers when they felt no call to mind their language and couldn't be none too particular about where they did what either.'

'I've worked for the WSPU with women from all walks of life,' I said. 'I'm not squeamish as to language.'

She looked me up and down unabashedly; it was not an ill-humoured look, just a frank assessment. 'We'll see about that,' she said again, but perhaps with a slight tempering of her tone. 'And as to Harry, you're not likely to hear a word out of him that's not perfectly proper. But there's a deal as he can't do for himself, and that he may not want you to do for him if he has any notions about you.'

'I'm here to be useful,' I said rather primly, 'and I should think Harry would want me to be useful.'

I had, I suppose, rather an exalted view of my own unselfishness in coming to Harry's bedside. I thus thought it highly unfair that I should be treated as if I had insisted, against all dictates of common sense and decency, to obtrude my presence on Harry like some hospital-haunting ghoul. Nurse Pine seemed to see only inconvenience in my presence.

'I suppose you'll be wanting somewhere to sleep,' she muttered.

'Why yes, I'm afraid so,' I replied, 'unless I'm to sleep sitting upright.'

She gave me a look that was clearly intended to be withering, and conferred with her deputy, a boot-faced young woman called Nurse Bromley, about 'what we're to do with the young lady'.

It transpired that there was, after all, no problem. One of the junior nurses had just left, and a small garret was available. Nurse Pine seemed almost disappointed when this was pointed out to her, and grudgingly allocated it to me 'for as long as we don't need it for a real nurse'.

I had no very clear notion of what was expected of me. I could hardly stay by Harry's bed twenty-four hours a day, and yet I had nowhere else to go. In the end I drew up an informal schedule for myself, so that I could be in attendance when there was likely to be no one else around, especially in the long afternoons and in the evenings until he went to sleep.

I was, I discovered, in the invidious position of a sick-visitor who wouldn't go home. The nurses bustled around me conspicuously, every rattle of a pan or clinking of a bottle intended to signal to me my own superfluity. This determined me to earn my keep, such as it was. The little nursing home was not abundantly staffed, and I resolved not to sit by and make some other woman perform functions that I was perfectly capable of performing.

But I had not foreseen, perhaps, exactly what this meant, in the case of a sick man paralysed from the waist down. Caring for the body in extremity, I soon learnt, entailed much more than wiping a feverish brow with a damp cloth or reading uplifting passages aloud to a dumbly appreciative patient.

Initially there was considerable awkwardness. There was in the first place the extreme artificiality of our situation: virtual strangers to each other, Harry and I were now confined in close

248

proximity in a room the size of a large kennel. In Manchester we had had the day-to-day business of the by-election to talk about; here we had to cast about for subjects, which, I soon found, can be hard to come by in a sick-room. The most salient subject – the sick person and his sickness – is not one that a tactful visitor would dwell on, and yet it's difficult to ignore. And then there was the simple physical fact of Harry's body, covered only with a sheet: impossible not to trace its lineaments, not to catch sight of an exposed flank, not to smell its warm rankness.

Fortunately there were many books by his bedside that Sylvia had brought, and Harry, whose eyesight was weak, enjoyed being read to. He was just then making his way through Jane Austen, who was also a favourite of mine. So I would sit by his bed for hours, reading to him, or talking about the book we were reading, or just sitting while he drifted off into a light doze.

At times I would notice that he was uncomfortable with something other than the usual pain. 'Would you mind calling a nurse?' became the tacitly agreed upon signal that I should absent myself. We both knew, though, that a nurse was not always immediately available, and when she was, I sensed that she resented being summoned by me to perform a function that I was, in her eyes, perfectly capable of performing myself. Nurse Bromley, in particular, one of the Boer War veterans, made no secret of her opinion that I was at best useless, at worst an encumbrance. Once, when I called her to Harry's bed, she said, 'I should think it would take as much of an effort to see to Harry yourself as to summon me.'

A certain obstinacy prevented me from explaining to her what she wouldn't have wanted to understand, that it was not a matter of squeamishness on my part or even shyness on Harry's: we were both considering the other. I assumed that Harry couldn't have wished for the woman he idealised to share in the squalid intimacy of the sick-bed, and he must have assumed that I would shrink from such realities.

In this respect, the pain that Harry suffered was fortunate – brutal as it sounds when put like that. It helped, in time, to remove the awkwardness, and to make social inhibitions seem pointless. Suffering such as Harry's brings emotions to the surface that might otherwise have been covered up decorously, and makes reticence seem trivial. It's natural to take the hand of a person in pain; it's natural to wipe his brow. And once one is comfortable with physical contact, the body loses something of the strangeness it had for young people of our generation. I would nevertheless still have refrained from proposing anything that might have embarrassed Harry; but in this he finally took the initiative.

'It's not something I would ask anybody else to do for me if I could do it myself,' he said, 'and it's not something I would willingly ever ask of you. But if you can face it, I can bear it.'

'I can face anything, I think,' I replied, though in truth not quite sure what it was that I was committing myself to. Harry, though, having become accustomed to having other people perform the most intimate of functions for him, was far less embarrassed than I, except on my account; and as with time I acquired something of his insouciance, it became progressively easier to perform those menial tasks I had so confidently mentioned to Nurse Pine.

In the course of these tasks, of course, I needed to touch him; and, my hands being cold on his feverish body, I noticed his bare skin quivering to my touch. 'I'm sorry,' I said, 'I know my hands are cold.'

'They are cold,' he said, 'but I'm not shivering because of that. I wish you could touch me forever.'

I was too taken aback by his sudden boldness to reply, and fortunately the business of tending to him covered up my confusion. There was in any case much of this business that militated against a romantic or erotic view of our situation. The exigencies of a sick-bed remain physically repellent even after one has made up one's mind to them. I sometimes had to

clench my teeth, even shut my eyes and my nose, and persevere. I could never emulate Nurse Bromley's enthusiasm in
seizing a bedpan, as if she were disciplining a recalcitrant animal, but I think I managed not to recoil visibly. Harry never
realised, I hope, with what mixed feelings I handled his body:
on the one hand so beautiful in its pale fragility, its planes and
concavities and cusps, its transparencies and its opacities; and
then again, what a centre of putrefaction and excretion, what a
seat of pain and distress, what a burden of mortality.

However much my presence by his bedside made Harry's situation more bearable to him, about the pain I could do little.
Indeed, as Nurse Pine informed me with a grim pursing of her
lips, my presence was complicating such relief as was available.

'You don't want to be giving Harry notions about keeping a
stiff upper lip and such nonsense, do you?' she said to me one
morning in the kitchen, where I was preparing Harry's tea.

I had no idea what she meant, and said so. 'It's just,' she
said, 'that Doctor Mills says as he's come up with some nonsense about not wanting the injections for pain because he
reckons it's unmanly. Doctor thinks it's because Harry doesn't
want you to think he's a weakling as can't stand no pain.'

'I really can't believe that my presence would have that
effect on him,' I protested.

'That's as it may be,' she retorted, 'but what you believe
and what Harry believes may be two different things. He's
always been a bit sensitive about that, you know, about being
a man. Funny, when you think about it, surrounded as he is
by all them strong women, that he should think being a man's
the most important thing on earth. Still, that's what he does
think, and your being here makes him think it all the more.
You can give an impression, you know, without knowing
you're doing it.'

It seemed unfair that I should be blamed for unintentionally
transmitting an impression to Harry. 'I'm afraid I don't see
how I can not do something that I don't know I'm doing.'

251

'Well you could be doing something that you're not doing to get him to have his injections.'

'What did you have in mind?'

'No, I don't have nothing in mind,' she said, banging a teapot on the kitchen table with unnecessary emphasis. 'All I'm saying is if you're going to hang around sick-beds you want to give some thought to what it means, being there. A sick person has a relationship with his doctor and nurses as he doesn't have with other people, and you don't want to get in the way of that. For you – for you, Harry is the Harry you knew out there, and you want to treat him the same as you did then; but for us – I'm not saying we don't love him, 'cause we do – but for us to do our jobs we have to see him as a sick person, a body we have to look after.'

'Are you saying I'm too personally involved with Harry?'

'I'm saying Harry's too personally involved with you. For you he wants to be well; for us he accepts that he's sick.'

On this, she bustled off, leaving me to make what I could of her inconclusive advice. I could see, on reflection, that what she was saying was perfectly sensible: for a healthy person to be of any use around a sick-bed, it's necessary first to accept that it is a sick-bed. And yet: if Harry really believed that he was recovering, was it kind to suggest otherwise by urging drugs upon him?

For me, the question was decided simply through witnessing Harry's suffering in his attempt to conquer his pain. Though he all too evidently wanted not to appear weak in front of me, his body refused to take its orders from his mind; pain convulsed his light frame and distorted his features beyond anything his will could control. Almost worse to witness than the physical agony, though, was Harry's distress at not being able to hide his suffering from me.

'I don't know why I'm being such a mardy baby today,' he said, as he tried to wipe his eyes surreptitiously.

'You shouldn't say that,' I said, 'for my sake.'

252

He looked at me in incomprehension, his eyes clouded with pain. 'Why for your sake?' he asked.

'Why, don't you see what it makes me out to be, if you feel you have to hide your pain from me?'

'No, I don't. What?'

'Some kind of sadistic gym mistress who wants to test your endurance. Wouldn't you rather feel that you can confide your pain in me, and share it with me?'

'I don't know. It doesn't seem right, somehow, to burden you with my weakness.'

'Oh, pish!' I snorted. 'It's not weakness, and it's not a burden. I don't know where you got this notion that you have to prove yourself by enduring pain.' In my indignation I became didactic. 'There's no virtue in suffering, Harry. It's an evil visited upon us by an unjust universe, and we must fight it with all the means at our disposal.'

'Mother says we're made strong through suffering.'

'Balderdash!' I said, my anger getting the better of my discretion. 'That's the philosophy of zealots and flagellants!' Then, seeing his shocked expression, I tried to qualify the force of my words. 'No doubt, when one has no choice, it's admirable to submit to such pain as one cannot avoid. But needless pain must be alleviated for the sake of one's soul as much as one's body.'

As much to calm myself as him, I took his hand in mine; it was wet with perspiration. 'And I don't want to feel that you're lying here in agony because I'm here. I'd far rather enjoy our conversation when I'm not sharing you with the pain.'

'You think, then, I should have the injections,' he said.

'I really do, Harry.'

'For your sake.'

'For my sake.'

It seemed Harry was incapable of doing anything, even of alleviating his own pain, for his own sake. And I was prepared to act the demanding woman if he needed a demanding woman to get him to have the injections. After that, Harry submitted to the injections, which made the pain tolerable, at least.

During this early period Sylvia and I had kept a polite distance, alternating our times by Harry's bed rather than sharing the watch. But though she had in fact asked me to come to Harry's bedside, I felt that she secretly didn't want me there – secretly even to herself. Her conscious mind and her moral nature told her that Harry wanted me there and that therefore my being there was a blessing; but somewhere in her something cried out against Harry's wanting me there. And not being able to resent Harry for this, she resented me.

Not that she was ever anything but civil to me. It was, indeed, in her very politeness that I sensed an effort; for Sylvia was not by nature polite. She was as natural as a door slamming in a high wind. But the considerateness with which she deferred to my presence, remaining in the background for the first few days, no doubt feeling that we'd be more comfortable on our own, testified both to her unselfishness and to the effort with which she was negotiating the loss of her own place by Harry's bed. In some ways, I caught myself thinking, simple selfishness would have been easier to deal with.

As Harry responded to my presence, though, becoming more cheerful and hopeful by the day, Sylvia took to spending more time at his bedside. We gradually established a routine whereby she and I took turns to sit with Harry on our own, and the three of us spent some time together for a while each day. Through these conversations I came to know something of Sylvia other than the tireless campaigner that the world knew, the obstinate, belligerent fighter against all injustice. She brought books to show Harry and me, books on Venice in particular, where she'd spent what seemed to have been an enchanted period, drawing, painting, making music with her landlady, Madame Sophie, a Polish countess. It was impossible not to notice how the plain face lit up as she recalled the days of wandering the alleys and canals of Venice, searching for subjects and finding them everywhere. She showed us some of her works, luminous watercolours of fruit sellers, a charming sketch of a boy in a black cape and red hat, a study of a young woman of the people intent on her labour of decorating pottery; only in the last of these was there a hint of the later work that she did in the slums and prisons of London, aimed not so much at pleasing the viewer as educating him in the lives of others.

'It's almost, I don't know, *wrong*,' she said, 'to have a city where even the most squalid parts are beautiful.'

'Why wrong?' I asked, in truth slightly irritated with such high-minded perversity. To my mind, beauty was rare enough; one should enjoy it when one could.

'I mean,' she said, 'that the beauty becomes a distraction from the poverty and the misery that coexist with it – that may even be caused by the same conditions as created the beauty.'

I was silent, still impatient with the solemnity of this, but Harry laughed. 'Dear Sylvia,' he said, 'you never will accept that beauty is a worthwhile thing for its own sake.'

She looked hurt; Sylvia was not good at being laughed at, perhaps because she herself would never have laughed at anybody. 'I don't think that's fair, Harry,' she said. 'I'm sure in an ideal society I could enjoy beauty as one of the blessings of justice and peace. But in a society as imperfect as ours, beauty is almost never created for its own sake: it's either a child of privilege or a servant of duty.'

My exasperation with her joyless philosophy turned to pity, seeing her there with the sketchbook on her lap, for once not fired with the vision of reform or the zeal of self-sacrifice, simply staring wistfully at an alternative vision that she was precluded from sharing, and not even allowing herself regret at her own renunciation.

'You shall go back with us,' cried Harry, evidently moved by Sylvia's recollection, 'all three of us will go to Venice when ...

when I've recovered, and you shall show us all the places you loved.'

'Of course I will,' she said, and for a moment she allowed herself to believe the impossible. 'There's so much I could show you. And I can introduce you – both of you – to Madame Sophie.'

I couldn't help wondering, at this time, at Mrs Pankhurst's absence, and neither Sylvia nor Harry offered an explanation. It was well known, of course, that she was touring America, and evidently taking it by storm. The tone in which her triumphant progress was reported in the feminist press suggested that it was the greatest thing since Christ's entry into Jerusalem, and I could see that political considerations might have weighed more heavily with Mrs Pankhurst than maternal concern; but it was difficult to look at Harry's blanched face and relentlessly wasting form without feeling awe bordering on horror at such consistency on the part of the mother.

A frequent visitor at this time was Keir Hardie, whom I knew and admired as a Labour MP. His presence brought a bracing blast of maleness into the sick-room, and his bluff manner was a welcome relief from Nurse Pine's dour presence and Sylvia's grief-fraught demeanour. Both Sylvia and Harry clearly adored Mr Hardie – and he, in his different way, both of them. He was too serious a man to be jocular, but he was too vital to be solemn; he gently teased Harry and could make even Sylvia laugh. It struck me, though, that Sylvia was nervous in their presence, and seemed reluctant to leave Keir Hardie alone with Harry. I didn't give it much thought at the time, but it was to return to me later, as Harry took me into his confidence.

Did any of us really believe that Harry would recover? Or did we all pretend for one another's sake? I could see from Nurse Pine and Dr Mills's behaviour that they didn't think Harry would recover: it's intangible but real, the difference between a nurse who expects a patient to get well, and one who's simply doing what she can to ease his going. So I held out no hope for his recovery, but I pretended along with Harry and Sylvia – for whose sake, I was not quite sure.

And Sylvia? What did she think? I can't believe that she truly thought Harry might recover, and yet she, too, formed part of the conspiracy, for Harry's sake. So that left Harry, the dupe of Sylvia's and my good intentions.

Or so I thought. But one afternoon I was sitting with him, when the pain was particularly bad. I was trying to help him to sit up to have a cup of tea, when suddenly he said, 'You know, on that smallholding where I was working …'

'Yes?' I said; he had returned more than once to the terrible conditions on the so-called co-operative to which Mrs Pankhurst had sent him.

'The saddest thing was the animals. They quite often died of neglect, for all that I … anyone tried to do for them.'

'Yes, Harry,' I said, not knowing why he was dwelling on the subject.

'You know,' he said, 'I've been thinking that with a dying animal nobody ever pretends to think that the animal isn't dying. All you can do is make the end as easy as possible.'

'Yes, Harry,' I said, still mystified as to his meaning.

'But with human beings the people remaining behind often need to think that they're fooling the dying person by pretending. They can't accept that he may know that he's dying.'

I waited for him to carry on, but he didn't; he seemed to be waiting for a response from me. I took a deep breath and said, 'Are you talking about yourself, Harry?'

He didn't answer immediately. Then he turned towards me with difficulty, looked into my face and asked, 'You don't really think that I'll get well, do you?' When I hesitated, he laughed, more a breathless gasp than a laugh. 'I'm sorry, that's not fair. What I mean is that I know I won't get well, and you needn't pretend otherwise.'

257

'How can you be so sure?'

He moved his shoulders in an attempt at a shrug. 'If I'm not sure, who can be? It's my body, and I can feel it breaking down every day.'

'Then why ... why don't you say so to Sylvia?'

'She needs to think that I think I'll get well. She needs to think that she has given me the will to live.'

'And don't you? I mean, have the will to live?'

'Of course I do, and now more so than ever, now that you are here. I'm not pretending that part, you know,' he added shyly. 'Of course I have the will to live, if will to live means wanting not to die. If I could, I would get well, and we would go to Venice, and we would take Sylvia along to show us her favourite places. So that part I'm not pretending. But as for believing that there's any chance of its happening – that part I have to pretend.'

I looked at him in amazement. 'Then why do you pretend?'

'I'm telling you. Because it makes Sylvia happy to think that I'm happy, and she thinks I can only be happy if I believe that I'll get well. And it even makes her happy to pretend that she'll be able to go back to Venice without feeling guilty about it.'

'So we're all pretending to one another?'

'Yes. Or we have all been pretending. From now on, you and I needn't pretend to each other.'

'But you have to pretend to Sylvia ...'

'That I think I'll get well, yes.' He considered this for a moment. 'And she pretends to me that she thinks I'll get well. And you have to pretend to Sylvia ...'

'That I think you think you'll get well.'

We looked at each other, both trying to swallow an appalled giggle; but catching each other's eye, we broke into fits of help-less hilarity, which I tried to stifle, for I knew what agony it was for Harry to laugh. That was how Sylvia found us; when she entered we tried to suppress our laughter and succeeded only in looking guilty, and as neither Harry nor I could think up a reason for our laughter quickly enough, Sylvia looked hurt in a way I thought of as uniquely Sylvia: a hurt not so much on her own account as on yours, a disappointment of her habitual high expectations of all humanity.

'I'm pleased,' she nevertheless said to Harry, 'that you seem so much better. It's good to hear you laugh.' I could see that she was displeased; she knew as well as I that laughter caused Harry pain.

'That's Helen,' he said, 'she makes me laugh.'

Sylvia was too unselfish to begrudge Harry anything that amused him, but in her quick glance at me I read an implication that my levity was irresponsible. 'I've come to tell you, dear,' she said to Harry, 'that Mother's back from America.'

This served very effectively to dampen our hilarity. Harry and I had never discussed Mrs Pankhurst or her return, but I'd sensed a certain trepidation in his very avoidance of the subject. As for me, I couldn't imagine that she would be pleased to find me by her son's bedside. I'd gathered from Sylvia that she'd not been informed of my arrival, indeed of my existence, and I was somewhat at a loss as to how I would account for my presence.

'Will she be coming here?' Harry asked, in a tone of apprehension rather than expectation. He suddenly seemed cowed, smaller somehow, and yet excited too, but in a fretful way. A muscle twitched next to his mouth.

'Yes,' said Sylvia, 'in due course. I've not seen her myself, but I believe there are to be receptions and photographs and interviews. The Union naturally wants to get as much publicity as possible from Mother's excursion.'

'Then when ...?' asked Harry.

'That I cannot tell you.' Her manner was more abrupt that I'd ever seen it in her relations with Harry. 'Nobody is prepared to risk a prediction. I asked Christabel, and she seemed to regard the enquiry as impertinent. She said the whole point of Mother's going to America was to raise awareness in this country. I said that I was pleased to have the point of Mother's going to America explained to me.'

Sylvia's constrained manner, then, was not a response to Harry's and my levity, but an after-effect of this interchange with Christabel. 'I shall not be able to wait here for Mother to arrive,' she continued. 'I have a meeting in the East End to address.'

'Would you like me to stay here with Harry until Mrs Pankhurst arrives?' I suggested.

'I don't know,' she said. 'Mrs Pankhurst does not require a welcoming committee here, I suppose.'

I could feel myself flushing with annoyance, but told myself that the barb was directed not at me but at the absent Mrs Pankhurst. Harry, as ever distressed at any sign of discord, said, 'It would help me if Helen were here when Mother comes.'

'*If* Mother comes,' Sylvia said, still not mollified. 'She may be very late and not want to wake you up.' Seeing Harry's anxious regard, she visibly relented, stroked his hand gently, and said, 'But of course, dear, if it would be of comfort to you, and if Helen really does not mind ...'

I, on my part, had no great desire to face Mrs Pankhurst, should she indeed arrive that evening. But Harry was clearly agitated at the prospect of his mother's arrival, and I spent the evening with him, reading and talking. We were reading *Emma* together, which he enjoyed greatly; the thought crossed my mind that strong-minded, managing women could never before have presented themselves to him as subjects of comedy. At nine o'clock he was given his injection for pain, and he drifted into a light slumber. He was restless, clearly still in pain despite the injection, and I sat as still as possible, trying, by the dim light of the bedside lamp, to engross myself in Jane Austen.

I may have dropped off, because I'd not heard footsteps approaching. I looked up from my book, sensing another presence in the room, and there in the door stood Mrs Pankhurst.

I got to my feet and extended my hand. I remember thinking how small she was, when one saw her face to face. And yet I felt intimidated by the clear gaze from those violet blue eyes, bright with the cold night air she had brought in with her. Her silence, too, was daunting. 'Mrs Pankhurst?' I said, with such assurance as I could muster. 'You may not remember me. I am Helen Craggs.'

She seemed not to absorb this information, indeed to be quite indifferent to it. She came towards me, though ignoring my extended hand. 'How is my son?' she asked, but I had the odd impression that she was avoiding looking at Harry. One glance, perhaps, but I thought she was almost relieved to be able to look at me rather than her son.

That voice, low and thrilling, which she could project over vast audiences, was surprisingly soft at close quarters. I looked at Harry to see if he was awake, but his head remained turned away in sleep.

'He suffers much,' I said in an undertone, 'but he is very cheerful and hopeful.'

'Hopeful – of recovery?'

'Yes,' I said, though of course I knew he was not, and suddenly I felt tears in my eyes; it was as if the untruth brought home the sad truth to me more sharply than anything else had yet done. I was annoyed with myself; I wasn't normally inclined to tears, and in front of Mrs Pankhurst of all people I did not want to appear weak.

Mrs Pankhurst looked at me sceptically, as if unconvinced either by my words or my tears. Then, without a word, she beckoned to me to follow her. I was reluctant to leave Harry, but Mrs Pankhurst wasn't an easy person to disobey.

I followed her to the waiting-room by the front door, where she sat down with much point in the only comfortable chair, leaving me an upright wooden chair. I considered for a moment remaining standing: if she was determined to treat me like a schoolgirl appearing before a headmistress, I would act the part. A barely perceptible lowering of her eyes, though, directed me to the chair, and once again I obeyed, though chafing under the presumption.

'I must confess myself puzzled, Miss Cragg,' she said in a tone not in the least confessional or puzzled, 'as to your function and identity.' Her voice, though pitched low, reverberated in the bare space of the little waiting-room.

I found her manner demeaning, the more so that I knew Nurse Bromley was on duty in the night-nurse room next to the waiting-room, but I tried to explain the situation to her as neutrally as possible. I couldn't avoid mentioning Sylvia's part in my being there. She stiffened at the mention of her daughter's name, her expression remarkably similar to Sylvia's earlier that evening when she'd mentioned her mother.

She was not an easy person to tell a story to – or such a story. It was my impression that she shied away from any mention of Harry in a personal vein, any recollection on my part that set him before her in his own right, as anything other than *her son*, conceived of more in a proprietary than a sentimental aspect. Although she'd demanded to know how I had come to be by Harry's bedside, she was visibly impatient with my recollections of our acquaintance. I felt I was lamely providing information to somebody who didn't want the information, and who yet insisted on being informed.

It was, if truth be told, a somewhat trying interview. Mrs Pankhurst seemed to assume that I owed her an explanation, whereas I was not convinced that she deserved one. Be that as it may, I controlled my own temper reasonably well until she referred to Harry's wish to see me as a 'whim' which Sylvia had 'indulged'.

'I believe,' I said, 'she did not see it as a whim as much as … as in the nature of a dying wish.'

If I'd intended to shake Mrs Pankhurst out of her complacent righteousness, I succeeded. She got up from her chair, and, short as she was, she *loomed* as she all but bellowed,

'Dying wish? But this is beyond all comprehension. On whose authority did Sylvia declare her brother to be dying?'

It took all such restraint as I could muster not to laugh in her face at her invoking of *authority* in the face of death itself. 'I don't know, Mrs Pankhurst,' I said as civilly as I could manage, 'I naturally did not question her as to that, but I must assume that she was acting on medical opinion.'

My civility was lost on Mrs Pankhurst; indeed, it produced another ill-tempered remonstration, climaxing unexpectedly in what was, for her, almost a polite request: 'Please just tell me without equivocation: *is* he dying?'

I couldn't help staring at her incredulously: it hadn't occurred to me that she would be ignorant of her son's condition. 'Don't you know?' I asked her.

'Of course I don't know, young woman, otherwise I would not be asking you. I have this day returned from America, and it would seem that I have not been kept informed by my daughters of the condition of my own son.'

I was about to point out that this was a matter between her and her daughters, when the front door opened and Sylvia came in, flushed and damp. Nurse Bromley, who approved of Sylvia, helped her with her coat and umbrella. 'I am sorry I'm so late,' said Sylvia, 'I was addressing a meeting in the East End and there were so many questions ...'

Mrs Pankhurst had got up from her chair and turned her back on me, and was facing Sylvia. Sylvia, after an initial hesitation, came forward to embrace her mother with what seemed like real warmth. 'I'm so glad you're back,' she said. Her mother's presence had evidently woken in her some filial feeling. Perhaps sensing some reserve from the other woman, who seemed to hold back from the embrace, Sylvia looked up at me, and as a reaction to the rebuff, greeted me more warmly than she had ever done; indeed, she came up to me with such overt affection that I kissed her on the cheek, which I'd never done before. For a moment, Sylvia and I were allies, united against Mrs

Pankhurst. Certainly, after the woman's imperious manner, I found Sylvia's warmth welcome.

She asked after Harry, and for a while Mrs Pankhurst stood by in the unaccustomed role of spectator. She soon found occasion, however, to make her presence felt, interrogating Sylvia as if she were personally responsible for Harry's condition, and of course for Mrs Pankhurst's own condition of ignorance. I remember thinking that she seemed more agitated about the latter than about the former, but I naturally had no part in an altercation whose origins clearly preceded the present crisis. I excused myself and returned to Harry.

When I entered the darkened room, Harry turned towards me.

'Has she gone?' he asked.

'Who?'

'My mother.'

'You were awake?'

'I woke up.'

'And pretended to be asleep.'

'Yes.'

'Why? Didn't you want to see your mother?'

'I don't think she wanted to see me. Not tonight.' He gestured at his body, as if trying to dismiss it. 'Not like this.'

'Like this?'

'When the pain is so bad.'

'You wanted to spare your mother the sight …?'

He smiled – a shadow of the merriment that used to transfigure his face. 'I wanted to spare myself the sight of Mother forcing herself to look at me.'

'Aren't you doing your mother an injustice?'

He shook his head. 'I don't think so. Mother went to America because she didn't want to see me die.'

'But why not?' I asked, appalled less by his theory than by his matter-of-fact way of stating it.

'She was afraid she would break under the strain.' Harry

had clearly worked it out for himself. 'She has a … horror of suffering. I think she'd rather suffer herself than have to witness suffering. There's a kind of selflessness in that.'

'I suppose so,' I said, without conviction.

'It is so.' I was surprised at his self-assurance. It was as if he'd gained in moral force as he lost bodily strength; indeed, he seemed to have gained also in vigour. His eyes were bright and his manner more decisive than I'd seen since the days of the four-in-hand: 'So now, when she's back – and, thanks to you, I'm still alive – she's feeling cheated. Only she can't say so,' he continued, 'and now she'll pretend that you're keeping her from my bedside when in fact she's only too relieved that she doesn't have to sit and watch me die.'

'Harry!' I exclaimed. 'Isn't that a very cynical theory?' I sat down on the chair next to his bed; his face was very close to mine.

'Well no, I don't think so,' he said, mildly but with unwonted firmness. 'You see, I'm not saying Mother is a monster, I'm saying just the opposite, that she's too … soft-hearted – for want of a better word – to watch me die. If she'd been callous, she could have faced my death with equanimity. But she doesn't trust her own emotions. She's afraid that she'll break down.'

'But why?' I asked. 'I mean, why should she *not* break down?'

'Because she's been brought up to believe that emotion is weakness, and that weakness is contemptible.'

If I was taken aback at his cynicism, I could yet not tell him he was wrong. Any protestations on my part would have seemed like the mere cant of convention.

'So you see,' he said, almost cheerful at the neatness of his own conclusion, 'you're doing Mother a service by sitting here. She can tell herself that she would be by my bedside if you weren't here.'

I had no idea whether Harry's theory as to his mother's conduct was well founded; it didn't seem to matter, if it was a theory in which he could take refuge from the implications of his mother's absence. I took a cloth and wiped his brow – wasn't that what I had imagined myself doing? – then I wiped the corners of his mouth, where his excitement had left traces of spittle. He closed his eyes.

'Will you try to sleep now?' I asked. 'I'll stay here until you sleep.'

I put down the cloth and he reached for my hand, his eyes still closed. He caressed it, gently; then slowly moved his hand up my arm, till it was cradling my elbow. I put my hand on his, not to restrain him, but to reassure him.

He opened his eyes. 'Where is Sylvia?' he asked abruptly.

'I left her talking to your mother. She may have seen her out.'

'Will you see?' he asked.

'Why? Do you want to see her?' I asked.

He shook his head. 'I just want to know where she is.'

I went out into the dark passage. There was no light in the night office; Nurse Bromley seemed to have taken advantage of my presence to get some sleep. The little room where Sylvia slept was also dark; it was unusual for her to go to bed without saying good night to Harry, but perhaps she'd not wanted to disturb him.

I returned to Harry's room. 'I think Sylvia's gone to bed,' I said. 'Her room is dark.'

He nodded. 'Come and sit down by my bed again.'

I did so; there was something unusually peremptory about his manner. 'Sylvia, you see,' he continued, now with some hesitation, 'Sylvia takes such a romantic view of my situation that she forgets I am, after all, a man – for all that I'm a dying man.'

I couldn't pretend that I didn't know what he meant, but I said nothing, just stroked his hand.

'She cannot know, I suppose, what I feel like,' he said, looking into my face. 'Perhaps she thinks that because my legs are paralysed, I've stopped feeling.'

He was unmistakably challenging me to a response. For a moment I resented this; not the challenge, but the indirection of it. Could he not trust me with an open declaration? Did he really want me to take the initiative in such a matter as this?

'What is that you feel, Harry?' I asked; I felt I was being manipulated, and was determined that he should name whatever it was that he wanted named.

I think he understood me, for – now without hesitation – he said, 'I feel the desire to touch you and be touched by you. You're very beautiful; I want to hold that beauty in my hand.'

I said nothing and he continued. 'You've been very kind and very brave in facing up to ... my condition. But at times I feel, in the very gentleness with which you touch me, that I'm not a *man* for you any more.'

'I'm not sure what you mean, Harry,' I prevaricated. 'I look after you as best I can.'

'Yes, I know that, and I'm very grateful to you, but I don't mean that, and you know I don't mean that. Or perhaps that's what I do mean ... what I mean, don't you see, is that you treat my body like an object entrusted to your care.'

'Then how would you want me to treat it?' I asked, even while knowing that was what he was willing me to ask.

'Like something you might desire.'

The word *desire* came as a shock to me: it was not one I had been brought up to use in reference to another human being – and in suffragette circles, of course, the only permissible desire was for social justice.

So I merely said, stupidly repeating, 'Desire?'

'Yes,' said Harry. 'Desire. Like a lover.'

'And how,' I asked, 'would I treat your body like a lover?'

'By touching it with your body.'

He was strangely calm now, and assured, a man making a claim rather than a boy being nursed. He slid the sheet from his upper body, baring the white, slightly concave chest with the small nipples; the body hairless except for the fair hair under the armpits; then, as he moved the sheet further down, a thin line of darker hair leading down from the shallow dimple of the navel to what, eventually, stood revealed in its aroused state.

'You see,' he said, 'my paralysis is not total.'

The sight was so unexpected and I was so tense that I had to suppress a sudden urge to giggle. My education had been comparatively liberal for the time, but dealing with the aroused male body had not been part of the curriculum. How strange, and yet how beautiful too, the strong arch arising from the vulnerable loins, the young body asserting itself in defiance of its own helplessness. I took a deep breath to overcome my own hysteria; then, unexpectedly, I found I could relax into the gentle domination of his manner.

'Will you take off your blouse?' Harry said.

Silently, I obeyed. He put his hand on my shoulder and moved the strap of my shift down my shoulder, first on one side then the other. He put his hands on my breasts.

'Touch me,' he said, and again I obeyed, though by now it was what I wanted as well. Without waiting for him to tell me, I leaned forward and kissed him. We kissed for a long time, with my hand on him. I tasted the medicine on his lips and tongue, I felt the silky skin of his sex, smoothly moving it against the urgent tension of his desire. I closed my eyes, but when I opened them again found him watching me, as if gathering an impression for all eternity. And then, suddenly, he caught his breath, sharply, as if in great pain, and I could feel that he had climaxed.

He kept me to him for a while, then slowly released me and lay back on his pillows. 'I love you,' he said, and closed his eyes.

'I love you too,' I said. I reached for a towel to clean him, my bodice still undone. As I did so, I looked up. Sylvia was standing in the door, a look of outrage on her face, or perhaps puzzlement, as if witnessing some alien rite of which she did not understand the significance. Upon catching my eye, she turned on her heel and left. Harry was lying with his eyes still closed, and had not noticed her presence.

I could see that sleep was at last upon Harry, though I think he would have stayed awake if he could, to keep me by him. I watched him drift away into exhaustion and narcosis, kissed him, and went to my little room.

Sylvia was there waiting for me, sitting on the upright chair next to my bed. I couldn't help noticing how tired she looked, and for a moment an impulse of pity took hold of me: she couldn't have had a pleasant evening.

She came to her feet as I entered. 'You are presuming too much upon my brother's weakness.'

My pity yielded to anger at her accusation. I turned my back on her, under cover of taking off the shawl which I had draped over my shoulders upon coming out of Harry's over-heated room. 'Why do you call it weakness?' I asked

'What would you call it?' she asked. 'Strength?'

'Yes, I would,' I replied, turning to face her. 'He had the courage for once to express a desire.'

'Expressing a desire takes no courage. All the world expresses desires. Courage is a matter of disregarding one's desires and doing one's duty.'

I sat down on my bed. 'And Harry's duty is to die without expressing a desire?'

'You don't understand. My mother has tonight confronted me with the impropriety of your position by Harry's bedside, and I laughed at her. Now I am to find that my mother was right. How can I face her, knowing that the woman I brought to Harry's bedside in defiance of her judgement has abused her position of trust?'

'I'm sorry to have proved your mother right. But perhaps you should leave it to me and Harry to face Mrs Pankhurst, if indeed you think it essential for Mrs Pankhurst to be informed of every detail of her son's personal life. For my part, I'm inclined to think it none of her business; there is, in any case, no need for you to assume responsibility.'

'Whatever I assume, my mother will hold me responsible.'

'Then that is a problem you have to address with your mother. It's quite immaterial to Harry's and my relationship. We're both adults and we know what we're doing.'

'Adults consider other people before they consider themselves. You have acted like two selfish children, considering only your own pleasure.'

'And pray what or who else were we to consider? We're answerable to nobody.'

'Can't you see that you are answerable to me and to Nurse Pine and to Mrs Pankhurst? That you are here by my invitation and as my responsibility?'

'No, I can't,' I retorted. 'I'm here at your request but of my own free will.' Strangely, I felt my indignation taking hold of me and issuing headily in effortless speech. This, I thought, is what it must be like, being a Pankhurst: fired with the conviction of one's own rightness. 'As for Nurse Pine,' I continued, 'I cannot imagine that she will be surprised that a young man and a young woman thrown together day after day in intimate conjunction should exercise their freedom and follow the dictates of their bodies. Heaven knows what you thought in bringing me to Harry's bed – that he was some kind of angel or eunuch? Did you not take him seriously enough as a *man* to consider that he might want something other than Jane Austen from the woman he loves?'

Sylvia stood looking at me with what in anybody else I'd have called hatred. Sylvia being Sylvia, it was more like profound disappointment. It was, in any case, wordless; a state to which I suspected very few people reduced her. 'Now, if you will excuse me,' I said, to my mind rather grandly, 'I would like to get some sleep.'

IV

I stop talking and look at Fred. He's leaning back, his eyes closed, but he's not asleep.

'And did Sylvia ever say anything more to you about this ... occurrence?'

'No, but she was visibly constrained with me. As indeed I was with her, I suppose.'

'I can imagine.'

He says nothing more, his eyes still closed. 'Are you shocked?' I ask him.

He opens his eyes. 'Shocked? Good heavens, no.'

There's something provoking about his equanimity. 'But shouldn't you be shocked?' I ask perversely. 'Your wife having sexual relations with a dying man?'

'You weren't my wife at the time, you were hardly having sexual relations, and Harry wasn't to you or to himself, at that moment, a dying man.'

'I wish you wouldn't always be so damned *reasonable*,' I say.

'Oh, you wouldn't want me to be unreasonable,' he says comfortably. 'I'm really horrid when I'm unreasonable.'

We sit for a while in silence. I am still under the spell of memory. He is occupied with his own thoughts.

He gets up from the sofa and walks to the window. 'It's such a lovely day,' he says, 'perhaps the last this autumn. Let's go into the garden.'

I get up and take his arm.

'You have a wonderful way of pretending that you need my support while you're keeping me from falling flat on my face,' he says.

271

'Let's say we keep each other,' I say.

Outside, the autumn sun has warmed the little garden. We look at the late-flowering roses, and the apricots ripening against the south-facing wall. Fred finds the birdseed in the shed and fills the bird feeder. His movements are careful, but with none of the tremulousness of old age.

He steps back from the feeder and watches as the birds swarm – as intently as if it's the first time he's seen such a thing.

'There,' he says, 'that's them seen to. Let's sit on the bench and watch them. There's something I must tell you.'

I look at him with concern. At our age, news is so seldom good. He notices my anxiety and laughs.

'No, it's not some horror,' he says. 'Just a confession.'

'Now *that* sounds like a horror,' I say, relieved. Ills of the spirit are more curable, or at our age easier to live with, than ills of the body. And getting married so late in life, you learn not to be surprised at evidence that the other person, too, had a life before you.

We sit down on the bench. He takes my hand in his. His skin has the transparency of age. He notices me looking.

'You can see it's never done an honest day's work, that hand,' he says.

'You've not done too badly for an idler, Lord Pethick Lawrence.'

'Oh, none so idle as the lords of the land,' he says. I can see he's delaying his confession.

'Please,' I say, 'confess your sins and have done.'

'It's not a sin; that is, the sin is quite venial: it was a sin of omission rather than commission. I didn't tell you the whole truth today.'

'What about?'

'Well, when you asked me how I could bring myself to speak at the unveiling of Emmeline's statue after her treatment of me.'

I think back. 'I don't think you actually gave me any answer.'

'That's what I mean. You see, there was an answer I could have given you.'

'An answer that would have satisfied me?'

'I'm not saying that. An answer, at any rate, that would have been an answer.'

'You're equivocating, Fred,' I say. 'What dark reason could there have been for your appearance? Were you blackmailed? Bribed?'

'No, fortunately one reaches an age when one is proof against both blackmail and bribes.' He raps the knuckles of his free hand on the arm of the bench. 'Well, dammit, don't you see: I was just, for most of my adult life, in love with Emmeline Pankhurst.'

Having delivered himself of this announcement, he leans back on the bench, clearing his throat to hide his embarrassment.

'My dear Fred,' I say, 'but how extraordinary.' This is only a fraction of what I feel, but it's all that I trust myself to express.

He seems relieved at my reaction. 'Why extraordinary? Thousands of people were in love with her.'

'Thousands of women, not men.'

'Have you never wondered why I was the only man in the WSPU?'

'I assumed it was because you had an unusually strongly-developed sense of social justice.'

'Well, I hope I had that too; but at the time that was perfectly compatible with being in love with Emmeline Pankhurst. In fact, I'm not sure that I didn't see in her an embodiment of every exalted aspiration of my youth.'

He says this with a certain self-deprecating irony, but I can see that he is serious. 'You must have been very much in love indeed,' I say. 'But how convenient – I mean if Emmie was in love with Christabel or with Annie Kenny, for you to be in love with Emmeline.' Again this expresses only a very little of what I want to say, but it will have to do for the moment.

273

'But, don't you see?' Fred asks. 'She was not the slightest bit in love with me. Couldn't stand the sight of me, if truth be told.'

'Oh,' I say, not knowing whether this makes it better or worse. 'That doesn't sound convenient, I must admit. But how do you know that?'

'She told me. Several times. The last time was on her death-bed.'

'She told you on her death-bed that she couldn't stand the sight of you?'

'In effect. Her precise words, if memory serves, were "If you want to grant a dying woman a last wish, please leave now and don't make a noise on the stairs as you go down."'

'Sounds inhuman.' In fact, it sounds downright brutal, but this is not the time to say so.

'We have agreed that she did not spare the feelings of others in her pursuit of the truth. Though you could say she'd had provocation.'

'You provoked her on her death-bed?'

'Yes. You see, I told her what I've just told you.'

'That you loved her?'

He nodded. 'That I'd always loved her.'

'Do you mean that was the first time you told her – on her death-bed?'

'You see what I mean by provocation.'

'I'm still not sure that I do.' I am not in a state of mind to find excuses for Emmeline Pankhurst. 'I can see that it would for various reasons not be an opportune moment to receive a declaration of love, but *anger* does seem like an extreme reaction. Of course, Emmeline Pankhurst was always extreme; it's what she was famous for. But how exactly did, you know, how did the situation develop to this point?'

He grimaces, then leans forward, his elbows on his knees. He seems to be staring intently at a bee worrying a rose. 'I can see that it must seem … well, to call for an explanation. I'm not

274

altogether sure how it came about; I was certainly not intending to come out with it like that when I went to see her. You see, I'd heard that she was not at all well, that indeed there was some doubt that she'd ever be well again. I knew of course that she was standing as a candidate in, of all places, Whitechapel, but I didn't know where she was living. So I wrote Christabel a note asking if I could see her mother. She replied after several days, saying simply that her mother had no wish to see me. Christabel could always be counted on to be direct.'

'You knew more than most people of Christabel's directness, I imagine. So you defied Emmeline's express desire not to see you?'

'You could put it like that. That was pretty much how *she* put it.'

I'm not sure that I want to know how exactly Emmeline Pankhurst put her final insult to my husband. 'How did you find out where she was?' I ask, in order not to say so.

'From Sylvia, who had herself seen her mother a day or two earlier. She said her mother was very weak, but that did not necessarily make her more approachable. I said I would risk it, and she gave me the address; she said that I was – if it was possible, short of lying – not to tell her mother that she had given it to me.'

'Strange, how Mrs Pankhurst could inspire fear even on her death-bed.'

'Yes, though I don't know if Sylvia at this stage, or any other, *feared* her mother. It was more that she did not want to displease her, if that's not the same thing as fear. In any case, she gave me the address. I was not at all sure that Emmeline would consent to seeing me – indeed, it seemed more than likely that she would not, after her peremptory message; but ... well, I suppose I wanted to feel that I'd made every effort it was in my power to make. A kind of moral vanity, no doubt. She was staying on the Ratcliffe Highway, above a barber's shop, with people called Chipperfield. It was decent enough, but not quite the style to which Emmeline normally aspired. The rooms were little boxes and the traffic noise was deafening.'

'Why would she have done that? After all, any number of people would have been honoured to put her up.'

He thinks for a moment, his eyes on two birds squabbling at the feeder. 'Who knows? Perhaps she had used up her credit with her supporters – she was always a strenuous house guest – and besides, her defection to the Tories would have alienated many of her former allies without necessarily moving her new allies to open their homes to her. My own theory is that she was trying to outdo Sylvia: after all, the East End was very much her territory.'

I get up from the bench where I have been sitting; I find it difficult to sit still when discussing the Pankhursts. 'I hope you're wrong,' I say. 'It would be too sad if that was what it came to in the end, the struggle for the vote for women: a mother trying to outdo her daughter.'

'No doubt I am wrong,' Fred says with the resignation of someone to whom being in the wrong has never held any terrors. 'But Emmeline's causes were never pure abstractions unmixed with the human element.'

'You haven't told me how she received your visit – if she received you at all.' I sit down again; something in Fred's manner tells me that we may be here for a while.

'Oh, she received me,' he says, 'after keeping me waiting downstairs in the barber shop for long enough to demonstrate her power to do so. If I'd not recently had my hair cut, this would have been a good opportunity to do so, at a fraction of the price my barber in Piccadilly charges. I was at length shown upstairs by Mrs Chipperfield, who warned me that Mrs Pankhurst was very poorly and couldn't see me for long. Emmeline was sitting bolt upright in an extremely uncomfortable chair in the little sitting room. I suspect that she had got out of bed for my visit, not out of consideration for me but because she didn't want me to see her in her weakened state.

She was, as always, carefully turned out, though nothing could hide the sheer exhaustion and emaciation. She looked again as she had looked upon emerging from prison after a hunger strike, although better groomed of course. The large dark-blue eyes seemed almost preternatural in the pale face. When I remarked that I was sorry to find her not well, she replied, "You may be sorry, but you can hardly be surprised: is that not why you came – because I am not well?"

'As always, I found myself absurdly incapacitated by her hostility. I've never had the Pankhurst gift of verbal parrying and swift rejoinder; so I merely shrugged, and probably blushed. She was huddled in her chair as if she were cold, although it was in fact quite a warm day and the atmosphere in the room was very close. While I was still trying to think of a reply to her last sally, she abruptly said, "I trust you have not come to ask me to forgive you after all these years."

'My first instinct, of course, was to ask her what she thought I might want forgiveness for; indeed, I suppose I had a naive notion that Emmeline might feel the need to express her own sense of having treated me with a certain lack of ceremony. But I could say none of this, and when I assured her that I hadn't come to ask anything of her, she merely sneered, "That, at least, is good to know."

One would have thought, you know, that I was a disreputable nephew who had made a habit of asking her for favours. But of course, she wasn't really interested in fairness or justice or any of those rather dull virtues; she wanted to put me at a disadvantage, which we know she was adept at doing.'

'But why?' I am moved to ask. 'I mean why should she *want* to?'

'Emmie's theory was that if Emmeline allowed herself to do us justice, or even showed herself capable of doing us justice, she could not live with herself. So she had to keep on proving to herself, or at any rate telling herself, how ungrateful, disloyal and emotionally rapacious we were. I, at any rate, was

277

not at this late stage going to contest Emmeline's version of events: having clung to it for sixteen years, she was unlikely now to abandon it. I meekly sat down on the only other chair in the room, and tried to look more comfortable than I felt.

'Indeed, I suddenly felt that I had nothing whatsoever to say to Emmeline, and for a moment I had a dreadful vision of our sitting there in tortured silence for as long as we, or rather Emmeline, could tolerate it. But to my surprise, she suddenly announced, as she picked up a letter from the table next to her, that she'd had a letter from Adela. She did this with a surprisingly positive emphasis, given that Adela when last heard of had also been relegated to the ranks of the unworthy and undeserving.

'"From Australia?" I asked. I knew of course that Adela was in Australia, but I couldn't think of anything else to say; it seemed inappropriate to display pleasure or even surprise.

'She didn't bother to answer my question. "I am pleased to say that she at least has come to her senses," she said, her mouth setting in that expression I remembered so well as marking her moments of victory, a satisfied little smile that in anybody else I would have called a smirk. It was a peculiarity of Emmeline's face, you may remember, that it was incapable of an unpleasant expression, however disagreeable or even downright nasty the content of her speech. Indeed, her face had its sweetest expression when she was at her most odious.'

Fred lapses for a moment into reminiscence, and I nudge him gently. 'So, did you find yourself celebrating Adela's return to the fold?'

'Well, I pretended to an interest I didn't really feel. "Do you mean politically?" I asked.

'"What else could I mean?" she asked, as if there were not at least a dozen points on which she had differed with Adela. She unfolded the letter. "She says ... here it is ... *Tom and I have come to believe in class conciliation rather than class conflict as the key to the future* ... which is as good as to say that she has given up

278

her absurd left-wing notions, isn't it?" She looked at me as if in happy expectation of my congratulations.

'"You forget," I said, "that I share Adela's absurd left-wing notions."

'"No, I do not forget that, Fred," she said. "But that does not make them less absurd."

'Hearing her, one would have imagined that my left-wing notions were a sudden perverse aberration from some self-evident truth, rather than the doctrine that she had herself embraced for twenty years. "I'm happy for you, Emmeline," I said, "if you and Adela have found a way of setting aside your differences. One of the reasons why I wanted to see you was the hope that we might also find some such course of … conciliation".

'She looked straight at me and said, in a tone of sweet reasonableness, "You told me not five minutes ago that you have not come to ask anything of me."

'I found myself, somewhat ridiculously, trying to explain that I didn't think I was asking something, as much as offering something. This hardly placated her, as you can imagine.

'"Whatever you offer you would expect me either to accept or reject, I imagine," she said, with that air of injured merit which had won her so many supporters. She was being truly impossible, and I was strongly tempted to say so and leave; but I told myself that this was no more than I could have foreseen, and in fact had foreseen in coming there – for how could I possibly have imagined that age or illness would mellow Emmeline Pankhurst?'

Fred puts this question to me as if I could enlighten him as to his own motives. 'If you had imagined it,' I say, 'that would hardly have been unreasonable. We do tend to think that people become less insistent on their own versions of reality as they approach the great grey area of death.'

Fred nods; I'm not sure how closely he's attended to my words. 'Be that as it may,' he said, 'Emmeline was clearly not in a conciliatory mood. So I had no choice but to carry on. It was a sensation I was familiar with, from my time in the House, the sense that one's audience was at best indifferent, at worst hostile, but that one had to carry on talking as an act of faith, no matter how futile. So I talked, disregarding her evident reluctance to be talked at. Her face was absolutely neutral, as if she were sitting in some inconvenient form of public transport; but her very body expressed rejection of me and what I had to say: it withdrew into the chair, not in submission, but as if in preparation to leap upon me and savage me.'

He hesitates again. 'But what was it that you told her that could so enrage her?' I ask.

'Well, it was not rage as much as a kind of aggravated irritation. I don't think she cared enough for me to be angered by me. But what I found myself telling her, in effect, was what I've told you, that I'd been in love with her for years. I made the point that I did not expect my declaration to give her joy, that it was if anything a kind of confession.

'She didn't seem surprised; she didn't even seem particularly interested. She said, "I cannot accept responsibility for such unlicensed expectations as you may have cherished towards me. I cannot see why people imagine their loving one gives them a claim upon one, as if it were a precious gift they were bestowing. What as onerous as an unwanted gift? What so little conducive to gratitude as the expectation of gratitude for an unasked and unwelcome attention?"

'She continued in this vein for some considerable time; Emmeline, as you know, could at any time pursue a topic to all its finest implications, complications and conclusions, and this topic clearly incensed or inspired or invigorated her. She waxed eloquent, as if my poor little confession had been some heinous plot to deprive her of her freedom; she could have been addressing the judge in the Old Bailey again.'

Fred subsides into silence, looking at the birds fussing round the feeder. 'Poor Emmeline,' I say at length. 'At the last to be confronted with her own failure.'

He looks at me. 'I thought it was my failure.'

'No; her failure to love and to respond to the love of others. I'm not saying she should have loved you just because you loved her, but in her place I think I would have felt, well, touched, somehow.'

'But you were never in Emmeline's place. I don't think, you know, that she would have felt that she had failed in anything in sending me away. Quite the contrary. I think I may have performed her a service, right at the end. I gave her a last opportunity to assert herself in opposition and defiance.'

'Is that what most people would want on their death-bed?'

'I don't know about most people. But I do know about Emmeline Pankhurst, and what I know about her is that she thrived on opposition. She was not a militant because she thought it was the most effective way of getting the vote: she was a militant because she was a militant in every fibre of her being. She was, in an old-fashioned word, bellicose. She needed somebody to fight; with her it was not a matter of finding that she disagreed with somebody and then taking up arms; she took up arms first and then found an enemy. So I provided her with an enemy when there was no other enemy within range.'

'And what else did she tell you?'

'Well, that was it, really. She told me to go away. But what struck me then, and what I'm trying to convey to you now, was the exultation with which she sent me away. No, she wasn't exactly sending me away, she was expelling me, banishing me, driving me out. She even looked the part; her eyes flashed as of old, the colour retuned to her cheeks, her voice rang out as if she were trying to reach the furthest corner of the Albert Hall. She was once again Mrs Pankhurst harrowing the foe. Her landlady came running up the stairs to enquire if anything was the matter; Emmeline got to her feet, adopted her grandest manner and said, "Mrs Chipperfield, kindly conduct the gentleman to the front door."'

'But how could you *tolerate* it?' I break out at last. 'I don't mean being shown the door by Emmeline Pankhurst's land-lady, but all those years of being humiliated, and to be thrown out of the Union as if you were some reprobate good-for-noth-ing. I suppose I'm saying, to feel so … *despised*.'

'Perhaps I needed to feel despised. I despised myself for being rich, for being a man, and for being so helpless to do anything about the injustice I saw all around me. And Emme-line relieved me of the money and punished me for being a man and took up arms against the injustice, and did not mind at all being one of the privileged, having quite literally suffered hunger and thirst and privation for what she saw as justice.'

I no longer feel obliged to suppress my indignation – at Emmeline, at Fred, I'm not sure which. 'I can't accept that,' I say, ' – that you should have *wanted* to be kicked about by Emmeline Pankhurst and her spoilt daughter, just because you were born into privilege.'

'Well, she had a way of kicking people about that made the kicked-about feel ennobled by it.'

'Those that she didn't destroy,' I retort.

'Are you thinking of Harry?' Fred asks.

'I was thinking of him, yes,' I say. But in thinking of Harry my anger yields to something else, and I think again. 'But then,' I continue, 'I don't know if she did destroy him. In the end he may have defeated her.'

'The end? You mean in his death?'

'Yes. In his death and in his dying. I don't know …'

V

I don't know how far I'd really thought when I agreed to Sylvia's request, but I do know that I had a very incomplete idea of what a death-bed is like. How could I have any other? I'd never been present at one, and the Death of Little Nell had not prepared me for any approach to reality. It's only in Dickens that young people die gently, murmuring of things that have loved the light. In real life, which is to say real death, the young body protests with every fibre of its being against its own obliteration, and its protest is registered as pain.

As Harry's condition deteriorated – and there was no fooling oneself now that it wasn't – he became too weak to sit up to eat, and I had to hold the bowl of thin soup that was his evening meal. As I lifted his head and brought the spoon to his mouth, he looked up at me and said, 'Forcible feeding.'

'Would you rather not eat the rest?' I asked. He was having trouble swallowing, and I knew it distressed him that he could no longer control his intake of fluid.

He gave me a grateful look. 'I really would rather not.'

'Then don't force yourself. You've eaten enough.'

I took the half-eaten bowl back to the kitchen. In the passage I passed Doctor Mills. He glanced at the bowl.

'Has he eaten?' the doctor asked.

'Very little. He doesn't want to. I think he is in too much pain.'

'But he must eat. You must try to persuade him.'

I thought the doctor's imperatives were inappropriate; Harry was not a fractious schoolboy refusing to eat his lumpy porridge. 'Why must he eat, doctor?'

'Why, to keep up his strength.'

'His strength to do what, doctor? To suffer?'

Doctor Mills was a patient man, if an unimaginative one. 'It's the duty of the doctor and the nurse to keep life going for as long as possible,' he said, with the air of explaining a self-evident truth to a slow learner. 'I took an oath that I would follow that system of regimen which, according to my ability and judgement, I consider for the benefit of my patient. I expect you to follow that same regimen.'

I did not reply, merely took the bowl back to the kitchen.

It was oddly as if, of all the people involved, Harry was most at peace, in spite of the agitation that shook his body – the frequent muscle spasms, the drooling, the difficulty he had breathing. When he was in pain, he submitted to the injections; when he needed anything else, he gratefully accepted whatever was done for him. He was always glad to see me, but didn't fret when I left to get some rest; after our brief moment of intimacy, there was something almost serene in his manner to me. The doctor had warned me that one of the symptoms of his disease was extreme irritability, even bouts of rage, but perhaps this was where Harry's schooling in self-denial stood him in good stead: if he felt any rage, he suppressed it with his usual fortitude.

Amongst those of us nursing him, at any rate, there was little of his serenity. It was as if, as we saw the end approaching, we all needed to stake our claim, not to be found wanting. Nurse Pine had never really warmed to me, and made no attempt to pretend otherwise; she bustled about, performing superfluous little tasks that, the implication was, I had neglected to perform. Sylvia did make an attempt to disregard our confrontation and to pretend to appreciate my presence; but Sylvia was never good at pretending, and, now that we could no longer indulge in visions of the future, she managed at most a constrained smile, more for Harry's benefit than mine. This in turn incensed me: after all, she'd told me to

284

pretend to love Harry; she could hardly hold it against me that I'd done so.

The one presence I did not often have to contend with at Harry's bedside was Mrs Pankhurst's. On one occasion, she did come to see him soon after her return from America. I excused myself, thinking to leave them alone, but Harry fixed me with such a pleading look that I decided to risk his mother's displeasure rather than abandon him, and I remained standing in the corner, leaving the chair by the bed to her. She took up her position there, as solemnly if she were guarding some shrine from desecration.

Harry was having a bad day; the polio was affecting his ability to breathe and speak and, never very articulate in his mother's presence, he now lay silent, his eyes roaming from my face to hers as if searching for something to say, or appealing to us to say something. I didn't want to put myself forward, even if I could think of something to say, and Mrs Pankhurst, too, uncharacteristically, seemed at a loss for words. She sat mutely staring at Harry, clutching her handbag to her chest. At one stage she put down the bag, extended her hand and touched Harry's hand, almost wonderingly, as if she couldn't understand its waxen pallor. Unfortunately, Harry's disease made him at times excruciatingly sensitive to touch, and he withdrew his hand sharply. For a moment her hand remained on the sheet; then she slowly put it back on her lap.

'I'm ... sorry,' he said, but lacked the energy to explain further.

'He is very sensitive to touch,' I tried to explain, but I might as well have addressed the wall. She sat staring at the hand in her lap as if wondering how it could have offended.

Perhaps under the strain of this tension, the muscle contractions that periodically beset Harry now came on quite severely, his neck and back going into violent spasms. Almost more distressing than these contortions was his evident embarrassment at having to suffer them under the appalled gaze of his mother.

He tried to talk, perhaps to apologise to her for his own pain, but could not form words without drooling. His tongue lolled ineffectually, and every breath cost him an effort.

I stepped forward, took a damp cloth and sponged down his face. I knew that he was suffering also from abdominal pain, and I wanted to apply a warm cloth to ease the discomfort, but felt constrained by Mrs Pankhurst's presence from such an intimate procedure.

'The pain is worse than usual today,' I tried to explain to her, but she seemed not to hear, merely gazed with a kind of horror at her writhing son. In the agitation the sheet had slipped from him, revealing his nakedness; she seemed unaware of this, too, and I rearranged the sheet as best I could. The sheet touching Harry's naked skin caused him acute pain, and he shuddered, suppressing a groan or even a scream.

At this point, at last, Mrs Pankhurst seemed to register my presence, and said to me, her normal imperious tone tempered by an unwonted quaver, 'Isn't there anything we can *do*?'

'I'll ask Nurse Pine for something for the pain.'

'No!' Harry almost shrieked. I knew that he was mortified at seeming to succumb to pain in front of his mother.

'He is very brave,' I said to Mrs Pankhurst, 'but the pain can be very intense.'

'Please, just *do* something,' she said. She seemed as much distressed as Harry. *Deeds not words* had been her motto; now deedless, wordless, she must have found her own helplessness unbearable. I left them together and found Nurse Pine; I explained to her that Harry was having a bad spell.

'I'll bring the lad something,' she said. 'I'd like to give him a bit of morphine, but Doctor says that will make the problem with the breathing worse.'

I returned to Harry's room to find Mrs Pankhurst standing by his bed, looking down at him with a ghastly expression on her face, of terror, even panic. He was still in spasm; his jaw was set with the effort of not groaning, but saliva was running out of his mouth and onto the sheet. I could tell also from the hand he held to his groin that he wanted to relieve himself – at the best of times a slow and painful process. I knew that he would not submit to the indignity of having his mother witness this, and yet I knew also what pain his bladder infection caused him.

'Oh, please,' I said to Mrs Pankhurst, without thinking what I was saying, and to whom, 'if you want to do something, won't you just *go*?'

She turned her blue gaze on me in wonderment; she was paler than I had ever seen her. I suspect nobody had ever spoken to her like that. I thought she would denounce me, challenge me, try to eject me from her son's room; but to my surprise, she bent to pick up her handbag from the floor, and silently obeyed me. I could hear her footsteps retreating down the passage; it sounded as if she was running.

After this I never saw Mrs Pankhurst at Harry's bedside again, not until the very end. I assumed that she had arranged with Nurse Pine to come when I wasn't there.

Harry died in the early hours of a freezing January morning. Since he'd seemed a bit stronger that evening, Sylvia had gone to bed, making me promise to wake her if there was a change in Harry's condition. I was alone with him. He'd been sleeping; he was heavily sedated, but very restless, and at about one o'clock he woke up. I had been dozing lightly in my chair, but I sensed his movement, and sat up. There was a shaded light next to his bed, and he was peering at me as if he couldn't see me clearly.

'What's the matter, Harry?' I asked, getting up from my chair.

He leaned back into his pillow. 'Oh,' he said, 'I couldn't see very well. For a moment I thought it was my mother.'

He was more lucid than he'd been for a while. I wanted to take his hand in mine, but was afraid it might hurt him. As if he could read my thoughts, he put his hand on mine. It was very cold. 'Should I have your mother sent for?' I asked.

287

He shook his head, the slightest of movements. 'It's too late.'

'Too late for what, Harry?'

'Too late … tell her…,' but he did not complete his sentence.

'I'll tell Sylvia you're awake,' I said.

He shook his head again. 'No,' he said, 'I'm tired and I want to be quiet with you.'

'I'm sure she would want to be with you,' I said, mindful of my promise.

'Yes,' he said, 'she would.' For a while he lay silent with his eyes closed, and I thought he might have gone back to sleep. But he opened his eyes, and in a stronger voice said, 'But she will understand.'

I said nothing, merely held his hand in mine, stroking it. In truth, I couldn't have said anything; I was too close to tears.

After a while, he said, 'And Mother … she wouldn't know what to say to me. If she'd been proud of me, she would have known. But now there is nothing.'

'She may want to tell you that in fact she is proud of you.'

He tried to smile, but managed only to twitch his mouth. 'For what? For dying without too much of a fuss?'

'But isn't there something you could say to her?'

He shook his head, or moved it as if to shake it. 'No. There was a time when I wanted to say to her, Mother I'm not as weak as you think; believe in me and I shall do great things for you.' Another tremor twitched his mouth, a swift brush of his former merriment. 'But this is hardly the way to convince her, and I've nothing else to say to her.'

'But perhaps for her sake, and for Sylvia's?' I quietly suggested. I could not rid myself of the thought that I was disobeying his sister by not calling her.

He pressed my hand. 'You think I'm being selfish, and perhaps I am. My father taught us to live for others, and I've tried to do so. But I don't have much to show for it, and now, perhaps, I can die for myself, with you.'

He lay back, then, and let go of my hand. I leaned forward

288

and looked into his face, so little boyish in its fierce contest with pain.

'Harry?' I said softly. He opened his eyes briefly, touched my hand again, and then closed them. In that touch I could feel him taking leave of me and of life; it was his last act of volition. His breath laboured, but he seemed at last free of pain. I bowed my head and waited.

There were hurried footsteps in the passage outside, and Sylvia appeared, looking more dishevelled than usual. She'd evidently lain down fully dressed, and her hair had come undone.

'How is he?' she whispered.

I made a gesture of resignation, and put a finger to my lips.

But Sylvia was not to be silenced. 'How is he?' she whispered again, more urgently. When I didn't reply, she seized his hand and held it between hers. Instinctively, I reached forward to prevent her, mindful of Harry's sensitivity to touch, then bethought myself: he could no longer feel pain. She looked at me sharply, wondering at my attempt to interfere. I stood up and fetched Nurse Pine. She had been sleeping sitting upright in a chair in her office, evidently expecting to be called to Harry's bed. Together we returned to his room. Sylvia was still leaning over her brother

'Harry,' she said, 'Harry, can you hear me?'

She leaned forward, straining, I suppose, to hear his reply. He was breathing with great difficulty, shuddering with every intake. His hands were twitching by his side, as if trying to find purchase on the sheet, the atrophied muscles on his upper arms contracting fitfully.

Nurse Pine stood by grimly, holding Harry's wrist to feel his pulse. She said nothing, but, catching my eye, she shook her head. Her lips formed the words 'Not long now,' as if to comfort me.

There was a movement at the door. I looked up. Emmeline Pankhurst was there, holding onto the doorframe with one hand. She looked withered, shrunken; her body seemed even smaller than it was, a finite bundle of bone and tissue, barely able to sustain itself. She seemed unaware of us; she was forcing herself to look at her dying son.

Harry's breath was now coming very irregularly. With each expulsion of breath we waited, thinking it might have been the last; but then, after what seemed an eternity, he would once again with great effort take a breath, hold it, and release it with a rasping sound. The pauses between each breath became longer and longer, until it seemed impossible that he could breathe again; and yet, time after time, the slow rasping breaths started up again. The four of us dared not look at each other. Sylvia was sitting by Harry's bed, her left hand on his right, her brow resting on her right hand. I was standing behind her, facing Nurse Pine, who stood absolutely still, monitoring Harry's pulse. Emmeline Pankhurst had remained standing at the door, like a pillar of salt. It was like a tableau vivant, Harry's stertorous breathing the only sound and movement in the room; the four waiting women almost oblivious of each other, their attention concentrated on the dying man. The room was kept stiflingly hot against the January cold, and in the dim light the sweat on Harry's face glistened, making it seem luminous.

There came at last one long expulsion of breath, more like a sigh or a sob than a breath; we waited, all four, for the breath to start again, but it never came. Harry's mouth lay open, a last dribble running down his chin. The poor wasted body lay limp, Sylvia and Nurse Pine each still holding a hand. Sylvia was weeping; Nurse Pine stood dry-eyed and grim, like the angel of death itself. She let go of Harry's wrist and wiped his chin. I exchanged some words with Sylvia, I hardly knew what. I suddenly felt light-headed, as if I were going to faint. I turned round and brushed past Emmeline Pankhurst, who was still standing by the door, and went out into the cold street.

290

VI

Fred has been sitting very still, listening, now and again shifting his position, once getting up to refill the bird feeder.

'And did you see Emmeline again?' he suddenly asks

'She came again, yes, that morning. He was still lying as he had died, looking very young and vulnerable. I'd come back from my walk and was sitting next to the bed, I don't know why; I felt, I suppose, that I couldn't just get up and walk away now that he was dead, as if that was that, and yet I didn't think that I was particularly wanted either. Nurse Pine had no more than tolerated me for Harry's sake, and even Sylvia, I could see, was impatient with my presence. I was about to get up to gather my few possessions, mainly the books from which I'd read to Harry, when Mrs Pankhurst arrived. She looked worse than I'd ever seen her or ever saw her afterwards, even after a spell of hunger striking in prison: then, however emaciated she was, she'd looked triumphant, the spirit victorious over the body, that kind of thing; now she looked simply defeated. Nurse Pine tried to console her, but she was beyond consolation or any human gesture: she was alone with her defeat.'

'Did she say anything to you?'

'I don't think she noticed me. She stood next to Harry's bed, looking at him, ... I don't know – as if she were *puzzled* by him, trying to make out what he meant. It was as if he incarnated some mystery. She was quite dry-eyed; I felt that even the relief of tears was denied her. At that moment I was intensely sorry for her – an emotion Emmeline Pankhurst didn't very often permit one.'

'No, indeed. And was that all? She simply looked at Harry's body?'

'She did say – I remember thinking it would have been a rather theatrical touch if she'd seemed at all declamatory about it – she said, as she pulled the blankets over him as if she were tucking him up for sleep, *Poor bare forked animal.*'

'If you say it wasn't theatrical, I'll believe you. But theatricality came naturally to Emmeline – if that isn't a contradiction.'

'It came naturally to them all.'

'Even to Harry?'

I have to think about this. 'My first impulse is to say no, he was too artless for that; but even artlessness can be artful. If so, Harry perfected the art of artlessness. I don't like that interpretation; I'd rather say that, without trying to, he discovered the power of powerlessness, the authority of the dispossessed. Harry dead was a more formidable challenge to Emmeline than all the massed male power of the law. And he defeated her.'

'But did he *want* to defeat her?' Fred asks, mildly. 'Isn't it your point that he wanted desperately to please her?'

'Yes, he did, or thought he did. But there comes a time, surely, when one has been trying to please somebody and failing, that one's desire turns to anger, and one turns one's back on the person one has been trying to please?'

He looks sceptical. 'I don't know. I think one may never stop wanting to please.'

I look at him and want to ask him if he ever stopped wanting to please Emmeline Pankhurst, but for once I hold my tongue, and he continues. 'And Sylvia?' he asks.

'What about Sylvia?'

'Did she reproach you with not having called her?'

'No. To tell the truth, I didn't much care, just then. It was only when Harry died that I realised how extraordinarily tired I was, and how sad. I think my youth came to an end there, beside Harry's bed. You can't watch someone slowly die, and yet retain the illusions of childhood.'

'Did you love Harry?' Fred asks the question so naturally that it takes me a moment to realise how strange it is that he has not asked it before.

'Yes,' I say, 'yes, I did. When I told him, that time, that I loved him, I realised that it was true, that I wasn't pretending – as Sylvia had asked me to do.'

There is silence for a moment. 'Do you mind?' I ask.

'Mind? No,' he says. 'He was your first love.'

He says this as a statement, but I answer all the same. 'Yes.'

'And your only love?' This time it is a question.

'Yes,' I say. 'In a sense. Sitting with him day by day I found that he came to be precious in a way that perhaps only something one is about to lose can be precious. And to have touched him and to be touched by him ... So though I loved Alexander, and I love you, Harry – Harry was, I suppose, the experience one can never repeat, the rapture one is always trying to recapture, not knowing that it's youth itself one has lost.'

'Did you realise this at the time? That you loved Harry?'

'I know why you're asking that. I know that memory idealises. But I do remember standing by Harry's bed and thinking: *This I will never know again.* Not just the loss, but also the sense of what I had gained; not the youth that Harry had taken from me, but the riches that he'd given me.'

There's a silence again, Fred looking pensive. 'It seems a pity that you could say none of this to Sylvia. It may have helped you, and it would have helped her.'

'I don't think so,' I say. 'Not as I felt then, and as she felt then. I really only wanted to leave, and, after what had passed between us, Sylvia didn't really want me around. She did, though, with good grace, give me a watch that Keir Hardie had given Harry.'

Fred looks up, surprised at last. 'She did? That is remarkable, if she felt what you say she did.'

'You see, Harry had asked her to give it to me. I think she found it hard. You know that she'd been romantically involved with Hardie?'

'I knew there was some speculation about it, but I for one never credited it. He was happily married, and I couldn't believe that two such puritans would actually, you know, indulge such an illicit passion. I could see them pining with love, but not burning with passion. The idea is wildly improbable, like one's grandparents romping naked in the clover.'

'But then, conceivably, one's grandparents did romp naked in the clover. And apparently Sylvia and Keir did indulge and burn. According to Harry, at any rate.'

'Would he have known?'

'He was convinced in his own mind. It had something to with his spending Sundays with them when he was at school: it's a long time ago, and the details escape me, but it seems that Sylvia lied to him about why she couldn't spend the day with him, and then he found out later that she'd spent it with Hardie, and he, you know, drew his conclusions from that.'

'It sounds so totally unlike Sylvia, to have told a lie to anyone, most of all to her brother.'

'That's what Harry said. "It's not like Sylvia at all," he said. "That shows how much she loved Keir."'

'Did he feel rejected?'

'No, he said he was disappointed at the time, and yes, hurt that Sylvia lied to him, but then he came to see, as he put it, that men and women are more to each other than brothers and sisters. It's possible that he used it as a rationalisation to have me rather than Sylvia by his death-bed.'

'And Sylvia never knew that he knew.'

'Oh, she knew.' I smile, suddenly amused at the thought. 'I told her.'

'When? There and then?'

'No, many years later. I've been thinking about it today. It was the last time I ever saw Sylvia, just after the birth of her son.'

294

'You went to see her?'

'Yes. She'd said to me, after Harry's death, that it was better that we shouldn't meet again, that she didn't want to blight my young existence with sad memories. I consented, though, as often before, I thought she was more absolute than necessary. But now, with this birth, I thought that I could share in her joy and, I hoped, efface the earlier sad memories. Besides, she was being ostracised by any number of her earlier associates for what was regarded as her flagrant immorality.'

Fred shakes his head. 'It was even rumoured I was the father, because one of the child's names was Pethick.'

I laugh. 'Of course. I'd forgotten that touch. Odd, how things have turned out. At the time, of course, it was just another bit of gossip about the Scarlet Suffragette ...'

VII

I found the house easily enough; I'd been told by Norah Smyth that it was 'somewhat rundown'. This turned out to be an understatement: the house was little more than a semi-detached weather-boarded cottage, ramshackle in the extreme, a shack, one would almost have called it. The garden was size-able, though of course overgrown. The whole set-up was exactly what I would have imagined a house of Sylvia's would look like, a kind of architectural equivalent of her personal style of dress and demeanour. Not that it was unpleasant: there was a quality about the place that suggested settledness, con-tentedness; now, in early April, the chaotic garden was in extravagant bloom, and the closeness to Epping Forest lent a rich dampness to the air.

As I opened the gate, the front door opened and two women came out. At first I didn't recognise them, but then one turned, and in the elegance of the movement and something almost disdainful in the wave of her hand, I recognised Christabel. She was dressed in a long black coat that made her look very grand – Christabel in her Late Phase.

Behind her was Sylvia. They were locked in intense conver-sation, but that did not surprise me: when the Pankhursts spoke to each other at all, they would no doubt do so with a certain emphasis. I nevertheless paused at the gate; it was an unwritten but absolute rule in the suffragette days, that one did not interrupt a Pankhurst conversation, any more than one would address Royalty without being first addressed.

The two sisters terminated their conversation, I couldn't help noticing, without any ceremony beyond the briefest of nods, and Christabel came *flowing* down the garden path in her voluminous dress. She peered at me, and I wondered if she was short-sighted; but of course, there was no reason why she should recognise me. We hadn't seen each other for eighteen years, and had never had much to do with each other, even then. She'd put on a considerable amount of weight, and the pink-and-white colouring had turned almost ruddy, but something of the grace remained – almost touchingly so, as if her body could remember what it was like being beautiful. As she approached, I could see her trying to place me. To spare us both the embarrassment, I put out my hand, and said, 'I daresay you don't remember me. I am – or was – Helen Craggs.' The way she extended her hand was a masterpiece of instinctive aplomb. She could obviously still not place me: her smile had the uncommitted generality of a celebrity being introduced to an admirer. If a *body* could be insincere, Christabel's was.

'It's been a very long time,' she said; a safe enough proposition, I thought.

'Yes,' I said, wondering whether I should refresh her memory or wait and see how far her self-possession would serve her. But I'd done her an injustice; from a sudden and instantly checked widening of the eyes, I could see that she'd placed me.

'You bring back such sad memories,' she murmured with graceful melancholy, 'but it's nevertheless a pleasure to see again someone so closely associated with my dear brother. So sad, so sad – such a beautiful life and such a brief one.'

She took my hand and squeezed it gently. Christabel had altered her style: in place of her youthful fervour and vivacity, not to say her pugnacity, she'd developed an air of dignified grandeur, of which the keynote was a kind of muffled tragedy. Poor Harry's death became subsumed into this manner and aestheticised into a melancholy memory, an occasion for mournful melodies.

I murmured something, I hardly knew what; I had no wish

to figure as a prop to Christabel's performance. I don't think she noticed: she was engaged in disentangling her voluminous scarf from the garden gate, where a splinter had snagged it. I left her to it, and approached the front door.

Sylvia had disappeared. For a moment I thought that she might have wished to avoid me, as well she might, given the tenor of our parting eighteen years earlier. But my knock soon brought her out, holding a baby. There were stains on her blouse, presumably the drool of the new baby. Her hair was so loosely looped that it seemed on the point of coming undone and collapsing. She looked at me so enquiringly that I thought she might not have recognised me.

'I'm Helen McCombie – I was Helen Craggs,' I said.

She nodded. 'I know,' she said. 'I did not recognise you immediately, but now I do.'

We remained standing outside. I wondered if she'd invite me in, then realised that she was looking at me interrogatively, evidently expecting me to state my business. There was something trying in the implication that my presence needed explanation, but it occurred to me that perhaps not all her visitors were well-wishers. So I said, 'I've come to wish you joy on the birth of your son. I'm so glad for you.'

Unexpectedly, her eyes filled with tears. 'Thank you,' she said. 'He is indeed a great joy. But others have turned him into a cause for reproach and bitterness.'

So my speculation had been well founded. Presumably Christabel had visited to express her displeasure at a birth that did not fit with her notions of propriety.

'What shall you call him?' I asked.

'Richard Keir Pethick Pankhurst,' she said, smoothing away the tears with the heel of her free hand, and leaving a smudge on her cheek. 'He is heir to all that has been best in my life.'

An impulse of conventionality prompted me to wonder whether the child's father might not have figured under this rubric, but I suppressed the impulse and availed myself of the distraction a babe in arms so readily offers in a strained social situation. I made appropriate noises, demonstrating to Sylvia that I was no stranger to children; she warmed noticeably and asked, 'Do you have children?'

I nodded. 'Two. So I understand ...'

The baby was becoming restive. 'Won't you please come in?' she said. 'I think he's hungry.'

We went into the little sitting room, in truth a book-filled room with three chairs, a table and a fireplace.

'Silvio has gone to London,' she said. 'Once a week he visits his Italian friends and they drink red wine and eat meat. The poor man cannot understand why in England socialists find it necessary to eat lentils.'

In truth, the compulsion escaped me too, but I refrained from comment. Sylvia merely busied herself with feeding Richard Keir Pethick; she sat down on a chair, opened her blouse and bodice, and was looking down at the little face tugging at her nipple. For a moment, in uncharacteristic repose, her face softened, and she instinctively adopted the mother-and-child attitude beloved of painters over the ages.

As if reading my thoughts, Sylvia looked up from the feeding child and said, 'Mother breast-fed only Christabel, of all her children.'

I wondered whether this was an obscure resentment expressing itself, but did not want to ask. She had not offered me a chair, but finding it awkward just standing there before the feeding mother, I sat down in an upright chair. Sylvia seemed unaware of my movement, absorbed in the suckling baby.

'I've brought Richard a gift,' I said. 'I hope you'll accept it on his behalf and one day bequeath it to him.'

'That is generous of you,' she said factually, without committing herself to any warmth of tone. Her tentativeness suggested that she was not used to receiving gifts or favours, at any rate when presented as such.

I got up from my chair and took from my bag the watch that

Harry had left me, that Sylvia had herself handed to me the last time I saw her. 'This has been precious to me,' I said, 'but I think it must go back, now that there is a Pankhurst boy to look after it.'

I held out the watch in front of the boy. He had stopped drinking. His eyes seemed to focus on it, his little hand waved at it.

I smiled. 'You see, he recognises it as his own.'

But Sylvia did not respond to my banal pleasantry. She was staring at the watch.

'You will accept it on his behalf, won't you?' I asked, uncomfortable at her silence.

She transferred her gaze from the watch to me; she seemed puzzled. 'Harry wanted you to have it,' she said, a flat statement of fact.

I nodded, 'Yes, of course. And it has meant much to me. But now …'

'Now what? What has changed? Don't you value it?' she demanded, almost fiercely.

'Of course I do. But there is now a young Pankhurst, Harry's nephew, who will in time value the watch for what it meant to Harry and … and to you.'

She wiped the baby's mouth and closed her blouse. 'How do you know what it meant to me?' she asked, a challenge rather than an enquiry.

'I think I know how much you loved Harry. And you have named your son after Keir Hardie. I must assume that you cherish his memory.'

She turned on me then. 'You can never know how much. He was the gentlest and kindest of men. They were both, both the gentlest and kindest of men. If you know what it cost me then to give you this watch – and now, after eighteen years, you return it as if it meant nothing to you.'

I reflected, not for the first time, on how exasperating it could be, dealing with a Pankhurst. 'Pardon me,' I said, 'you mistake my meaning. I don't know why you assume I would give away something only because it meant nothing to me. Have you never given away something that was precious to you?'

Sylvia's anger subsided as abruptly as it had flared up. 'Yes, yes, of course I have. We were brought up with the idea of the nobility of sacrifice.' Was there a tinge of dryness to her declaration, a suggestion that Sylvia might with age have grown to question the Pankhurst doctrine of self-denial?

'Then surely you can accept that other people, too, may be capable of sacrificing a treasured object?'

I think she was startled at that; it's possible that she had become accustomed to not being challenged on her assumptions and certainties.

'I beg your pardon,' she said, in the tone of someone who seldom begged anything of somebody else, least of all pardon. 'I only meant that, as you did not know Keir Hardie, you couldn't know how very highly I treasure his memory.'

'I did in fact meet Mr Hardie, though yes, I never knew him well. But Harry always spoke very highly of him.'

'Did he?' I was surprised at the eagerness with which she seized upon my conventional enough utterance. 'Do you think Harry esteemed Keir Hardie?'

'Why yes, very much so. Surely everybody did, who knew him or of him.'

'No, many people hated him. He was not a man who sought popularity. But yes, Harry loved him like a father, and he loved Harry, like a son.'

'Then,' I said, 'the watch belongs with you and your son.'

Sylvia shook her head. 'You don't want to give away your only reminder of Harry.'

'No,' I said, 'I don't *want* to. But nor do I want to keep it, now. I think Harry would have wanted you to have it, now.'

I held out the watch to her; she looked at me as if wanting to judge whether I was serious, then, tentatively, she took it.

She turned it round and rubbed the dents on the back. Then she looked up at me again.

'This watch brings back memories of some of the happiest times in my life. But it also brings back other memories, painful memories.'

I looked at her, not saying anything. It was clear that she was under the spell of the watch and its associations; I had ceased to matter to her, except as a medium through which to access her own memories. I knew that if I prompted her, she would withdraw, become conscious of me as a possibly unsympathetic onlooker, as someone who had taken her place at her brother's bedside.

'You see,' she said, 'Poor Harry ...'

She got up, I thought in an attempt to master her own emotion. 'I'll put Richard down. He'll go to sleep now.'

She went into the next room, leaving me alone in the haphazard little sitting room. There were books everywhere, books and baby clothes. On the wall was a watercolour portrait of Keir Hardie, possibly slightly idealised. It was very quiet in the cottage.

She came back, sweeping back the loops of hair falling over her face.

'I'm afraid I cannot offer you any tea,' she said, 'Silvio is not here at the moment, and I never make the tea. Or we could go round to Mrs Powter's.' A head movement indicated, I assumed, the occupant of the other half of the cottage.

'Oh no, no,' I protested, though I was in fact thirsty, 'I had some tea before I came away.'

But I could have saved myself the lie; Sylvia was no longer listening.

'I shall not refuse your gift on Richard's behalf,' she said. 'I am not used to investing material objects with value, but this,' she shook her head, as if in disbelief, 'it means more to me than you can know.'

I suppose we are all jealous of our own secret sources of

302

emotion, but there was something provoking in Sylvia's assumption of the inaccessibility, the exclusiveness of her feelings.

'Pardon me,' I said, 'but perhaps I do know something of what you feel.'

'How can you?' she asked with a lofty disdain that for a moment made her resemble her mother.

'Through ordinary human sympathy,' I replied. 'But also –' and then I hesitated, thinking I'd been driven too far by my irritation.

'But also what, Helen?' Sylvia asked.

'But also through what Harry told me.'

She sat down abruptly. 'What could Harry possibly have told you?'

'That you … loved Mr Hardie.'

'And how did Harry know this?' She asked this as a challenge, as if I were answerable for Harry.

'That I cannot tell. But he knew you well enough, surely, to have guessed.'

'But he told it to you as a certainty?'

'Yes. He said something about … about your spending time with Mr Hardie one Sunday; I'm not sure what the details were, but he somehow deduced from that that you … cared for Mr Hardie.'

Sylvia sat staring in front of her, absent-mindedly brushing her hair from her face.

'So Harry knew,' she said at length. Then she looked at me. 'Was he angry?'

'Angry at what? Your … relationship with Mr Hardie?'

'That too. But the lie I told him that Sunday. Did he mention it?'

'He did. But not as something that angered him. He said … it's a long time ago, but I think he said that it was proof to him of how much you loved Mr Hardie, and that he could understand it, because Mr Hardie must be the finest man alive.'

'He said that?'

'Yes. As I say, it's a long time ago, but that, I'm sure, was the gist of what he said.'

She got up then and came to where I was standing. She took my hand in hers.

'So, in your opinion,' she asked, almost formally, as in a court of law, 'in your opinion, Harry forgave me?'

'I don't think Harry saw it as something requiring forgiveness.'

'No,' she shook her head, and tears came to her eyes. 'Harry did not harbour grudges.'

We stood like that for a moment. Then she let go of my hand and took the watch from the table where she'd put it, and stroked it. 'Thank you. Thank you for this and for what you have told me. It has been … on my conscience. I shall cherish the watch and pass it on to Richard when he is old enough to understand.'

'I think, perhaps, you should keep it yourself. You can leave it to Richard in your will.' I knew that Sylvia was little accustomed to appropriating anything for herself. 'You really must take custody of it yourself.'

'But you want Richard to have it?'

'Of course. Eventually. And I want you to have it for your lifetime.'

She closed her hand around the watch. 'Thank you,' she said. 'I shall keep it for myself.'

VIII

'And that was the last time I saw Sylvia,' I say.

'I see,' Fred says pensively. He is quiet for a while, pondering my tale, rubbing his eyes with his thumb and index finger. I want to tell him not to do it, but refrain.

At length he says, 'It was generous of you, to give her the watch.'

'That's like you,' I say, 'to think it was generous.'

'Well, wasn't it?'

'No, I don't think so.'

'You don't *think* so? Don't you know?'

'No, not really. I wish I could say that I simply wanted her to have something that belonged to her by right. But I'm afraid it may have been more petty than that. Perhaps I'd been slightly irritated with Sylvia's righteousness, and wanted to let her know that I knew about her … lapse.'

'I see.' He nods. 'Yes, there was something about Sylvia's selflessness that made one almost wish she would do just one thing because she wanted it for herself.'

'My dear Fred, that's not what I'm saying. I'm afraid you're going to have to accept that my motives were a good deal less pure than that.'

This at last moves him to protest. 'How impure, for heaven's sake, can one's motives be, in giving someone a watch?'

'Consider it not as a watch but as an emblem, a symbol, if you like.'

'I'm considering,' he says, and he really does look as if he's considering, 'but I'm flummoxed. A symbol of what?'

'Can't you see – a symbol of the value attached to it in the

305

first place by Harry. He gave it to me because ... because he loved me, and because I'd come to his bed, and – been generous to him, as he saw it.'

'I can see that, yes. But that still doesn't explain –'

'Why I gave it to Sylvia? Why, because in her mind the watch was associated with Keir Hardie and her –'

'Her coming to his bed, as it were?'

'As it were. And by accepting the watch, she was acknowledging an equivalence between my relationship with Harry and hers with Keir Hardie.'

He looks at me quizzically. 'And this was ungenerous on your part?'

'Yes. I was getting even with her for her high dudgeon when she discovered Harry and me ... when she discovered us as she discovered us.'

Fred is silent for a while, absent-mindedly tugging at the sleeve of his cardigan. I take his hand to stop him. 'You'll stretch the sleeve,' I say.

After several minutes of silence, Fred says, 'No.'

'No what?'

'No, I don't accept your interpretation.'

'My dear Fred, it's not an interpretation, it's a declaration. I know what I was doing and why I was doing it.'

'And yet your giving the watch to Sylvia gave her pleasure.'

'I suppose so,' I admit. 'But I didn't really *want* to give her pleasure. Or rather, I wanted her to reflect on the reasons for her pleasure.'

'Which no doubt she did.'

'No doubt.'

'And was still grateful.'

'And embarrassed.'

'But more grateful than embarrassed.'

'How do you know that?'

'I knew Sylvia. And I know you. I think I understand.'

'What is it that you understand, Fred?'

'Why you told Sylvia that Harry knew about her lie.'

'Yes?'

'I think you knew that Sylvia would want to know that Harry knew, that knowing it would set her mind at ease.'

'You're assuming, as usual, what is most to the credit of all parties involved. You're determined that both Sylvia and I will emerge from this with honour, and I'm determined that there must be at least one thoroughly selfish person in the equation.'

My tone is intended to lighten the conversation, yet Fred remains serious. 'But why?' he asks, with unusual intensity. 'You say that your account is not an interpretation, but pardon me if I point out that in listening to you, what strikes one most is that it's in almost every detail just that, an interpretation, and is in almost every detail open to a contrary interpretation. That is, of course, in the nature of interpretations. But my point is this: given that you're assuming so much about everyone's motives, why not, while you're about it, assume that everyone was, within the bounds of their opportunities and the limits of their insight, selfless?'

Fred's heat ignites my suppressed anger. 'Do you know how *sick* I am of selflessness?' I all but shout at him.

'Still?' he asks, his surprise the only concession to my heat. 'After all these years?'

'What do you mean, after all these years? Don't I live with you, who every day demonstrates to me what it is to be bloody selfless?'

'I'm not aware of demonstrating any such thing.'

'No, of course you're not,' I reply. 'You're too bloody selfless for that.'

Suddenly, I want to hurt Fred, hurt him into crying out and protesting. I want him to acknowledge, now, the hurt and resentment that he could not acknowledge then, to admit that he had been shamefully treated.

'You spend your life in a cause that spurns you for your pains and ruins you financially,' I continue, 'in love with a woman who treats you like dirt, married to a woman who's in love with everyone except you, and then you write a book called *Fate Has Been Kind*. Just what the hell do you mean, Fate has been Kind? I should think Fate must be laughing up her sleeve at you *thanking* her for dealing you such a hand. Aren't you being grateful for very small mercies?'

If I have been trying to stir Fred to anger, I have failed. He merely turns over my question as he turns over every request for information: unhurriedly, serenely. 'I don't think so,' he says at length. 'I've had a life full of incident, I've worked for hopeless causes, I've seen some of those causes triumph. I've known the most exceptional people, I've been in love, I've loved, I've been loved, and now I have you. You won't, I hope, think of yourself as a small mercy.'

I ignore his attempt at humour. 'You're evading the issue. I wish you wouldn't be so impossibly high-minded. Did it never rile you to be condescended to by Emmeline Pankhurst and Christabel? And didn't you want to kick Christabel when she turned against you and Emmie after all you'd done for her?'

'Yes, it riled me, and yes, I wanted to kick Christabel. At one stage, in fact, I was obsessed with the injustice I considered had been done to me by mother and daughter. I do believe I was tempted to take a horsewhip to them.' The words sit oddly with his placid manner; it's impossible to imagine Fred with a horsewhip. 'But when one enters a battle like that,' he continues, 'one realises that it transcends the personalities of the participants, even of the leaders. It becomes an abstract thing, if you will.'

'But how can it be abstract, with Emmeline more or less spitting in your face?'

'What would you have had me do?'

'It would have been refreshing, and indeed productive, if you'd just once spat back in good, honest anger. It's not natural to be so ... so *abject* in the face of such treatment.'

'What is to be achieved by anger?'

'What is not? Do you think Emmeline and Christabel achieved what they did through equanimity and fair-mindedness? No,

308

they were driven by anger – anger at their fathers for not loving them enough, anger at their mothers for marrying their fathers, anger at nature for making them women, anger at the whole bloody world for not going down on its knees in front of them. If they'd believed in God they could have been angry at him; in his absence they were angry at everything, and out of anger they changed everything.'

'That, too, is an interpretation,' he says imperturbably.

'What is an interpretation?' I ask.

'That Emmeline and Christabel changed everything.'

'You mean you don't believe that they did?' I look at him to see if he's serious, but he's still regarding the garden placidly, not giving away anything. 'That is heresy, surely?' I say, to prompt a response.

'Well,' he says at last, 'there is quite a strong body of opinion nowadays that holds women would have got the vote anyway, indeed would have got it earlier, had it not been for the WSPU and its militancy.'

I am caught off guard: *he* has been defending Emmeline and Christabel, *I* have been arraigning them; now *he* is calling into question their achievement.

'And you?' I ask, in order not to have to argue Emmeline and Christabel's case. 'Are you part of this body of opinion?'

'On balance, no. But I'm just pointing out that their claim to posterity's veneration is also an interpretation. And then, you know, you said yourself that Emmeline was defeated by Harry.'

'Yes,' I admit. 'And by you.'

'Oh, that I don't believe. But if you believe it, then there you are. In the long run, anger's achievement is … well, illusory.'

I don't want to accept this. I've been angry too often, and acted on my anger. 'I still think,' I say, obstinately, 'if you'd been angrier, they'd have taken you more seriously, Emmeline and Christabel.'

'But what difference would that have made, their taking me seriously?'

I reflect a while. 'Perhaps,' I say, 'you wouldn't have married me.'

He rubs his eyes. 'My dear Helen, I don't follow your logical leaps. How would Emmeline's treatment of me fifty years ago have inclined me to marry you or for that matter not to marry you?'

'Ah, you see,' I say, warming to my theme, 'I'm thinking you may have married me to get even with Emmeline.'

He looks mildly surprised. 'Good heavens. I married you because I loved you.'

'I believe you. But that needn't prevent.'

'Prevent what?

'Prevent your marrying me to get even with Emmeline Pankhurst.'

'I can't see how I could achieve that, so many years after her death; you mean I was offending her shade?'

'I don't mean anything vulgar like revenge; just getting even in your own mind, balancing the books.'

'I still don't see how my marrying you would do that.'

'Fred, consider,' I say, starting to find my own theory plausible. 'I was the woman who, Emmeline believed, kept her from the death-bed of her son, the woman, if you like, with whom her son avenged himself on her, an accomplice of Sylvia's. Now she rejects you and you marry that woman. Is there not a neat poetic justice to it?'

But if I was hoping that the sheer outrageousness of my charge would at last move Fred to protest, even to anger, I am once again disappointed. He gives, or pretends to give my suggestion the balanced consideration it may not deserve. 'As an interpretation,' he says finally, 'based on the agency of anger, it will do, give or take a decade or five. But if neither Harry nor I were motivated by anger?'

'Perhaps our devious minds devise things we're not conscious of.'

The idea of Fred's having a devious mind is one that in all conscience I can't seriously entertain. But Fred, being Fred,

310

does gravely attend to the charge. 'Well,' he eventually says, 'if my devious mind led me to marry you, I'm grateful to it.'

'Oh, so am I.'

'Well, then. You see, fate has been kind.'

I sigh. 'You're incorrigible. The truth is, you're too good for this hard-hearted world you were born into. I suppose you were made so.'

He says nothing. Then I ask him: 'Did you tell me about being in love with Emmeline because I told you about Harry?'

'I've always known about Harry,' he says.

'Not that we'd been … intimate.'

'So many years after, it can surely not signify. We both had very long and very full lives before we married each other.'

'They're the worst, the infidelities before the fact.'

He seems amused. 'Why? Because you can't be angry about them?'

'I can be angry about whatever I have a mind to.'

'Are you angry about Emmeline?'

'Yes, I am.'

'Well, by your logic we are both now avenged.'

I look at the garden in the late afternoon sun, and feel the warmth on my skin, hear the birds, their piping more subdued now, smell the damp earth; and I feel Fred's hand in mine, the papery skin over the delicate bones.

'As revenge goes, it will do,' I say.

'As revenge goes, it will do very well,' he replies.

But in another moment the low autumn sun has moved and we are sitting in the shade. I shiver.

'Come,' I say, getting up from the bench. 'It's getting chilly. You don't want to catch cold. Let's go in now.'

He looks up as if to object, but I take his arm and help him up. For a moment he leans on me, as he delicately shifts his weight onto his legs, and then he assumes responsibility for his own body. As we negotiate the uneven paving of the garden path, he takes my hand, like an obedient child being taken home.

Acknowledgements

This novel started life as a project for Marlene van Niekerk's Creative Writing seminar at the University of Stellenbosch. My thanks are due to Marlene for her expert guidance and to the Department of Afrikaans and Dutch for allowing me to attend these seminars. My thanks, too, to my fellow class members for their advice and support; I am particularly grateful to Stephanus Muller for his encouragement.

Thank you to Lynda Gilfillan for a meticulous but sympathetic editing job. She is not, of course, to be held responsible for those tics, whims and solecisms I persisted in despite her advice.